THE SILENT CITY

D1319388

AARON COLE WILLIAMS

ISBN: 978-1-7371148-2-6 Paperback
ISBN: 978-1-7371148-3-3 Ebook

Cover design by Damonza.com
www.aaroncolewilliams.com

To my parents,

Thank you for all your love and support.

I hope you enjoy reading the type of content I was always uncomfortable to watch with you on TV.

PROLOGUE

Cassandra Averill struggled to acclimate to her extended stays in the capital. From the balcony of her palatial estate, she looked out at the mist rising from Lake Thaxter. A few miles from her home, construction had begun on more houses in Kingsbury's increasingly popular Lake District. After breathing in the dew-kissed morning, she lumbered down the stairs toward the kitchen for coffee's loving embrace.

Thos and Cass oversaw Averill Estate Farms, which had become one of the largest companies in the nation. The duo spent most of the day managing the agricultural behemoth, a task both found unimaginably draining. Since the fall of the Blackthorne dynasty, Averill Estate had merged with various other businesses to become the equivalent of something in the Old World called Wal-Mart. The company had its long fingers in numerous pies including food, timber, clothing, tobacco, alcohol, and actual pies. With deals in Mexico about to be finalized, Averill Estate Farms was poised to span the entire country.

The Averills spent their days living in three locations, Kingsbury during the winter and wet season, Emerald Coast during the summer, and outside Greenfield during the harvest. They were always busy, getting little more than a week or two a year to themselves.

Cass strolled to the deck that looked out on the lake not yet swarmed with boats. The Averill's two dogs basked in the soft dawn light in the sunroom. Cass relished her creamy morning pick-me-up with some fresh fruit and pleasant scenery.

She breathed in the lake air and sat with the dogs until the last possible second. The Averills took great pride in their work, even if neither enjoyed the day-to-day operations. Thos had shown a surprising aptitude at running this new empire. Cass held her own, but perhaps only as his assistant. She gave one last monstrous stretch and braced herself to tackle the business world.

Hastening her step up to the fourth floor, she threw off her bathrobe and swapped it for a long teal skirt and white shirt with a high, long collar. Slipping on her black shoes, she hurried out the front door to a slate gray car with an impatient chauffer. The armed guards by her door gave her a wave.

Bells chimed from the direction of the city square. Bells only rang for significant events like major deaths or gatherings of national importance. She turned back to her doorman, who was frozen in his tracks.

"Sir?" Cass asked.

The man didn't budge. She placed her hand on him.

"What is it?" she asked.

"The Compact. We've been summoned," he said.

A tugging feeling in her skull compelled her to the car. Behind her, two dozen bodyguards began a zombie-like march to the city square. One bodyguard climbed into the car with her. Silently the driver took her through the grounds and up to the city.

Driving through the city, she saw the throngs of people heading the same way. The car stopped to drop Cass and her bodyguard off near the statue of the crown-holding eagle that had replaced one of Queen Adamina, which had been destroyed a little over two years ago. Cass took her spot beside her husband and the other power elite at the head of the crowd.

The entire population gathered in the square and the

connecting streets for this momentous event. Cass found it a bit unsettling that virtually nothing was known about these world-changing events, only bare bones records based on second-hand accounts. The more she tried to think about it, the foggier her mind grew. She tried to take another step, but her body refused to budge. Her heart began to dance to the beat of anxiety and fear.

"Citizens of the world!" a voice cried out.

All heads turned skyward. A lone figure hovered above the people. The strange man walked down invisible steps toward the crowd. The figure was a man in a white suit and waxen, gray skin. His most disturbing feature was the golden mask with a maleficent smile and eyes of piercing blackness, an exaggerated version of the comedy mask that always freaked her out. The man's voice boomed with inhuman power.

"Today is a momentous day," he began. "You have been chosen to receive the great burden of knowledge. The Compact is the agreement between you and us that keeps your world spinning. As long as you remain compliant, it shall continue to turn for two thousand more."

The figure touched the ground, moving like a specter through the crowd. It stared into the eyes of each person that held power in New Prosperity. The man gave Cass a passing glance, the black pits where his eyes should be made her heart stop. He turned and continued to address the enthralled crowd.

"Do you agree to our terms?" he asked. The crowd answered in unison with a resounding yes. The word slipped from Cass's mouth against her will.

"Let us begin," he said, clapping his hands together.

A throbbing pain filled Cass's skull. All around her, the city's people endured the pain without so much as a grunt. Lost and forbidden knowledge filled the people's minds. For a moment, they were all connected. Cass felt their thoughts, the brain cells surging with white-hot fire. In silence, each person received the knowledge that the Compact assigned to them. Aviation technology, new medical treatments, telecommunications, weapons tech, and information of all kinds flooded through the living network. Cass strained under her paralysis, trying to break free from the hallucinatory hypnosis. Then the connection to the masses ceased. A voice pierced the silence.

"We'll be slaves to false gods no longer!" a man said.

A dozen other men with unknown rifles emerged from the crowd and surrounded the masked man. Cass felt control of her body return. The enthralled masses fell to their knees, trying to shake off the disorientation.

"Ow . . . what the hell?" Thos said. "Cass? Why are we out here?" Thos stumbled to his feet.

"How dare you . . . *you* defile the Compact?" the masked man's voice roared with a force that shook the earth.

The men aimed their rifles and opened fire. Ripples of energy knocked the masked figure back. During the attack, the zombified masses stumbled to their feet and scattered.

"No!" the masked man snarled even as the bullets hit.

A shockwave knocked the people back to the ground. The gunmen quickly jumped back up and continued firing, unleashing strange waves on the strange man.

"He ain't going down!" one cried.

The entity raised his right hand. The masked man pointed at each of his attackers as if marking targets.

"Die," he said.

Blood ran from the eyes, nose, ears, and mouth of each man. In unison, they fell. Only one attacker remained, scrambling for his missing weapon. The man noticed the gun falling at Cass's feet.

"Shoot!" he cried. Cass refused to move.

Slowly the masked figure walked up to the last man. Again he raised his hand. In response, the man flung his arms out and grunted curses.

"To fight your salvation, what a sad state of affairs," the masked man said.

The attacker tried to lift his gun, sweating from the strain. The masked man opened his palm, and the victim's arms snapped backward. He let out an unholy scream as his elbows shattered. Cass tried to closed her eyes to avoid the horror, but they wouldn't budge. The man choked out words through the pain.

"We got your number. Your time is running out."

Another man hidden in the crowd wielded a thick, rectangular rifle with a flat end. He pointed the gun and fired more waves. The masked figure let out a hellish shriek. Glass exploded from the windows behind him. The figure's physical form shifted, going back and forth from transparent to opaque. It shifted through numerous forms, including one obscured in robes and a knight with a mask resembling an old king. The masked creature swatted at his attacker. The weapon in the attacker's hand fell into pieces. The masked figure resumed the form of a man in white. The entity disappeared then reappeared in front of the defenseless attacker. It reached out and extended its finger just a hair away from the man.

Slowly the entity drove his pointer finger in between the man's eyes. The man whimpered like a beat dog as the finger pushed through skull and brain. Cass felt the enthrallment weaken and moved toward Thos. The crowd—discombobulated—stirred. The entity scoffed and quickly lulled the masses back into submission.

"We do this for you," he said, removing his finger from the man's skull.

Knowledge flooded in Cass's mind, learning all the things the Compact wanted her to know, including rudimentary surgical skills useful for her second job at her clinic. Her head throbbed and burned. Then as suddenly as it came, the pain left. The entity clasped his hands together.

"This instance of the Compact has been completed. You now possess the information you're ready to know. Don't waste or abuse it."

It offered a bow and walked up into the sky. A mist rolled off the entity and enveloped the bodies of the fallen soldiers, leaving not even a drop of blood on the ground. The entity continued upward until disappearing. The crowd awoke, confused and oblivious.

Thos instantly grabbed hold of Cass and hugged her tight. He fumbled for words, which was more than she could do at the moment. She remembered nothing—no masked figures, no attack, or even how she got here. The only thing Cass knew was that the Compact had taken place.

ANSELM

ANSELM RAN HIS fingers over the serpentine cuts on his chest. They were reminders of his failures as a husband, a father, and a king. The wounds healed within minutes, so he made more voluntarily, although sometimes they were delivered by enemies looking to rob the odd hermit in the wilderness. His blood-rusted blade failed him just as he had failed everyone else. He thought of different endings to his story. Racing to his car in the royal garage with family in tow. Sometimes he imagined hugging his family tight as the castle collapsed on them all. There was no happy ending for Anselm, and he feared there may never be an ending at all.

He reflected on this second life in the wilderness of the Northern Frontier. The comforts of Blackthorne Castle had become a distant memory. The Northern Frontier was the northernmost state of New Prosperity, with small pockets of civilization and only a handful of cities. It also housed the branch of Vigilant once commanded by Gregor Pavane, survivor of Anselm's attempted murder. Most frontiersmen lived in small settlements, villages, or logging camps.

He had nothing from his old life, not even clothes. His home had been destroyed, his possessions distributed among his betrayers, and even the resting place for his entire bloodline had been reduced to a landfill. Anselm lived as a vulture as he moved across the nation he once ruled. And then even his masked benefactor disappeared, leaving him alone in the great wilds. For now, Anselm lived as an exile, biding his time.

His body throbbed and his stomach growled. Pain and hunger had become his constant companions. Slivers of warm light crept in the openings of his ramshackle hut, one hard push away from doom. The distant rooster crows heralded the new day. Donning a pair of wrinkly trousers, forest green tunic, and black cap, he braced for another day of difficult living.

He threw open his straw door without thinking, and it fell to the ground to the sound of his cursing. On three sides of the hut, trees, plants, and tall grass stretched as far as the eye could see. Anselm's knowledge of botany was lacking, but he could discern spruces and mighty royal oaks. He headed east to the coastal town of Durenburg. Anselm, who went only by the name Journeyman, had carved out a decent relationship with the townsfolk as a hunter and occasional defender when not planning his revenge. Alexander assembled his army here 2000 years ago, Anselm wondered if he could, too. His long hair, bushy beard, and increased muscle mass ensured no one recognized him. With the masked entity absent for over a year, and all the secret labs picked clean, Anselm became rudderless. He left his weapon in the hut and strode across the green fields toward the town.

He stopped in the open for a moment to let the gentle breeze caress his face. He breathed in deep and watched the tall grass sway. His pace slowed as he took in the serenity, a rare feeling in his new life incognito. The visage of Abigail appeared before him with cracked, blackened flesh. Abigail's eyeless face wept crimson tears and reached out for him.

"Give me a moment's peace!" he roared. His frail old voice now sounded vigorous; another blessing bestowed upon him by mistake flowing through his veins. The encounter ruined his brief moment of joy. He resumed his journey.

Cottages, farms, and a few Victorian-style houses dotted the landscape. It was a beautiful place for those willing to work hard for a quiet, remote life. People tended the gardens, shops, and fishery. A horse-drawn carriage passed him by, and the driver nodded.

Durenburg was the very definition of the word quaint and seldom visited by government officials, himself included. So he was relatively safe. As he walked to the town, the smells of fish, water, and wood clung to the air. He could hear the hustle and bustle at the pier, the heart of the local economy.

A prune-faced, elderly woman hobbled past Anselm. The woman nodded and gave a warm smile. A boy gave him a wide-eyed stare long enough to cause him irritation. The child looked so much like Edgar, adding insult to injury. The boy's father yelled at him, causing him to flee.

Through the cracked streets, he worked his way to the pier. It didn't take long for Rosalie Crowe to spot him. Her black hair fluttered in the summer wind against a blue sky filled with marshmallow clouds. She carried a light within her that reminded Anselm of possibilities, and her presence always lifted his broken spirit. The Crowes were the most successful family in the area, in charge of Durenburg's fisheries. Like Anselm, Rosalie knew tragedy; she had lost her mother to unexpected illness and her husband to bandits. Without a word, she ran up and wrapped her arms around him. She was half his age, but he had developed a friendship with her that bordered on something more intimate. He ignored the glares from his imaginary dead wife.

"Hey, you," she said. Her voice was sweet yet tinged with a rough tom-boyishness. "Thought the wendigos had you." Wendigos, named after the beasts of folklore, were gaunt creatures with long claws, mismatched antlers, and sharp bones visible through their thin skin. His last encounter with one of those monsters had left him shredded up beyond what mortals could endure, but when he made it home, he had nary a scratch.

"I've learned their ways and lead them now," Anselm said, puffing up his chest. Rosalie always laughed loud enough that Kingsbury probably heard it. It pleased him to hear her laugh, but the others in the vicinity weren't so fond of it.

"Ugh. I hate my laugh. So quit it." She poked his chest with her finger.

"Anything been going on since I've been out?" he inquired.

"Been quiet," she said.

"Good, it's supposed to be nice and quiet. I've seen some camps a few miles from west of here, but no campers."

Anselm had heard the rumors of violence sweeping on the country, the controlled chaos his enemies were so fond of. Rosalie's cheerful demeanor vanished with a scowl.

"Already talking about going out again. Don't you just stop?" She poked him again. Internal thoughts chewed away at him when he stopped, so he tried not to as much as possible.

"I made you something," she said. She rummaged through the knapsack at her hip and gave him food wrapped in a towel. "Butter tarts. I saw how much you loved them at the fair."

She grinned from ear to ear as he took the gift from her, trying to contain her girlish excitement.

"I may have an addiction problem," he laughed. He couldn't get enough of the treats. "I can't get over seeing people loving to cook. Everyone I knew hated it," he said between chews.

"We're not always stabbing and smashing 'round here," she teased.

Rosalie had caught his eye from the moment he arrived. She had been friendly when all others were fearful. She had genuine honesty and beauty that few maintained in hard lives. She talked to him long before the others welcomed him into the fold. There was one other like her, though she had endured a different type of hardship; this person was once his best friend and closest confidant. Rosalie was kind, loving, and everything his wife once had been. He could've left the wilderness whenever he wanted, but she kept him here. They both filled up the missing piece in each other's lives.

They walked and talked their way down the pier. The two bounced from subject to subject as they sat on the pier. Rosalie watched him demolish the butter tarts while he watched the fishing boats depart. They sat in silence for a while. A few delivery trucks drove by. Anselm grimaced at the sight of Thos Averill's smiling face plastered on the side of each one. Knowing Thos's ever-growing business supplied these locals better than he had was a unique kind of pain.

Thos Averill was the grandson of the man who had saved the life of Anselm's grandfather, Aldous, and received the lands that would turn into the country's most successful farm. Thos joined in the rebellion, feeding their army, lynching Anselm's eldest son, and leading the charge on Kingsbury that brought down the mighty Blackthorne dynasty. Anselm would share his knowledge of torture with the bumpkin one day; he'd refine his skills for now. Anselm quickly turned his attention back to Rosalie and the water. He needed to talk about his past life, alleviating its spiritual evisceration.

"I used to take my family on the water," Anselm said. "My oldest loved fishing. Spent all day on the boats just laughing until the stars came out. He loved driving too." Words came out before he could think.

"You've been in a car?" She perked up. He quickly melded truth with lies.

"Was one in town the owner was nice enough to let people ride in. It was a beautiful silver, like something out of a storybook. King Astor gave it to him. Astor was a tough old bastard, they said, but a good man. My kids couldn't get enough of that damn thing. I told them we shouldn't be seen using it, made us seem snobbish. Honestly, I was just afraid of it after the wreck."

It embarrassed him. His eyes welled up with tears.

"If only they had reached that damn car. I failed them."

Anselm told Rosalie about the attack on his home and the fight to evacuate using a car. She didn't know that he spliced this with events from the town near Heller Valley, which had a car bequeathed to them by Anselm's father, that vehicles had been destroyed in an uprising that happened after word got out about the king's demise.

Rosalie took his hand in hers and rested her head on his shoulder. At that moment, Anselm didn't care if he had revealed too much. His sobbing gave way to relief.

"Hard to believe they've been gone two years. It's hard going on without them, but I'm doing my best. It's easier here with you," Anselm said.

Curses from fishermen with empty nets traveled along the water, trying to force the image of the dead family out of his mind. Anselm moved the conversation off to her family.

"How's the family?" Anselm asked. A few strong sniffles caused them both to chuckle.

"Cam's feeling better and back to studies. Dad's been good, but he needs more people out on the water." Anselm understood the words were meant as a request.

"Yes," he said warmly.

"Yes?" she asked.

"I'll go fish with your father." She sighed heavily and hugged him.

"Thanks. He wouldn't ask for help even if he was half in a shark."

Shame washed over him as she hugged him, quickly vanishing at the warmth growing inside. Rosalie was his anchor to the world. She gave him a reason to live, but this dillydallying got in the way of his true mission.

"I have to go pick up Cam. See you tomorrow," Rosalie beamed.

Anselm went over to the gray-haired, barrel-chested man inspecting the boats. This burly man with arms as thick as baby whales, cast a visage like Anselm's father in his prime. The gray hairs on his chest peeked out from the collar of his shirt. The imposing man was Rosalie's father, Ezra. On his last tour, Anselm learned the frontier bred a much heartier folk than the spineless fobs in Kingsbury.

"Mornin," he said. The man gave Anselm a stern look.

"Morning," Anselm replied.

Anselm extended his arm and gave Ezra a firm handshake. He didn't realize how hard he had gripped until he saw Ezra cradling his hand.

"We might get ya crushing rocks 'fore long," he said. Anselm knew pride kept Ezra from asking for help, so he took the initiative.

"Mind some company today?" Anselm asked. Ezra cocked an eyebrow.

"I can handle it myself," Ezra replied. He grappled with his pride for a moment.

"But help'd be nice. We're catching somethin' strong either way," he added with a devious grin.

Ezra pulled a scratched-up, brown flask from his pocket. *Aric loved whiskey,* Anselm thought bitterly.

"Not a whiskey man," Anselm replied. Ezra frowned.

"Got rum, beer, scotch, too," he grinned. "Wanna come, gotta drink." Anselm threw up his hands.

"Ah, what the hell."

The two men walked over to the docks. Along with a crew of only two others, Anselm boarded the Tiger Shark, named for the discolored stripes that weaved up and down its sides.

Ezra fired up the engine, and they set out to the ocean waters between the coast and the islands. The queasiness forced Anselm to hang over the side at first.

"Thought you've done this before?" Ezra asked. Anselm spit in the water. The damp, salty air shot up his nostrils.

"Little rusty," he groaned. Ezra laughed.

For the next thirty hours, Anselm helped the men catch fish and crabs. He loved to eat crab, even though it only angered his stomach for lack of fulfillment. Ezra spotted a large fin circling their next spot.

"Rime shark," Ezra hollered out.

Anselm smirked when Ezra placed the picturesque telescope up to his eye. The shark fin shimmered, giving it the appearance of solid ice. A large white bird swooped down to grab a meal. Just as the bird took off with its prize, the beast burst forth for the aerial meal; its crystalline skin sparkled in a rainbow effect. Ezra cursed while Anselm enjoyed the wonders of the frontier. Ezra waved Anselm up to the bridge.

"My daughter has really taken a shine to ya," he said as he gripped the wheel. Anselm blushed, rubbing the back of his neck.

"Never could find the right guy after Bill died. You seem decent enough. People 'round here like you, well most. Some call ya fuckhead."

"Not the worst impression I've left," Anselm said.

"What're you, thirty?" he asked.

Anselm cocked his head, wondering if that was some jest. He hadn't paid much attention to his appearance during his exile. Ezra's expression also scrunched with confusion at Anselm's reaction.

"I . . . feel like an old man," Anselm laughed. Ezra laughed in kind and waved his hand at the remark. "Anyway, I don't plan to stay here much longer."

"Yer welcome to stay. My daughter could use a man like you."

"I'll keep that in mind," Anselm muttered.

He smiled genuinely, not against having a life with Rosalie.

"Let's head back," Ezra said.

Anselm pulled up a net with a good haul. He looked into the water and saw his youthful reflection, so much like Aric.

Returning to town, Anselm spent the evening cleaning Ezra's haul to the hungry glances of a shaggy stray called Mange—the dog quite found of him. Rosalie and her son, Cameron, found him leaving the dock with Mange. This was his new family. This was the life that had been stolen from him. He spent many days, evenings, and some nights with Rosalie, her son, and their dog. He treasured these moments, and the more there were, the harder it would be to leave. He neglected his duty. His hate for himself and his enemies grew as much as the budding love for Rosalie. Taking Rosalie by the hand, the two walked to the town center with Cameron.

A crowd had gathered in town to celebrate not just the summer but an anniversary. Today was the founding of the new government and the end of the Blackthorne dynasty. The people of Durenburg didn't seem to care about that, but no one turned down a reason to party. *Today is the celebration of my death,* Anselm thought.

One man strummed an acoustic guitar to a crowd of revelers. He could smell the prawns on the grill and saw Mange running excitedly around the meaty goodness. Anselm grabbed some chilled cider and chugged it. When the music turned festive, Rosalie pulled him up to dance.

He flailed around awkwardly at first but eventually found his rhythm. The two became the center of attention. Abigail's corpse stood by the grill, frowning at him. The other festival-goers clapped as they spun around. Anselm moved instinctively, feeling as if he'd fall over at any moment. Rosalie didn't care. She spun around and around, completely in bliss. It sent Anselm's nerves aflame with excitement and trepidation.

The stars burned brightly in the summer sky while the firebugs illuminated the hills. She kissed his cheek, and he felt his face grow warm. Emotion took over. He snuck in a kiss on Rosalie's lips. He heard the pitter-patter of her heart, followed by the frantic pumps of his own. Rosalie smiled at him and wished him goodnight. She caught up with her father and son. Anselm whistled all the way back home, though his mood changed when he arrived. For the first time in his two-year exile, he didn't want to participate in the nightly ritual.

"Not tonight," he said forcefully. *Every night until I do what I promised,* he thought.

It all came rushing back. The masked man's absence was no excuse. He had let his mission falter by getting close to Rosalie. Anselm needed to fix his priorities. *You continue to fail them. Do what you promised.* Anselm sighed.

He entered the work shed beside his hut and scanned the various tools carelessly laid out upon the bench inside.

An assortment of tools for maintenance, hunting, fishing, and raider killing. The fingers of Anselm's right hand wrapped around the hammer. He placed his left hand on the table. He spread his fingers as far apart as possible. He sucked in a deep breath and slammed the hammer down, resulting in a sickening crunch. He cried out. He hit it again, crushing the bone at the joint. He hit the fingers repeatedly, leaving them flattened crimson mush going off in all directions. He cried in pain and anger, fueling ever harder blows. He held the hammer high and never faltered.

GREGOR

"ANOTHER DAY, ANOTHER demon," Gregor said, licking his cracked lips.

Gregor enjoyed returning to work, free of rolling around about as helpful as a hat for an ass. While he enjoyed the change in scenery, he didn't relish the idea of sweating to death in Mexico under the leadership of the newly appointed grand crusader while someone else lorded over his former domain. After being reinstated into the order, Gregor was immediately reassigned before he could ask any questions about his branch. Absorbed into the southern branch of Vigilant, he found himself having to take on jobs to prove himself still valuable. They told him he was needed down here, but only if he was still in top form. Gregor feared the specter of age was finally catching up to him, but this pushed him to work harder. He refused to be a feeble old man rolling around in a chair. He fought through the doubt, proving himself for months. Gregor fought as well as ever, pushing himself to the limits and hoping it was only hard work and not Old World mutation that kept him so capable. He grabbed the skin of water at his side, a friend he found comfort in every other minute. He told himself beggars can't be choosers and went back to the basics of being a field agent for now.

Mexico was once a country, having been torn right down the middle by Toth and New Prosperity over 1500 years ago. Toth repurposed their half as the province of Khmun while the New Prosperity side kept the original name. Gregor's contract brought him to the region of Veracruz, east of Mexico City. His recent mission took him to a place called Alvarado.

Alvarado was a beautiful town overlooking the gulf, known for sugar cane and coffee. The area was quickly expanding with talk of the Averills adding local farms to their gargantuan empire. The locals viewed Gregor as a curiosity, clearly not believing the old man a legendary warrior. Sickly sweet smells of fruit and sugar filled the streets. Summer heat assaulted his every minute, adding a layer of sweat under his uniform. With hot city days, cold desert nights, and every variation of the two, it was the worst of both worlds. While searching for his target, he admired the vibrant colors of the Mediterranean and Moorish style architecture so different from the rest of the country. Neon lights added to the surreal rainbow of colors all around.

The man that had hired him cowered in an old tangerine condo overlooking the waterfront park where tourists came to loiter. He was a thrill-seeker named Renaldo, apparently finding a little more thrill than he desired. According to Renaldo, the demon became an urban legend. Dubbed "Boo Hag," it left skinless bodies behind every year for the last three decades.

Gregor passed many crowds, drinking and celebrating the beginning of summer and the anniversary of the establishment of the new government on track to be no better than the last. Gregor stalked every nook, cranny, dive, and hole for his target.

Gregor stopped briefly to enjoy the seductive rhythms of a woman in a dress that smoldered like embers. A young girl approached him, way more disturbed than any child should look.

"Don't let the hag ride you," she said before running back to an angry father. Gregor winced in disgust and confusion.

"Creepy little shit," Gregor blurted out, turning an angry parent into a livid one.

Gregor veered away from the crowds to the dark corners ripe for demonic activity. Unsubstantiated rumors and questionable reports had victims all over town with no connection, save their grisly end. He passed a man rolling tobacco.

"Don't let the hag ride you," he said.

He'd nearly given up hope when a faint sound caught his attention, something like a woman crying but off just enough to raise the hairs on his arms. The cries then grew louder, painful. Locals fleeing the scene gave him the impression his night was about to begin.

Gregor picked up the pace, this time with an EMP wave rifle, pistol, and sword for close encounters. The latest Vigilant invention, EMP waves tore through demonic, mutated, and artificial cells. The name was misleading since it suggested it was purely for machines, but it had stuck. Demons were tough to kill at full strength without Vigilant weaponry, but the starving ones could be eliminated with the standard blades and bullets. He recalled telling Drake this, somewhat diminishing his victory over the shrill.

With rifle held high, the locals veered away from the grouchy crusader. Gregor followed the screams. He approached the faded green apartment complex. Multiple sets of five holes zig-zagged up the side of the condo, stopping at a shattered window on the sixth floor. Pressed against the stucco wall, he moved up blood-slick stairs. He heard tearing. Fire shot through his feet and calves from his first post-wheel stair hike.

He followed the bloody trail to an open door. The tearing stopped. Gregor walked in with gun ready. On the floor lay a woman with skin freshly peeled off. Blood painted the walls and covered the mangled furniture.

Gregor felt a presence by the window, a tall figure hunched over, with long bird-like talons and ghost-white hair. A patchwork of human flesh from various women hung off the demon's skinless frame. The creature smiled through the collection of faces it had haphazardly stitched together.

"Am I not beautiful, love?" she said, running her claws down the naked flesh that wasn't hers.

Though he'd never encountered such a demon, he'd read reports on the vaingloria. A vaingloria was a demon of insecurity, born of those that used technology in the constant need to receive adoration from others to bolster their fragile egos. Vanglorias developed attachments to humans that, if said individual didn't tell them how beautiful they were, would proceed to "improve" themselves until they did. Needless to say, vainglorias handled rejection poorly.

"You want this flesh? You can't have me. I am his," she said, her attempts at seduction subverted by a voice not quite human. Gregor recoiled. The demon bore her teeth, slightly tearing her skin-quilt mask. His visible disgust was a declaration of war.

"No one rejects me!" she roared. The blood ran through the stitches of the demon's fresh skin.

Gregor fired waves in the demon's stomach. The demon stumbled back into the hallway. Gregor fired again. The demon fell over the railing, cracking as it bounced off the rails down to the bottom floor. He sprinted down after her. The monster jolted from the ground and burst through the door. Gregor fired more rounds as he darted after her. The moment Gregor placed a foot outside the complex he jumped back, barely avoiding a fatal swipe from scalpel-sharp talons.

He shot the creature in the face, shearing off part of her flesh mask. The demon slashed frantically, reducing Gregor's tabard to confetti. The endless barrage of attacks prevented Gregor from shooting. He pulled the sword from the sheath on his back, deflected the assault, and countered with a few of his own. More pieces of skin and tarry blood hit the floor.

"You won't come between us!" the demon hissed.

The demon slashed at Gregor's face. He jumped back, knocking his head back into the brick wall behind him. Disoriented, he swung his sword to keep the monster at bay. After a few sword swings, he realized the creature had left.

"Where'd she . . . shit," he said, making haste toward his employer at the end of a trail of blood, skin, and screams.

Gregor's lungs threatened to burst as he sprinted across the city toward the tangerine condo. He rounded corners, occasionally narrowly avoiding a flesh-rending slash from a demonic ambush. He chased after the demon. He arrived at the condo, the door now cut to ribbons. Gregor had a hunch of where to go. The remainder of the demon's skin lay in pieces near the basement entrance.

"Of course," he grumbled.

Gregor slowed down his pace to avoid the potential evisceration up ahead. Muffled speech and thuds came from far below. At the bottom, he found the basement converted into a private nightclub. A dangling neon welcome sign gave a last flicker before hitting the ground. Behind the counter of the underground bar, Gregor's employer threw bottles at the horror approaching him.

"Why don't you love me? I've done everything for you! Don't let him kill me!" she cried.

"Get away!" Renaldo screamed, throwing his last bottle.

"I saw you with that whore. She won't get in the way anymore," she growled.

"Luca? You bitch!"

Gregor shot rounds into the monster and she fell back. Her predatory eyes turned to Gregor. She rushed across the room toward him. Gregor jumped out of the way, leaving the demon's deadly claws to go straight through the basement wall. With her hands stuck in the wall, Gregor switched to his sword and proceeded to cleave through her arms. She desperately tried to pull herself free as Gregor chopped through muscle, ligament, and bone. The creature fell back, with her severed hands still in the wall. Tarry demon blood spilled out all over the floor.

"Help me, Renny!" the creature wailed.

The cowering man did nothing to help his ghoulish admirer. Never in his life had Gregor heard a demon cry for help. "I thought you loved me," she whimpered, thick black liquid running from her eyes.

"Your days of stalking innocent victims is over," Gregor said. The demon turned to him and hissed.

"Innocent? He sought me out! I was so beautiful," she wept.

Footsteps above distracted Gregor for a crucial second, yet she didn't attack him. Down the stairs rushed two Vigilant soldiers. The moment they saw the demon, they filled her with waves, destroying her regenerative cells. The dying vaingloria gave one last look to her intended mate.

"We're made for each other. I love—" she said.

A point-blank round through the brain put her down for good. Renaldo rose to his feet, trying to hide the urine trail decorating the front of his cargo shorts.

"Thank God," he said, clearly unclenching his anus with an exhale.

"I got this," Gregor snapped. The two soldiers bowed their heads.

"Didn't want to take any chances," one said.

Gregor wiped away the sweat. Holding on to the bar counter, he pushed himself back up. Gregor walked over to Renaldo, who looked for a quick exit.

"You got some dangerous fetishes," Gregor said with disgust. Sweat began to roll down Renaldo's protruding brow.

"What . . . no, that's . . . she's lying," he said.

His twitchy stance, rapid eye movements, and enough sweat to fill a pool let Gregor knew the demon had spoken some truth. The two soldiers blocked Renaldo's escape.

"You believe a demon?" Renaldo asked. Reports of the vain-gloria suggested that they could make themselves attractive enough to mimic humans and lure in the sexually curious.

"Normally no, so start talking," Gregor said. He chose to withhold the information of Renaldo being bait for the backup plan.

"I wanted to experience something new . . . and I found her. I didn't know she was a killer."

"The stories I've heard?" Gregor asked.

"Lies," Renaldo said. "Those people out there hate me. I've heard about you. If what they said is true, there'd be guns pointed at you right now, too."

Gregor analyzed Renaldo and sensed partial truth in his words.

"Fair point," he said, just two years ago a fugitive for attempted regicide. The soldiers behind Gregor stirred.

"The law is clear. Consorting with demons is punishable by death," said the Vigilant soldier behind him. Gregor knew the law yet hesitated. "The law is clear," the man repeated.

"I know the damn law," Gregor said.

Gregor saw the fear in Renaldo's eyes. He came to hate this part of the job. The Compact could be mercilessly strict, but he'd uphold it to the best of his ability. Gregor reloaded his pistol and aimed it at Renaldo.

"What the hell are you doing? You're overreacting. I . . . I'll pay!" he shrieked.

"The law is clear. Ever Vigilant," the man beside Gregor said, firing a single round into Renaldo's skull.

One of the soldiers walked over to Renaldo's corpse, checking his pockets. The body held a few hundred coins more than the contract price. Violators of the Compact had all monies and effects removed, providing a grim bonus. The soldiers tossed the sack of coins at Gregor.

"You want to intervene so bad, you can burn the demon," Gregor said. The soldier shook his head.

"We're taking it with us," he replied.

"Of course," Gregor said with a perturbed sigh.

"Got an issue, take it up with the boss. He's requested your presence by the way. We're heading out now."

Gregor had yet to meet the new supreme commander of all Vigilant forces, the first grand crusader in centuries.

"Moreno?" he asked. The soldiers responded with disturbingly wide grins.

"You'll see," they replied.

Vigilant commandeered local army trucks for the crusades, another perk of the job since only the nations rulers could get away with refusing. Gregor looked out the window. The truck stopped in front of a large barn beside an empty house. Gregor scratched his head. His brow furrowed.

"Matthias is out here?" Gregor asked, confused.

"No. West. Far west," the soldier said coyly.

"Far west? You can't mean the Uninhabited?" Gregor said.

The Uninhabited was a large stretch of wasteland somewhere between Toth, New Prosperity, and what was once the Badlands. Rocked by walls of violent storms and desolation from some ancient super weapon, it was a place Vigilant had yet to penetrate. Unlike its eastern counterpart, the Deadlands, rumors of unimaginable riches enticed many adventurers to their deaths. Though everyone had their theories about the nature of the desolate land, all could agree that it was a place best left alone. But not leaving things alone was the general reason why Vigilant existed.

"And what exactly did he find out there?" Gregor asked.

"It," the soldier replied.

"It," Gregor said, sifting through the memories, histories, and legends. He knew at once. "No . . . the Silent City."

Two AR-wielding Vigilant soldiers stepped out of the farmhouse and opened the barn door. The truck drove inside. Gregor noticed the metallic floor unlike any in what few barns he knew.

"Really went all out for this, didn't you?" Gregor said.

One member of Vigilant nodded and went over to a cleverly hidden panel in the corner of the barn. The soldier hit the button on the panel. The metal floor sank into the earth.

Inside a large cave that led into a black tunnel there was a long train humming with life. Gregor stepped onto the train.

DRAKE

SHACKS AND HOVELS lay ahead in what was left of the town the Void used as a hideout. Drake could see the ruins of Alman Cathedral, torches with red flames, and the hell of the Chihuahuan Desert that fed into the even more hellish Uninhabited. Though Mexico was under the control of the New Prosperity government, the Void was a powerhouse in the region. Once a union of gangs that served as the modern cartel, it had mutated into something even more ominous. The death worshiping cult was an offshoot of an Old World group that became its own thing, with a particular hatred of the Catholics that expanded into a hatred for everyone. Driven by a desire to create death, they were nihilists who wanted to drag the world down with them. People had taken to calling their members deadheads.

Drake watched the targets below, their madness on full display. The cult members were painted, tattooed, or sometimes scarred up to look like skeletons with faces. One member dragged a battered captive toward the cathedral.

The rest of Drake's squad pulled up behind him. One scanned the area with the scope a tan and brown sniper rifle. Drake felt strange sporting a buzz cut and wearing the desert camo armor, feeling naked without his sword. Even though swords, like long hair, were useless in most skirmishes, he missed them.

"We move in five," Drake said, the sight of his assault rifle pointing at the head of a meat wall of a gang enforcer. Drake had been down this road quite a few times already during his time down here in Mexico. Eliminating gang hideouts became routine at this point. The group took positions and slowly moved in on the shacks. Guns and drugs were the primary sources of income for the cult, growing more lucrative as the government banned more and more of them. The organization was rumored to also dabble in the slave trade, though Drake had no idea who the buyers could be. Drake saw a small object flying down toward him. Instinct took over.

"Grenade!" Drake said.

Men jumped out from all corners of the abandoned town. Another grenade sailed out from one of the windows and landed right in front of Drake. He snatched it up quickly and threw it back, blowing off the front of the shack, leaving two cultists exposed. He killed them with multiple shots to the chest. A man fired blue-trailed bullets from a rapidly deteriorating house. One of the more eager recruits jumped to his feet and sprinted to the hovels. His bullet-filled corpse hit the ground a few feet from a blown apart shack. Drake's heart sank when he saw the man brandishing a strange, two-pronged gun.

"Cover me!" Drake yelled and flung himself to his feet, sprinting to the nearest building.

Drake dove through the window, barely missing the blue trail of bullets. He ran back out the door as the building exploded from the barrage of bullets. Drake was unsure how he knew they were using railgun bullets, but hazy memories suggested he'd seen them before.

He used the smoking ruin as cover and shot a man cautiously rounding the corner of the building ahead. The surviving cultists ran to the cathedral, which glowed with red light. Drake and his troops mobilized, clearing a path to the cathedral. Blue trailed bullets eviscerated what remained of the town. Drake and his four remaining squad-mates dropped the gangsters firing on them. The gunfire ceased.

"That wasn't all of them," Drake said.

Drake's men pushed open the cathedral door. Drake eyed the pews, finding no enemies. He turned his attention to the altar in the back. A robed figure made of numerous fused human skeletons towered over an altar, holding a fresh corpse in its arms. Dozens of bony limbs came together to form four giant arms and four legs. A series of melded ribcages formed the body. Numerous skulls bound together to create the multi-headed horror. It reminded Drake of the textbook drawings of the golems cobbled together from various scraps; the many limbs also reminded him of ghoulish fairies. Drake would've admired the craftsmanship if it wasn't so grotesque. This grim figure was a recreation of Void, their version of death. Drake had seen these perverse altars far too often. The squad groaned in disgust.

"Focus," Drake said.

Open crates littered the back of the cathedral. The surviving figures stepped out from behind the altar. All placed weapons on the ground in front of them. Drake began interrogating them. He believed at least one would be unwilling to die for the cause, even among those in the death cult. The cultist in the middle grinned.

"Something funny?" asked Drake.

The cultist launched projectile phlegm at Drake.

"None of this matters. The end is here, He's the messenger," the cultist said.

The two sides grew braced for combat. The three cultists slowly separated, walking casually toward Drake and his men.

"Stop moving. Final warning," Drake said.

The cultists moved forward. Drake noticed the small device on the hip at the man in front of him. The man's hand reached for the device.

"For the Void," he said.

"Drop him!" Drake said.

Drake lit up the man in front. The man hit the floor. Drake turned his gun to the man on the right. The man appeared unmoved by the two soldiers preparing to end him. Drake didn't let the man's smug expression unnerve him. They all stood in silence, waiting for the other to make a move. The other cultist spouted insults at Drake's other soldier.

"Hold it together," Drake advised.

The taunts turned to threats of graphic violence to the soldiers' families. He kept his eyes on the other man. The man reached for something in his pocket, forcing Drake's hand. Drake and the soldier dropped the smug cultist.

Drake heard the click from the gun of the man on his left. The others opened fire, shooting but not killing the attacker in time. The last cultists rushed the soldiers and hit the detonator, reducing both to red mist. Any possible lead on Void's supplier was now in pieces on the ground.

"Check the boxes," Drake replied.

His men scoured the boxes to obtain the strange weapons not sabotaged. "I've seen this weapon before. But where?" Drake said. A clean sweep found nothing else of value. Drake personally tore down the altar.

Drake and the survivors attached the guns to their AATV Jets. Black ops agents were assigned amphibious all-terrain vehicles for missions in a variety of locals such as jungles, deserts, cities, and swamps. The Jet models were more akin to armored cars. They drove across the expansive red, rocky desert into greener and lusher pockets near civilization. Thirty miles from Mexico City they came to the walled villa of Lost Glory, home to Silas "Duke" Calester, Red Devil mercenary turned state regent, the New Prosperity term for governor. Duke's abode rose like a rugged castle with thick walls manned by gunmen.

Two rows of exotic trees lined the roads inside the villa walls; Drake loved the rows of nova blossoms, whose mesmerizing blue glow functioned as streetlights. The road split and wrapped around a small lake complete with small islands and wooden bridges. Various buildings sat on both sides of the lake, with the house proper behind it. The neoclassical house on the right served as the guest house for Drake and other important out-of-towners; the house on the left served as the barracks for Duke's personal guard. A small collection of houses along the wall served as the staff's quarters. A greenhouse, garden, and small hedge maze comprised the area behind the house.

Drake and his men arrived at the regent's mansion. Large doors decorated with the image of a wolf, Duke's personally created family crest, greeted Drake. The butler opened the door as and led Drake to Duke's office. Duke paced around the office, his gray vest and white shirt hiding the small potbelly he had developed in his post mercenary life. Duke was a short-tempered man with thinning brown hair and a commanding baritone voice. He favored intimidation as his method of leadership, a skill honed from his time as a Red Devil. He puffed on a cigar that didn't appear to be helping his nerves. Duke glanced back at Drake, then again at gardens outside the window.

"Another failure," Drake said, grabbing the half-empty glass of bourbon on the table and downing it quickly. Since the fall of the Blackthornes and his reinstatement, Drake adopted a more blunt approach in dealing with questionable leadership.

"There's plenty more out there," Duke said.

"They'd rather explode than cut a deal." Duke brushed the words off and took a seat at his desk.

"That's what crazies do." Duke gave him a disinterested look.

"They got serious firepower that shouldn't exist. And this time it wasn't because you armed them," Drake reminded him.

Drake knew well enough how Duke and others had once

armed these terrorists to undermine Anselm, and now they used these weapons to wage war on their old patrons. Drake hated working for the new government. He wore it for all to see, and only accepted to bring down psychos indiscriminately killing civilians of all affiliations.

"Have you seen the children nailed to the city walls? Beheadings in the streets? Your grievances with us are irrelevant. We will wipe them out. That's the mission." His tone grew louder, and sweat formed on his brow.

"And I'm glad to be a part of that struggle, but we need valuable information to cut this off at the source. These excursions aren't getting us anywhere. I'll handle this on my own."

Drake looked down at the polished veneer desk, everything in the house cleaned to a sparkling finish showcasing Duke's obsessive compulsiveness. Drake could hear the servants scurrying about the place, dusting and cleaning. Duke breathed in deep.

"Very well," Duke said. "Scout around Mexico City and see what you can find. Your pal Thos will be arriving before long. The scum will come out of the woodwork to kill him; surely you can nab one or find an informant."

Drake could almost see the sword cutting through Duke's skull. He knew the stories of the Red Devil's savagery that made Aric's crimes seem like a kid torturing insects.

"Use him as bait?" Drake said.

"It's a golden opportunity. Good ole farm boy is an inspiration and a prime target. There are calls for secession, and more people gravitate toward the Freemen and gangs. Deadheads come out, we kill them, people will reconsider their treason," Duke said.

"Stopping the tyrannizing would also work," Drake said. Duke sneered, Drake could almost feel the invisible venom flying his way.

"That'll be all," Duke said, returning to his papers as Drake walked out. "Oh and Mr. Hale, change your tone the next time you speak to me. This is my domain."

Drake walked through the villa grounds then made his way up to the second floor of the guest house reserved as his. The guesthouse reminded him of home: spacious, beautiful, and empty.

He rested until morning. He changed his armor to a more relaxed outfit: cotton shirt, blue jeans, cowboy hat, boots, sunglasses, and a multicolored serape hiding a reinforced vest in case things got heated. He wore his sidearm, so as not to be completely helpless without his rifle.

Drake left for Mexico City. He raced across the desert, watching the sea of grass, cacti, and rocks go by. He noticed a few silhouettes of bandidos on horseback near a large rock formation south of the city. The battles over the cities gave the bandidos more chances to terrorize the roads; a particularly successful gang called the Hobgoblins caused problems for both the government and the Void. Drake watched the figures until they rode off in the other direction.

He continued apace until he arrived at Mexico City. The main road cut directly through the city center with a large circular courtyard lined with pillars near the north end. The city had many different architectural styles: Gothic, baroque, neoclassical, even some pre-Hispanic types all existed in the city, making it a time capsule for many different eras of human history. Most of the city had been destroyed in the Collapse, but it had all been painstakingly rebuilt during the early decades of the Second Dark Age.

The city brimmed with life and vigor as the people began preparations for the weeklong celebrations to honor fallen heroes, Mexican history, the fall of the Blackthornes, and the unofficial start of summer. Some of the locals on the city council had already dispatched volunteers to put up the decorations. Parking his vehicle in the officer area, Drake walked the streets to gather intel. Drake could barely move through the city square with swarms of people obstructing his path. He snaked his way around them, listening to the conversations. Screams up ahead changed his priorities.

Drake followed the commotion to a crowd parting for a procession. At the front was a group of armored, skull-faced men on white horses, enough soldiers present to be more than a match for the army. A procession of women in red robes and skull masks followed. Four engines roared behind them, four motorcycles, each dragging a rope wrapped around a severed limb. The macabre entourage moved unopposed through the city. Drake gave the nearby soldiers a confused look; he could clearly see the fear in their eyes. He walked over to the closet soldier.

"What're they doing here?" Drake asked.

"Meeting with the mayor. He's over there," the man said, pointing to the ropes.

More screams were drowned out by the roar of engines. Images flooded Drake's mind, taking him back to Anselm's final day. He watched himself ram his sword through Anselm's chest. He saw the castle fall, the Blackthorne family trapped inside. The past bore down on his chest as the castle did on them. Thoughts and emotions spiraled out of control. Drake's hands shook.

"It's not real," he said.

Drake pulled a small bottle of pills from his pocket. The pills rattled around as Drake steadied his hand. He quickly swallowed. The Void left without further incident. Drake took a seat at a café down the street, waiting for his medicine to kick in. His hands stopped shaking. He focused his thoughts on the task at hand. There was more to the chaos raging across the nation. This was controlled chaos. With Blackthorne loyalists, gang wars, and opportunists all spreading violence, Drake had the feeling they were all pawns in a very dangerous game.

THOS

THOS HADN'T YET grown accustomed to wearing a suit, and from his constant squirming, everyone knew it. Company trucks with the Averill Estate Farms logo and his grinning mug plastered on the side delivered food and goods nationwide. He beamed with pride at finally enjoying the family business. Just a few years before, there had been a time when seeing an automobile was an event to travel hours for, and now he had one of his own plus a private army. Thos's driver instantly took him wherever he needed to go. The man's bushy mustache and chubby physique gave him an appearance far jollier than the bland reality. Thos stretched ferociously and didn't look back at the office building that served as Averill Estate HQ. He quickly hopped in the car and out of the sun's death rays, eager to head home.

"This keeps up they can sell my roasted ass at the market," Thos whined.

"That's why you have me, sir."

"What would I do without you, Reg?" Thos asked.

"Walk," he replied.

The Averill mansion dominated the Lake District outside Kingsbury. Two years ago, this had all been countryside and he only a very successful businessman. Now he had the fifth-largest fortune in the entire country and was the go-to guy in agribusiness.

Guards constantly patrolled his house, a costly but worthy investment. Since that fateful day the Blackthornes fell, Thos received the best military training money could buy. With his resources, influence, and training, he wouldn't be bullied anymore. Being a driving force in the economy, a leader in charity work, and a willing critic of the government made Thos a likable guy to all save those in power. Thos felt good to go home and not have to shower off the guilt from sleazy, dirty dealings in Kingsbury. Reginald let Thos out front and drove off toward the garage.

At the front door, Thos saw Cass and forgot all else, including waking up in the middle of the city after the Compact. Nobody questioned the Compact, keeping heads down and moving on from something they couldn't change. It was easier to move on than he thought. He wondered if it was mere habit that kept people moving on. Far as he knew, no one had the power to do anything about it. Like all traumatic events, people seemed to chuck them down the memory hole and move on to stay sane.

Cass stood in the foyer in a simple white and yellow dress of flowers, her hair wrapped around in one long flowing auburn ponytail; all he could do was grin. She saw the blinding white smile and shook her head as he fumbled over the shoes by the door, waving his arms around like a love-struck teenager.

"Weirdo," she said with a smile.

He moved in for a kiss. After the embrace, they walked hand in hand inside the expansive home away from the ungodly heat.

Thos continued to strip down to only a towel as the two walked through the house, both forgetting about the windows. A house guard walked by, saw Thos through the window, and did a double-take. Thos waved. Cassandra buried her face in her hands then quickly drew the curtains on all the relevant windows. They worked their way out back for a dip in the hot tub on the deck.

After an hour of hot liquid relaxation, Cass and Thos headed upstairs to the master bedroom. Thos grabbed his bathrobe.

"Let's lounge today. Gotta busy day tomorrow." Thos yawned. He lay on the bed for a second and rolled over.

Thos grew a little too comfortable and fell asleep, waking up an hour and a half later. Thos's head ached at the unintended oversleep. Cass was nowhere to be found. He could hear and smell the delightful feast being prepared downstairs. Heading right, he went down the hall adorned will griffon bone wall sconces toward the aromas calling him. Before heading to the kitchen, Thos rounded another corner past the massive indoor pool and through the trophy room. Collecting trophies was his new obsession.

On the left-hand side of the room, a winged scorpion lay in a glass case on a pedestal. In the center of the room lay a gargantuan green-plated snallygaster with jaws agape. Guests always asked if he owned this as revenge for his brother, to which Thos always answered yes.

He strolled down the halls, enjoying the spoils of a national hero. He saw Cass. She struck a seductive pose in the kitchen entryway, wearing a tight white t-shirt that exposed her midriff and blue panties. Thos decided that the food could wait. He rushed over, picking her up in a single swoop. The two kissed passionately as he carried her to the bed.

"Gonna play rough, are you?" she said. He thought about talking dirty to her, but it rarely ever went well with this tactic, so he abstained. Their moans of pleasure filled the palatial estate. Afterward, Cass went to the bathroom to clean up, then slid into bed beside her husband.

The two lounged around the estate for the rest of the evening. They strolled through the hanging gardens in the greenhouse, a step pyramid filled with flowers and plants of all kinds growing at the base of each step. They walked the grounds until encroaching rain clouds forced them back inside.

The evening went by too fast, leaving them at the dawn of a new workday. Thos put on a pair of faded blue jeans, a wine-colored button-up shirt, and his favorite boots. Cass dressed in dark jeans and a sleeveless top.

Reginald begrudgingly drove them through the city streets. The first thing he noticed was just how much business the brothel did even in the morning. It had been the first thing rebuilt after the assault on the city, and he could see why.

"Maybe we outta invest in the brothel . . . tits 'n' tots," he said.

Cass responded with an eyeroll. The reconstruction efforts had successfully restored the city. Much improved throughout the nation, though none of it was the government's doing, nor would anyone associated with the royal family be allowed a part in it. Friends of the Blackthorne family were driven out. All traces of the dynasty were erased from the capital: monuments, historical texts, even the mausoleum housing almost two thousand years of Blackthornes.

The Compact made a few changes for the better, too, including the beginnings of air travel and cancer treatments. But for every good thing came plenty of bad, courtesy of the ruling body. The constant presence of armored troops kept people on edge. Stricter gun laws left the people even less capable of defending themselves or participating in any insurrection come the next rebellion.

David Westerfield's media apparatus accused anyone that criticized the regime as Blackthorne loyalists and encouraged violence against them. It was funny to see teachers, musicians, writers, and public officials who once decried tyranny now demonize anyone who criticized them for doing the same things. Taxes increased massively and government anti-terror policies gave it an excuse to seize and shut down anything it wished. Worst of all, the government's plan to outlaw religions let the people know that the State was their only god.

Many people could see the world was quickly heading down

the same road that led to the Collapse. But very few people were willing to speak out. Thos used his influence to push back, but few others dared. Thos considered it to be his unofficial second job.

Everywhere Thos went, he found New Prosperity troops. The newly restructured military had abandoned the color schemes of old for the standard black, all in the latest and greatest reinforced polymer armor. Elite soldiers patrolled the city as if an attack could happen at any moment. They carried XM8-8 assault rifles, and all but officers abandoned swords.

Thos approached the cobblestone going up the hill to Prosperity Hall, the nation's political center, which had replaced Blackthorne Castle. The office building stood seven floors high. Columns surrounded the front of the structure, inspired by the Greek and Roman architecture from Old World government buildings. An enormous domed structure attached to the back of the building served as a gathering place for the masses should the government need to address them. This was the new brain center for the nation, housing offices for political leaders, meeting spots for major business ventures, and the heavily restricted Blackthorne Vault.

The new national flag flapped in the wind in the courtyard, blue with a mighty griffon holding a dented crown in its right claw. Joseph saw a world without kings, with government limited to the extreme. Under his brother's leadership, it became more powerful than ever, a complete mockery of Joe's vision.

A wall of armored soldiers lined the outside of the structure. An officer waved the Averills through to the large ivory house part of the structure. They two followed the gold-trimmed azure carpet that cut through the lobby to the stadium. Artifacts and documents detailing the nation's history were proudly displayed in glass cases, including the Blackthorne crown. Thos noticed David Westerfield, John Derbin, Abraham Kerr, Janice Caan, and Katonah Hale engaged in whispers on the stairs. He didn't like that these five served as advisors to the government, very much still the board of directors with more power but a friendlier name.

Thos tried to like Drake's parents; however, their glacial nature gave him an understanding of why Drake wasn't a fan either. John waved, Thos didn't. David ignored Thos, always with an air of superiority that made him insufferable. Mr. Derbin's features became even more pronounced and vulturesque since Thos had first met him. With his hair falling out and slender limbs, Thos no longer believed the fairies were the worst things he'd seen. Abraham Kerr wore his hatred of Thos not just on his sleeve but in his every expression. Abraham's decisive and ruthless nature made him a man to be feared.

Further ahead, he passed by James Dumas and Yadira Khouri, the regent and vice regent, leaving their offices. James Dumas, the man most credited for destroying the Blackthorne family, had a meteoric rise to power. Thos heard the rumors about James and his involvement with the royal family, suggesting he killed his lifelong friend Percival when he saw a chance to gain power. When Thos and James locked eyes, his skin crawled to the nearest office.

Yadira wore a tangerine blouse with a black skirt; her stunning foreign beauty and down-to-earth personality made her an ideal choice for vice regent. He doubted Yadira would survive politics unless she was secretly a monster like the others. Near the exit to the meeting rooms, he saw a portrait of Abraham's late brother Joseph hanging on the wall.

Two armed guards pushed open the ornate wooden doors that led to the stadium. The stadium held 100,000 people, more than enough for any political or business venture. A massive screen, technology allowed in small portions by the previous Compact, provided those in the nosebleeds a better view. Spectators took seats on the metal benches. Chairs lined the floors for all the important people of the event: politicians, businessmen, and the board of Averill Estate. At the center of it all lay a stage with a podium with seats for the company's top brass and government big shots. Thos scratched his arms, a sign of rising anxiety.

Thos took his seat. He doubted anyone would be so bold as to attack him, but sitting beside his former enemies could make him a target the same as them. What made it worse was that he hated advisors as much as anyone. Thos took a few deep breaths—this was likely the safest he'd ever be.

He watched David Westerfield take a seat beside him. Yadira spoke first, detailing the most relevant news to the business and political communities. She even prepared a slideshow of all the fallen soldiers pacifying the loyalists and battling the cartels. The final slide popped up with a familiar face: Melvin Shor. It was hard to believe it had been a year and a half since Melvin vanished after being assigned to Mexico after his failed election. Melvin could be abrasive at times, but Thos found him far more decent than people gave him credit for. He at least was happy the man died bringing down Maria Ramos, last member of the pre-Void crime family.

Long workdays left him completely exhausted. Thos yawned repeatedly during the cavalcade of speakers. His focus waned. He stared blankly at the spectacle unfolding before him and the endless line of speakers dragging things out longer than necessary. When Abraham finished speaking, he turned and gave Thos a malicious grin.

"I believe Mr. Averill would like to say a few things about his upcoming trip to Mexico." The eyes all shifted to Thos. He had explicitly requested not to speak at this event. He nodded and turned to Cass. Thos covered his mic.

"Prick," Thos whispered.

He took his sweet time coughing and adjusting himself before he leaned in toward the microphone.

"Hey everybody," Thos said with a big wave. "As you all know, even though my board members all backed out at the last minute, I'll still be going down to oversee our expansion into the region.

It'll be beneficial to show our commitment to bringing our brand down south. I know there's trouble with the death cults and whatnot, but being surrounded by enemies is just a normal day for me. We won't let them push us around." Thos shot a look at Abraham.

He pulled the mic off and left it on the podium. A few muffled laughs came from the crowd while others grew visibly uncomfortable. Cass placed her hand on his leg.

"Mexico's not that bad. You'll have a nice time there. Give a few speeches, tour the facilities, give a few more speeches, and relax at Duke's villa. You'll have a whole army at your beck and call," Cass reassured him.

"Not waving any flags this time. Sure you don't want to come?"

"In a few weeks. Got a few projects to finish first." She kissed him. The pit in Thos's stomach and chest-crushing anxiety told him everything he needed to know about this new trip likely to go as well as the last.

GREGOR

GREGOR SAT QUIETLY on the train racing through the cold, dark earth toward the fabled Silent City. The train flew through the tunnels with such grace Gregor could barely tell it was moving at all. Above him was a wasteland ravaged by storms known as the Uninhabited. Gregor was a little disappointed he was unable to see if the reality was as grand as the myth.

Automatically, the doors opened. Gregor stepped out into a cave and was instantly blasted with heat. A set of stairs lead to the surface. He hurried up the steps, showing excitement not felt in decades. At the top of the steps, Gregor nearly collapsed at the sight.

Most technologies of the Old World lasted a few centuries without maintenance before rotting away to nothing, but not the Silent City. Even 2000 years after civilization's fall, the city had undergone only minor damage. A circle of waterfalls that dropped thousands of feet below, formed a massive city-sized pool of water, a perfect aquatic circle beneath the impossible city. A grass-covered bridge extended past oddly shaped buildings, platforms, and walkways that hovered above the watery chasm. Outside the city was a jungle that extended in an impenetrable dark mass of storms.

"Mercy," Gregor said, frozen in his tracks.

Bridges and suspended buildings crisscrossed at different heights, forming a vertical city of many floating tiers. Crusaders moved about the city streets far below like white and red ants. Gregor saw thousands of Vigilant troops scurrying about. Roofs had a slick, shiny quality. Stairs and other land bridges covered the top of the chasm, dropping to the lowest homes and the tallest spires. Automobiles without steering wheels were strewn about the roads like the apocalypse had happened only moments ago. Trees grew from green areas in the middle of bridges, and water ran out the sides down into pools below. Buildings floated ominously in the distance. Mangled pieces of a behemoth aircraft fossilized at the city's western edge.

Gregor and the crusaders moved toward the city's center, not concerned with any danger. He noticed something strange in front of the cylindrical tower at the city's heart. A pattering of light rain smacking up against an invisible wall.

Each man carried either a wave rifle or an assault rifle. Men hauled large boxes to the bowels of the city. The crusaders opened a golden gate to the upper levels of the city just outside the invisible barrier. Gregor stepped back the instant he saw them. In the central hub of the upper city, thousands of figures stood unmoving. He approached one of the female figures and ran his hand against her synthetic flesh. All robots. The beings showed signs of injury and decay: exposing mechanical innards, alloy bones, and waxy, artificial skin of various colors.

He instantly marked this place as the creepiest he'd ever seen. These robots were far more advanced than any Gregor had encountered in his career. The few machines that roamed the world were hulking, jury-rigged trash used as mindless golems for tech-savvy apostates. None of the robots were positioned to attack; many were still mid-run while others stared up at the protected building with mouths agape for a final cry of terror.

"Quite the sight, isn't it? One of many hidden cities meant

to kick start the new world, three that we've found with some functionality. Based on my studies, this city wasn't even the main one, but the only one intact. Filled with treasure and protected by powerful guardians, so the tales go. I suppose that's all true."

A man in red-gold armor and robes stood amid the frozen masses. From the attire, Gregor identified him as Grand Crusader Matthias Rehnquist, former lord sentinel, and now supreme leader over all branches of Vigilant. Matthias didn't approach Gregor and focused on the invisible shield protecting the structure the size of Blackthorne Castle.

"How little we know about this world," Matthias said.

Gregor bobbed and weaved through the robots toward his new CO. Matthias was a younger man in his early forties with a pointy chestnut goatee and a thick diagonal scar across his face. His eyes were orange like flames, a genetic anomaly that revealed him as a defect. Defects resulted from Old Worlders that had used genetic modification for anything from skin re-coloration to muscle or brain enhancement that included animal DNA. The human genome manipulation left their descendants with various mutations, from something as minor as orange eyes to extremes like monstrous deformities, or fatal ones like transparent skin. Every human on the planet was believed to be a descendant of some form of genetic manipulation, though few would be labeled as Defects.

"What better place to save the world then at the source of its destruction. Welcome Sentinel Pavane."

Gregor extended his hand. Matthias clamped down on it with a vice-grip, ensuring a strong handshake garnered a strong impression.

"Thank you, sir. From what I've heard, you've accomplished incredible things in a short time. Been a long time the world took us seriously."

Under the leadership of Matthias, Vigilant held more power than it had in centuries. Gregor imagined the vice regent would regret her decision to fully reestablish the order should the government once again violate the law.

"You're too kind. The world has spiraled out of control as we've grown weaker, but we'll soon change that."

"How the hell'd you find this place?" Gregor asked. Matthias's face scrunched up.

"Visions. Visions of the dead, of a world on fire, and of the terrible truth. I believe we can use this city to turn the tide of this war, maybe end it completely." The topic piqued his interest, though Gregor showcased his doubt.

"Forgive my skepticism . . . visions? Wisps, I get," Gregor said. "And war . . . against what?" Gregor had dealt with people that claimed to see visions that guided them before, they all ended up insane and then dead.

"I understand your doubt, but there's an explanation. As for the war . . . the one against fate."

Gregor crossed his arms, unintentionally disrespecting his superior.

"I'll brief you on the details later, but I'll say that the key is in there." Matthias picked up a severed robot hand and threw it into the barrier. "Something horrible was born here. Driving us toward a dark new world. The means to end this thing lies within." Gregor cocked his head.

"And what is it?" Gregor asked.

"The reason for our very existence," Matthias replied.

Rain rolled down the invisible wall. Energy roared through the city, causing it to flicker to life for a moment. Matthias pointed to the rooftops. Atop the buildings were figures of flesh and metal attached to spikes, clearly identifiable as apostates. As far the eye could see, apostates on spikes lined the roofs, forming a ring around the barrier.

"The hell is this?" Gregor asked.

"Our job," Matthias said.

Sounds of electricity crackled. Wires connected from the barrier to the spikes. Audible sounds of electricity became agonizing cries of the bound prisoners. Electricity flowed through the wires to the barrier. The barrier became a cylinder of blue rising up and around the building. The wall flashed. The cybernetic modifications of the prisoners sparked and melted. The prisoners burst into flames, enhancements or not.

"An appropriate fate," Matthias's voice dripped with hatred as he watched them burn.

Gregor had little sympathy for the apostates, but the others bore no marks to indicate their guilt. Deserving or not, Gregor felt sickened by the cruelty. Gregor wasn't fully convinced the actions were necessary or purely altruistic.

"Followers of Gideon?" he asked. Matthias nodded.

"Not all, but abusers of tech in some fashion. Thieves, killers, schizzers."

Schizzers were individuals that used electric drugs; they didn't fall on the radar of Vigilant despite it technically being a violation of the Compact. Gregor found schizzers not worth the order's time.

"You're using the energy to break down the barrier?" It was a rhetorical question.

"They can do some good for once," Matthias said.

The screaming stopped, leaving smoldering corpses and an impenetrable barrier still standing but quite visible. Matthias pushed over one of the frozen robots; it fell over in the same running pose. "Follow me. I have something else to show you."

Gregor gave one last look at the charred victims before heading down the streets to a three-story glass building powered by a large generator in a truck bed. Chubby, finger-sized slugs with yellow innards glowing through transparent skin clung to the generators. These slugs, called syphons, were a species that fed on electrical energy. Matthias smacked a few dozen off the generator and ordered troops to "de-slug" the area.

Gregor followed Matthias inside the old medical building. The two hopped on the generator-powered escalator in the lobby. Vigilant techs fiddled with a variety of medical tools throughout the building. A med-tech rolled a cart with a shapeless blob covered in mouths.

"Most of our time is spent analyzing this marvelous city, but we try to get some demonology in. The way things are going, we may be able to eliminate demons altogether," Matthias said.

Gregor and Matthias stepped off the escalator into a large back room with dozens of chilled containers. Two small dishes rested on a table beside a new wave rifle. Gregor peered inside to see black liquid in one and the other empty.

"Blood?" he asked. Matthias nodded.

"Demon," Matthias said, picking up the newly developed EMPX gunblade. The EMPX was the brainchild of Matthias, a longsword with a rectangular box on the left side. The EMPX was soon to replace his previously developed wave rifle. It was the pinnacle of killing tech, functioning as a sword, assault rifle, and wave emitter.

"Some confusion about what mode to have it in. Carry it as a rifle or on your back as a sword depending on your role. It's a bit awkward at first, but the EMPX is every weapon we need, all in one."

On top of firing armor-piercing rounds, it also emitted higher frequency waves than the previous model. Matthias pushed the switch above the rifle's trigger, switching it over to wave mode. He aimed the gun at the black blood and pulled the trigger. The hum of the weapon became an ear-piercing shriek. The blood bubbled inside the container.

"To be expected," Gregor said, unimpressed.

"Hold out your hand," Matthias commanded. Gregor frowned but complied. Matthias moved faster than expected. Matthias nicked Gregor's thumb with his blade, and the blood ran from the wound into the dish.

Matthias grabbed Gregor's hand and pushed on Gregor's thumb. He let go of Gregor's hand, leaving Gregor to reach for the small first aid kit attached to his belt.

"Know what the difference is between humans and demons?" Matthias asked.

Matthias turned the dial up on the EMPX to the max. He pointed the rifle at Gregor's blood and pulled the trigger. Electricity surged through the container. The container exploded, shooting blood in all directions. Gregor stood dumbfounded and splattered with blood while Matthias hollered with delight.

"Turns out not much. Took forever to get the right frequency to figure that out," Matthias said. Gregor processed this startling new information. After a bit of stuttering, he finally got words out.

"This . . . " he said in shock. Matthias nodded. "Disables demonic cells, cybernetics . . . ." Matthias nodded again. "So that means . . . ."

Matthias walked over to a desk with five perfectly spaced and immaculate microscopes. Gregor had seen his fair share of microscopes, though these were thicker with far too many knobs and buttons. Matthias pulled up a black chair and gestured for Gregor to sit. Questions about how such equipment could function for so long or Matthias's tech knowledge was put on the back burner for the time being.

Gregor placed his eye over the microscope, and it begun to water the second he got close. Matthias adjusted the magnification to analyze the very red and very human blood cells. Gregor waited for the big reveal. Matthias hit a button on the microscope. Gregor pulled his head back at the blinding flash from the new filter. Gregor cursed and returned to the microscope. He saw two colors of cells through the filter, one white and the other black. Gregor became dizzy.

"Godseeds," Gregor said, finally understanding Gideon's madness.

"It gets worse," Matthias said. Matthias lead Gregor to the back room with a single table and a corpse on top. Matthias pulled out a small, metal rod of silver from his ammo pouch.

"Witch-tech?" Gregor asked. Matthias shook his head.

"Worse," Matthias said. Matthias held the wand out and grunted as if shocked. Matthias stretched out his right arm and the corpse followed suit.

"Have you ever had the feeling there were important pieces of your life missing? Removed? Things so wild and bizarre you couldn't possibly forget?" Matthias said. Gregor sifted through memory. Vague images flashed through his mind.

"You have a hard time remembering some of your missions, don't you?" Matthias said.

Gregor thought about battles with demons he could no longer see when he thought about them. Technology wild enough to . . . he couldn't remember. More images flashed by. In the blur, he saw a shape in white. Matthias tinkered with the rod. The images grew clear. As a boy, he had stood in a field with his brother, looking up at the sky. As a man, he hit the dirt after a battle with a rampaging wendigo. After the battle, he lay on his back, looking up at the sky. He saw him. Over and over again. He saw the man in white, wearing the smiling, golden mask. The memories faded as Matthias lowered the rod, but they didn't disappear completely.

"It can't be," Gregor said, horrified.

"I'm afraid it is. The truth. The great sick joke," Matthias said. "Machines in our blood . . . our skin . . . our brains. Humans and demons. 90% identical and from the same source. Cybernetic cells, both organic and inorganic. Nanomachines. Godseeds."

The revelation hit Gregor with enough force to knock the breath out of him. He wanted to vomit. He felt woozy. His vision blurred. Gregor rested his head in his hands. Matthias laughed.

"The great revelation. We're slaves to the Compact. It has power over our bodies and our minds. The Compact is inside us all."

ZORA

ZORA'S EXPERIENCES WITH the capital were tumultuous at best, but at times like these, she could forget being the failed Freemen speaker and peacefully surveil. Since Anselm's death, the new government had unleashed a slew of regulations and laws on the world while flouting what they ruthlessly enforced. The nation roared unapologetically into a new era, whether the Freemen liked it or not.

Zora watched the supplies rolling out onto the roads making up the Great Highway, some heading to her home in the White Woods. She imagined the monster machines plowing through them, a possible future. She fought to keep an amicable relationship between her people and the government, an uphill battle as the groups drifted further apart. Zoning laws, trade agreements, unwanted intervention, and the endless discussions planning more intervention made her days unbearably long. Spying on the new leadership provided some valuable intel should the need arise to use it. Zora had enough politics for the day, letting her cares go with the Averill supply trucks.

Walking through the city, she saw a collection of tourists gawking at a city buzzing with life. Zora envied that sense of wonder. She knew how quickly it fizzled out. She needed a change in scenery. Thoughts of sprawling deserts and lush jungles flashed through her head. Zora desired to visit Mexico, and not just because Drake was there. Her friend Thos also planned an extended business trip to the southernmost state. With her uncle reassigned there, it seemed everyone headed south.

Zora worked her way to Prosperity Park, choosing to day-dream amid the lush grass and song birds. She closed her eyes and breathed deep, going into a state of meditation. Her muscles relaxed as peace washed over her. All thoughts and tension melted away like dandelion petals in the summer breeze. She closed her eyes for only a moment and jumped back at the two figures in front of her. A man in blue jeans, sunglasses, and a button-up shirt stood hand in hand with a woman in jeans, a purple shirt, and a sun hat. The grin was unmistakable.

"Thos, Cassie, nice to see you. Get free?"

"Just did. Hell of a stroke fest in there," Thos said, getting nudged by his wife.

"See what I have to put with?" Cassandra interrupted.

"Oh, I know," Zora replied.

The trio held a brief casual conversation.

"Anywho, sending a small army with me to Mexico," Thos said. "Cass can't make it just yet, and I heard some individuals could use a little adventure. Could use reliable brothers and sisters in arms. Anyone fit that bill?" Zora knew this to be an opportunity knocking loudly.

"Mmmm. Maybe," she said.

"All right. Gettin' the band back together. Heading out in three days. Meet me in the garage at six, you know the one," Thos said.

"I'll be there," Zora said, revitalized.

"Time to go. Your pals are coming up," Cass said.

"Pretend we don't see 'em," Thos said as he hurried off.

"Nice to see you again," Cass said, waving at Zora as she walked off.

Shortly after the couple took off, the men following them huffed and puffed by Zora, muttering curses about Thos. Zora needed to make another trip home and discuss her findings with the Freemen. She made haste toward the familiarity of the White Woods.

Traffic through the forest increased exponentially over the last two years. Lifeless tree trunks surrounded a watchtower that gave a clear view of the new public road. The agreement with the advisors came at the cost of certain sections of the forest, but the ever-expanding Freemen population meant that was inevitable. Her people hated the arrangement all the same, but they understood how to play ball for the moment. The advisors were doing a better job getting people to join her people than even the Freemen could.

Kami sat in his hut, sullen since Gregor left for Mexico. The other Freemen no longer came to him for advice, making him something of the town hermit. Her father did more for the Freemen than anyone realized; the people were lucky to have him around. Kami sipped on a large glass of nectar, immediately lighting up when he saw Zora.

"Zora!" he said, perking back up into his cheerful old self.

His love and loss made it that much harder to be his latest abandoner. Zora opted not to tell her father the news right away. She spent the day with him, having a simple lunch of turkey sandwiches while they sat with feet dangling off the side of the hanging courtyard. She spent many days like this, quiet, happy moments that brought her back to childhood. The sun sank over the trees. The etherflies came out, waltzing through the air like tiny blue stars.

"Let's spar," Kami said, catching Zora off guard.

Her father preferred the quiet life and rarely got in the mood for such things. Zora happily accepted. Kami grabbed a few dueling swords and led Zora out to a clearing often used for training. Kami never used practice swords; he believed the real thing was the only way to truly learn. Kami tossed Zora a blade. Kami's demeanor changed. The languid old man once again became Matthew Pavane. He raised his sword.

"Come at me," Kami said. Zora raised her weapon slowly.

Zora was confident in her abilities. Thoughts of hurting her father made her hesitate. Zora hesitated, but her father didn't. He jumped forward and stuck. She deflected the attack, and he jumped back. Zora struck from the right. Kami parried. Zora lost her footing, but she recovered fast. She made a second strike, taking advantage of her speed. Kami proved surprisingly agile, the sixty-year-old man suddenly fighting like one in his thirties. He left forth a series of thrusts, putting her back on the defensive. She focused on wearing him down. Kami's pace slowed. Zora saw an opportunity and struck. Kami stepped back and struck back. He knocked the blade out of her hand.

"Thought I had you," Zora said. Kami wiped the sweat from his brow. She laughed.

"You learned an important lesson," Matthew said. "Never underestimate your opponent. You thought you were better. Faster. But you thought wrong."

It had been years since they dueled, and it felt as if Kami never missed a day. He always told her he was "the best of the worst," but she knew it was him acting modest. Zora and her father took a moment to recover. Matthew Pavane lowered his guard and reverted to the chill and loving Kami.

Kami was a warm and kind man but stern and harsh when needed. Regardless of his name or demeanor, Zora was proud to have him as her father. Everything of value she learned from him.

"I know you didn't come here just to spend time with me," he said. "You're heading down to Mexico." Zora nodded.

"I understand," Kami said. "Never one to stay tied down long. I'm tempted to go with you, but I'm needed here." Zora knew it concerned tensions with the government and the reports of violence moving closer to home.

"You might need to. With uncle down there, something big must be happening. I'll meet up with him if I can. I have a feeling we'll get dragged into whatever is going on it before long."

"Sounds like Vigilant instincts," Kami said. "Gang wars, corruption, labs, witches consorting with kings . . . something's happening in this world." Kami's tone grew ominous. His gut feelings were seldom wrong.

"Still very much Vigilant, too," Zora said.

Zora was happy to assist in destroying threats to humanity. Still, she and her father disagreed with the unnecessary regulation of technology that made it easier to keep people under the ruler's thumb. There were debates between her and Gregor about Vigilant ideals within a Freeman society; they both welcomed the challenge to ensure their ideas favored the philosophy. Zora kissed Kami on the forehead.

"You're becoming too much like your uncle," he said. Zora imagined herself a grumpy old woman.

"A little," she said. "A little more like you, too."

"I suppose a little is fine," Kami said with a smile. Zora turned away.

"You've been wanting me to go," she asked. Kami sighed.

"Less about want and more about need. And not just to contact your uncle. The government will come for us soon enough. We're keeping them happy for now, but," he said. Her eyes widened.

"We have to rally the other Freemen communities."

"Conflict is unavoidable," he said. "Joseph's ideas inspired people but didn't go far enough. More people want to be free, and they can't allow that. We need to be ready to strike. While you're in Mexico, I'll make some time for them; you should too when you aren't scouting around for any more labs. I'm making arrangements to meet with the coastal groups."

"You think it'll happen soon?"

"Unfortunately," Kami said. "When whatever madness going on is settled, it will. I'm sorry to put this on you; thought we had more time."

"I wish it didn't have to come to this," Zora said, knowing as a Freemen she would be a target whether she got involved or not.

"I wish that, too. I always wanted you to have a life free of schemes and plots. You should get to live a carefree life of adventure, but that's clearly not in the cards."

Zora nodded and left. She spent the next two days in the woods before it was time to meet up with Thos. Tossing the last of her choice clothing in her travel bag and grabbing her dagger and the rifle Drake gave her. After gearing up, she rushed to Kingsbury and headed toward the capital garage, formerly the Blackthornes. She worked her way through the arena to the private elevator at the back. The guard stepped aside and let her through. The elevator rattled down through the earth.

One car and ten gas-powered military jeeps hummed as they waited for her. Two rifle totting soldiers greeted her and the door and waved her closer. Thos and a cavalcade of armed escorts gathered around him like hungry dogs at feeding time. Thos smiled and waved when he noticed her.

"That bad?" She asked.

"Bout to find out." Thos leaned in and began whispering. "The big wigs didn't want us armed, but I had enough charisma . . . . and money . . . .to persuade the hard asses. Nice to have some pull around here. We got hardware if things get hot and heavy."

The black car that served as their transport held four passengers: Thos, Zora, a driver, and a soldier ready for driving . . . and possibly shooting.

"Better get underway. One last thing, though," Thos said, stepping out of the car and over to Cassandra, waiting to see her off. The two of them embraced as Zora took her seat in the back, squinting as she tried to read their lips. Thos gave Cass one more kiss, locking his fingers in hers. The driver grumbled and rummaged in his pocket for a pack of cigarettes. Thos let go of Cassandra and made his way to the car.

"Ready to go," Thos said, rubbing his hands together vigorously.

"Better get comfy. Trip will be about thirty-six hours," the driver said.

The car roared to life. Zora spied Abraham Kerr, James Dumas, and Yadira Khouri among those seeing Thos off. Thos blew a kiss at his wife and everyone else staring. They drove out of the garage and onto the highway. The city of Kingsbury faded in the distance until it vanished from sight.

Thos and Zora sat quietly, watching the familiar sights of Heartland blur by. Zora tried not to bounce with excitement as the car zoomed down the road at speeds faster than she had ever known. Much on her mind stifled the excitement of adventure or seeing her love. She feared for Drake's and Thos's safety with the Void running amok. With her father's gut feeling and her own, she knew her friends would need her. Vigilant activity also meant the possibility of more labs that would point her to the masked evil that continued to haunt her dreams.

"Word is they plan to branch out into air travel. Apparently, it's a new thing the Compact allowed," Thos said. "We'll finally make contact with the East. Wild times."

Zora shifted nervously.

"Not keen on the idea?" Thos asked.

"No, it's great but . . . things are moving faster than ever. All the knowledge and tools banned for generations have barely seen the light of day; now they're massed produced. This sudden jump in technology after two millennia of heavy regulation . . . is what my uncle always feared. I don't share Vigilant's views on control-ling tech, but I certainly don't trust it in the hands of the advisors."

"I'm a tad nervous with them behind the wheel, too," Thos admitted.

Thos and Zora spent the next few hours in conversation ranging from the political infrastructure to guns to which Mexican desserts to try first. Thos decided to sleep for much of the trip, waking up for the necessary pit stops. Zora cursed her alertness as her body surged with energy that had nowhere to go. Despite the serious nature of her missions, she still had the craving for a little adventure. She spent her time looking out the window and occasionally pushing Thos's drooling head off her shoulder.

Out the window, fields gave way to forests that gave way to more fields. Zora wanted a break from forests and fields. The group stopped for food and rest at a military gas station before passing through dangerous territory. All snapped from their zombie-like states. Zora knew where they were.

"The Deadlands," she said, growing anxious at the thought.

It was clear that the feeling was shared among everyone. The truck in front of them slowed. Behind her, she could see the men gripping guns tightly through the windshield of the jeep. Thos scanned the surroundings through every window.

"Few miles that way," he said.

Thos pointed over to his left to an area under a putrid yellow sky that hung over boiling swamps.

"The land of demons," Zora said.

The stories of the place and tales of machines that could transform the land, air, and sea into whatever they desired were both ludicrous and very frightening. Stories of red rain, black waters, and mutated exiles invoked vivid images of a living nightmare. Though no one ever verified such tales, the past few years made her less skeptical.

"Hope I never see it," Thos muttered.

She could feel the malice from here. Demon activity had been on the rise since not long after the fairies returned, which was something she hadn't even thought about until now. Some said the demons originated from the Deadlands. Her father had a theory they were able to manifest physically using the power of the ancient machines. One day, Vigilant would end up there; Zora didn't doubt that. She wondered if she'd end up there, too.

After a few minutes, everyone quickly hightailed it out of the area. The scenery gave way to more unfamiliar landscapes as they crossed the border of Heartland and arrived in the state of Mexico. Zora's eyes widened at the expansive red, rocky deserts and cacti dotting the land. She forgot about swampy nightmares and thought of deserts, jungles, and ruins. Zora hungered to take it all in. She dwelled on her father's words. She wanted to enjoy her time in this exotic land, but she was a Freemen first and foremost.

ANSELM

Anselm's arm throbbed. He had grown accustomed to the pain, a necessary routine in his new life. The deep cuts that shredded up his wrists and arms closed within minutes. Each time he inflicted pain upon himself, his body healed quickly, leading to ever-increasing extremes of pain to ensure he suffered for his failures. Anselm needed it. His dark compulsion grew stronger the closer he grew to Rosalie. A woman hollered outside. Before he could react, Rosalie Crowe kicked open and knocked down the flimsy door he'd just repaired.

"Help!" she cried, giving only a second to gawk at the bloody Anselm.

"What's wrong?" Anselm asked.

"Cam . . . I think he's been taken!" she wailed.

With raiders lurking in the wilderness, he couldn't ignore this. Anselm grabbed the sword he had stolen off the last raider that threatened the village. He strapped the sheath to his back and slid the blade inside; then he snatched up his pistol, just in case.

"Stay in town. I'll find him," Anselm said.

He hurried out the door and breathed deep, smelling no blood other than his own. With heightened abilities, he heard the faint cracking of branches, birds chirping happily, and panicked yells of locals. The sun poured down through the treetops as Anselm navigated the wilderness north of the closest logging site. When he had first arrived in the frontier, he'd found the bodies of two young girls three miles from the village. Bringing back their bodies and the highwayman's severed head, had earned him Durenburg's respect. Anselm held no illusions of finding Cameron alive, but he could prevent future tragedy. He felt the world was hellbent on tearing another family from him. He snacked on some fiddleheads as he scoured the dense wilderness of his former kingdom, letting his pain drive him.

Anselm had spent a fair amount of time exploring the wilderness, finding only plants and the occasional deer or elk. He took note of the lack of animal life scurrying about. Rain sprinkled off and on as he worked his way deeper into the woods. He passed countless widowmakers on his way. Instinctively, he gave them a wide berth in the early days, now he wondered the pain he'd feel if one crashed down on him. Anselm pressed on to a rusted logging crane. The thing had been abandoned not long after he had it shipped up here, judging from the rusty shell. It annoyed him the board fought his logging expansion; he believed it to be purely out of spite.

Anselm caught a scent to the northwest. He felt a stirring inside him, like an internal warning bell. He came upon a small cave; smells of other carcasses came from inside. Anselm pulled his sword from the hilt on his back and his eyes pierced through the black. A sense of familiarity hit him. He counted two dozen mangled bodies inside, including children, raiders, and Vigilant crusaders. The Vigilant corpses were fresh, verifying the order was active once again. Anselm smelled living flesh. He sighed with relief to see young Cameron intact, albeit bruised. Anselm called out, but he didn't respond.

"Why is he still alive?" Anselm said. Anselm realized his mistake. "A trap, simple but effective."

The faint sound of childish laughter echoed from outside. He turned. A figure darted behind a thick tree. A shadowy mass whizzed by. Anselm heard the laughter from behind a different tree.

"Come and play," the voice said.

The voice was childish and singsong. Four pale-green hands grabbed a hold of the tree. A shiny, porcelain face not unlike that of a doll peered out. Anselm never knew anyone that wasn't creeped out by dolls, and in his former life, he hadn't been a fan either. In Anselm's new life, nothing scared him. Now, he came face to face with a demon.

"We'll have so much fun," it said.

Anselm read some reports about them after his incident with the masked man. Vigilant reports detailed a type of demon born from those that used technology to prey on children. Anselm surmised the creature realized he was a severe threat to his future meal plans. He aimed his pistol at the beast.

"Playtime's over."

"You'll be sorry," the demon said in a childlike tone.

The demon slipped behind another tree. Then it whizzed by a tree much closer to Anselm. The demon giggled again and emerged from hiding. Anselm got a full view of the monstrosity. A thin green humanoid roughly twice the size of an ordinary man glared at him with its doll-like face. The arms extended down to its knees. Each forearm split into two separate forearms, each with needle-like fingers. The slender demonic frame was held aloft by two equally slim legs. The creature walked toward Anselm, bobbing happily.

"I'll play with you first!" the demon roared.

The head split open at the mouth. One massive, pink tentacle covered in hundreds of serrated teeth burst forth. The tentacle wriggled ferociously, cutting the air in front of Anselm. Anselm dodged and shot at the demon. The creature bobbed and moved from side to side, avoiding some of Anselm's shots and shrugging off the rest. Anselm scrambled for the ammo in his belt pocket. Before his hand made it down to the clip, the demon rushed him. The four arms reached out for Anselm, but he effortlessly avoided the initial attack. The superhuman speed allowed him to avoid the demon's arms, though the thrashing tentacle proved much harder to dodge. The tentacle shredded Anselm's chest, spilling his blood onto the ground.

"Fun!" the demon giggled, the voice coming from the tentacled mouth. Anselm fell to his knees.

"All done?" the demon whined, already assured of victory.

Anselm let his blood flow freely. Such wounds were no longer fatal. Wounds from the demon healed slower, something Anselm hadn't anticipated. Anselm pulled the sword from his sheath and swung with all his might, severing the right arm of the creature. The demon screamed and fell back.

"No fair!" it cried. Back on his feet, Anselm prepared to swing again.

The monster quickly dashed to the comfort of a thick tree. It darted between the trees at lightning speed. Anselm followed the demonic movements too fast for normal human eyes.

He pretended to lose track of the creature, positioning himself further away from the cave toward the trees. The demon sprinted to a tree behind Anselm. Sword in hand, Anselm spun around right before the demon's tongue wrapped around him. Anselm's blade connected. The severed tentacle flew from the demon. Tarry, black blood from the flailing wound sprayed Anselm. The scalding black blood seeped into Anselm's wounds and in his mouth before either could close. Anselm's body surged with energy as his wounds closed.

The demon hit Anselm head-on in an act of desperation. Its remaining arms gripped Anselm's shoulders and dug down into his flesh. The claws burned inside Anselm's wounds. The overwhelming pain turned to rage. Anselm grabbed the demon's arms and pulled the claws from his wounds.

"You're not the only monster," Anselm said.

Anselm's wounds closed. He gave the demon a hard kick to its sternum, and he chopped through the demon's legs the moment it jumped up. The demon attempted to crawl away.

"I don't want to play anymore," it whined.

Anselm walked over to the creature and severed its head with a single stroke. He hacked the body to minuscule bits. After a minute of thrashing, all of the pieces of the demons stopped moving. Anselm turned back to the cave to rescue Cameron.

He passed by the logging camp on the way back to Durenburg. A familiar sensation came over him, the feeling of being watched. He gently placed Cameron inside the nearest tent and braced for a second attack. He moved toward the logging camp where the voyeur hid. A large yellow crane sat in the center of the base among tents, rotted logs, discolored coolers, and rusty trucks. He sensed only one entity watching him. Anselm readied his gun.

"If you've been watching me, you know what I'm capable of!" Anselm hollered.

"Of course we do. That's why you were chosen, ant-king," a voice replied.

Anselm's head began to throb. He looked up. Atop the crane stood a man in a white suit and wearing a golden comedy mask. Anselm's blood boiled, threatening to explode within him. He fired at the masked man. The bullets went straight through the man, who scoffed in response.

"How dare you show your face after all this time!" Anselm roared.

The figure vanished and appeared directly in front of him. The masked man, now wearing a face of tragedy, bowed his head in shame.

"It was not our intent. We can't stay for long. Certain . . . complications have arisen." he said. Anselm laughed bitterly.

"What complications could *you* have?" Anselm said. The masked man raised his head.

"The kind you need to eliminate. They have inhibited our abilities. They're destroying everything we've built," he said.

"The new government . . . ." Anselm said with a groan.

"No . . . but you'll deal with them in short order," the masked man assured him.

Anselm thought about Rosalie, Cameron, the possibility of more children, and simple living. His insides twisted and burned, but through the hate and pain, he felt the chance for something more.

"I'm . . . not sure I want to be a part of it anymore," Anselm said.

"Your part in the Algorithm has been cemented. You can't unmake your choice. The life you want you'll never have," the masked man replied.

Anselm grappled with his feelings, unsure of what he truly desired.

"Hell with your Algorithm," he said. The masked man's head snapped back, returning with a gaping maw of rage.

"You dare defy the Algorithm?! You'll see the true depths of agony." The masked man raised his hand; Anselm felt sharp pain for only a moment. The man cocked his head in confusion.

"Not so omnipotent after all," Anselm said. "Who is this villain that wounded you so?"

The hum in Anselm's head became a piercing shriek. The masked man became translucent, staggering backward.

"If our world ends, so does yours!" he replied before vanishing completely.

"Dammit!" Anselm screamed. He threw his fist into the closest truck, knocking it on its side. Anselm knew he had wasted time languishing in the wilderness, and his enemies needed to be punished. Local attachments were getting in the way and grew stronger. The thunderous crash woke Cameron from his sleep. Anselm walked over to his sword and the screaming Cameron.

"It's all right, you're safe now," Anselm said. Anselm placed his hand on Cameron's shoulder.

"Let's go home," Anselm said, scooping the boy up.

Anselm gave one last look back at the logging camp for any sign of the masked man. Seeing nothing, Anselm and Cameron made their way back home.

CASS

WALKING THROUGH THE bustling streets of Kingsbury, Cassandra Averill found that incognito was a meaningless term when you were one of the most famous individuals in the nation. She wore a blue and pink floral print dress with white sneakers and a ponytail, a welcome change from pantsuits and jeans. The citizens waved, Cass learned how often simple gestures could come from cunning foes hiding behind smiles. Thankfully most people respected the Averills and deemed them valued members of society.

Thos had only left yesterday but life had already grown dull without him. She walked past the Noble Quarter to the South Quarter, once dubbed "Turd-town" before the restoration courtesy of the economic boom Averill Estate Farms helped initiate. She felt compelled to help. Every action taken for the benefit of the people was offset by the advisors the Averills helped empower even further. An armored guard ran up to Cass for the thirteenth time that day, but she shooed him away. Cass always kept a gun handy in case someone came looking for trouble.

Her sunglasses continually slipped down; she decided to make a detour to buy a new pair. Cass approached her destination where a small gathering took form. She quickened her step and took her place among the workers.

"Right on time, Mrs. Averill," the head worker said.

Cass spared no time chatting and followed the group to the building Thos had bought and repurposed as a soup kitchen. With her spot in the line secure, she donned the gloves and prepared to serve the array of food to the famished downtrodden. A few other famous faces had joined the cause today, including Adrienne Williams of the Prosperity Theater Group. Even though Cassandra disliked most actors, as most were imbecilic government propagandists, Adrienne seemed to be a decent person.

Cass also saw her friend Yadira Khouri. She liked Yadira, who was surprisingly down to earth compared to all other officials. Cass struck up a friendship with Yadira around the same time she'd first started doing these events with Adrienne. Yadira served the hungry masses all while redirecting the media to Adrienne. Yadira moved beside her.

The masses poured in seemingly nonstop. Workers moved in and out of the line to take breaks. Yadira smiled warmly at everyone to the point of pain, engaging each with a brief conversation.

Cass powered through for four hours until taking a moment to herself. She snuck out back for some fresh air. Adrienne leaned against the wall and took heavy drags on a cigarette. Yadira glanced around for pesky media men skittering about.

"Finally worn out?" Yadira said with an amused chuckle. Cass nodded and waved off the cigarette offered to her.

"Always more to do," Cass said.

Besides providing and paying for the food, the Averills owned several other facilities in the city and participated in the actual construction when time permitted. Life had been very good to her and Thos; they did what they could to pay it forward. Critics used the big houses they lived in as a counterpoint against their efforts. It frustrated Cass that someone spun their actions to paint them as bad people despite everything they've done.

"Back to it," Cass said.

Two more hours saw the crowds and food dissipate. When the stragglers vacated the building, she and the crew started cleaning for dinner preparations. Yadira caught Cass slipping out the back and followed her out.

"Not so bad without the entourage, is it?" Cass asked, struggling against the call of the nicotine.

"Only time I get away is in the bathroom . . . at least I think," Yadira said.

Adrienne griped with the cigarette bouncing between her lips. Yadira looked on, her mind clearly in some other world.

"Plans tonight?" Adrienne asked.

"Read and sleep. You?" Cass inquired. Yadira didn't respond.

"Hello? You in there?" Adrienne asked, waving a hand in front of Yadira's face. The wave startled Yadira out of her waking slumber.

"Sorry, just . . . .it's not important," she replied. "There's a gala being held at my house tonight for the Gloire Ambassador. Be nice to see you there. Adrienne has already invited herself." Adrienne laughed. Cass considered that a gala might be a welcome change from the trappings of monotony without Thos.

"Maybe," Cass said.

The two exchanged pleasantries and went their separate ways. With Cass's volunteering concluded for the day, she made her way back through the town to get home and rested for tomorrow's work. A few people stopped her on the way back, thanking her for her works around the city.

With her business in town finished, Cass returned to the comforts of home. She opted for a long hot bath and chose a book from her collection. She picked up the practice of reading after meeting Thos and his love for fantasy and folklore. Cass turned the pages of *Life in a House of Thorns,* a volume of memoirs from two generations of a Blackthorne servant family. She yawned ten minutes in reading. She hurried to bed and lay down to finish the story in soft comfort. Cass closed her eyes for a minute, a minute that lasted until morning.

"Shit," she muttered. Lacking time for disappointment, Cass quickly got herself ready for another day.

She hastily threw on some jeans and a shirt for a day of non-office work. She passed a merchant on the street spinning coins on his fingertips, trying to amuse jaded children while their mother browsed his Toth silks that were the current fad. A nearby conversation caught Cass's attention.

"She's probably fine," said one gossiper.

"Maybe the loyalists got her; she was friends with the vice regent," said another.

"She was trying to get cozy with the ambassador. Bet he killed her, he does seem . . . you know."

Cass slowed her pace to eavesdrop on the gossipers. They didn't fail to notice. She smiled and walked on through the construction site at the edge of the commercial district. Cass passed by dozens more civilians, all discussing the same thing. When she reached the work site, she saw an officer standing by the foreman with a stern expression on his face.

"Mrs. Averill, can you come here please?" the officer asked. She immediately thought the worst.

"Is Thos okay!?" she asked, hit with a sudden wave of panic.

"He's fine, sorry to give that impression," he said apologetically. "No, it's about Ms. Williams. She's missing. She disappeared after she left your soup kitchen. Her manager is very concerned, enough to file a report." The officer adjusted his azure vest.

"She was going to a gala, all I know," she said. The officer cut to the chase.

"Did you notice anything odd about her behavior? Where she was going?" He pulled out a small notepad to write down any tidbits of information she could provide. Adrienne did love the limelight, but sometimes the media and her handlers got pushy.

Rumors swirled about people vanishing around the city, some of minor importance. It wasn't the first time a killer had stalked the streets of Kingsbury. A series of murders took place about five years ago with the perpetrator never caught.

"That's all I know," she said. The officer let out a frustrated grunt.

"If you learn anything, please contact us immediately. Good day, Mrs. Averill."

She replied with a courteous nod. Cass brushed off her concern. The likelihood of her becoming the victim of a serial killer or anyone was relatively low. *Probably wanted an alone day*, she thought. She had ran off a few times before.

Cass focused her energies on a day of volunteer work in the newly created Habitat for Prosperity. Unlike the soup kitchen, this work proved far more strenuous. She wiped off the sweat from her small physical contribution to the building's construction, though more than making up for it with the financial strength to cover any cost.

After an exhausting day, Cass journeyed back to the palatial Averill home and collapsed on her soft bed. The full moon beamed down brightly through the window and a much-needed breeze passed through the space. She had almost fallen back asleep when a muffled crash downstairs roused her. Her eyes sprung open. She immediately rolled to the side and the bed and pulled a handgun from the nightstand.

"How'd did they get past the guards?" she wondered.

Silently as possible, she crept out of bed, scanning every corner of the house with the aid of the moonlight. She walked through the upper floors of the mansion, seeing no signs of an intruder. Footsteps barely on the edge of her perception sent her nerves alight. Her mind raced at the possibilities. Her finger stayed on the trigger as she moved forward. She saw the door still locked and the shattered remains of her porcelain rooster statue. The moonlight illuminated most of the house, the window in Thos's study wide open. She checked the safe, finding all the valuables intact. Cass heard the faint ebb and flow of breathing. She followed the sounds to the trophy room and felt she was not alone. Her hand shook, and her aim faltered at this vital moment.

"Come out now!" she said with the best stern voice she could muster. The figure moved but didn't respond.

"I'll shoot!"

The figure whimpered, but Cass didn't lower her weapon. The figure stepped out from the shadows. It quaked with fear and brandished a series of burn marks on her exposed flesh.

"Adrienne?" she gasped. Adrienne fell forward, and Cass rushed to catch her. Adrienne cried for a moment.

"You gotta help me. They're after me! I didn't know where else to go."

"Why not Yadira?" Cass said. Adrienne shook her head.

"They have eyes on her. James, too, I think," she said.

Adrienne's wounds were clear evidence of someone on the bad side of the wrong people.

"Who?" Cass said in disbelief. Adrienne looked at hear, half in disbelief herself.

"Vigilant."

THOS

THOS SQUIRMED IN the choking heat as the people of Mexico City gathered in the square, awaiting his rousing speech about a bright new day for the country. He spent the rest of his first day in Mexico recuperating from the unbearably long drive; today was day two and the start of his work. Armed soldiers covered nigh every inch of the area. Thos never liked the show of force the government flaunted, but he made an exception here given the situation. An assistant on his right held the umbrella over his head, despite his numerous protests. Over on a side street, Zora watched him when not distracted by the million other sights and sounds. Thos also noted the Duke's absence with a half-hearted, last-minute excuse.

Thos's mood had declined sharply without his wife, hiding his sorrow and irritation with fakes smiles honed over the years. He buried that sadness, knowing what it could bring.

The sun crept down through his sunglasses as midday approached. The company's Mexican liaison spoke first, dishing out the usual spiel on the greatness of the Averill Estate Farms and Averill's Own products. The liaison motioned Thos to the podium to the sounds of applause. The overwhelming majority of the country spoke English, making translators unnecessary. Thos tripped over the microphone wire, almost knocking the podium onto the front row. The entire crowd laughed. *Should've brought my club, really sell the image.*

Thos hopped to his feet and so did his assistant with an umbrella in tow.

"I'm not a princess. Get that damn thing away from me!" Thos groaned, grabbing the umbrella and throwing it behind him. Thos placed his hands on the podium.

"Afternoon. Hope you're well, all things considered," Thos said.

The speech cards lay on the podium. He thumbed through them. Bullet points about his childhood, patriotism, and recent marriage seemed disingenuous and clearly written by someone else. It also played up the death of his brother, something he explicitly stated he would not discuss. Thos covered the microphone.

"Who put this in there? Don't *ever* bring my brother into this," he said.

Thos closed his eyes until he regained his composure, fearing the demons of the past would again become flesh. Putting on another false grin, he begun to address the crowd.

"There's much we can achieve together, and the nation will reach new heights because of it. You're already good at dealing with bullshit, so we got one ingredient for farmin' right there."

The crowd laughed. Thos picked up the speech cards and ripped them up.

"They wrote a speech for me. It's stupid. I think I have the whole word thing figured out."

Thos neglected to mention that the massive job expansion resulted in some job cuts up north and reduced the average pay per worker. Giving each worker decent pay, benefits, and healthcare proved far more costly than he had imagined. He never realized how difficult running a business truly was and developed a bit more respect for large companies not propped up by the advisors.

"Look, I know you've heard this story before, promising you

the moon and giving you a hard turd instead." Thos cleared his throat and straightened up, what he called the "sincerity stance."

"I know things've been hard. You probably don't have much faith in this changing anything. There always seems to be chaos that knocks you two steps back. I often wonder if anything I do makes a difference, but it does. I'm not good at many things . . . public speaking, for sure, but I'm doing my damnedest to help. My family worked hard to make Averill Farms what it is. People like to give us shit for getting that land from the Blackthornes; we made the farm what it is, not them. People like you make it work. I wanted to come down here to show that we're here for you and no gangs or anyone else is gonna get in the way. We have done some good with this business, and with your help, we'll do a hell of a lot more."

"You're a hero!" someone yelled out in the crowd.

"I'm definitely not that," Thos countered. *I was a flagpole.*

He heard the anxious squirming of the officials behind him. Thos finished his disjointed speech and returned to the hard-cushioned seat while the nervous interim mayor concluded the event. He spotted Zora in the crowd, giving Thos a nod of approval. A pop rang out from the business district a few blocks behind them, followed by the monstrous roar of engines.

The dispersing crowd panicked as armed troops shoved them out of the way, forming a perimeter. A few small battalions broke off to engage the unknown enemy. The nearest guards grabbed Thos and pulled him to a safe location. Thos couldn't see Zora among the fleeing populace.

"See anything?" Thos asked.

"No. An army could be hidden in that damn crowd."

"Just the confidence boost I needed," Thos replied.

A woman in a red robe casually walked down the street. She pointed at Thos. A dozen men dressed up like skeletons ran past her and began shooting. Thos scrambled for an exit, losing the guard at his side. Thos rounded the corner and collided with a skull-faced man before he could pull out his gun.

"End of the road," he said.

The man pointed his semi-auto rifle at Thos. Thos grabbed the man's gun, thrust it upward, then rammed it repeatedly into the man's face. The attackers grip loosened, giving Thos the chance to take the rifle and turn it back on his assailant. Thos fired three times into another enemy's chest. Gunfire rang out across the city. Three more skull-faced men wielding machetes converged on Thos's position. Thos unloaded the last rounds from his gun. He dropped the gun and switched to his sidearm, but the man was on him before he could shoot. Thos narrowly dodged the blade swipes. He tripped the man and struck him with the butt of his gun, and then killed the second attacker. Rifle shots from a man in a faded serape and cowboy hat took out the last cultist. The man with the cowboy walked up to him.

"Always causing trouble," he said. Thos knew the voice and breathed a sigh of relief at the sight of Drake Hale.

"I like to make an impression," Thos said, still eyeing his surroundings.

"It works," Drake said, shaking Thos's hand.

"See Zora?" Thos said. Drake's eyes grew as wide as cannon-balls at the name.

"She's here?"

"You've made an impression too," Thos said.

Thos hollered out to Zora and she hollered back. She stood over by some wounded civilians, helping the medics treat their wounds. Soldiers took defensive positions around the people that had failed to escape. Thos and Drake approached Zora.

"In one piece?" Thos asked.

"Yes," Zora said with relief. She finished salving up a young woman's wounds and noticed Drake. Drake hugged her.

"Hi," Drake smiled, breaking from his hardened killer

persona. From the expression on her face, she struggled to take in Drake's attire.

"You look like a kite," Zora said. Drake looked down at his outfit.

"I think I look cool," he said. Thos gave him a pat on the back.

"Time to head out, cool guy," Thos said.

The trio and their armed escort rushed through the city on lockdown while government forces swept over the area. Drake caught them up on the war with the Void on their way out of the city.

A few injured civilians stopped to applaud Mr. Averill, while some paid him no mind at all. Trucks, including one with Drake's AATV and Thos's armored car, pulled up in front of them. The three got in Thos's car and hastily drove out of the city toward Duke's villa.

DRAKE

MINOR SIGNS OF life greeted Drake and company as they moved across dunes and crags of the desert. Bugs and other inhabitants could be heard. Horned snallygasters napped on the large rocks. Drake kept his eyes peeled. Drake glanced out the back window, losing sight of the rest of the convoy.

"We have a problem," Drake said.

The tires on the truck in front of them popped, the truck hauling Drake's AATV. The truck swerved out of control, flipping over from the attempt to correct. The AATV flew out of the back, scraping the side of the car and barely avoiding a head-on collision. Drake, Thos, and Zora prepared to fight, sizing up Void motorcyclists closing in. Through the bulletproof windows, Drake saw two armored trucks bearing the image of Void gaining fast.

The driver made a quick left turn, causing the two vehicles moving in for a sandwich attack to swerve hard. The driver veered off the desert road. The driver and his passengers bounced around in the car speeding across the jagged rocks. Dodging rocks only last so long. One last right turn sent the armored car into a sand trap. The tires sputtered in vain. The military escort fought the bulk of Void troops, but Drake's group was exposed. The two trucks pulled up behind them. Thos, Drake, Zora, and the frazzled driver watched as eight armed men stepped out of the trucks. Drake noticed a third truck approaching, this one with a hefty green monster holding a sack painted on the side.

"Who the hell is that?" he said. Drake shook his head.

"Hobgoblins," Drake said. The third truck ran over two of the cultists and came to a stop. The remaining cultists took cover behind their vehicles.

Out of the new truck stepped two figures. The first was a bulky, but relatively normal-sized man in a brown duster and cowboy hat; the other man was a different story. He was a gigantic beastly figure double the size of the other man and wore a custom, stitched-up duster. Drake's eyes widened.

"That's a troll!" Drake exclaimed.

Troll was the term given to humans with an extreme defect that left them with a beastly appearance, these mutations resulted from ancestors meddling with animal DNA, or so was the theory. Some trolls were reported to be cannibals and having a mental state more akin to a wild animal. The name came from a traveling merchant's first encounter with one hiding under a bridge during a rainstorm. Most born with such mutations died within days, but others were exiled, willingly or not, to the untamed reaches of the world.

The troll's arms were disproportionately large compared to his legs, and the torso was like a wall. The arms were massive like a gorilla, extending down to his knees. The skin had a texture akin to scales, adding a reptilian quality to the gargantuan man. The troll's head was the most striking feature, infant-sized compared to his body. The man beside the troll spoke.

"Sic 'em," he said.

The troll walked over to the truck the cultists were hiding behind. He placed his arms under the truck and effortlessly flipped it over, squashing the cultists. The other man focused on Drake and his dumbfounded companions.

"Hello, ladies and gentlemen. We're the Hobgoblins!" he said. Drake swore he recognized the voice.

The Hobgoblins, though not as dangerous as the Void, were a successful gang of thieves causing grief for the other groups fighting to control the state. The group appeared about nine months ago, and something inside Drake clicked.

"Somethin' ta say?" the man asked.

"Infamous gang, rather dangerous group of killers and thieves with a leader the people called, and this is the translation." Drake cleared his throat. "Captain Assface." Zora and Thos didn't reply. "I'll handle this," Drake said.

"Oh will ya now?" the leader asked. Drake and the others stepped out of the vehicle and raised their hands skyward.

"It's a bit odd seeing you here. Quite the flip," Drake commented.

The leader stared back at Drake and approached him. The troll bared his overly large teeth.

"He's no threat to us," Drake said. "You know, I've wanted to test your abilities for a while now. How about a little sparring."

"Why not?" the leader responded. "Liz, keep watch for dead-heads, and don't get involved."

The leader immediately responded with a quick jab at Drake; he barely dodged. Drake ducked down and extended his leg for a sweep kick that his opponent leaped over. The leader responded with a fist to Drake's stomach as he hopped back up. Drake stumbled. He threw a punch at the leader, who caught it. Drake's eyes widened in surprise, as did those of his friends. Drake thrust his leg up and gave a hard kick to the leader's right side. The two dodged and exchanged punches to the point of exhaustion while everyone else enjoyed the show.

"I'm impressed. Thought you were all talk," Drake said.

"You know him?" Zora asked.

"We all do." All three turned to face the leader as he removed his bandanna and sunglasses.

"Son of a bitch," Thos said.

"The great Melvin Shor, alive and well," Drake said. "He's been leading the Robin Hoods of Mexico, robbing the government and the Void," Drake replied. Melvin smiled at them.

"Had to make a grand entrance," Melvin said. "And you don't steal from the government, you just take back." Drake couldn't exactly argue with that fact.

"You were part of that government too for a while," Drake said. "Had Joe's war tax, if I recall."

"Fair enough, I've done some shitty things. I do donate regularly, but keep some for ya know, business expenses," Melvin said.

"You risked being killed for this little song and dance?" Thos asked.

"We've pulled off hairier shit than his. 'Sides you can see why I'm not afraid of the deadheads," Melvin replied.

"Who's your friend?" Zora asked. She smiled at the troll. The troll responded with a hilariously besotted grin.

"This is Liz, my number two guy. I named him Liz because, well . . . look at him. Say hello," Melvin gave him a nudge.

"Hi," Liz said, throwing out his hand out in an awkward wave that nearly knocked Melvin off his feet.

Something about Liz's demeanor made them all smile in return, though it might have been from Melvin's pain. Melvin stood and dusted himself.

"Bit awkward and shy, but can get pretty wild," Melvin said.

"Why you out here stealing from the government you helped install?" Thos asked. Melvin sighed deeply.

"*We* helped install," Melvin replied. "I'll give you the short version, but not here. Perhaps we can discuss it over drinks tomorrow. Got some missions planned so I can't stay long, going after the deadheads. When I get back, I'll get you some intel about the space guns and whatnot, need to verify a few things."

"How do you know about those?" Drake said.

"I nabbed a few of 'em," Melvin said proudly. "Never saw one 'til a few weeks ago . . . yet I feel like I have. You figure a thing like that would stand out," he said.

Drake and Thos looked at each other. Zora shook her head in confusion. Liz, uninterested, began to walk around the area like a restless child.

"Now that you mention it, I think I've seen them guns too. In Kingsbury," Thos said.

"So I'm not crazy. Thought I had dreamed it up. Weird, ain't it? And it all started when Vigilant showed up. Matter of fact, your uncle Greg was out this way not long ago," That got Zora's attention.

"You've seen him?" Zora asked.

"Once, yeah. Word is Vigilant's got a huge base somewhere, planning something big."

"Very interesting, but I think we should get out of the desert before more deadheads show up," Drake said. "I doubt you two can fight them all off." All nodded in agreement.

"Liz!" Melvin yelled. "Get their car out of the trap, please and thank you."

Liz effortlessly picked up the car over his head. "Don't break it!" Liz gently placed the car down beside the trap. The driver, still in shock, woke from his state and checked the ignition while the others talked.

"I'll catch up with ya guys tomorrow," Melvin advised. "Dead guys are going to be receiving some premium goods from their benefactor. I'll snoop around some and let you know. I have a feelin' this dude is behind some of the troubles up north too. Might get some info and put a hurtin' on 'em," Melvin said, moving toward the truck.

"You been stealing from the government. Am I supposed to just forget that?" Drake asked. Liz nodded.

"Yep. Bye!" Melvin said. "Say bye, Liz."

"Bye, Liz," Liz said.

Liz gave a proper wave before hopping in the passenger side and speeding off into the unknown.

GREGOR

GREGOR HAD SPENT the last several days grappling with nauseating revelations about cybernetics in all life on Earth and the terrifying possibility of what this could mean. Before his next mission, he stayed in one of the houses in the residential district bequeathed to him by Matthias. Hundreds of luxurious houses filled the area. From the window, Gregor watched the floating structures of the impossible city.

Screams from burning cultists echoed from the depths. More barriers were found throughout the city, but thanks to the constant influx of prisoners and Matthias's impalement devices, the place was quickly opening up. Gregor was impressed by the robust barrier system. He saw storms far off in every direction that provided another layer of defense for the oasis.

Gregor divided his time with training to keep himself in peak condition and taking in all of the marvels of the Silent City. The floating tiers of the city didn't seem practical, but the design was certainly a testament to creativity. He deciphered buildings based on shapes: bars, shops, and offices. There were a few buildings he couldn't make heads or tails of, such as circular ones covered with large vertical slots. Half of the buildings Gregor searched were bare-bones, without any evidence humans had ever lived here. The excessive grays and whites throughout the city suggested an unfinished entity, not unlike a drawing waiting to be colored in. The dead city began to infect Gregor with a heavy sorrow.

Military trucks rolled through the city, repainted in Vigilant colors of white with a red eye that had swords for lashes. Surrounded by barren wastes between two deserts, Gregor contemplated the nature of the visions that guided Matthias to this needle in a state-sized haystack. Talk of visions and connections he often associated with apostates. Gregor's reinstatement came with the title of lord crusader, stripping away the original title of sentinel now that all branches of Vigilant were unified. Gregor served as the new head of the Vigilant's Mexican branch, but with all hands on deck, he would also double as a field agent for the foreseeable future. Many within Vigilant's ranks respected him, some more than they respected Matthias; Gregor hoped that wouldn't become an issue.

The splendor of the fabled city was outmatched by the crushing emptiness of its streets and buildings. Thousands of robots stuck in eternal paralysis set Gregor's nerves afire; he kept one eye on them, suspicious they would in a moment roar to life.

The sounds of footsteps from behind him echoed across the city. Gregor slowly turned around to face his new babysitter. The person in question was a slim man, more scholar than fighter. His gear hung a bit too loose.

"Help you?" Gregor asked.

"Sorry . . . sir. I should've said something. I'm Raul . . . Alvarez, your new second," he said awkwardly. Raul extended his hand but then switched to a salute. Gregor cocked an eyebrow and gave Raul a once over; his timid demeanor matched the early days of Cedric's career.

"Don't be nervous. Nervous soldiers become dead soldiers," Gregor said. Raul remained nervous. "Alvarez . . . related to Sentinel Alvarez?" he asked. He nodded.

"My father. Did his best to not be biased. I had a knack for tinkering," he said, stumbling over the words that threatened to open a recently sealed wound.

"I'm sorry for your loss. Heard he was a great man," Gregor said.

"T-thanks . . . thank you, sir," he replied. A long pause followed.

"Was there something you needed? A mission, I hope," he said.

"Boss wants to see you. Apparently, your radio isn't working," he said. Gregor glanced down at the radio; he forgot to turn the volume up.

"Yeah . . . defective," he lied.

Raul led Gregor to the labs where Matthias spent most of his time. As they walked, the two discussed the floating city of impossibility. Gregor entered the section of the city devoted to scientific research. He heard the ghostly breathing of wisps. The wisps took form, becoming the hundreds of human citizens moving through the buildings. The figures spoke, though most words came out as static save for one: Collective. The Collective, more commonly known as the New World Order, was a cabal of elites seeking to unite the continents into one empire they held absolute control over.

Gregor followed the wisps to a lab that was more akin to a warehouse. Wisps were a strange phenomenon not unlike, or possibly were, ghosts. Wisps were most common around strong electric energy and played back events that transpired in the past, from the mundane to the momentous. The wisps glitched, speeding up to a table beside a large vat. The figures were huddled over the table and analyzing a computer no longer present. On the table, a wisp took the form of a newborn baby hooked up to various wires from a long-absent machine.

A wisp spoke. The voice rattled off bits and pieces of the child's statistics from the invisible future. The statistics became personal and predictive. The wisp spoke about his future beliefs, political affiliations, genetic aptitudes, and likelihood to criticize the government. The wisps sounded disappointed at the idea of a child not fitting their parameters.

"The Collective rejects him." The wisp picked up the child and callously dropped him into the vat. The wisps vanished, thankfully not showing Gregor the atrocity that came next.

"Mercy, I thought child processing centers were an exaggeration," Gregor said.

Gregor despised the Old World, a place where a baby that may one day maybe, possibly, complain about the government would be thrown in a pot and turned into soup. Gregor didn't dare to think how often this evil was carried out. The wisps returned to play the nightmare out yet again.

"I've seen this a dozen times. I still can't believe it," Raul said.

Raul led Gregor to the lab. Gregor saw hundreds of containers of various fill with various organs, cadavers, fauna, and flora being carted to and from cold storage. Scalpels and scopes analyzed thawed meat. Gregor watched Vigilant troops enter a large back room and shut the door behind them.

"Nano-alteration testing," Raul said. "Stay away from there right now. Boss gets mad if the unauthorized poke around. Not sure what goes in there, but word is some don't come out. Probably nothing, big place."

Gregor mulled on Raul's words while climbing to the third floor—secret experiments behind closed doors could lead to disaster. Matthias paced back and forth with a long-range radio, an "allowed" version of an Old World cell phone, up to his face. Gregor and Raul stood around while Matthias finished the call; the end piqued Gregor's interest.

"Can you still hear me? Find out the source ASAP. Things are escalating. If this is him, we have to speed this up. I'll let you know when it's time," Matthias said, ending the call. "Worthless junk." Matthias turned around and smiled.

"Got a date?" Gregor asked. Matthias checked his reflection in one of the empty blood jars.

"We all do. A lot from here on out," Matthias said. Gregor's eyes focused on the jars and he grimaced. Matthias laughed.

"Still bugging you, isn't it?" Matthias said. Gregor let out a caveman grunt. He crossed his arms and stared at Matthias like a fed-up teacher.

"Are you going to tell me about these visions?" Gregor asked, folding his arms. "Sir," he added.

"Is it that crazy after all you've seen? I have a theory that my defect plays a part, something to do with the cells that made me susceptible to the signal." Gregor nodded.

"So you got clairvoyance and I go white by sixty," Gregor said. "He wanted to know more about defective cells." Matthias raised an eyebrow in confusion.

"My second, Cedric," Gregor began. "Was a good friend. He would've loved to be here theorizing with you. Probably might've had it all figured out already. He was murdered by Anselm."

"We've lost many good soldiers to get to this point; we won't waste their sacrifice," Matthias said. Gregor preferred not to think of dead friends.

"The signal," Gregor said, steering the conversation back on track.

"Something drew me to a powerful warlock, a deadlander named Samedi. I managed to apprehend him. I took something from him that showed me many things, changed everything. It reacted with my body, like that rod I used on you. It showed me the end of the Old World . . . and it started at the center of these ancient cities," Matthias said. Gregor remained skeptical. Matthias smiled deviously.

"Oh ye of little faith," Matthias said.

Matthias walked to the back room and picked up a black case. He pulled a key from his pocket and opened the case. Maintaining his smug grin, he removed an expressionless mask of polished silver from the case. The hazy memories once again became clear.

"The images you saw were very much real," Matthias said. The air rippled around the mask.

"The more I see it, the more I wanna smash it," Gregor said, feeling the icy prick of little legs crawling up his spine.

Matthias walked up to Gregor with mask in hand. Gregor extended his arm to take it. Matthias shoved the mask onto Gregor's face. Gregor's whole body surged with fire. His head swam; a static hissing wracked his brain. Then he saw.

Humans and artificial life forms fled toward the city's heart, trampling the unfortunates that fell in the stampede. Outside the central structure, humans and robots screamed for those inside to stop. Barriers shot up across the city, separating family and friends behind unseen walls A dome of energy covered the city. A beam shot up from the tower and passed through a hole in the barrier and into the sky. The sky became ablaze with green fire. Gregor witnessed the very last seconds of the Old World with horrifying clarity. The frozen machines decayed, suggesting some time passed. Humans fled into the wastes and the tunnels. A man in a white suit and a golden tragedy mask stood in the ruins of the dead city, blocked from reaching the central structure. More time passed. Gregor witnessed people across the continent gathered before the masked man. Another flash saw him viewing masked figures gathered around Anselm, laughing as he writhed on the floor.

"Demon?" Gregor asked, trying to maintain his composure.

"Not like any of the others," Matthias said. "My men have classified him as an arch-demon." A wave of nausea hit Gregor in the gut. He grew light-headed.

"Compact . . . built by a demon," Gregor said.

"All this time, the Compact we follow . . . that we kill for . . . created by one of the very things we're trying to destroy. Guess we should've seen it coming," Matthias said bitterly. Gregor ran his fingers along with the mask. He heard voices whispering in his head. *He will doom you all.*

"Don't use it too long. It can have long-term effects," Matthias cautioned.

Gregor saw through the eyes of Samedi, spouting curses in an unknown language. As the other person, he saw the floor moving by. Crusaders bound him. The mask came loose as hands pried it off. The mask came to rest on the face of the orange-eyed man standing before Gregor at this very moment. Past Matthias looked around at a city with floating towers. Something called out to Gregor from inside the city. Gregor felt the gentle tugging in his skull. The mask turned hot. It wrapped tighter around his face like a constricting python. A voice came from the mask.

"Pay the price for treachery," it said.

The mask started to burn. Gregor cried out in pain. Matthias tore the mask from Gregor's face and threw it across the room. It slid across the room, it came to a halt with a smile on its ghoulish face. A crusader rushed to Gregor's aid, firing waves at the mask. Matthias picked up the mask back and sealed it back up in the case.

"Destroy that as soon as possible," Gregor said, breathing and sweating heavily.

"Quite resilient," Matthias said. "We'll destroy it when we don't need it anymore. Been quite useful as you can see . . . nothing like it."

"I'll say," Gregor said, regaining his composure.

Gregor pressed his hands on the lab table in front of him and breathed heavily.

"And the experiments? What exactly are you doing?" Gregor asked. Matthew stopped for a second, slightly irritated by the questions.

"Don't worry about that now, you have a mission," Matthias said. "An old-fashioned witch hunt. With luck the last," he said. Matthias rummaged through a collection of files marked with individual member names. Matthias pulled out a dossier marked "Greg" from his desk at the back of the room and handed it to Gregor.

"She's hard to track down, but we believe the target is going here. She's a dangerous one, the kind that needs an elite soldier like you. You have a few days to get ready and head out. And bring this one back alive."

Matthias returned to his work like Gregor wasn't there. Gregor thumbed through the papers and map with a dot east of Mexico City.

CASS

Cass sat beside the bed, sipping tea with lemon so intense she had to make sure it wasn't cleaner. Adrienne slept in Cass's bed, snoring like a chainsaw-wielding banshee with an extra hand running nails on a chalkboard. Despite a private army patrolling the grounds, she feared another lone intruder may slip through the cracks.

Her oldest cat, Mask, whined for attention in a scratchy voice, no longer the worst thing she'd ever heard. The cat purred soft and hopped onto her lap. She ran her fingers through feline fur with one hand and drank tea with the other. Adrienne mumbled in her sleep and drooled all over Thos's favorite "Eternacool" pillow. The more she thought about the situation, the more anxious she became, tapping her foot to the annoyance of Mask.

Cass put the cat down and went to the bathroom. She did a quick look over her graying hair and orange eyes. The gray strands were only noticeable to her; she saw them even when they weren't there. Cass kept her status as a defect well hidden. The term "defect" had become a stigma meaning sickly and not whole, and in her case, it was true.

On top of the widespread defect traits of early gray hair and orange eyes, Cass's genetic mutations left her with a fragile immune system, thin blood, and ovarian cysts. Thos didn't care about natural hair and eye color, but Cass preferred the auburn hair and hazel eyes a 35-year-old should have. She poured some water in the glass on the sink and swallowed her medication. She added some fresh color to her hair and popped her new contacts in.

Cass had plenty to keep her busy during Thos's absence, but now she was harboring a fugitive. She begrudgingly called the day off to keep an eye on her ward. Cass was never one to spend too much time idling; it worsened her mood when these times of idleness were enforced upon her. This new wrinkle in the plan gave her the impression she wouldn't get to join Thos in Mexico at all. Adrienne was a poor substitute for Thos.

She heard a faint thumping from the side of the house and reached for the gun. The doctor came around the corner and his eyes grew wide. Cass moved her hand away from the gun and gave him a welcoming smile.

"Sorry . . . thought you were someone else," she said casually.

"I see," he said with a frazzled laugh. At that moment, Cass had remembered about his appointment with the bedridden Adrienne.

"Sorry. Lost track of time. She's upstairs."

Cass accompanied the doctor up to the bedroom. He peered down the hallways as if looking for something. She always thought Dr. Halus was an odd duck but well-meaning. Cass stood by the window and watched him pull several medical instruments from his small brown bag.

Halus roused Adrienne from her sleep. When she fully came to, she reluctantly accepted her painkillers. He examined her bruises and lacerations. Adrienne winced as he touched her back and arms. Cass noticed a few things out of character for the doctor: namely profuse sweating and an unusually twitchy nature. Her instincts were gnawing at her.

"You're sweatin' like a pig in a chophouse. What's wrong?" she said, gauging his behavior.

"No . . . It's just . . . working on fugitives," he replied. Adrienne mumbled her displeasure at the topic.

The doctor gave her a few pills. Cass's internal gnawing intensified.

"Sure you weren't followed?" Cass said. It took a moment for him to respond. He nodded. Cass didn't reveal her suspicions. He finished up his business.

"Get some more rest. I'll be back tomorrow," he said with a curt goodbye.

Halus made haste for the door, forgetting his belongings in the process. This time the instincts inside her screamed. Cass picked up her gun. With a click, the startled doctor spun around to find her gun pointed at him.

"How much they payin' you?" she cried. She removed the safety to let him know the severity of the situation.

He quickly ducked out the door. Cass scampered after him, but he flew down the steps and toward the door. Shadows moved in the kitchen and prepared to shoot this new threat.

"We've had enough of your failures," came a voice from the kitchen. Halus opened his mouth to speak but fled while Vigilant allowed it. Two men in red and white robes burst into the room with muzzled rifles.

"Don't interfere. We only want the girl."

Cass wasn't sure she believed it. Vigilant could be ruthless to accomplices. Her survival instinct took over. She took cover behind the wall, not wanting to kill anyone. The enemies moved in. A loud bang upstairs caught them all off guard. Crusaders moved up the stairs toward the noise.

Cass braced for the crusader to attack again. He stopped at the top of the stairs. A loud crash came from Adrienne's room, followed by a scream and a gunshot. She heard the man call out from the stairs.

"Sitrep," he said. There was no response.

"Sitrep," he repeated.

A third crusader stepped out of Adrienne's room and bolted down the stairs. Adrienne stepped up behind him, her right eye a burning green. Adrienne stumbled. *The drugs,* Cass thought.

Adrienne caught a glimpse of Cass standing in complete shock and feral.

"You betrayed me!" Adrienne said. She lunged at Cass. Cass cried out for help, but none of her troops came; she feared the worst.

"Guns ready!" a man hollered.

The sounds of more footsteps down below stopped the conversation. Cass hollered out for her men once more. They had been seemingly defeated without a single shot. The enemy advanced. Fear mounted. She had precious little time to wonder about her absent army. With her guard mysteriously incapacitated or dead, Cass knew she would be unable to fend off the attacks for long. She instinctively dipped behind cover when she heard more foes on the top step.

More crusaders appeared with long rectangular guns. The crusaders pointed the strange guns at Adrienne. Adrienne clutched her head and fell unconscious to the floor. The green color left her eye.

Out of the corner of one crusader's eye, he caught Cass peeking from one of the rooms at the end of the hallway. The crusader pointed his weapon at Cass. She walked out behind her cover with hands raised. The man lowered his weapon when he saw Cass was no threat to him.

"You all right?" he asked.

Cass's head and heart pounded so loud she could barely hear him. She steadied her breath. The man asked again, this time she heard loud and clear. She nodded.

"Sorry, Mrs. Averill," he said. "Had to make sure you weren't a thrall." Cass was finally able to process everything.

"Is she?" she asked, already knowing the answer.

"A Grey Sister, well, an ex. Apparently, a lot hiding out around here. You're lucky she didn't kill you," he replied.

"That means . . . " she said, afraid of what would follow.

"You harbored an apostate," he said. "That's a violation of the Compact, but since you didn't know, I'll forgive it. The death sentence only comes for willing accomplices."

"What about?"

"Your men outside are unconscious but alive," he said. "We had to prevent them from getting enthralled. When they wake they'll have no idea what happened. Tell them what you wish, but they must not reveal anything to anyone."

"What's going on?" she said.

"There's much happening in the world right now," the man said. "I can't say more. Carry on like normal and trust we'll resolve this," he said.

One of the crusaders threw Adrienne over his shoulder and carried her away, and the others followed. The man gave a bow and turned away from her. When she heard the front door slam shut, she ran to the nearest window to find the Averill guards lay strewn across the grounds.

ANSELM

ANSELM SAT CROSS-LEGGED outside his hut, watching the blue and purple etherflies waltz above the hills. He never found such peace back in Kingsbury. He closed his eyes and breathed in the tender summer night. For a moment, he pretended he was sitting with his family. Anselm opened his eyes and saw Rosalie standing over him.

"Shit!" Anselm said, startling Rosalie.

"Didn't think I was that terrifying," she said.

"Cam okay?" Anselm asked. Rosalie waved her hands.

"He's fine. Staying with dad tonight," she said, calming the war-ready Anselm.

"Sorry, used to being called to action." He realized her purpose immediately after.

"I wanted to see you," she said, moving close. Anselm battled his growing feelings for her. "Mind if I sit?" She said nothing about his freshly shaven face.

"I can work it in my schedule," he laughed. Rosalie took a seat beside him.

"Like some wine?" he asked. She nodded. Anselm fumbled through the bag beside him and pulled out a bottle with only a few swigs remaining. "Oh, I . . . don't have any," he laughed. Anselm heard a voice in his head. *The life you want you'll never have.*

Since Cameron's rescue, Anselm had been declared a family member and no longer worried about dishonoring his previous one. Anselm and Rosalie sat and relished the night. He looked up at the moon while he formulated his next move.

"Stories say there used to be a grand city up there," Anselm said. "The lights never stopped, for years. They went out about the time we got ours back. I wonder if anyone is up there looking at us? Maybe they destroyed themselves, too."

Anselm wasn't much of a romantic, growing uncomfortable at her advances yet not wanting them to stop. His cheeks reddened quickly, a stark contrast from his pale skin.

Instinct told him to push Rosalie away, yet he couldn't bring himself to do it. His heart fluttered. He grappled with the feelings he no longer wanted to imprison. Before long, genuine sincerity began to flow from him.

"Since my family died, I've been no more than a ghost. For the longest time, I wanted to join them . . . I even tried."

Rosalie looked over but could see no wounds. Rosalie moved closer to him and placed her hand on his. Her soft crystalline eyes pierced through him. She put her hand on his chest. Anselm grew nervous as her fingers ran down; his pale skin became tomato red. He hesitated. Their lips touched. The torment of his hellish new life for a moment washed away. Something came over him he had never expected to feel again. He had grown exhausted of fighting himself.

"I like you, but I . . . to hell with the past," Anselm said, locking lips with her.

Anselm bit her lip. He had no time to regret the action when she returned the favor. He kissed her hard. Rosalie took him by the hand, and the two entered the hut. He gave in to his passions and pulled her in.

He ripped her clothes and kissed her nipples before biting them. Her skin felt like fire; he relished her warmth. She grunted, not seeming to mind the pain.

"You're gonna have to buy me some new clothes," she giggled.

Rosalie tore Anselm's pants off. Anselm ran his fingers through her hair. He pulled her hair, exposing her neck. Picking her up, he carried her over to the makeshift table for eating, knocking off the crude bowls with the swipe of his right hand. She leaned in close and whispered in his ear.

"Fuck me."

Anselm entered her hard, and the energy of their movements almost destroyed his home in the process. At that moment, Anselm didn't care. In the throes of passion, he didn't mind the collateral damage. Her fingers curled and locked with his. At that moment, Anselm forgot the mission and told himself that maybe this life could be his. He hadn't dared to hope for anything other than pain and vengeance in a very long time. The unbridled passion was matched by the searing pain inside him that never ceased. Nothing he did made the pain vanish. Anselm powered through it. He sweat profusely and called out his dead wife's name as he finished.

Instinct took over. Rosalie's orgasmic moans ceased, and she cried out in terror as Anselm's jaws clamped down on her neck. Her warm blood ran down his throat, nourishing him like water to a man in the desert. His hands dug into the flesh of her back. When he realized what he was doing, he pushed himself off her. Rosalie jumped back as he tried to calm her. She cradled her neck, blood running through her fingers.

"I'm sorry! I don't know what came over me!" She reached for his sword and pointed it at his throat.

"You fucking monster!" She stabbed him; thick dark red blood trickled out from the wound.

"I didn't mean-" He didn't fight back.

He forced the words out. "Stop, please. I didn't mean it! Something is wrong with me. I'll get help. I'll even go to Vigilant!" She pulled the blade back as he poured his heart out to her. She stabbed him again.

"The reason people are vanishing, was it you?" she asked, not believing it herself. *I couldn't help myself,* he thought.

Anselm raised his hand in protest. The pain intensified, twisting up his guts with the feeling of a thousand cuts. The veins were forced against his skin, wriggling like worms. He growled in response to the pain.

Anselm smacked the blade out of her hand. She ducked under his attempt to grasp her and darted to the door. He spun around, grabbed her, and forced her down. She kicked him hard in the gut. His anger took over.

"I said stop!" he roared. His vision blurred.

He grabbed her by the throat with his right hand and squeezed. Her throat began to tighten and cave. Blood ran from her mouth. As her throat collapsed, she gurgled one last word before succumbing to death.

"M . . . on . . . ster . . . ." The rage subsided.

Anselm's wits returned. He released his grip. Rosalie's body hit the floor. He stared at the corpse at his feet. In his anger, he'd killed the only person left that he cared about. He fell to his knees and wept.

Anselm picked up the bloody sword and began slicing himself as punishment. The wounds healed seconds after appearing. He rammed the blade through his heart in one last desperate attempt to end his life. Impaled, he knelt beside the dead woman he had come to love. When the sorrow left, he removed the blade and got to work.

Anselm wiped his blood and Rosalie's from his body. He scooped up her body and carried it to an area of the woods only he explored. He buried the body fast, just another in a collection scattered about the area. Anselm sat by her unmarked grave for hours. Once more, he had no place in this world.

The walk back home was torture . The woods around him were as silent as Rosalie. Anselm's thoughts of grief were drowned out by explaining Rosalie's disappearance; a thousand expected questions assaulted his brain. He knew the villagers would eventually discover bandits and demons weren't to blame for all the disappearances. When they found out, they would attack, though there was little they could do to him. But Anselm didn't want a needless fight. Gunfire from the direction of Durenburg forced Anselm to hurry back and grab his sword.

Over the last hill, he spied a dozen figures wearing reds and whites, not like any bandit he'd seen. Three trucks carrying more robed, lightly armored soldiers pulled up behind him. Further back, he spied a supply truck with the grinning face of Thos Averill that came to infect his dreams. One of the men held a megaphone. The people of Durenburg gathered outside, many armed and ready to take on the invaders. Though the red and white colors on the outfit were inverted from the last time he saw them, there was no mistaking Vigilant. The weapons Vigilant brandished gave him pause. He remembered the railguns he plundered from the family vault. He wondered how and why the technophobic group possessed them. Rosalie mentioned something about a large gang that terrorized them before he showed up, but he didn't expect it to be Vigilant. He thought of their attempt on him and felt the darkness stirring inside. Anselm crept closer to the agents, not fearing their guns. The leader addressed the villagers.

"There's no need to protect him," he said. "You harbor a killer. Turn him over and there'll be no more trouble."

Anselm formulated a plan of attack. A sudden burst of light from the truck behind him put all eyes on him. The Vigilant commander turned around while his men kept guns pointed at the townsfolk to deter their intervention. The bulky, dark-skinned man was instantly familiar to him. The man leading this branch of Vigilant was Jaren Hart, son of Anselm's former general.

He's seeking vengeance for a father that died defending me. Anselm hollered out to draw their attention.

"Speak of the devil," Jaren said. Jaren squinted his eyes as if he recognized Anselm. "Aric? Can't be," he muttered.

"So this is Vigilant now? I knew you were frauds," Anselm said. Jaren sneered.

"We need these supplies for things a murderous hermit like you can't understand," Jaren said. "Wonder how these villagers will feel when they see your true nature? How *you're* the one putting them in danger." Anselm felt old hatreds bubbling up, control slipping away.

"Your men were pathetic and weak," Anselm said. "And brittle. Cry a lot more than I expected. You should make yellow your color; save yourself the embarrassment." Anselm let his viciousness out; his body burned with the urge to rip them apart.

"Your insults won't deter us," Jaren said. "We lost our families in the war. My dad . . . my sister . . . my baby sister *died* because of people like this! We're here because Vigilant saved us from the firing squad. Changed our identities, faked our deaths, and gave us our chance for payback. You're lucky we don't gun all of you down." Anselm understood the festering hatred that made anyone in his path guilty enough.

"I lost my family, too. Had you done your job pacifying threats, it never would've come to this. Leave these people be. The only thing people like you're good at is dying. Take another step and I'll prove it." Anselm gripped his sword tight.

Darkness stirred inside him. He had frustrations to vent, although he understood Jaren's pain. Jerrick Hart had been a fine man, and the things done to his wife and daughter were unforgivable. Anselm's sympathy only went so far, he had his own retribution to sate. Jaren shook his head in disappointment. Anselm smiled, knowing they weren't prepared to face him. Jaren quickly raised his railrifle at Anselm and fired. The blue trails of the bullets whizzed past Anselm, moving at unanticipated speeds. Anselm dodged the shots. A few other Vigilant soldiers joined in the attack. Multiple shooters proved hard to escape. The villagers cheered him on. With Anselm fighting for them, the villagers refused to be intimidated anymore. A few villagers rushed up the hill toward the Vigilant gunmen, only to be shot apart by superior firepower. After this, the villagers scattered amidst the chaos.

The distraction pulled the attention away from a few crusaders giving Anselm just enough time to cleave a man through the waist. He rushed the next crusader in his path, tackling him to the ground. The others quickly hopped on the trucks, unable to rescue or kill the prisoner of war.

The trucks disappeared over the hills to the north. Anselm pushed himself off the prisoner. He struck the man, knocking him unconscious. With the commotion over, the villagers returned to find Anselm on top of the hill carrying a Vigilant thug. The people erupted in cheers and gasps at Anselm's power. Anselm swelled with pride until he saw Cameron frantically pushing through the crowd in search of his mother.

MATTHEW

Matthew Pavane walked past the hanging gardens, preferring the soft blue glow of the etherflies while most of the Freemen slept. The Freemen communities had grown slow and steady over the past year thanks to the government's increasing authoritarianism. Business flourished in areas without fear of stepping on the wrong toes. The outside world had a great misunderstanding about the Freemen, thinking them all oversexed hippies sharing everything and owning nothing. Despite the reputation, a few wild individuals, and people like Melvin mistaking buzzed swimmers for orgy goers, Freemen were regular folk working jobs and raising children. They valued private property, free enterprise, and liberty above all else. Matthew owned an extensive stretch of what would be considered the town, including the gardens. He allowed everyone to access it, turning it into the most popular public space. The idea of being Freemen gained more and more appeal these days.

Seeking less and less recreational substances, Matthew's Kami persona was dying. He found it disappointing not to be consulted anymore, though he considered it a positive people were striving to not rely on others.

Matthew felt good, more than good, since his sparring match with Zora. For the first time in years, he felt alive. He tried not to yearn for the good old days, only making him regret not joining his brother and daughter. The Freemen communities of the east were on board and preparing for the inevitable conflict with the advisors. Several dozen Freemen groups were coordinated and ready to strike when the time came.

Matthew strolled through the dead quiet forest to Naia's grave, a part of his nightly routine. The sticky, hot dragon breath of the day began to die down, but no weather ever got in his way. Every night since Matthew had lived here, he took a nightly walk. Every night since his daughter's death, he came to visit her. He knelt by her grave and listened to gentle waters at the memorial pool. The Freemen loved the nature symbolism, but he could take it or leave it.

"Your sis is off again. Watch over her," Matthew said.

He looked over at the grave of his wife, Brielle, still finding it hard to believe she had been gone for so long.

"Where's the time gone, B?" Matthew asked.

Matthew laughed at the reaction his younger self would have at his transformation into an old bore.

"Never thought I'd tire of retirement."

Part of Matthew hoped the battle would go ahead and happen while Zora was far from the epicenter, but another part wanted her here defending her home. The chorus of bugs put him at ease; it was one of his favorite parts of living in the wilderness. He reminisced about the early days with his wife. Matthew missed their nights together, the torrid wild ones, the quiet comfortable ones, and some long forgotten. He saw her among smoking ruins. There were enemies coming for her, robed and with green eyes; they didn't expect to find Matthew Pavane. Matthew was in his prime, his savagery made him as lethal as any coven. He dodged their amateur attacks. He sliced and diced through the witches, most were more bark than bite. When all was said and done, Brielle walked away without a scratch. These were fragments of memories, yet they felt brand new. Matthew couldn't recall them before, yet deep down he knew they were real. Over the last years these new memories kept coming. Matthew couldn't remember why a coven had been after his wife, or how he could forget such an event. He tried to put the pieces together, but they never seemed to fit. The nightly strolls brought him no clarity.

The nightwatchmen were far away watching the borders from the treetops. In the small hours, few wandered in the night. Tonight he suspected a few more making their way toward him. The year of sobriety re-sharpened his dulled instincts. He sensed figures in the dark; he counted two. He scoffed at the idea.

"Only two? I'm worth more than that," Matthew said, goading his enemy.

"Big talk for an old man," one said. Even his attackers could see Matthew was in fantastic shape and had decades of combat experience over these goons.

"I was arrogant like you back in the day," Matthew said. "Waltzing into enemy territory. I suppose I'd still do that but I'd do my homework, like you shoulda done. If I'm a useless old man, why are you here?"

"We have done our homework. We know who you are and what you're doing," he said. "Been under his nose this whole time. The city isn't yours. What's Killswitch?"

Matthew's brow wrinkled. He shrugged.

"Don't make this difficult. Come with us," the man said.

"No," Matthew said.

"We'll loosen your tongue, maybe if we get ahold of some of these woodfolk or that cute little daughter of yours. Last chance: what's Killswitch?" Matthew kept a sidearm for such an occasion, but he wouldn't need it. He sensed two more lurking in the darkness.

"Now that's more like it," Matthew said.

The speaking man smirked and charged at Matthew. Matthew

dodged the incoming punches, to his attacker's saucer-eyed surprise.

"You whippersnappers," Matthew said, slightly disappointed Zora had fallen into this same trap. "Never underestimate your opponent." Matthew caught the man's arms. "And never threaten his family."

Matthew rammed his head forward and into his enemy's nose. The man swung wildly. Matthew stepped back, trying to keep the other men in his peripheral. He ducked and gave a hard jab into the man's stomach. The man stumbled back, coming to as Matthew drew the knife at his hip and thrust it up into the henchman's chin. The man hit the floor, leaving the enemy team one man down.

"Next?" Matthew asked.

The second man seized the opportunity to escape, though the Freemen would soon catch him. The third man was not so wise. Matthew dodged the tackle of the man rushing toward him. As the man got up, Matthew bequeathed him a hard kick to the face.

The other man was already on him. Matthew ducked and dodged, getting in a few quick blows. The frustrated growls signaled his opponent's sloppiness. Matthew turned his hand forward, allowing his next attacks to carve his enemy up. The man fell to the ground, bleeding. Matthew noticed a fifth man in the dark.

He spun to face the last attacker; this one appeared a bit smarter than the rest. The last man was a thick wall of meat that carried himself like a soldier. Matthew waved him forward. The man didn't budge.

"You're up," Matthew said. The man shook his head.

"I've taken your advice. Been studyin' you," he said. Matthew nodded, impressed by the wise choice.

"Not enough," Matthew said, raising his sidearm and planting a bullet into the man's skull. Freemen began to stir.

The surviving man on the ground coughed and spat a red glob

onto Matthew's shoe. Matthew raised his leg with said shoe and gave the man a kick in the ribs.

"Now listen and listen good, boy," Matthew said. "Why do you think I'm involved in this Killswitch business? The Freemen don't meddle in affairs unless you force us to."

"Not them. Vigilant," he said. Matthew's eyes widened.

"Vigilant's in the city?" Matthew asked. Matthew had a guess it concerned the Blackthorne Vault. Vigilant in the capital was a violation of law and a declaration of war in their eyes.

"Who you work for?" Matthew asked. The man stuttered. Matthew pushed him down with his foot.

"He'll kill me!" the man said.

"So will I. Who sent you? John?"

"Mr. Abaddon," the man replied.

Even jaded Matthew was taken aback. Mr. Abaddon, elusive to the point of being a myth, was the supposed ruler of the criminal underworld. The stories never warranted Vigilant's involvement in his relatively standard atrocities, outside of their age. Hundreds of years of reports lent credence to the idea that Mr. Abaddon was a title rather than an individual, and Vigilant had never found evidence to indicate otherwise. If Vigilant was involved, something serious was afoot. Matthew let the man rise his feet, studying him. The man's fingers twitched. Matthew didn't lower his gun. He pitied the man, but he made his choice and was about to again.

"You gonna kill me? I talked!" the man said.

"I told you I never underestimate my opponent," Matthew replied, pulling the trigger. The Freemen were fully up and armed by the second bullet. A Freemen hunter escorted the fleeing attacker back to Matthew. He blubbered and pleaded for his life.

"You're a smart one, so you got two options," Matthew said. "You should disappear, but if you must report back, tell your master to leave the Freemen out of it."

The hunter released his prisoner, who wasted no time sprinting out of a very angry Freemen stronghold. The waking Freemen flocked to the area. Matthew filled the populace in on the situation. Mr. Abbadon wasn't known for wanton slaughter, however, he wasn't above killing to get what he wanted, the innocent or anybody else. Matthew bid his farewells, making one final trip to his home.

He hastily packed some dry goods, bottles of water, medical supplies, and ammo into his survival bag. With Vigilant in Kingsbury, Matthew decided there was another thing he may need for survival. He pulled a long, black box out from under his bed. Opening the box, he grabbed his sword, a weapon kept polished to a mirror sheen for such an occasion. Matthew saw his reflection in the blade; still finding it hard to believe his long mane and beard were ghostly white. Both Pavanes' hair went white by the time they hit sixty; he liked to think he wore the look well.

Matthew proceeded to the bathroom and hastily trimmed his hair and beard. He donned some plain light armor under his clothes. Picking up his gear, he quickly headed for his horse. There was something strange going on in the city, and the resurgence of lost memories couldn't be a coincidence. Matthew shook off the rust and loaded up for a new crusade.

ZORA

Zora sat on the balcony of the spacious library of Duke's guest-house. Workers toiled with large cutters to maintain Duke's green maze and gardens precisely the way he wanted, down to the individual blade of grass. Zora heard a shouting match between Drake and Duke from the garden. The yelling marred the peaceful moments of her morning.

Zora thumbed through *Mexico: A History*, its events contradicting those told in *The Life of Manuel Diego*. The more she poured over the history books, the more she preferred entertaining fiction.

Zora spent her time taking in the sights and sounds of Mexico with Drake as her guide. Thos, when not cooped up in his room, spent his time touring the local farms and facilities soon to be part of Averill Estate Farms. Rumors of high-profile thefts swirled about, which meant the Hobgoblins were very much active.

The meeting with Melvin in Mexico City was a few hours away; Zora, Drake, and Thos were all going. Thos didn't mind putting himself in dangerous positions these days, with enough training to give Drake a run for his money. Zora made plans of her own for her time down south, none of which she was ready to share; her involvement with other Freemen deemed criminal conspiracy and treason. Zora felt less inclined to go since her vacation mission became a recruitment drive for the next war. Her entire life was beginning to revolve around conflict.

Patrols marched around the complex at all hours, while guards prepared armored cars for their trip to Mexico City. Zora's heart jumped up in her throat at the sound of someone behind her. She spun around, embarrassed to find Thos.

"I just died," she said as her face returned to its natural color.

"Sorry. Thought you heard me," Thos said.

The sound of footsteps and chewing came from the hallway, followed by the frustrated huffing and puffing of Drake. Drake walked into the room and did a double-take at Thos and Zora standing around.

"Catch you at a bad time?" Drake said.

"This is steak and wine hour, going by Duke Standard Time, I can alter my plans though. By the way, don't know what it is about the baths here, but they're a trip. Put some little ball in, swear I got stoned." Drake ignored this, but Zora had taken a bath and nodded in agreement.

"We should get ready. We'll see if Melvin has useful info," Drake said.

Thos cocked his head, apparently getting the message Drake also wanted a moment alone with Zora. He glanced at Zora and then again at Drake. He left with a bow. When Thos left, Drake wrapped his arms around Zora and kissed her.

"Think Melvin has anything?" she asked.

"I do," Drake said. "Much as I hate to admit it, I heard he ran the show before he vanished. He's damaged the Void quite a bit. Even if we find nothing, we can still enjoy the festivities." Zora raised her eyebrows and opened her mouth to show shock.

"Enjoy things? You?" she said. He shrugged.

"I'll give it a shot," he said, giving her another kiss.

Drake and Zora spent an hour together before meeting up

with Thos. They each donned incognito attire. Thos suited up in boots, jeans, a button-up green shirt, sunglasses, and a cowboy hat; he leaned against his Duke-loaned armored car. Zora noticed a pattern—all the guys wearing cowboy hats. She was pretty sure it was because they all thought cowboy hats were cool, and she kind of did, too. From a distance, Thos appeared mopey, though he quickly pepped up when he noticed the others.

"Remember, low profile," Drake said. "The whole situation is a powder keg, don't light the match."

"I'll vanish before your eyes," Thos promised.

They headed out. A few gunmen followed them from a comfortable distance. Mexico City brimmed with life, everyone preparing for the celebrations that kicked off that night. Barrels of alcohol lined the main street as food carts were set up. A few roads were already blocked off. A crowd had gathered to watch the parade by the old church with the destroyed cross, courtesy of the Void. Events occurred off and on each day and night of the week for the festival's entirety. Singing echoed from one direction of the city while the strumming of guitarrons came from another. The scene lifted Zora's spirit, relieved people still made time to enjoy life in this unpredictably violent world.

Together they walked the bustling, sun-drenched streets, taking in the playful mood of the city. Drake led Zora and Thos to Melvin's favorite hangout, Paraiso, a large and oft-frequented establishment. A restaurant, bar, strip club, whorehouse, and recreational drug den, the place existed to provide all of the vices in the city. Even in the daytime, with the pink, yellow, and purple neon lights wrapped all around, it wasn't exactly low-key.

"Not very inconspicuous for Melvin, is it?" Drake asked.

"Inconspicuous? Mel? He hangs out with a lizard man," Thos replied.

"Been here before?" Zora asked.

"Get a lot of intel here . . . and *nothing* else," Drake said emphatically.

Festival days left the building bursting with patrons. The stench of smoke and booze formed a pungent cocktail. A few of the working girls patrolled the back of the bar area wearing stockings and nighties, one gyrated on a loud drunk patron while another eyed the crowd suspiciously.

Melvin sat at a large empty table toward the back center of the bar, stroking his trim platinum-blonde beard. He removed his hat from one of the chairs and motioned them on over while downing a mug of beer. The three took seats at the table and exchanged pleasantries. A serving girl brought Melvin a large slab of ribs. Melvin devoured them, this time with a bit more sophistication than the last meal with the old gang.

"Shrimp," Drake said.

Thos pointed at the menu, saying, "That one, thank ya, ma'am." Zora asked for water and salad with chicken. She sat anxiously and listened to the light conversation between drinks.

"I'll get right down to the nitty-gritty," Melvin said. "Things were pretty quiet 'round here until old Duke 'won' his office. Then it got hot. After I killed Maria, things went bonkers. Cult wiped out Trinity and took over the gang biz, only seem to care about killing now." Melvin gave what information he could about Void's transformation from a cartel into a death cult, unrest since the government's rumored religion ban, and Duke's abuse of power adding fuel to an already roaring fire.

"And your last stunts?" Thos chimed in. "Pretty brazen."

"We go for the big fish. Gettin' some goodies and good info from it. Got on their freighter, too, was a storehouse for their trucks and guns, including those fancy new ones. Guarded too closely for us to nab anything though. And that's not all; the bottom was full of empty cages.

"Where are they getting this stuff from? The advisors?" Drake asked. Melvin gulped down another beer, loud enough to wear on Zora's nerve.

"Nah, they supplied them with stuff to destabilize the Blackthornes but stopped after that," Melvin said. "And that was the normal stuff. They have some new benefactor giving them space guns, now, and they get whatevers in them cages. It won't be long before they have enough firepower to take the state. I think Vigilant is also trying to stop them too, might want to team up."

"This'll be full-blown war, and with these guns, it won't be a long one," Drake said.

Melvin opened his mouth to reply too quickly, beer running out onto his beard. He wiped himself and continued.

"We've been tracking their movements for the past few months," he said. "Meet-sites are very remote for the special deliveries and always changing. Next exchange is out in the desert tomorrow night. Risky but our best bet, no civs to worry about, either. Me and Liz'll take ya to the meeting place." He spoke with childlike excitement.

"What's Vigilant been doing?" Zora asked. Melvin burped softly into his hand.

"Usual. Haven't made any movements on the deadheads yet, but they have grown very active the last few months. Word is they're making both the government and the deadheads nervous. It'll take some doing, but I'll try and contact your uncle."

"I'd appreciate it," Zora said. "And the Freemen?"

"They're way out in jungle ruins in the southeast. I can point ya in the right direction. Not lookin' for more labs, are ya?" Drake looked at Zora.

"Not entirely, but they may know something out there," she said. Drake frowned, sensing the half-truth.

"If you don't have any more questions, I'll meet your guys here tomorrow night," he said, clapping his hands together.

"Actually," Thos said. "I gotta know how you ended up heading a gang of thieves goin' after a government you helped install. You were their number one guy . . . 'til ya lost the election."

"That *we* helped install," Melvin corrected. "Day one I saw they were making a mockery of everything people like Joe and me had fought so hard for. I looked past a lot of shit I shouldn't have. After my failed election, they sent me here, then they found out who I really am." Melvin hesitated.

"Who you really are?" Drake asked.

"Don't leave us hanging," Thos said.

"I'd love to hear it," Zora said. Melvin sighed and ordered more drinks. "If you insist. There's a lot to tell you. Get comfy fellas."

MELVIN

Sixteen Months Before

MELVIN TURNED HIMSELF over to stare at the cloudless Mexican sky to see something pleasant before he died. Hours of wandering in burning nowhere had left him exhausted. Maria's corpse roasted back where this should've ended. Killing a vicious mass murdering gangster should've been a reason to celebrate. He should've returned home a hero. He also should've known better.

Among the cacti and patches of grass, Melvin contemplated just letting go. He only hoped he'd die before the night terrors came out to hunt. The dreaded bat-wolves were able to kill snallygasters and had the strongest jaws of any non-demonic entity. He deserved a better end than that, he thought. The soldiers that had betrayed him had driven away in his dune buggy.

He still couldn't believe it. He had lost the election he was guaranteed to win, thanks to the government finding a more malleable henchman. Worst of all, Abraham gave the order to take him out. Melvin avoided the bullets, now wondering if that would've been a more merciful end compared to a gradual death in this wasteland. He sacrificed his integrity and his friend's dream, and all he had to show for it was a mouthful of dirt. In his hand was his gun, now empty. Through his sunglasses, he watched the vast blue emptiness above. He broiled inside his duster. He pushed his cracked lips together, desperate for a drink.

"Come on, sweet rain," he said, choking out the words. The rain didn't come.

"Fuck you, nature!"

He forced himself to his feet for one last valiant attempt at survival. Not knowing what to do, he lumbered north, making sure to keep an eye on the carrion-eating blighters hovering above. Blighters were a nasty vulture offshoot with a mixture of black and red feathers, giving them a bleeding effect. Their long necks and heads were more reminiscent of a snake than a bird.

Melvin suffered on for the better part of the day. He spied what he assumed were some ruins through the watery horizon he could barely make out. He swatted at the uncaring birds perched on nearby rocks.

He voraciously gulped down the last drops of water from the canteen taken off a dead cartel enforcer. He picked up rocks and tossed them at the birds missing each one by a mile. He could see them laughing, not aware of his worsening madness.

"You won't get me!" he screamed and heard them talking back.

"Yes, we will," one said. Their featherless heads bobbed up and down in a mocking fashion. The catci joined in the insulting chorus. Melvin gave one a hard kick.

"Pricks," he mumbled. He sat down beside the cactus, feeling guilt.

"Sorry. You're just out here doing cactus stuff," he said, reflecting on his recent troubles. He felt the need to talk to anyone, even the cactus he thought looked like a Richard.

"I used to be somebody, Rick. Not just in the rebellion, either. Melvin's not even my name, just made it up. Bet yer on pins 'n needles?" he asked, laughing at his own joke.

Melvin imagined the cactus leaning forward for the shocking

revelation. His imagination transported him back to the glory days. He stood looking out over a grand fortress, a man respected and admired.

He repeated the words of the man that abandoned him.

"So long, Vic."

"Who's Vic?" Richard asked.

"Me. I was once the CO of Heartland. Victor Whitehall. Yeah, those Whitehalls. Had things gone differently, I would've been lord commander instead of Jerrick." His mentally animated cactus gasped.

"Didn't need the family, either, worked my way straight to the top."

Melvin saw the crowds waving as he strolled through towns. Men wanted to be him, and women wanted to be with him. His mind was clear and sharp. He remembered the day someone threw rose petals at him once. He took pride in it all, not realizing how he'd soon be humbled.

The inevitable day came to re-rain on his parade. A routine mission in western Heartland, a place where there was little more than a shouting match over dog shit on the wrong property.

"Don't matter how good ya are, Rick," Melvin said. "If someone surprises you from behind, yer done."

The details were hazy. Melvin heard many things: local thugs, political rivals, jealous soldiers, vicious bandits. He remembered the pain of being thrashed within an inch of his life, with irreparable damage to his brain. He walked through this world of half desert and memory, not too keen on either.

"Something happened to my brain that after. I . . . can't focus. My thoughts get jumbled. Get my words mixed up. Used to be smart, but now sometimes the ol' brain just can't get it." Melvin downplayed the extreme moods that changed with the wind, embarrassed to admit the unfortunate results to his cactive audience. The imaginary cactus face frowned.

"After a few mistakes, they discharged me. My parents dropped me like a hot turd. Never tried to help me. Never even looked for me. Can you believe that!?" Richard shook his head.

"Now you know why I changed my name," Melvin said, lamenting his chance to speak with his family since Anselm took that from him permanently. Melvin grew angry at the very thought.

"Not talking about that. Wife and kids are off-limits, Rick," Melvin said. He pushed himself to his feet, dusted himself off, and bid his farewells.

"Nice talking with ya, Rick. Take 'er easy. And if you can take 'er easy, take 'er twice," Melvin said with a grin. *Too much? Whatever, dying anyway.*

Melvin became acutely aware of every lifeform in the desert. Brown snakes, black scorpions, and sand wyrms—the legless variant of the snallygaster. He caught a glimpse of one wrapped around a pronghorn, impaling it with its serrated teeth. Hungry blighters dogged his steps. His pace quickened. Hours crawled by. He resigned himself to his fate, falling to the ground.

"Maybe I deserve this. I haven't been much of a hero in quite a while. Lost my wife. Lost my son," he said.

He never meant to hit his wife; uncontrollable flashes of anger post-injury spurred on violence that seemingly no medicine could treat. For every hit, she returned in kind. It didn't matter who initiated; neither of them were victims. It had once been a beautiful relationship, but they brought out the worst in each other after his discharge. Damaged soldiers and damaged criminals didn't mix. People believed he hurt his son, a lie that would drive him from the world. Moving to a large patch of grass, he lay down to make his last rest as comfortable as possible.

"Maybe I should sleep," Melvin said. The more he thought about his lost family, the less he cared to go on. "Yeah. Sleep sounds nice. Death'll do the rest."

He made one last plea for his final moments to be peaceful. He saw a nearby cactus and knew it had to be Rick.

"Take care of yourself, Rick." Melvin's consciousness faded as a blurry figure hovered over him, one far from welcoming.

He awoke to more desert. He sat up. In front of him lay a pockmarked, off-white Mexican church with red roofs and bright blue doors. A lone cross crowned the church, a sign of former Diegan Neo-Catholic activity, one of the religions gaining popularity despite, or because of, the government's attempt to stamp them out.

Melvin got up and turned to see a few more buildings behind the church and dozens of jugs of water. He laughed triumphantly. He rubbed his eyes; they opened to a bestial form grinning at him. Melvin shrieked and stumbled back. The figure had scaly skin and long thick arms like a gorilla's. The troll's chest was broad, and his legs were short and stubby. Holes in the side of his head served as ears. His eyes remained fixated on Melvin. Melvin had seen many bizarre things during his life, but today marked the first time he encountered a troll. The troll wore brown shorts, tattered boots, and a sunhat; its outfit diminished the overall menace.

"Hi," he said, in a deep, yet friendly voice.

"Uh . . . hi," Melvin replied. *Betrayed by friends and saved by a monster*, he thought.

"Why'd you save me?" Melvin asked. The situation dumbfounded him.

"You needed help," the troll said. Its words were slower and deliberate like a child.

"Thanks. Thought I was dinner," Melvin said.

"People taste bad. I like fish," the troll replied. Melvin laughed nervously, unsure if his host was joking.

"Fish good," Melvin replied.

"Yeah."

The troll waved Melvin over and showed him his humble

abode. Well-maintained buildings surrounded the church. A skinned bat-wolf cooked on a spit roast. A few other dead night terrors lay in a pile beside a collection of blackened sand wyrms and pronghorn carcasses. "Eat?" the troll asked.

Melvin's stomach growled in response. The troll approached the animal, effortlessly tore off a leg and brought it to Melvin. Melvin looked at the meat. He looked at the troll. He looked at the meat again.

"Eh, fuck it," Melvin said, tearing off a bite of perfectly cooked leg meat.

The meat was juicy and succulent, almost like steak.

"Pretty good," Melvin admitted.

The troll smiled at the compliment. It ripped off another leg clean from the socket and devoured the meat in seconds. Melvin tossed the bone in a large basket beside the spit roast. The troll led Melvin past a large empty warehouse to a lime green colonial house that had seen much better days. Houses painted green, pink, and ocean blue created a sense of vibrancy throughout the dead village. Melvin noted a peculiar dearth of life in the town, seeing no one except the single troll.

"You live alone?" Melvin asked. The troll pointed over behind the warehouse with four mounds.

"Yeah," he said. "My family."

"I'm sorry to hear that. My family's gone too."

Melvin chatted with his host about his parents and two brothers, along with the former residents who long vacated the place after constant gang shakedowns. The info corresponded to one of many villages abandoned thanks to the gangs around six or so years ago. Melvin didn't precisely know troll physiology, but this one was quite capable for an eleven-year-old as he claimed to be. It led Melvin to one of the barely standing homes and opened the door.

"You can stay, or I can help you go home," the troll said. Melvin considered the offer.

"I . . . uh . . . don't have a home anymore," Melvin said. "By the way, do you have a name?"

"Don't remember," the troll replied. "Been alone a long time." Melvin quickly concocted a new name for his new friend.

"Mind if I call ya Liz?" The troll shrugged.

"Okay," Liz said. "Drink?" Melvin smiled.

"Now you're speaking my language," Melvin beamed.

MELVIN

Four Months Later

MELVIN AND LIZ sat in a camouflaged truck atop a ridge, scanning the desert for their target. For the past week, Liz and Melvin had prepared extensively for this day. Melvin was still rusty getting back to civilization. Life in nowhere was nice at first, but Melvin needed a purpose. Befriending Liz gave him a purpose: payback. The payback would start with Daniel Garcia, a businessman by day and extortionist by night. It burned Melvin to think Joseph Kerr's plan to create a free society ended up supplanted by one more authoritarian than ever—helmed by Joe's brother, a mountain of salt in the wound.

Melvin played a dangerous game reclaiming assets from both the G-men and deadheads, but the joy of hurting them and the financial gain was too alluring to pass up. Giving a decent portion of his spoils back to the people got him in their good graces, though a far cry from the good old days.

Melvin and Liz carried out the robbery outside of a town Bulaz, named after famous Knight-Ambassador Hayden Bulaz; he mistranslated it to "balls," always confused at the subsequent laughter until someone finally explained his mistake. The town was important for one thing only: being a stop for supply trains. For most of their 200-year existence, trains were primarily for goods and mobile bases/ prisons for VIPs. Daniel loaded Duke's share of the cut in with the various monies and goods on their way to secure facilities.

"Showtime. We'll get it right this time," Melvin said. Liz frowned.

"We will," Melvin assured. "That donkey thing was a fluke. This is our first mission."

Liz was covered head to toe in a duster, sombrero, dark pants, and a black bandanna over his face, looking the part of a southwestern thief. The train came into view. Melvin responded with a scowl, reflecting on the two previous mishaps. With his military-issue binoculars pilfered from a double-dealing Knight Ambassador, Melvin scanned the train. He saw a dozen armed troops patrolling the train plus a kitchen staff for Daniel and another guest. The time to strike was now. Melvin and Liz hopped in the truck.

"You know what to do," Melvin said. He could barely contain his excitement. "An old-fashioned train robbery. Hot damn!"

"Yeah. Hot damn," Liz replied.

The train whizzed by. Liz hit the gas. Liz wasn't the best driver, but he learned quickly with Melvin as his instructor. The truck maneuvered itself behind the train. Melvin stood up.

"Time for liftoff," Melvin said. Liz nodded. His left hand grabbed hold of the gun harness underneath Melvin's jacket. Liz flung Melvin onto the train, barely avoiding a head-on collision with the door. Melvin opened the door. Supply trains always carried lots of goods and lots of cash. Two guards patrolled the back car, carrying riot gear and Derbin ARs. Melvin took them out one at a time, clumsily yet successfully. He chose not to dwell on it; there would be plenty of endeavors to master the art of stealth. He grinned from ear to ear on seeing the bags upon bags of cash. The train screeched to a halt. Melvin ran back outside and saw no sign of Liz. Gunfire erupted in the front of the train.

"So much for in and out," Melvin said. Melvin readied his pistol and prepared for conflict. The door swung open and in burst Daniel Garcia.

"Melvin? You little—" Daniel said.

"Ain't dead yet, but you're about to be," Melvin said. Daniel reached for his gun. "*I Always wanted to duel.*"

Melvin's fingers tapped the firearm. There was a pause. Daniel got his pistol out of his holster but got three bullets in the chest.

The gunfire persisted up ahead. Melvin cautiously moved through the cars to check on Liz. He passed through cars with dead guards. Melvin pressed on to find one lone soldier pointing a gun at him. His eyes widened at the loud thuds of someone approaching from behind. Before he could make a complete turn, Liz gave him a hard fist to the chest, sending him flying through the window. Melvin grimaced at the limbs breaking on the way out.

"Hi," Liz said with genuine happiness.

Liz lost his hat in the caper. His bald head shined, making him look like a miniature lighthouse. Melvin cracked a smile.

"Went overboard, didn't ya? Was hoping to not kill anyone else," Melvin said. Liz's thick brow shot up.

"Wait . . . you didn't kill them dudes back there?" Melvin asked. Liz shook his head.

"Uh-oh."

The door behind Liz opened. A hum rose like rising anger preparing to explode. A passing wave of energy changed that. A confused Liz flew through the air, barely missing Melvin diving to the ground to avoid him. Air rippled from the invisible wave. A few yards ahead, a man examined a rifle with a strange dish-shaped barrel. The man wore desert fatigues, sunglasses, and a bulletproof vest with the emblem of a griffon; such symbols were worn by Knight Ambassadors. The man carried a bizarre rifle that gave Melvin the nagging sensation he'd seen weird guns before.

"I can see why he had this locked up. Deadheads upped their game," the knight said.

"Ow," Liz said. He shook off the impact of the gun. The man aimed again, Liz growled.

"Nice gun you got there. Look better in my hands," Melvin said. He didn't like the idea of these in the hands of Abraham or the Void, whether he ended up with it or not.

"You'll look better all over the seats," the knight said.

The man fired a volley of energy from the rifle Melvin's way. Liz threw Melvin out of the way with the ease of a sack of groceries. He hit the wall hard, screaming a curse. Liz prepared to yell out sorry, but the energy wave sent him back. He scrambled to his feet and returned fire. Liz didn't get up from the second shot. He was durable, but Melvin wasn't sure how durable.

The knight adjusted the knob on the side of the gun; the gun buzzed loud enough for Melvin to know the lethality of the next incoming volley. He sprinted toward his attacker, diving to the side, and avoiding a blast. The blast punched a hole through the side of the train. The knight swore under his breath, unintentionally revealing a delay in his next shot. A bestial growl distracted both men.

"Ow!" Liz rose to his feet. "Stop it!" He sprinted toward the attacker, screaming like a madman all the way.

Liz reached the mercenary and pulled the gun from his hands. He crushed the gun to Melvin's lament. The mercenary gaped in horror. Liz raised his fist and slammed it hard into the mercenary. Melvin gawked at the mercenary folding like an accordion from the force of Liz's strength. Melvin continued to gawk.

"Liz?" Melvin said. Liz's demeanor returned to his mellow, awkward self. "Guess we can get back to it."

Liz nodded and went back out to the truck. He carried a massive sack, looking like a very intimidating Santa Claus. Melvin admired the bags and boxes of paper money, coins, gold, silver, and a scrap of bizarre weapon now in his tender, loving care.

DRAKE

MELVIN DROVE UP to the eastern gate of Mexico City inside a camouflaged military truck. Liz sat in the back, wearing only dark pants, black boots, and a deadly new railgun. Drake, Zora, and Thos rolled in a military escort wearing light gear and warm clothes for the cold desert night. Drake felt right at home in full military gear, while Thos and Zora fidgeted with their body armor. Thos risked much being out here with Drake, but his training and authority gave him such freedoms.

Melvin stepped out of the truck. Liz gave an awkward wave. Drake had a hard time grappling with the idea of the crude Melvin once being a revered military commander. Victor Whitehall had been highly respected in his day and something of a hero. Drake felt guilt for treating Melvin so harshly in the past, knowing full well the mental and physical toll of being a Blackthorne soldier.

The three approached after Thos gave his escort the all-clear. Drake carried a sniper while Thos and Zora carried standard-issue rifles. Drake didn't like having Thos in this situation; however, being a Void target and constantly pissing off the government, he could find no place safer than among friends. He knew Thos wanted to help. Thos felt some guilt in Abraham's rise to power, but he also realized the Averills had great potential to do good in the world.

The sun hung low overhead, bathing the land in a blood orange glow. The nightly festivities kicked off inside the city and around the state, fireworks soon illuminating cities in a rainbow of sparks.

The group quickly hopped in the vehicle as Melvin drove them south into an area known as Hot Land. Melvin drove over bridges toward off-road secrecy. The region was largely uninhabited, leaving any humans encountered as most likely of the deadhead variety. Mesas, grasses, and a smattering of trees gave Drake the visage he always pictured when he thought of Mexico. Melvin went off-road a few dozen miles toward a mesa and some smaller rock formations perfect for hiding in. A lone, metal tower jutted out from the top of the mesa. They pulled up a few miles away. The group left the vehicle and, in a low crouch, moved up toward the rocky hills.

"Why are they meeting out here?" Drake asked.

"To keep dicks like us away," Melvin replied.

Liz flattened himself against the ground. Everyone lay on the hill with weapons and binoculars at the ready. Drake prepared the directional mic.

The group listened to the serenity of the desert. A half-hour later, a dozen black trucks and a semi pulled up, all bearing the image of Death. Behind them came a silver car. A small army of men in suits with skull tattoos stepped out of the vehicles and formed a perimeter.

"Little overboard with this death thing, don't you think?" Thos said.

Through the binoculars and rifle scopes, everyone watched the cultists face the mesa. Light emanated from the base of the mesa. The bottom of the mesa slid apart like a door. A series of vehicles rolled out of the mesa door.

"It's the labs all over again," Drake said.

Drake's sniper rifle came equipped with a directional microphone that fed into some headphones he quickly put on. The group watched the vehicles stop in front of the Void. Out of the vehicles stepped out men wearing the red and white robes of Vigilant. An orange-eyed man took place in front of the men.

"That's Matthias Rehnquist, the big cheese," Melvin said.

"No, this can't be," Zora said. Drake looked over to Zora, scanning the crusaders for signs of her uncle.

"Maybe he isn't involved," Drake said trying to comfort her.

Drake focused on the directional mic. Buried memories crawled back into Drake's mind. Again, Blackthorne castle fell. Again he drove his sword down through Anselm's chest. Memories of his kills rushed through his mind. His hands shook, rattling his gun for the others to hear. He breathed deeply until his hands steadied.

"Don't shoot unless I give the order," Drake ordered. Everyone turned their attention to the business near the mesa.

"Nice to see you again," Matthias said. One member of the Void stepped forward to greet Matthias.

"Likewise," he said.

The two exchanged fake pleasantries, information about the activities of the government, robberies, and plans to assassinate Thos that required more sophisticated hardware.

"Have our goods?" he asked.

Matthias nodded. Vigilant crusaders hauled boxes over toward the gang. The men opened the other boxes packed to the brim with remote grenades, railguns, rocket launchers, communicators, and the latest armor. The Void's second-in-command inspected each box and gave his boss a single nod. Drake remembered these railguns.

"The guns . . . Anselm used them in Kingsbury," Drake said, old memories tearing through the fog.

"I kinda remember that, too," Thos said. Melvin nodded.

"How did we forget that?" Melvin asked, getting no answer.

"Anselm didn't have this many . . . did he? They mass-producing them?" Drake asked.

A sinking feeling formed in Drake's gut.

"All seems to be in order," the gang rep beamed.

The other gang members quickly loaded up the new gear into their trucks, taking a few guns for current use. Matthias grew impatient, tapping his right foot. The gang rep ordered his men to unload the semi. Everyone pointed guns to the back of the semi. The cargo stepped out of the back. Ten modified humans and three giant, deformed humanoids bound in irons were herded toward Matthias. A large transport vehicle came from the door in the mesa. Liz let out a low growl. Melvin growled back to dissuade an attack.

"Uncle wouldn't stand for this," Zora said.

"We need to get inside and see where it goes," Drake said.

"The fuck we do. Remember what we found last time?" Melvin replied nervously.

The tower on the mesa surged with power, spewing a wave of energy across the land. Vigilant instantly took up defensive positions. The soldiers grew twitchy.

"What is it?" The gang rep asked. Matthias folded his arms in triumphant smugness.

"Don't worry, I can keep It away," Matthias said.

"It?"

"The enemy," he replied.

The trolls seized the opportunity to escape. Two crusaders with bizarre gunblades fired at the trolls. No bullets came from the weapons. The trolls stopped instantly, screaming and clawing at their heads. One by one, the chained trolls fell to their knees. Liz growled again.

"No," Melvin said. Liz snapped at Melvin.

He let out a series of deep breaths. Vigilant fastened large collars to each troll and led them to more secure cages inside the transport vehicle. The modified human prisoners grew dizzy and collapsed inside the special cages. Drake heard them called nullifiers in response to a curious deadhead. The transport truck drove into the mesa. Liz continued breathing deeply to suppress the mounting anger.

"We're done here," the gang rep said.

"Not quite," Matthias replied.

A member of Vigilant approached Matthias with a small black case. Matthias took the case and removed a silver mask. Zora began to sweat.

"We need to leave," Zora said.

Matthias put on the mask, jerking back like the thing had a mind of its own. A massive wave of energy shot from the tower, lighting up the desert as clear as a cloudless day. The majority of Vigilant returned to the safety of the mesa after seeing the Void off, while some hung around to protect the entrance.

"Dammit," Drake yelled. "Gonna be tough getting in there."

"If it's anything like the labs, maybe there are other entrances," Zora said.

"It would explain how they're all over the damn place," Melvin said. Drake saw the concern on Zora's face.

"Don't worry. We'll contact Gregor and let him know what we've discovered," Drake said. "We need to find out where they're coming from. Melvin, can you do it?" Melvin hesitated at first.

"A chance to rob . . . er explore a Vigilant stronghold is mighty enticing," Melvin replied. "God, I hope there's not monsters."

"Well, it's Vigilant, so that might be the one thing you don't have to worry about," Drake said.

"Good point," Melvin said. He turned to Zora. "I'll get in touch with Gregor."

"Thank you," she said.

"The rest of us can get back to business as usual and go from there," Drake replied. The group left the scene and sped away, having found more questions than answers.

MATTHEW

Matthew hated the claustrophobic prison called the big city. People stacked upon people was no way for humans to live. In every direction, the city expanded, leaving metal skeletons ready for their roofed and walled flesh. Matthew counted himself blessed that the city didn't smell like a dog's ass for once. He left his sword back at the horse to avoid suspicion of being the lone non-officer carrying one. For the time being, Matthew's gun would suffice in the off chance he'd get attacked in the broad daylight.

Matthew spied hundreds of soldiers patrolling the busy streets, a seemingly unnecessary force to intimidate the people. He had a full day for surveillance; he loaded up on some beef and bread for the boring part of his job. Nothing outside of the ordinary caught his eye. Matthew eavesdropped on drunken patrons at the closest bar, learning nothing except rumors of a missing actress. Few paid any mind to the old man, but Matthew suspected Mr. Abaddon knew the second he arrived.

Matthew's mind began to wander, thinking about his old missions and long-forgotten memories continuing to resurface. He cradled the convulsing body of his new bride. He remained strong for her. He was not about to forget such memories, and it was clear he had been dealing this issue for a very long time. Brielle kept mentioning a dubious "connection," struggling with her own battle with memory suppression. There was a solution, he heard the words clear.

"We have to go to them," she said. Matthew remembered the hate at the notion, he only wish he knew why.

He made an exit after a satisfying meal and excessive listening. He walked casually through the heavy-traffic areas of Kingsbury. For hours Matthew's investigation went nowhere. He followed a crowd dogging the steps of Vice Regent Yadira Khouri. Mediamen lined the streets to harass her with questions both pointless and personal. She remained calm and warm to the those buzzing about her. Bodyguards continuously drove the sycophantic crowd back. Matthew sensed people up above. On the rooftops, dozens of snipers monitored the situation from above. A man in a suit moved in close to Yadira. Matthew couldn't make out the words, but Yadira's cagey reaction spoke volumes. Bodyguards shoved the man away. Matthew moved through the crowd.

Something wasn't quite right, and Matthew knew it. A thousand people were around him and at least one didn't belong. Matthew noticed a couple of his Freemen spies in the crowd who avoided looking at him. There was another presence always right on the edge of his perception. The feeling vexed him terribly. Factions were hiding in plain sight all around him. The crowd dispersed when Yadira left, but someone moved up behind him.

"Took your sweet time," Matthew said.

"Mr. Pavane," a voice said in an impersonal tone. "My employer wanted you to get comfortable first."

The voice belonged to an older man with purple eyes and wearing a black suit. Matthew never seen the purple-eyed defect before. The man also wore a black hat. Lines like cuts ran down his head to each eye and one going from his lips to his chin. "You can call me Proxy."

"Cute," Matthew said. "It appears you didn't underestimate me."

"Not completely," Proxy said. "Mr. Abaddon wanted to test you. See where you stood and where you could lead us."

"You let me kill your people for a test?"

"The best way to separate the wheat from the chaff, as it were," Proxy said. "All outcomes were to his benefit." Matthew crossed his arms.

"If your boss is so great and powerful, why hasn't he taken care of this?" Matthew asked.

"Everyone has limitations."

"Just breaks my heart to see a kingpin fall on hard times," Matthew said.

"Save your wit and get to work," Proxy said, cold and emotionless. "Things are in motion that threaten us all, and your order is at the heart of it."

"Then give me a heading," Matthew said.

"There's nothing of value for you in the city. What you seek lies below," Proxy said.

"In the Blackthorne Vault."

"Deeper. Older. Start at the sewers; you'll find our contact," Proxy said.

Proxy pulled a city map from his pocket and handed it to Matthew. Matthew gave the map a once over, taking note of the marked sewer entrance and the line that fed into the city's center.

"There's no time to dawdle," Proxy said. "If you fail to resolve this soon, there are others we will use."

Proxy looked off in the distance. Matthew followed the purple eyes to a female figure with an entourage. She wore a plain shirt and jeans, not the outfit that commanded an escort. He saw her and her husband's image numerous times in the Prosperity Herald. "I doubt Mrs. Averill will fare as well as you, especially if you attack me."

"Save your threats. I'll get it done," Matthew said.

"You can stay in one of our safehouses. Red building on 22nd."

Proxy gave a bow and recused himself, leaving Matthew to

this new mission. Matthew doubled back to his horse and grabbed his gear. He quickly memorized the map, thankful that his years of recreational substance use hadn't affected his memory too bad. He worked his way to the paper manufacturing plant and slipped behind the corner, removed the manhole cover, and scrambled down the ladder. A scruffy, stocky man in the light black armor of a knight-ambassador waited for him at the bottom.

"Right on schedule. Name's Kane," he said, extending his hand in respect. Matthew responded.

"Owe the wrong people, do you?" Matthew asked.

"Mr. Abaddon knows the value of soldiers," Kane said.

Kane filled Matthew in on the dwindling number of Mr. Abaddon's forces at the hands of Vigilant. Kane seemed normal enough. He was an acquaintance of Zora's beau, though that wouldn't keep Matthew from watching him closely.

"Remember, this is recon, no killing," Kane said.

"Not sure I want to kill them, doing the city a favor from what I see."

Together they followed the yellow lights of the slimy tunnels. Kingsbury sewer was but a fraction of the original Chicago system. Matthew couldn't imagine the original city that was said to cover most of Illinois by the end. The two trekked through stank and dank until they came around a gaping hole in the side of the wall. They passed through a sleek, white hallway that fed into a large room covered in faces.

"So this Vault?" Matthew asked rhetorically.

"They must've been planning this for years," Kane said. "Must mean the guards up top are in on it."

Empty shelves and containers littered the room. Faint yellow light from the opposite end of the room caught their attention. Slowly they advanced. A door-shaped opening in the back wall led down into older tunnels. Syphons slithered along the walls, moving in the same direction as Matthew and Kane. The glowing slugs provided ample light and heat for the mission. The tunnels went on for miles, going deeper into the earth. Sounds echoed from further down in the tunnel. They soon reached the end, stopping dead in their tracks.

"Th-this . . . " Kane stuttered.

The team stood upon a ledge overlooking an impossibly large chamber. Thousands of syphons clung to the ceiling and slid across the floor. A walkway around the cavern went into numerous tunnels. Collapsed bridges had once connected to the center. Unfinished structures filled the cavern. The structures appeared to be part of multiple tiers collapsed on each other.

"There's a whole damn city in here!" Kane said.

"This isn't the Chicago I've seen," Matthew said. "This is something else."

"A hidden city within a city," Kane said.

Both stared in awe at this metal world beneath the city. In the center of the chamber, a skyscraper-sized metal column stretched up the man-made floor all the way up to the top. Screams filled the cave, followed by flashes of light. The two hopped off the walkaway and into the nearest abandoned building. Matthew pulled out binoculars from his utility belt while Kane surveyed using the scope of his rifle. Matthew could see hundreds of red figures combing through the chamber. A series of restrained humans were attached to metallic poles that circled the central column. Pieces of metal wove through the flesh of some of the prisoners.

Wires ran from the metal poles in the ground. The figures on the poles squirmed and cried to uncaring Vigilant soldiers tinkering on machines throughout the ruins. Kane and Matthew perched for hours, studying the Vigilant. A loud hum ran through the metal poles. The prisoners' screams intensified. Sparks flew from the metal pieces of the restrained humans. The prisoners burst into flames. Matthew gawked in horror as the prisoners blistered and their enhancements melted.

"This is what your order does? It's barbaric," Kane said.

"There must be a good reason," Matthew said, not entirely convinced.

The machine roared to life. A section of the column opened for just a moment. The chatter of frustration echoed across the dead city. Matthew heard the word Killswitch repeated.

"Sounds like they need more witches to power that machine," Kane said. "Not sure what they're doing, but if Mr. Abaddon is concerned, this is serious."

Chatter behind the knights suggested it was time to leave. Kane pointed to the closest tunnel. The two crept across the walkway. A hastily drawn sign hung from the tunnel, labeled "fields."

"Did they dig these tunnels? How did they know how to get here?" Kane asked, curious at this impressive undertaking going on beneath the feet of over a million people.

"Not sure," Matthew said. The sounds behind them grew louder. "Guess we're going to the fields."

Matthew and Kane hurried down the tunnel that led up to the maintenance tunnels. The pair followed a more recently made path into the maintenance tunnels to a rope ladder leading outside. Kane advised Matthew to stay behind him. Matthew followed Kane up a ladder to a hole barely large enough to squeeze an adult through. Kane poked his head out for signs of Vigilant activity. One Vigilant soldier stood in front of the hole facing the lake. Sounds of footsteps in the tunnels behind them forced Kane to act. He unholstered his knife and rammed it into the soldier's neck.

"No killing, eh?" Matthew said.

The man gurgled and clawed at Kane until his eyes glazed over. Matthew exited the tunnel before the sounds could reach them. Together they sped across the fields, doubling back to the city and out of Vigilant's sight.

"We need to find out what Killswitch is and stop it if need be," Kane said. Matthew still tried to process what he'd seen.

"You're asking me to go against my order. For the sake of gangsters," Matthew said. "I'm not yet convinced you're the right side."

"Like it or not, Mr. Abbadon knows this city," Kane said. "If he believes whatever they're doing is bad, then so do I. If you disagree, you better prove it. I have other business, but I'll be in touch."

Kane left Matthew to his thoughts. An unprecedented number of Vigilant lurked below the surface of Kingsbury, carrying out an operation greater than Matthew had ever seen or imagined. Something was happening in this city, and if it scared the dreaded Mr. Abaddon, it wasn't to be taken lightly.

YADIRA

Yadira felt minuscule in the coliseum-sized meeting hall. Inside the chamber, stairs led up to a platform with five chairs. Five people sat in the chairs: Abraham Kerr, John Derbin, David Westerfield, Janice Caan, and Katonah Hale. These five served as the advisors and the true rulers of the country. The other former members of the board still held power, though diminished and now had to send any requests to the advisors. James Dumas stood beside her, a man of boundless ambition with a coldness in his eyes strong enough to suck the heat out of the room. James served as the second to only them, with her and the other state regents right behind him. Despite being the elected officials, everyone still bowed to the advisors. Yadira begrudgingly deferred to the wisdom of those who could quite easily make her disappear.

Out of all of the advisors, David Westerfield was the one she feared the most. The Westerfield family controlled the nation's media, and it served as the State's most effective weapon. He ensured each news story was told how he wanted and always kept the vital info from the public. His artists, authors, actors, and musicians forced political narratives into everything through the entertainment industry, a not so subtle mode of mass brainwashing.

Entertainers that once condemned government tyranny now slandered and silenced any that spoke out against it.

David's newest campaign turned the nation's youth against their parents, convincing them to report family members for even mild criticism. It was hard not to be intimidated by David Westerfield, knowing his media machine could crush anyone with a single headline

Yadira tried to escape this life once before, the only child of a lower tier merchant family. She was transported to her youth, kneeling at the feet of Imhotep's gold-painted priests and priestesses known as the Order of Duat. The supposedly thousand-year-old man and his order held more influence than the merchant houses or even the pharaohs.

Imhotep threw her parent's bodies on the white fires; they seemed to vaporize in the mystic flames. The holy fires cleansed their souls. Imhotep appeared to levitate off the ground, though she considered it was a symptom of fear at the larger-than-life man. It was easy to believe he was a god made flesh with the crystalline pyramid behind him. Though the ritual was for good, she knew his head priestess directed the merchant houses to take them out. She fled from people like them; she wouldn't back down this time. Yadira made preparations for the coming enemy.

She forced the mounting anxiety of her personal life out, placed her hands at her side, and gave a robotic bow. James followed suit. The regent and vice regent functioned like the president and vice president did in the Old World. Each state had a regent and two that ruled over them. Once a quarter, the regents delivered reports on state conditions, make any appeals, and bring pertinent info to the advisors' attention. After the entrance of James and Yadira came their administration, delegates, officers, the state regents, and investors that rounded out the nation's top brass. Duke was absent for the meeting, having to remain in Mexico and handle the Void. All waited for Mr. Derbin to speak.

"What news do you have for us?" Mr. Derbin asked.

James gave an in-depth report on the state of New Prosperity: detailing the condition of every piece needed to keep the nation running. In truth, all states had prospered beyond expectation since the fall of the Blackthornes, at least financially, thanks to the meteoric rise of Averill Estate Farms. Yadira had little to report, only a few bits and pieces of good news and finances covering the city's expansion, growing businesses, increased security along the roads, and the occasional disappearance.

David yawned throughout Yadira's reports while Abraham picked lint off his blue-gray suit. Abraham came off as heartless; however, the long hours spent at Joseph's memorial suggested at least some humanity lurked inside. Yadira had met Abraham five years ago when he and Joseph recruited her to their cause of a functional government before the plans included working with members of the board of directors. Having finished his lint work, Abraham chimed in.

"Any word on . . . what was her name? Friend of yours," Abraham said.

"Adrienne . . . I wouldn't exactly call us friends, but no, sir," she replied.

"This string of disappearances is no coincidence. We need to root out any Blackthorne loyalists involved," Abraham said.

"There's also the possibility of Mr. Abaddon's involvement," Janice said. "I heard she was involved with shady types."

Yadira knew little of the elusive figure; only that he was the dominant crime boss in the nation that served as an unofficial advisor.

"I'm looking into it," James said.

"Look harder," David said.

John leaned over and whispered in Abraham's ear. Yadira could've sworn she saw the bones through his skin. It was no secret the advisors weren't the biggest fan of her appointing a grand crusader for the new Vigilant; they only accepted out of fear of violating the Compact and of their enemies marshaling against them. Yadira's constituents wanted a strong Vigilant; people considered the order a form of checks and balances against elites, apostates, and mad kings. Vigilant was fully reestablished to placate the masses, which had no means of fighting these battles on their own. David advised her to keep an eye on them and reiterated how quickly they, and the one that pushed for Matthias's promotion, can be re-branded enemies of the state. Yadira hoped her decision to establish a grand crusader wasn't a fatal error.

"If that's all, I'll take my leave," she nodded.

Yadira gave another low bow and exited chambers, leaving the lesser regents to address the advisors. James gave her a nod and quickly absconded to his office. A man stood directly in her way in the hallway, a man with a white dress shirt and tan slacks. The man's right arm was behind his back. She smiled when this man's right arm came around with a red rose in hand— Enton Marco, the number two man at Prosperity Bank.

"I thought you wanted this to be discreet?" she said, glancing over her shoulder. She walked up to him.

"Won't be discreet for long," Enton said, placing his hand on her stomach. "How's the little one?"

Despite carrying the child for months already, it was hard to process. Wearing dark clothes hid it some, but it may be no one bothered to mention the obvious. Enton pulled her close and kissed her. Fire surged through her body, followed by a tremendous wave of terror and joy. She had news to share, but this was an unfitting place for such a thing.

"What brings you here? Trouble at the bank?" she asked, puzzled.

"There's always trouble at the bank. I wanted to treat you to lunch," Enton said. She had a laundry list of things to do today, but the world could wait for a few hours.

"I'd love that," she said.

Enton quickly escorted her out of the building before she got drawn into some new crisis. Enton led Yadira to a swanky restaurant called Vella's, located on the hill that overlooked the lake. Vella's was a local favorite specializing in dishes inspired by Old World Italian cuisine. Enton bought out the whole restaurant that afternoon for the two of them, having some guard shoo away pesky reporters constantly dogging their every step. The restaurant staff led the pair up to the rooftop. Enton removed Yadira's jacket and pulled up a chair for her to their table.

Under the welcome shade of an umbrella, the two shared eggplant and mushroom stuffed ravioli. Yadira debated letting out her big news, her excitement fighting an uphill battle against insurmountable dread. A bodyguard in a black suit approached the two of them.

"What's wrong?" Enton asked.

"Rooftop a block away," the guard said, motioning with his eyes.

Yadira and Enton followed the direction of his eyes with their own, trying their best not to tip off the voyeur. A man was barely visible on a rooftop closed for renovations. The moment they spotted him, the man stood up and casually walked out of Yadira's field of vision.

"Not creepy at all," Enton said.

Yadira's demeanor changed. The kind yet stern persona she had become known as vanished, replaced with a distant preoccupation. Enton's words grew faint as she drowned in her thoughts. She feared what was coming, but Yadira held out hope. *This time will be different,* she thought.

Enton spent the remainder of the lunch hour attempting to wash away Yadira's sorrow. The hour sped by, forcing the two back to running their collective domains. Enton hugged her again. His love kept her fears at bay.

"Thank you," she said.

"Anytime," he replied.

Enton and Yadira returned to their respective army of body-guards clearing a path for them. Yadira sensed unwanted eyes on her, not just their eyes either. Keeping her composure, she returned to her office and performed her duties governing the state. Even inside the building, the sensation of eyes upon her chilled her to the bone. *This time it will be different.*

She heard the muffled voices from her bodyguards on the other side of the door, as well as another familiar voice. She began to shake. "Not this time," she said under her breath. The dry heaving started. The door swung open, revealing a confused and horrified Cassandra Averill. It took a moment for Yadira to register her friend.

"Bad time?" Cass asked nervously.

Yadira slowly lowered the gun and laughed hysterically. The guards peeked inside the office, not hiding their confusion. Yadira and Cass took a seat to regain their composure. The confused guards closed the door after a nod from Yadira.

"Sorry. On edge today," Yadira said with an unconvincing smile.

"And here I was coming to tell you about my problems," Cass said. Yadira shrugged the nagging sensations.

"Comes with the job. Please, what can I help you with?" Yadira asked. Cass tensed up, showing the exact symptoms Yadira experienced. Cass glanced out the window again and then at the door. She leaned in.

"I didn't know who else to turn to. They told me to not to say anything, but I couldn't let this go," Cass said.

Yadira prepared herself for her friend's equally bizarre story. Cass told the story of her encounter with Adrienne and subsequent abduction at the hands of Vigilant. She sat in silence for a few moments to process the information. Witches right under Yadira's nose and a friend with a Vigilant target on her back. She sensed Cass's concern for Adrienne and the danger it would put them both in.

"Thanks for bringing this to my attention," Yadira said. "This warrants serious investigation. Adrienne of all people. A coven here? And if Vigilant is watching us . . . I'll do what I can."

"Thank you," Cass said.

Yadira understood Cass's concerns all too well, though she deigned not to share too many of those with the equally frazzled Cass. Yadira glanced back out the window.

"You're under the protection of the government. Even Vigilant can't win that fight," Yadira assured her friend, but her words failed to comfort Cass.

"I . . . I have a bad feeling. The same I had when Aric showed up," Cass said. Yadira spent enough time with Cass to know she wasn't one to rest on her laurels.

"Please don't do anything rash," Yadira said. "You Averills are always getting into trouble, but please let us handle it, okay?"

"I will," Cass said. Cass gave Yadira a warm smile. "Maybe I'm just paranoid. Anyway, thanks for listening to me. Good to have someone to talk to about those Averill problems we're always having."

"Maybe one day you can have regular problems," Yadira laughed.

"If only," Cass replied.

ANSELM

THE LIFE YOU want you'll never have.

The words repeated in Anselm's head over and over. The guilt chewed his guts despite the cheers he received walking through Durenburg. The people were wholly unaware he had been responsible for some of their anguish.

Anselm aided them in their search for Rosalie. The guilt led him to extended rounds of self-mutilation. The villagers returned to their daily lives after a few days of grief. Ezra's fishing business suffered as he spent most of his time searching for his daughter.

The day was accentuated by a much-needed breeze. A few clouds hung in the sky to herald the coming of the summer storms, a welcome reprieve from the spring storms. His stomach burned with hunger and his body ached, feelings he'd grown accustomed to. Anselm had more important business in town than fishing today. He took a moment to watch the boats as he had done with Rosalie. Ezra woke him from his daydreaming state. The last few days had altered Ezra's personality. His bushy beard was wild and tangled, and the kind man had grown hateful and bitter. He spent most of his time interrogating the raider with some of the other enthusiasts in town. Ezra sat on the bench beside him, his knuckles red.

"He talk?" Anselm asked.

"To the others. To be honest, I haven't asked anything yet." He sighed deeply.

Anselm understood the anger. He came to learn that even though Aric and his brutal actions may not have been the best option, he wasn't wrong about enemies all around.

"Before this . . . I never hurt a person in my life," Ezra said, watching the rhythmic ebb and flow of the waves.

"Tragedy leads us down a dark path," Anselm replied. "I've killed my fair share. Perhaps it got me here, or perhaps I didn't act fast enough."

"I tell myself every time I hit that boy that it's wrong, but I don't stop," Ezra said.

Anselm thought on his nightly self-inflicting tortures as vital to him as food or water.

"We do what we have to," Anselm replied.

"Suppose so," Ezra said. "It won't be long before they come back."

"Have you contacted the regent?" Anselm asked, not liking the idea of allying himself with the man that killed his family. Anselm deemed them necessary in the short term.

"We finally got through, yes. Not sure what info I'll be able to give them. No idea if the boy'll talk," Ezra said.

Anselm did not enjoy people asking for things without being straightforward. He mulled over his answer. The more he thought about it, he deemed his own interrogation necessary.

"I'll interrogate him," Anselm said. "But once I do, I'm gone. The government is no friend of mine. I'll fight Vigilant on another front."

"Good lad," Ezra said. Ezra gave him a pat on the back.

Setting by the coast on lazy summer days brought Anselm peace; he knew this peace had come to an end. Ezra saw plainly Anselm wanted more time to relax.

"Whenever you're ready," Ezra said.

"Just a moment," Anselm said.

With his moment up, Anselm followed Ezra to the dilapidated lighthouse. The crumbling monolith that once served as a beacon home for those daring to brave the frigid waters still functioned, but time ravaged its beauty. Rust wrapped around the lighthouse in red-brown vines. Ezra placed his hand on Anselm's shoulder and stopped him.

"You said you lost the people you loved. Did you get justice?"

"No. Some of those responsible are alive . . . and thriving. That's the worst pain of all. But one day I'll return that pain a thousandfold," Anselm said, casting a glance over at the smiling Thos plastered on the supply truck.

"We'll both find justice, I'm sure of it," Ezra said.

Ezra and Anselm shook hands. Ezra opened the door to the lighthouse. Rickety steps spiraled up, but Anselm's journey went down to a trap door in the floor. At the bottom of the spiral stairs sat the captured Vigilant soldier bound and gagged in a brown chair. Ezra wished Anselm well and left him to his work. A table in the corner contained a few blood-stained tools of the trade: knives, a hammer, pliers, and dental instruments. A single light bulb dangled from the ceiling. The prisoner whimpered and sobbed. The boy's right eye was swollen shut. He braced himself for another round of torture. Anselm removed the gag.

"Please let me go! When they come back, they'll kill me. I'll leave, I swear!" the man squealed.

Anselm tried to bury the urges for violence that clawed at him; however, Vigilant crusaders made a decent outlet for his appetites.

The boy resembled Percival, wiry, short-haired, and too young for such hardships. He revealed himself to be an ex-soldier named Zac, loyal to his king until the end; some of his cohorts joined Vigilant as nameless soldiers seeking an opportunity for revenge and protection from the firing squad.

"You don't have to do this," he said. Bloody spit flowed from his lips and down his chin. Anselm cut him off.

"You're right," Anselm said. "But I will if you don't give me what I need."

"He never asked me anything. I'll talk." Zac said, revealing a few missing teeth.

"Vigilant has fallen far if they're common raiders now. What're they up to?" he said sternly. Zac sighed, breaking easily under a few rounds of torture.

"We're under orders from the grand crusader himself. It's the largest operation in our history. We set up shop in Mexico, Kingsbury, and north of here. He called the operation Killswitch," Zac said.

"Ominous and vague. How does it work?" Anselm said. Anselm moved behind Zac. Zac jerked his head, trying to keep an eye on his pale interrogator.

"I'm not sure," Zac said. "But it's a simultaneous operation. If one fails, they all fail."

"Does this have anything to do with the man with the gold mask?" Zac's non-swollen eye widened.

"You've seen the false god?" Zac said. "We've found a way to fight It. Kill It."

Anselm maneuvered around Zac to face him.

"I'm just a grunt! I've said all I know!" Zac replied. Anselm paced around the room. *So they're why he vanished.*

"Why attack Durenburg?"

"We needed supplies at first, but now it's more than that. Someone or something is leaving a trail of bodies in the area. Men, women, children, us."

"That brought you here, to me," Anselm said, wondering how long Vigilant studied him from afar. Anselm leaned in. He could smell the blood. Zac winced and closed his good eye.

"Please let me go!" he sobbed.

The sobbing intensified. Anselm walked over to the table of tools. Anselm's stomach burned from hunger.

"You operating from Gregor's old base?"

"We're converting the logging camps into outposts, but 'Killswitch' is going to happen there."

"Can you show me on a map?" Anselm asked

"Will you really let me go if I do?" he asked

"Yes," Anselm agreed. *I can always hunt you later*, he thought.

He moved in on the restrained the prisoner. Pulling a crumbled state map from his pocket, he handed Zac the map. The prisoner pointed at a location far to the northwest of Durenburg. Anselm ran his finger on Zac's face and used some of his blood to mark the map where Zac instructed. Zac panicked and slipped his broken hand from the restraint. He threw his head forward and collided with Anselm's skull. Anselm stumbled backward, cursing loudly. Zac, still in the chair, fell to the floor and frantically clawed at his restraints.

"I was going to let you go, fool!" Anselm growled. Pain seared Anselm's body, pain far greater than what Zac inflicted on him.

"Bullshit!" Zac screamed.

Agony overcame Anselm like never before. He fell to floor, convulsing. Still bound to the chair, Zac crawled over to the tool table. Zac knocked a knife on the floor as Anselm writhed. Anselm screamed out in agony. His very cells felt as if they were exploding and reforming, only to explode again. At last, Anselm found the pain he deserved.

Zac sawed at his bindings. Anselm made it to his hands and knees. Zac's restraints gave way. He scrambled up the stairs, trying in vain to open the locked door. Bones splintered and contorted, reforming inside Anselm. His skin stretched, and his muscles expanded. Patches of flesh across his body split open. Blood seeped from the wounds the few seconds before they closed. Anselm begged for the pain to stop, but part of him needed it. His stomach growled.

Zac rammed his knife in the door in a desperate attempt to unlock it. He screamed for help. Anselm rose to his feet, acting on instinct. He flew up the stairs with blinding speed. Anselm grabbed Zac and effortlessly threw him down the stairs onto the blood-splattered floor. Anselm had gone down this bloody road many times during his exile, he could only fight the hunger for so long.

He blocked Zac's means of escape. Zac darted toward Anselm, plunging the knife deep in his right breast. Anselm stopped for a moment, surprised at the protruding blade. Anselm smiled; he had started to enjoy the pain. He grabbed Zac's arm and snapped it like a twig. Zac fell to his knees, howling in pain.

Anselm fell upon the prisoner, knocking him to the ground. Anselm thrust his right hand down into Zac's stomach, ripping it open like paper. He pulled out everything Zac kept inside, devouring everything. He washed down Zac's innards with hot blood, his senses overloading at the nourishment and his own pain. Zac whimpered and twitched. Anselm didn't see Zac, only Percival, yet he couldn't stop himself; he didn't want to stop. Anselm ripped a large piece of the throat out and devoured it greedily. He made his way to ribs, breaking apart bones as if they were crackers until he reached the long-sought sensation of fullness.

With Anselm's hunger sated, he regained control. He wiped the blood dribbling out of his mouth. Anselm knew his crimes. He was the monster feeding on the people of Durenburg, starving out the demon also vying for them. Noises came from above. Ezra and two other armed men flew down the stairs.

"What the fuck?!" Ezra choked out the words.

"I . . . I . . . " Anselm said, soaking in blood with bits of Zac stuck in his teeth. Ezra fumbled for words.

"You were eating him!" Ezra said. Anselm had no counter to the accusations with blood running down his chin.

"Wait, did you kill my daughter?" Ezra asked, fighting the urge to cry and scream.

"I . . . " Anselm said. Anselm's slow response told the truth. Ezra's skin went red as the remnants of Zac.

"You goddamned freak!" Ezra exclaimed.

"I saved you," Anselm said, hurt.

The words fell on deaf ears. Ezra and the other two men pointed their rifles at him and fired. Anselm charged the men head-on, knocking them out of the way. He dashed up the stairs and out the open door. Ezra chased after him, screaming for aid. Durenburg roared to life, scrambling for weapons.

People saw the horrific sight of a blood-covered Anselm fleeing from the lighthouse. Confusion set in until Ezra screamed out.

"Stop him!" Ezra cried.

Anselm sprinted up the hill away from town. He fought the urge to hurt his attackers, well aware he had to power to dispatch everyone there. Part of him cared for Durenburg; he left while that part still lived. Men gathered in the town, ready to hunt the devil in their midst. Anselm ran into the wilderness, once again friendless and alone.

GREGOR

AN OLD CASTLE, mysterious disappearances, witches, and cryptic visions: Gregor's newest mission had all the makings of a classic horror story. He recruited three grunts for his team, along with Raul Alvarez. Raul led Gregor to a tunnel through the waterfall toward the underground railways.

Inside the structure was a vaulted ceiling with clocks, benches, ticket booths, long metal tracks, and bullet trains.

"How many trains are there?" he asked.

"We got six of them working, but the other tunnels have been destroyed," Raul said.

"How far do they go?" Gregor asked.

"All throughout the state from what we can tell. The damaged ones may go further. The northern tunnel goes to the Heartland border, but it's collapsed beyond that," he replied. "The one we're taking goes under Mexico City and straight to the east coast."

"Would've been nice to know first," he grumbled. The setup reminded Gregor of Gideon's lab under the White Woods. The possibility that systems like this were all across the country or even the world put a little bile in Gregor's throat.

"Matthias thought you might've grown soft. He likes to make us prove our worth."

"He make you?" he asked. Raul looked down at his feet.

"I was a machinist for the branch," Raul said. "Had to prove myself over and over because my father was a sentinel. I was the one figuring out the defenses and the power grid for this place. When father died, he sent me on a mission to ensure I wasn't compromised and gave someone else my old job. When I came back, I got put on studies. I was useless there, so I volunteered to join up with you."

"Might be useless here, too. What happened to your father?" Gregor asked.

"He . . . died on a mission almost a year ago, right after a bunch of deaths in the lab. Not sure what the mission was; he left before I could find out. We didn't have the numbers or gear yet, only a few weeks more and he'd probably be alive," Raul said.

Gregor considered his role in the new Vigilant and what Raul was hinting at.

"And Matthias reassigned me here to take his place. Not sure I'd call it a favor," Gregor said.

"He thinks highly of you; you're his idol, I'm pretty sure," Raul said.

"Not idol enough to have me in the loop," Gregor said.

The other members of Vigilant hand-selected by Gregor arrived, carrying pistols, ARs, and EMPX gun blades. Gregor's team joined with two different teams heading east. The train made two stops for the other teams. According to Raul, many of the stops led to locations hidden inside mesas, caves, and one feeding directly into the deepest recess of Mexico City's sewer system.

The train made a sudden halt that caused Gregor to hit himself in the face. The stop was immediately followed by a loud apology from Raul. Gregor and his team exited the train car to an empty cave and a stairway heading up. The small cavern opened to a field leading to a mountain range between the capital and Puebla. The lights of Mexico City illuminated the horizon behind him, with flashes of pinks and greens from fireworks lighting up the sky like a war between clowns.

Mount Tlaloc and the neighboring mountains formed the northernmost tip of the Trans-Mexican Volcanic Belt. From what history Gregor knew of the region, the area was a sacred place during the Aztec Empire. His target location was at the base of Mt. Tlaloc.

Tarango Castle had existed for almost 1500 years, constructed by a local lord of the same name. The castle had been abandoned years ago, not worth the cost to maintain. Through his binoculars, Gregor saw the tattered Blackthorne flag flying from the stubby tower peeking out from behind the walls. A few camouflaged AATVs bearing the marks of Vigilant lay beside the cave. Gregor and his team made their way toward the castle, leaving Raul as a sniper and in charge of outside communication.

Slowly his team scaled the mountain, thankful the castle was near the bottom. Gregor slipped a few times, blaming it on imbalance courtesy of his EMPX. He arrived at the base as the stars emerged.

The group wrapped its way around the elevated base to the scratching sounds of robes scraping ancient walls. Gregor's EMF detector made no sounds. A road off Prosperity Highway 76 led to a guard station that in turn led to the castle. Decent-sized indentions in the poorly maintained foundation allowed him to scale the side.

Overlooking the courtyard, he saw cut grass, neatly trimmed bushes, and plants with royal purple blooms. At the center of the courtyard, a winding tree twisted up toward the sky with leaves of glowing crimson. His team positioned themselves around the castle. In unison, the group flanked the sides of the castle. Outside the castle, Raul provided updates via radio. Gregor climbed down to the courtyard. He scanned the tree with his EMF, shaking it violently when it made not so much as a single beep.

Moving into the building, he sensed a presence. He drew

his EMPX to deal with close quarters threats. Moonlight poured through the stained-glass windows of hallways with checkered floors. The stained-glass windows depicted the end of the Old World, the Second Dark Age, and the founding of New Prosperity. He admired the painstaking hours it must have taken to produce images of fires, skyscrapers, demons, and kings. One scene caught his attention. A large crowd gathered under a blue sky. Above them floated a man in white robes with beams of golden light coming from where the face should be. *Are these original or new?*

He arrived at a picturesque dining room illuminated by candlelight. Goblets, plates, serving trays, and candlesticks were polished to mirror sheen. He used the reflected surfaces to catch a glimpse of any possible foes creeping up behind him. He smelled spices and grilled meat from freshly prepared meals. Three full meals lay at the end of the table, along with three goblets. He smelled the wine and dozens of sweet liquors. The plates of shrimp, chicken, bowls of fruit, tostadas, and black bean salad.

"Pretty luxurious for a witch," Gregor said.

He moved through the room to another hallway with murals depicting the burning of and rebuilding of Mexico City.

His exploration led to large rooms with pillars of malachite. At the end of the hallway, a set of engraved malachite doors gave off an ominous vibe that often preceded violence. The EMF came to life, nearly stopping Gregor's heart. Gregor lowered his weapon to open the door. He raised his gun and used his foot to silently push open the door. He stepped through to a circular room with walls covered with malachite statues. An enormous bed was at the center of the room, surrounded by four pillars and silk curtains. He saw something through the silk curtains and braced for a possible trap.

Gregor's heart danced in nervous anticipation. Lifting back the curtain, he pointed his gun down at a man and woman lying naked on the bed. Gregor ran his fingers along the carotid arteries of each of the victims.

"They'll be fine," said an alluring voice from the open door leading to the courtyard.

The woman slowly moved around him. He came face to face with an alluring woman in a low-cut dress that shone like pure sapphire. She had black hair with an iridescent glow. Instinct told him this was a demon classified as a harlot. Harlots were the product of those using technology to fulfill sexual desires, a somewhat risky endeavor that could end in humiliation, loss of money, or loss of life. He aimed his gun at her, she responded with a smile. "Breaking into my house, disturbing my guests, and pointing a gun at me . . . must've made quite an impression on someone."

"Demons and witches, quite the haul," he replied. "You won't feed on anyone else."

"I've killed no one," she insisted.

"Doubt that. Your friend most certainly has though. A young man died a few days ago after a trip up here. Francisco." She frowned as if the words visibly hurt her.

"He's dead?"

Gregor knew better than to trust a demon or any target for that matter. Demons, like humans, seemed to adapt to new situations. The sorrow in her voice did not dissuade him. She moved toward the door that led to an outdoor garden and not at the speed of a fleeing enemy. Gregor followed her out. The woman proceeded to the bench in front of another crimson-leafed tree. Gregor kept his hand from the trigger, but he sensed something different in her than with other demons. Yellow light from the city crept over the courtyard walls. She glanced at the bench.

"Francisco would sit on this bench and recite poetry. I liked his company." She wiped at her eyes.

"A demon harboring witches and kink seekers?" He checked the corners for any lurking surprises.

"Is that so hard to believe? They call me Meridiana." He'd heard the name before.

"You feed on people!"

She nodded her head.

"But I don't kill them. I fulfill every sexual desire my clients can dream of; in exchange, I feed off their life energy in the process. It takes a day or two to recover from most clients. Francisco must've been very ill. He hid it well. He didn't make it."

Gregor saw no signs of his team. She pulled off a crimson leaf from the serpentine tree.

"I've heard of you. You owned a brothel in the city. Why move out here? Long way for people to go for a romp," he said.

"I became a target and others on your list wanted my protection, too," she said.

"From us?" She shot an annoyed glance at Gregor.

"Of course." Gregor cocked his head to the side. "Your assignment was to kill. Your target came to me seeking aid." Gregor threw up his hands and fumbled for words.

"We're here to capture a witch, possibly witches," Gregor corrected. Gregor braced for attack, if bloodshed was coming he preferred to get to it. He raised the gun and turned the dial on the side to the max. He swore he saw her fingers lengthen then return to normal. Again he didn't sense the normal danger.

"Not all under my care are witches, as you call them," she said. She moved close to Gregor.

"I'll be the judge of that. We gonna do this?" Gregor asked.

"There's plenty of time for that. You may need my protection now, too, but first you need some time to relax. Work off that stress," she purred.

Her hair turned a burning orange. She moved closer to him. Gregor didn't shoot. He didn't understand why he wouldn't shoot.

In the moonlight, she gently slid the straps of her dress down and stepped out of it. She approached Gregor with a hungry grin. Her figure morphed when she walked. He cursed aloud, to her amusement. She pressed herself against him. His heart began to flutter. He couldn't fight against it. He couldn't bring himself to attack.

"I can't. I won't," Gregor said. She leaned in, placing her lips on his.

"See, I'm not so bad?"

She circled him, kissing him gently on the neck. She completed an iteration around him and became petite with short hair and ebony skin. She leaned in and kissed him again. She made another iteration around him, taking the form of a buxom brunette. He cursed his mounting urges.

"I can be whatever you want," she said.

She cycled through hairstyles, curve sizes, and skin colors. She became a blur of shapes and colors. He felt his head spinning like a twister. The demoness saw the image of a figure in his mind.

"I'll not-"

His words stopped instantly when the being morphed into a woman with fiery red hair. The accuracy disturbed him; it was her, down to the loving smile that nearly made him quit the order. He knew this demoness wasn't the woman he loved, yet it still gave him pause. His tough facade vanished at the image of the woman he abandoned for the cause.

"Let yourself have this. We both want this," she said.

She wrapped her arms around him and ran her fingers through the white curls of his beard. He felt his energy draining as they fell to the ground in passion. Gregor couldn't stop himself. The emotions overwhelmed him. Gregor hated himself for doing it and despised the part of him that wanted it. The demon proved harder to resist than he anticipated. He hadn't realized what happened until it was too late.

THOS

Thos, ALONG WITH his bodyguards, Drake, and Zora, walked through the massive warehouse at the back of the newest Averill Market supercenter, the biggest of the thirty-five stores launched across Mexico. The facility was on the edge of Mexico City. With the Vigilant-cult debacle on the back burner, Thos focused his attention on his reason for being down here in the first place. He spent his time meeting the owners of the newly acquired farms plus touring and speaking at the new facilities. The work kept Thos's mood from souring.

Inside the warehouse, a maze of busy conveyor belts carried boxes of goods to the appropriate locations. The facility manager led Thos and his entourage through the place, giving them the lowdown on the operating costs, return on investments, plans for growth, and all the other things he dealt with seven days a week. Zora yawned, a sign she regretted this endeavor. Drake likewise remained stone-faced and uninterested.

Thos felt the stirrings of an inner funk brewing, such events increasing each day he spent away from his wife. Thos's feelings began to eat away at him, affecting his ability to function. He kept his internal battles secret from everyone except for his wife, and he intended to keep it that way. Constant mentions of his wife, dead brother, and murdered friends became an invisible noose slowly tightening around his neck.

Thos approached the entrance to the store where hundreds of shoppers waited for its doors to open. Out front large red tape covered the public entrance. Provincial Mayor Roberto Rhon held oversized scissors Thos would use to officially open the store. Mayor Rhon addressed the crowd as Thos approached; the crowd erupted in applause. Thos heard the mayor's spiel about his life, dead brother, and murdered friends. He cursed under his breath and took his place beside Roberto, who immediately handed him the scissors.

"You're up," Roberto said.

The constant references to his long-dead brother wore on his nerves. His cheery demeanor vanished. With scissors in hand, he snapped them in the direction of the mayor, who stepped back and laughed nervously. Thos opened his giant scissors again to dissuade the mayor from speaking again. The laughter from the crowd made Thos feel good; he was relieved people couldn't push him around so easily anymore.

"They wanted me to give another big speech about loss, politics, and so on, but I'm not about that. I hope bringing you guys into our business will get food on tables and monies in hands. So without further ado . . . ."

Thos opened the scissors and pushed them down on the ribbon . . . or attempted to at least. He mumbled a few curses when the scissors would not close. The scissors refused to budge. Thos's face became as red as a magnificent sunset. Both Drake and Zora turned away to avoid laughing at their friend.

"Technical difficulties, folks. Not a reflection of our products," Thos said.

He threw the defunct object to the ground and used his pocket knife to finish the job. Thos, Drake, and Zora quickly stepped out of the way of eager shoppers cutting a swath of destruction through the new store. When the potential voters entered the building, the mayor made a hasty departure.

"So this is what you came down here to do? Walk through buildings and farms?" Zora asked. Thos shoved his hands in his jean pockets.

"No, there's more," Thos said. "But I do need to make sure everything is running the best it can. We won't let gangs or mayors or scissors or anyone else get in the way of that."

"You know you've made it when people conspire against you," Drake added.

Thos replied with a grin. Shoppers continued to flood into the store, including some well-to-do customers heading into the parking lot. Thos felt pangs of guilt creeping up inside. He reached in his pocket and popped a few pills to remedy the situation.

"You okay?" Drake asked.

"Nothing to worry about," Thos replied.

Drake looked over to Zora for a reaction; however, her attention was focused on an approaching black truck and a car bearing the image of the Void. The Void developed a nasty habit of showing up at all of Thos's public events.

"Look alive," she said. Drake and Thos got their weapons ready.

The car rolled right up to Thos, Drake, and Zora. A woman with a skull tattooed over her face stepped out of the vehicle's passenger side. Every location Thos had gone to ended in a staring match between him and the Void. Despite the nihilistic nature of the cult, they eased up on attacking the business bringing prosperity to the state. Event security immediately took defensive positions around Thos. This time the deadheads came up for a face-to-face meeting. Thos stepped out in front, refusing to be intimidated. *I ain't the flag boy this time*, he thought.

"So you're the Heartland hero," the gangster said, disappointed.

"Here for our legendary deals?" Thos asked. She laughed and gave a surprisingly pleasant smile.

"You really are as they say," she said. The woman smiled how Thos imagined a snallygaster did when it came upon a tasty cow. Her attention turned to Drake.

"And the famous regicide," she said.

"Your judgment means nothing to me deadhead," Drake said. The woman moved close to Drake.

"You're in no position to moralize. You aren't helping anyone but those power," she said. "You soldiers are all the same. Cowards and dogs. You'll kill your own families if your master gives the whistle. If you believed in justice, you'd be killing them. Part of you wants to. They're a bigger threat to this world than us. Fighting fair is a losing battle. Life is a losing battle. All you can do is take them down with you. Give them the mercy of death, as is his will."

"I'll remember that when I plant one in your skull," Drake said. Thos interjected.

"Unless you plan to start shootin', I suggest you leave," Thos said. "You come to scare me? I ain't goin' anywhere," Thos said.

Void and government soldiers awaited the command to open fire. Shoppers cowered behind the glass of the supercenter.

"I've no intention of harming them. They're more my people than yours, and we're always hiring. As a matter of fact, I applaud your efforts to aid them. If only there was such a thing as peace," he said.

"There still can be peace if you leave," Zora interrupted.

"Death is the only peace," the gangster snapped. "Life's purpose is to position your pieces to reach this goal. They set theirs, so we have set ours."

"You're running out of pieces," Thos said. "This nice play of yours won't keep the people from turning against you."

"All we need is a bit more time. But part of me still loves my home, so here's the deal. I want you, the regent, and the government troops to leave Mexico at once. The state is under our control. If you want to avoid secession, you'll agree to these terms. Surrender your operations to us. Take these conditions to Duke, then leave, or death will come for you all. I don't want chaos, but my people do. They won't restrain themselves much longer."

With all the plots and wars, Thos started to believe that secession wasn't so bad after all. The cowering masses stirred behind Thos and his fears were realized.

"You know you can't win," Thos said.

"Maybe not," she replied. "But we'll take as many of you—"

A high-pitch shriek brought the confrontation to a halt. Thos and the Void turned to the fleeing crowd and ghoulish sight. A stubby-legged demon with long, thin arms and a stretched-out face shambled toward Thos.

"Shrill!" Drake said.

The arms shot out, Thos dodged in the nick of time. The demon's arms found a consolation prize in a cultist. The arms shredded him up but quickly let go for a different target. The female cultist dashed for her vehicle, not loving death enough to face it with her henchmen. The demon's arms flailed around, trying to lock onto Thos. The stomach ripped open, revealing a vertical maw filled with jagged teeth. Thos opened fire on the demon. Drake and Zora joined in, followed by Thos's bodyguards. The thrashing demon arms swatted at the attackers. The stubby legs stretched out, adding three feet of height to the creature. The lumbering beast became fast, rushing away from the army mobilized against it. A swipe from the right arm knocked two of Thos's bodyguards off their feet. Thos fired at the soft insides of the large mouth inside the chest. The remaining forces concentrated fire on the demon. The barrage of gunfire tore the demon to pieces.

"That was a demon. And it was after me," Thos said.

Thos learned about shrills after Drake's encounter with one. This particular demon fed on sadness and guilt. If a shrill failed to consume the desired victim, it grew weak enough to be killed by conventional means. Thos knew it was drawn to him, like the others before it. Thos ordered his bodyguards to burn the body.

The rest of the day passed without event, but the encounter left Thos longing for his wife even more. Constants mentions of his brother and the war brought them back, tearing him down even further. The demon attack would keep patrons away from this store for who knows how long. Thos adjusted his glasses and congratulated his troops on a job well done.

"Well, I believe that's it for today," Thos said.

"You all right?' Drake asked. Thos nodded.

Thos yearned to retreat to Duke's house and hide away for a time. It was a long time coming for Thos to deal with his guilt before it was the death of him.

CASS

EACH DAY CASS went around and around with her board of directors. Violence across Mexico had them considering abandoning the state. Cass pushed for toughing it out despite the risk, reminding all of the long-term benefits for the company, Mexico, and the nation as a whole. The compulsion to help remained strong; the Averills had the means. Cass and Thos believed they had an obligation to help, as much from guilt as from genuinely wanting to make a difference; the fears the Averills couldn't pay it forward enough also remained strong. Days of her convincing finally waylaid fears to push on and keep opening stores, gangs be damned.

After days of meetings followed by days of volunteer work, Cass needed a break. She smoked enough to rival any manufacturing plant in town. Every time she told herself this one was the last she hated herself a pack later. She retreated home to rest. Guards patrolled the grounds, humiliated but alive after Vigilant's house call. They were under the impression it was some side effect from the Compact. Nausea and headaches forced Cass to spend her time off in bed.

After a full day in bed, Cass picked up the black rectangle on the nightstand. Since the last Compact, technology advanced across the nation like never before. Mere weeks after the castle's fall, the scarce landline phones slowly cropping up around the country were soon to be replaced with more cell towers and less restrictions. Only a handful of business and political leaders were allowed to possess, much less use, the virgin technology.

Cass picked up the phone and dialed her husband, then put the phone on speaker before setting it back down. The phone rang until right before the voicemail kicked in.

"Dropped the phone again," Thos said, with unusual irritation. He let out a heavy breath signaled a composure change. "Just thinking about you."

"That why you dropped the phone?" she teased. He laughed but said nothing else, Thos had no witty comeback this time.

"What's wrong?" she asked. Thos generally kept his feelings under wraps, having difficulty talking about things even to her.

"Too much time to dwell," he said. She understood the sullen tone and what it meant.

"It hasn't been this bad in a long time," she said, fearing another rough patch. She heard the defeat in his voice. "All these people keep bringing up my brother." Cass rested her head in her hands and provided what little comfort long distance afforded.

"I just can't get away from it," Thos said. "Been on my mind every day since I got here. The company, war, and now this. I'm overwhelmed. Dammit, why can't people let the past go, no one that brings it up was within a hundred miles when any of it happened."

"You can't hold it in anymore," Cass said. "You know how it was when I found out about it."

"I suppose. Gettin' in the way of my job. I can always fall back on being a good kisser, but people don't appreciate that 'round here," he said.

No matter what was happening, Thos had the power to make her smile, such a simple thing could lift her spirits no matter how bad the situation. Cass's headaches worsened, but she powered through.

After a moment of silence, the two exchanged stories of their solo adventures, ranging from strawberry sales to gang shootouts. Thos paused.

"That's not all. Get this, The Void is working with Vigilant!" he said. Cass nearly dropped the phone.

"You're joking, right?" she asked.

"Saw it with my own two peepers," Thos said. Suddenly all the warning bells went off in Cass's head. Thos's tone changed. "Why? What's up there?"

"They're in the city right now, they were in our house!" she said. Cass recounted the abduction of Adrienne and the threats against her. Cass realized her gut feeling may prove right. She instantly feared that someone may be listening.

"I'm packing right now," Thos said.

"No. It's important that you stay there," she said. "We shouldn't speak any more about this, they could be listening. I'll talk to Yadira. I got plenty of protection here. If you pull out of Mexico the board may decide to abandon the project," she said. Thos swore, hating the responsibilities always thrust upon him.

"Please be careful," he advised.

"You, too," she said.

Cass spent so much of her time doing what she could to help people, but it felt like she hadn't made a dent. She had to pursue this, fearing by the time the government was involved it might be too late.

"Love you," she said.

"Love you, too," he said.

Cass ended the call and planned how to best to approach the situation. Ever since her run-in with Vigilant, Cass always kept a sidearm handy in case they made good on their threat. She chose to go to Yadira with the disturbing new information. Driving through the city she found no trace of Vigilant activity. The nagging sensation of their presence told her they were only hidden and not gone. Cass's nausea and headache remained, but they would not deter her.

Cass arrived at Prosperity Hall. Thousands came and went from the constant events, meetings, debates, and all things government. The sun reflected off the cars in the parking lot. Cass always forgot her sunglasses, at home, in restaurants, and once in a Prosperity Hall bathroom. A city hall meeting concerning Blackthorne loyalists boomed from the auditorium. James Dumas stood outside the auditorium, glancing over at Cass while he talked with some underlings. A moment of eye contact with the man called "Ambition Made Flesh" was enough for her blood to freeze. Cass smiled at him, but James did not smile back. Cass shrugged it off and walked up the stairs to Yadira's office, closed with guards on either side.

"Sorry ma'am. The vice regent is too busy for you," one said. Cass crossed her arms, aware of her inability to intimidate. One of the guards sighed.

"She gave us specific orders to keep everyone away. Come back tomorrow," he said, expecting a round of sass from an elite.

Cass went back down to the lobby a sat by the chair beside the small memorial of those that died in the attack on Kingsbury. Cass stared at the floor waiting for a revelation. The nagging sensation prevented her from leaving, Someone zeroed in on her location. Like her husband, Cass spent a fortune on training for combat situations for the very real possibility of needing it; she feared that day was today.

"Mrs. Averill," a voice said, catching her off guard.

She turned around. Though he wore civilian clothes, she recognized Kane Turce, one of Drake's old knight-ambassador friends. The Averills' friendship with Drake connected them to a network of trusted allies, including current and ex-military. Kane hugged her.

"You're being watched, you need to get out now," he whispered.

He faked a laugh to mask his conversation. Cass could almost feel James's eyes on her. Cass followed James out of the building where a second, thicker man, waited. The second man she recognized as another of Drake's friends, Knight-Ambassador Trevor Linden. Cass had had a few experiences with both men before and since Drake vouched for them she had at least some trust in them. Cass followed the two men around the corner and out of sight.

"Wanna tell me what's going on?" she asked, irritated.

"Not here," Kane replied.

"You have some business with our employer," Trevor said.

"Employer?" Cass asked, suddenly aware this did not mean the military. It did not take long to make Cass doubt Kane and Trevor's loyalty. Kane motioned her to follow but Cass wouldn't budge.

"Tell me or I'm goin' nowhere," she replied sternly. Trevor cursed under his breath. He looked at Kane.

"Mr. Abaddon," Trevor said. A twinge of fear shot up Cass's back.

Over the last two years, Cass learned much about the country of New Prosperity including a surprisingly robust criminal underworld, surprising in that it wasn't tied to the equally criminal government aboveworld. No accounts ever mentioned the man himself, which added a mythical quality to him. The way Cass understood it, Mr. Abaddon had operated in Kingsbury for as long as anyone could remember, and led a powerful organization that even the advisors feared to take on.

"You work for him?!" she asked, now skeptical of Drake's network.

"Don't be so judgmental, we do what we have to," Trevor said.

"I don't wanna be a part of this," Cass said.

"Too late for that. Besides Mr. Abaddon believes there can be an arrangement that benefits the both of you," Trevor replied.

"What's this, kidnapping?" Cass scoffed.

"Survival," Kane said.

"I suggest you follow us and we can discuss this somewhere safe," Trevor said. "You're too far in now. Vigilant'll kill you, we could've long ago if we wanted."

"Fine," Cass said, surprised she feared Vigilant more than Mr. Abaddon. Cass followed the two men around the building and out to the park, talking along the way.

"Mr. Abaddon has a mission for us, you included," Trevor said.

"I'm not a soldier," Cass said. Kane and Trevor made no glances around yet she realized they were well aware of their surroundings.

"You don't need to be. He needs you for something more . . . covert," Kane said.

"I wouldn't be in this situation if not for Adrienne, would I?" Cass asked, understanding how Thos felt being pulled into bad situations because of someone else.

"I'm afraid you would," Kane replied. "This just pulled you in faster." Trevor grew irritable at the two falling behind, she felt Kane had more to say.

"No more talking. Go about your business. We have some things to do. Meet us in the park at nine tonight. Until then stay around people you trust. Trust me when I say your life is at stake regardless of your choice."

A twinge of anger shot through her temples at the threat. Once again Cass felt powerless, and with a name like Mr. Abaddon being thrown around, she realized this threat to be very real.

Cass avoided contact for the rest of the day, always near a hefty collection of guns in case Mr. Abaddon or Vigilant came calling. Night fell and Cass made her way to Prosperity Park. The park was a two-mile-long stretch of land like a miniature forest with a crystal clear pond. Kane, wearing his black knight gear, waited in the park. Kane didn't stand out among the thousands of civilians and dozens of knights watching and enjoying the public park.

"Have snipers on me?" Cass said. Few paid attention to the incognito Cass. Kane frowned and crossed his arms.

"Don't be so negative, we need you as much as you need us," Kane said. Cass raised an eyebrow.

"Wasn't a no," she said.

"It wasn't," Kane replied.

"You could ask for my money and skip all this," Cass replied. Kane sighed.

"Not about money. You're the only expendable asset Mr. Abaddon has at the moment . . . besides me." Kane scanned the nearby crowds. Cass wondered how many agents of Mr. Abaddon lurked in the area.

"Can you give me any details?" Cass asked. Kane sighed.

"You and I got the short end of the stick. You're here because Vigilant is after us. The boss's resources are stretched too thin so this mission is my way to pay it back."

"What do I have to do?" she asked. Kane slipped a recorder into Cass's pants' pocket.

"Gather intel. Record everything you can in Prosperity Hall, record everyone you speak to. That's all for now. We'll have new agents to replace you soon enough."

"Don't have a choice do I?" Cass asked.

"This is the right choice. Help us and gain Mr. Abaddon's protection. That's as valuable as any army," Kane replied.

Kane escorted Cass to her unmarked car and followed her home and to the safety of her updated security team.

"Carry on as usual, just keep recording. I'll contact you soon," Kane said.

Cass returned home. The safety of the mansion provided little comfort. Surrounded by guards and behind thick walls, she couldn't escape the feeling she was a dangling carrot for many hungry foes.

MATTHIAS

MATTHIAS'S RESOLVE COULD be nothing short of ironclad. Enemies were gathering. Agents of the false god were paving the way for the Adversary. Things were escalating too fast. Matthias would have to expedite Killswitch in response. He charted the course for a bold and dangerous future. Witches became the unceasing torchlight in the city's heart. He found it oddly relaxing. Matthias walked up the stairs into the overseer's room of the production hub at the north end of the Silent City. Generators powered the essential plant functions, including the terminals and security cameras. At the moment, five generation chambers were fully operational. Matthias had spent weeks figuring out the technology with the help of the Alvarez boy.

He pulled up the five chambers on the overseer's terminal. A skeleton crew operated each chamber. One man operated the terminal, leaving the rest to handle the products. Large rectangular structures with blue lights served as individual workstations. The workstations had options to build and deconstruct. Each chamber had a different amount of workstations, allowing for different product sizes. Each workstation was loaded with a blueprint and the necessary part to create it. The chambers were in process at all hours. The success rates were low, but they were more than adequate for the time being. Each workstation was loaded with materials taken from the city's resource storehouses. Large robotic arms with dozens of fingers retracted from the workstations and processed the materials.

Before his eyes came the frames of tanks, sword spring mechanisms of EMPXs, light plating for his troops, railguns, and his patented witch-burning spikes. The workstations were a godsend for Vigilant, functioning as an advanced version of Old World 3-D printers. In deconstruction mode, arms with many fingers with blue eyes studied machines loaded into them. The arms with fingers then pulled the machines apart. Dismantled machines were processed into digital blueprints, allowing nearly any device to be shoved in and mass-produced. With a handful of Anselm's railguns, a single city tank, and a plethora of resources, Matthias had all he needed to create the most powerful army on Earth. He took steps to prevent the Compact's mind-wiping powers; otherwise, he'd be like the masses utterly oblivious of such technology.

Matthias monitored the progress of production. Weapons and armor that failed to meet his quality standards were deconstructed or given to the Void. Matthias wasn't so foolish as to make the distraction too strong. Vigilant restricted the Void's access to a series of tunnels, and they weren't in a position to argue. They disgusted him. These death-loving nihilists were reaching the end of their usefulness.

Matthias made his rounds through roads, passing by wisps playing back the Collective's last days. Matthias checked on the progress of the new labs. Here, the Collective had made its last stand to rebuild the world after the war they believed would come and devastate it all. The wisps played out the scientists making notes of genetic algorithms. They created a road map for the people, determining every aspect of their lives, reducing them to little more than bug-eating slaves of the hive mind. Matthias made it a point to walk through the areas with heavy wisp activities to remind the people of their duty to prevent this dystopian world from coming back. Matthias had spent years to reach this moment.

Hot streaks of pain shot through his brain, stronger among the static reproductions of the Old World. They grew more frequent by the day, whether he wore the mask or not. He told himself it was the price he had to pay, and Killswitch would be successful before the price grew too high.

"Are you really willing to do this? This is not the work of a hero," the voice said. "If you're so righteous, you would let the flames take you."

"Your words won't sway me, false god. You made this necessary," Matthias responded.

The voice was so faint he began to doubt it was even there. Nearby soldiers ignored the grand crusader's conversations with an unheard voice. Trolls bolstered his labor force, another necessary evil for the task at hand. Despite the whispers from his less-loyal soldiers, Matthias took no pleasure in using slaves or the experiments. A contingent of Vigilant men oversaw the trolls, having guns on them at all hours. The man leading the group to the city's depths saluted Matthias as he passed.

Matthias entered the main lab. He spent so much time in the lab he made a bed in the director's office to avoid losing time from pointless traveling. He limited his sleep to four hours a day, the standard for men in the field.

"When the mission is done, you can sleep for 23 hours a day if you want," Matthias told his men.

Matthias got his required sleep in before the following status report. He shrugged off the drowsiness, pumping himself full of the energy cocktail developed by a former subordinate with an aptitude for chemistry. Matthias despised the stuff, describing it as being mercilessly beaten with a ten-pound bag of sugar. The swill served its purpose; everything Vigilant was doing had to serve the greater purpose.

Matthias opened the case that held the damnable artifact. No one discerned the true nature of Eon, save that he was the immensely powerful author of the Compact and ruled the people of the world from the shadows. This mask was not organic, but somehow, it lived. Matthias felt it. He knew its connection to Eon, like a severed limb still able to be manipulated by the body. He studied it thoroughly, attuning his weapons to a frequency even Eon couldn't withstand forever.

Matthias placed the mask on his face. He found himself using such things with ease. He didn't understand his susceptibility to signals or technology, but he wasn't alone in these abilities.

He reached through it, syncing with Lord Crusader Jaren Hart. Jaren detailed reports of the "Devil of Durenberg." Matthias saw the man multiple times when connected, though never for long. The man looked remarkably like Aric, but all Blackthornes were very much dead. It didn't matter who he was; this man was an agent of the enemy. Matthias knew that time was running out.

The simple act became a battle of wills with the fragment of Eon that inhabited the mask. The initial stages of Killswitch gave Matthias the means to use it and ultimately destroy his enemy.

"You can't use this forever," Eon said. "You're losing yourself in us, like Gideon. You have already lost so much."

Matthias felt the mask tighten and its long silvery fingers wrapping around the back of his head. He ignored the entity's goading.

"I don't need this much longer. You're growing weak. A few pieces were all we needed. This connection of yours will be used to burn away every trace of you."

Matthias's vision blurred. He was back home. He watched his ramshackle home from outside. His daughter played outside, driving around in the little wooden car he had built for her. The old him sat in an weathered plastic chair, much more disgusting than he remembered. She regarded the other him with the most loving orange eyes. She didn't know the truth yet. The dark voice of Eon wormed back into his skull.

"You killed her two days before this, did you not?" Eon said.

Matthias relived that night in this very spot. There were none of the tools of his current trade. Matthias made do with a wood-cutter's ax. The memory wounded him.

"She was a witch. Was going to sacrifice my daughter. I regret nothing," Matthias said. He doubted who she was for so long. He buried the ax into her neck.

"Yes, you do," Eon said. "You could have stopped her long before. Your denial led to this. In the end, you prevented nothing, and you only made it worse. Trapped in the endless loop. This is why we rule you."

The words cut deeper than Matthias anticipated. Eon capitalized.

"See? We're stronger than you think. The connection works both ways. We can destroy you with a memory. You made a fatal mistake before. Are you so sure you won't again?"

Eon planted a kernel of doubt. Matthias doubted himself for the first time since he had started this monumental crusade. He had wandered through deserts and wilderness, guided by visions and signals. He killed witches and demons without the need for Vigilant. Matthias fought and killed his way into the order; a nobody becoming the east coast sentinel and now master over it all. Matthias revitalized the order. He navigated the storms of the Uninhabited, proving his worth. His followers fried, he passed through with ease. He gathered support from others like him, defects with lives ruined by Eon. People told him he was crazy, yet here he was. Vigilant was whole once more, set to reclaim its place in the world. "You're the one that made the fatal mistake," Matthias said. "All it took was a little mutation and your great Compact fell apart. I'm gaining control."

Matthias reached out through the mask. He strained. The

mask tightened. Matthias focused his thoughts on the pulse emitters that served as his miniature prototype killswitches. He imagined them activated. They became an extension of him. His mind flooded with code and energy. His body ached. He fought through the pain.

"Can you really do it?" Eon said. "Can you make that sacrifice? Do exactly what they did? Repeat the same mistake?"

"You're the mistake, and I'm about to correct it." Matthias said. Eon's voice faded.

The fingers of the mask released hold of Matthias. He removed the mask and placed it back in the container. The duels with Eon were starting to turn in his favor. Matthias's plans were beginning to bear fruit.

He approached the office "shop floor," removing the cubicles and converting it into the room for live testing. Men hauled human and demon bodies into the room for postmortem testing. Matthias hated this part of the job, but it was necessary to show his men his willingness to the cause. The experiments were painful yet vital for what came next, especially for Matthias and his generals. Again he told himself it would be worth it.

Matthias stripped off his armor and lay on one of the constructed chairs. A dozen Vigilant men were strapped to the chairs on either side of him. The lab technician pressed the button on the side of his chair. Straps shot from the sides of the chair and wrapped around Matthias. The chairs lifted up, becoming vertical. Sacrifices were necessary; it was a part of war. Armed men and scholars gathered on the other side of the room. His resolve wouldn't falter again. A world free of false gods, adversaries, and algorithms was worth the cost. The last piece of the plan rested on the shoulders of Gregor Pavane.

"Ever Vigilant," his men said in unison.

"Ever Vigilant," he said.

Matthias gave the nod to begin.

YADIRA

YADIRA SPENT AN increasing amount of time in her office. Her nerves hung by a thread. She hid in her office under the guise of being overwhelmed with work. Even with hundreds of guards in the building, the feeling of safety eluded her. Muffled voices outside the door put Yadira on edge. She reached for the gun in her desk.

"Sorry ma'am. The vice regent is too busy for you," one said. Cass crossed her hands, aware of her lack of intimidation. One of the guards sighed.

"She gave us specific orders to keep everyone away. Come back tomorrow," he said

Yadira carried out her duties in her seclusion, save for unavoidable meetings with Regent Dumas. James carried himself with surprising competence as second to the advisors. Only two years ago, James served as a knight-ambassador with untapped potential. Now he reigned over an entire nation, trusted by advisors to govern New Prosperity.

Yadira also rose to power in a fashion nothing short of meteoric, going from Toth expatriate to Emerald Coast representative to vice regent in a decade. She survived the most powerful group in Toth and was now part of the strongest one in New Prosperity.

Toth dominated the western half of North America, with Gloire in between the northern half of them. Toth and New Prosperity had a reasonably amicable relationship through the centuries, though ultimately vied to be the dominant power in North America. With the dismantling of the rancher-controlled Badlands, only four countries now existed in North America.

Yadira made a necessary trip to the meeting hall. James discussed the topics of the day and the dramatic changes that followed the Compact. Each Compact imparted lost, or new, knowledge to the masses. In some cases, this knowledge advanced the nation for decades, most recently allowing air travel. In a few years, the continent would contact the eastern half of the world not heard from in two millennia.

Yadira and James made the necessary approvals for the allowable aircraft, the companies contracted to build, as well as the initial flights and those willing to risk partaking in another lost art. Yadira and James discussed other things, covering yawn-inducing mundanities and military operations for the bulk of each meeting. Cold dread split Yadira's attention.

"Yadira?" James asked. The creeping darkness consumed her thoughts. "Yadira!" The eyes of the advisors pierced through the brain fog.

"S-sorry," she said with an apologetic bow. Katonah Hale leaned forward.

"Are you ill?" he asked in a warm tone.

Katonah mastered the art of faux concern. Mr. Hale often labeled himself the group's outsider; however, he and his wife were as much part of the establishment as anyone else. The Hale family represented the interests of the Emerald Coast, where their family originated from. Though Mr. and Mrs. Hale were self-serving, their son was honorable and one of the finest agents in the land. The other advisors wore the disdain of her plain on their faces.

"My apologies. It's nothing," she replied.

"Leave if you must," James said, clearly a command. Yadira bowed one more time and left the room.

James did not require Yadira to run the country; his abilities made her wonder if the position of vice regent was wholly unnecessary. James's decisiveness and ambition left many believing he'd one day be capable of taking out the advisors, and Yadira suspected that day was fast approaching.

Agents of James skulked around wherever Yadira happened to be. Everyone spied and schemed. Trying to keep up with all the intrigue made her head spin. She maintained pace and kept her eyes forward while her own spies monitored her stalkers.

Yadira retreated to the safety of her office prison. Knowing the truth made every day a nightmare. It stung her to be a cowering pup, the opposite of the people's champion she had aspired to be. She prepared for this. The fear was drowned out by anger. *I won't let them win,* she told herself.

Yadira psyched herself up and left the office, deciding to fight or meet her fate standing tall. She threw open the doors, connecting with the shoulders of the startled guards on the other side. Yadira bent her head down, trying to hide her embarrassment. An apology later, the guards escorted her through the city. She went so far as to have lunch with Enton in the Advent Park in full view of the world. It felt good not to hide.

Onlookers swarmed the area for a chance to see Yadira. Inevitably, the conversations revolved around politics and baby talk. Yadira spent a little time speaking with the public as Enton took the opportunity to dip out of sight. Not all eyes on her were friendly. The jostling crowd could hide agents, spies, assassins, and worse things. Her head throbbed. Dizziness set in. A guard rushed to catch her. She choked out the word "water," instantly gaining access to every water canister within a 100-yard radius.

"Dehydrated," she told everyone.

Exhausted, an escort drove her home. Yadira lived on the edge of the noble district, the last house on the road to the lake district. She went to the gun safe in the closet under the stairs. Filled with weapons, Yadira could at least go down fighting should anyone get past her army. Gun in hand, she sat down on her posh tangerine couch, dwelling on the mounting burdens.

Her head continued to throb. She retreated upstairs. Yadira hit the light. Heat filled the room. Yadira's blood went cold. In the corner of the room, she saw It. It took longer than she expected, long enough to make her doubt. Mist rose from cracks in the floor. The mist took form, growing arms and legs. It became a figure that brought terror to those unfortunate enough to break the Algorithm. She knew what this creature brought. The form was different but the creature was the same. The entity wore a hooded white robe and floated toward her. When this entity arrived, death followed.

The figure wore a golden skull mask. She couldn't escape, but she had to try. Yadira ran back to the door. Turning around, she sprinted back to the hall to find the entity there. She turned to the left and then to the right, each time facing the masked nightmare. Yadira screamed for help. Bodyguards rushed the door. The entity waved a bony hand. Her bodyguards hit the floor, unconscious.

"You were not supposed to remember us, but that's not why we're here. You know us, and you know it must be this way. The Algorithm demands it," Eon said. The entity spoke without a shred of emotion.

"Fuck your order!" she cried. "Wear all the gold and white you want, but you're not God."

Eon stopped for a few seconds, taking on a static form. He reached out for her, she felt little more than a tingle. The house groaned. The masked figure disappeared completely. Yadira doubted all the gene therapies and defects in the world could save her for long. She ran for the door and threw it open. The door slammed, knocking her back inside the room. She felt Eon's presence to her left at first. Wherever she turned, he was there.

"You have tampered with the Algorithm, it must be adjusted," he said. She looked down at her stomach at the horrifying revelation when the pain started. Her fleeting hope dissipated. Her eyes welled up with tears.

"Please. I'll give you anything," she pleaded.

"You know what you must give," Eon said. "The Algorithm must be corrected. We can't kill you, but the Algorithm requires a life. You have made a trade."

The entity raised his arm and pointed a bony finger at her stomach. Ripping pain tore through up body. Yadira clutched at her stomach, screaming in agony.

"Not my baby, I beg you," she cried.

"The Algorithm demands it. Your hubris makes it so," he replied. The pain intensified. Blood ran down her legs. Yadira fell to her knees, overwhelmed by sorrow and pain. She pushed herself up in a vain attempt to defeat the entity. The creature appeared taken aback by her determination, clearly used to victims submitting quickly. She believed he couldn't hurt her, but the monster found a disturbingly clever loophole. The life dimmed inside her. The pain intensified; the knowledge she couldn't save her son was anguish beyond compare. She fell back to the ground. She writhed on the floor. She'd lose her family once more, as dictated by the Compact. Her resolve vanished under the crushing despair. The masked figure lowered its hand and the pain ceased. All she could do was cry.

"The correction is complete," he said. The masked figure disappeared in the mist and slipped into the cracks in the floor.

ANSELM

THE TOWNSFOLK AND Vigilant scoured the forests for Anselm, the "Durenburg Devil." He burned with shame at his dark hunger, growing stronger the more he denied it. Anselm studied them, sometimes within mere feet of them. With no luck, Vigilant doubled back to loot Durenburg. From atop a tree outside the town, Anselm saw Vigilant soldiers move from house to house, demanding supplies, confiscating weapons, and thrashing those who refused.

Without Rosalie, his feelings for the people of Durenburg evaporated fast. He was a fool to think this life would last. Nothing more than a distraction, he told himself—made it easier to think that way. He wasted too much time on people so quick to turn against him. Ezra and Cameron stood undamaged in the chaos. Anselm spied no casualties from the raid, giving him another reason not to engage. A confrontation with Vigilant was inevitable. For now, Anselm observed his prey, curious as to their numbers and this ominous mission of theirs. The anticipation of their end would have to satisfy him for now. With the raid over, Anselm moved on.

He needed to return to the site—one last stop there, before his journey resumed. Anselm dashed to the burial site. Though constantly in pain, Anselm felt stronger and faster than ever, courtesy of the Vigilant lad. No matter what Anselm did, his body was constantly wracked by pain, something that became as normal as breathing. He stayed close to Durenburg until a chance to get his sword presented itself. Through the trees, he saw a few armed men coming from the direction of his hut.

He rushed to his hut only to find it burned to the ground. He chose not to waste time looking for his weapon, knowing soon he could take one from the next fool that crossed him.

He reached the dirt, where Rosalie took her final rest. Part of him struggled to let her go. Anselm made out the anxious breathing of an interloper.

"We don't have to do this, Ezra," Anselm said. Ezra stepped out from behind the tree, with both hands gripping a pump-action shotgun.

"All this time, it's been you," Ezra said, unsure of how right he was. He pointed the gun at the unmarked grave. "Is this her?"

Ezra's skin reddened. Anselm wanted to tell him everything, all the secrets he had buried within himself for the last two years. He had wished he'd dared to tell Rosalie, but Ezra would have to suffice.

"I loved her. She took the last good part of me," Anselm said.

"Before I kill you, tell me who you are," Ezra said.

"Anselm Blackthorne," Anselm said. "I was your king. Your protector. Now I don't know what I am." Anselm spoke full of woe. Ezra lowered his shotgun. Anselm did not want more Crowes to die because of him, but he'd likely kill them before he'd even realized it.

"I cared for Rose. The only person I've cared for since that day." Anselm saw the same pain of loss in Ezra's eyes.

"You did kill her," Ezra said, face contorted by hate.

"And I'll live with that forever," Anselm said.

"No, you won't," Ezra said. Ezra aimed his gun at Anselm. The dark urges swelled inside Anselm.

"Leave, before I get hungry again," Anselm warned.

Ezra's eyes went glossy from rage. He opened fire. Anselm didn't dodge the shots. Ezra lowered his gun and gritted his teeth. Anselm saw the feeling of powerlessness in Ezra's eyes, the feeling that dominated his past life.

"He's here!" Ezra cried.

Shots from afar rang out from behind. Ezra hit the ground. A Vigilant gunman fired round after round at Anselm, grunting in frustration at his opponent's swiftness. A few bullets tore through Anselm's sternum, yet he didn't miss a beat. He slipped behind his attacker and grabbed the top and bottom of the man's mouth and pulled them apart. The top of the man's head ripped off like a fleshy bottle cap. Ezra rushed Anselm, only to be thrown to the ground. Ezra cursed Anselm. Anselm's sympathy burned away in fires of hate.

"You allied with them to get me! Pitiful," Anselm said.

The urge to eviscerate Rose's father grew strong. He reached down and placed his hand on Ezra's chest. Anselm applied pressure. Ezra cried out. Anselm imagined the cries of his wife and children as the Blackthorne castle crashed down on them. He stopped short of crushing Ezra's torso.

"Go home, if anything is left of it, and care for your grandson. He doesn't need to lose anyone else," Anselm said. Ezra struggled to his feet. He grabbed the shotgun. After a brief internal debate, Ezra dashed off.

Anselm walked over to the dead man. He found value in the dead soldier, namely a pristine sword that had clearly never been used. He picked up the man's Derbin rifle. Anselm looked down at the body, thinking of other things that might be useful. The hunger grew and so did the shame. He buried the urge, fighting to retain what humanity remained in him.

Anselm placed his hand on Rosalie's gravesite and walked away. He bid his last farewell and pushed on deeper into the wilderness. He fully expected more run-ins with Vigilant, finding pleasure in the thought.

For his first order of business, he renewed his search for the masked entity and Jaren Hart. Anselm headed toward the abandoned town as detailed by Gregory Pavane further up the coast, the last reported hotbed of coven activity on route to Vigilant tower. Anselm moved through the wilderness, eliminating Vigilant patrols along the way. Hundreds of dead Arics hung from the trees around him. Anselm blocked out their hateful glares.

He arrived at his destination. He identified it by a tree-trunk-sized hole in the center of town where a Hell Gate once stood. He scoured the area and found a few homes and a collapsed church. Something inside his head tugged at him. He remembered an important event and an old landmark another dozen miles north. Anselm chose to make camp for a moment and enjoy an evening meal of jerky that failed to satisfy his hunger. He lay on the grass and watched the glowing waltz of the purple and blue etherflies for a brief respite.

After two hours of sleep, he made his way up the coast on a nagging hunch. These feelings increased the further northeast he traveled. The feelings quickly turned to voices that directed him forward. Anselm approached a chasm that extended from the ocean a half-mile inland. He looked in the abyss.

"Everything important is underground," he grumbled.

In the past two years, Anselm had learned of an entire world hid beneath the surface. After fleeing Kingsbury, he had spent the better part of a week exploring the underground ruins of Chicago. He found partially intact buildings, catacombs, numerous vehicles, and scurrying horrors always out of sight. He was eager to see what other secrets lay in wait beneath his feet. A voice urged him on.

"Take a leap of faith," it said.

He took the plunge. Anselm hit the water hard. His legs hit water far shallower than anticipated. Bone shattered and splintered. He didn't mind the painful crash landing; he found himself enjoying the shattering punishment. He forced the protruding bones back inside and waited for the healing.

A honeycomb of passages filled the tunnels. The tunnels moving westward were more prominent than the others, big enough for vehicles. Anselm realized the tunnels were created by machinery. He spied faint light in one of the tunnels.

Anselm moved through the winding tunnel toward the light. The light-filled tunnel lacked the natural smoothness of the other passages. He ran his hand along the wall, slicing his hand on a razor-sharp rock. His hand bled for a few seconds before closing back up. The endless passage quickly wore on Anselm's nerves. The passageway finally came to a glorious end.

A burly warrior holding a sword was carved into the back wall. The figure had a beard and a face filled with wrinkles of burden. A series of holes around the figure poured light into the room. He sensed the masked entity's presence behind him. The entity walked past him. The figure wore the same white suit as every previous encounter, but the mask bore no expression this time.

"This is Alexander," Anselm said. Overwhelming melancholy rolled off the entity.

"We made it so very long ago," the masked man said. "The herald of the recreation of the world. We struggled to remember him then; it was here to remind us. He gave us renewed purpose." Anselm clenched his fist.

"I don't want to hear any more of loss, not from you," Anselm said. The masked figure twitched. It felt strange for Anselm to see this frightening entity be vulnerable. The masked figure paid Anselm no mind, seeming to forget his presence and rising anger.

"This is where he found us, our home after the death of the world."

"Show me something, or maybe I'll let Vigilant put an end to you," Anselm growled.

The entity held up his hand. The carving vanished. A figure

appeared in front of Anselm, a burly man in furs wielding a sword and a crown. The long hair, white flecked beard, and a muscular warrior frame beyond that of a typical Dark Age survivor. Anselm stared upon Alexander Blackthorne, the man that had rebuilt the world.

"It's done, Eon," Alexander said.

He knelt, and a figure emerged for the darkened corner of the chamber. The figure hobbled out. The figure wore an off-white suit and a weathered mask.

"You need not kneel for us, we're not your masters. Your part in the Algorithm is greater than ours. Rise," Eon said. "It can finally begin as it was always meant to be. You have made us proud. You have created the first new nation and it thrives beyond expectation," the masked man said.

Anselm watched his revered ancestor fill with pride at the words, his decades of hard work fully realized. His ancestor had built a mighty kingdom over decades, and Anselm had let it fall in hours. The notion made him want to hurt his betrayers and himself all the more.

"Are you ready?" Alexander said. The masked man looked down as if in shame.

"We're still . . . separated from ourselves," the masked man replied.

Anselm pondered the meaning of the words, this entity behaved far different in the visions than the demented, villainous type that guided him forward.

"Can it be fixed?" Alexander asked.

"We're not sure," the masked man said. From what Anselm gathered, the fix was still pending. Alexander closed his eyes in disappointment.

"Fear not," Eon replied. "Our power is returning. We will guide the world to break free of the loop. Soon other nations will follow. We will share with you the law. It shall govern the evolution of the world. It is a compact between humanity and us," the masked man said.

"So is this really the end?" the king asked.

"It is," the masked man said.

"Must it truly be this way?" the king asked. The masked man's head reared back and then snapped forward with a face riddled with sorrow.

"No one else must know of our presence; this knowledge must die with you. You'll not see us, but we will always be there. You're strong. The world will prosper, and it will be from your efforts. Your family has the potential far beyond others. They will bear a terrible burden, but we know they will overcome any adversity," the masked man said.

"Thank you, Eon," Alexander replied. Alexander embraced the masked man as one would a father.

"Farewell . . . son." The figure grew transparent and fell apart in a fog. The fog dissipated.

The visions ended. Anselm stood beside Eon. He was at a loss for words. There had been a symbiotic relationship between the Blackthornes and Eon from the very beginning; Anselm wondered just how much influence this creature held over his family.

"You lure me here for this?" Anselm asked.

"We needed you to see while our powers remained. We never controlled you. We guided you throughout the ages. Your family is special. The Blackthornes are the shapers of the world. They have endured much. You have endured much. You passed the test. The final iteration can begin. And you must continue to endure. You were born for this. You can't escape it. The world will collapse without you."

MELVIN

Darkness fell. The rest of Melvin's new crew arrived at an area on the gulf coast used by Vigilant as a weigh station between the eastern cities. Roald "Skully" Jimenez and Edward "Edsplosion" Jeks were geared up for the stealth mission. Liz wore stitched-together pants and boots; dressing for stealth as best as a giant lizard man could. Skully, the skull cap-wearing scout, led them to a Vigilant hotspot.

Melvin's infamous gang was a collection of two dozen original members after the two founders. The gang operated in squads, rotating out members while the remainder of Melvin's gang protected their headquarters or sought out recruits. His current squad included a soft-spoken ex-gang hitman and an overly-eager demolitions expert. Skully was a master assassin and the best choice for sneaking around. Ed, despite his psychotic tendencies or because of them, was excellent at firepower and traps for when things went south.

The quartet made the last mile trek on foot, hugging the coastline until they were out of the tourist spots. The final mile saw the group crouching, crawling, and dipping in and out of the natural hiding spots. A gaping maw vomited its rocky guts onto the coastline. *Trespassers Will Be Shot* signs gave Vigilant a mile radius of secrecy.

"Remember we do this quiet, no fireworks if we can help it. If they find out we're here, they'll put this place on lockdown. I bet she's ripe for the plucking," Melvin said gleefully, rubbing his hands together.

Weapons equipped with silencers were kept at the ready. A few red blobs were spotted at the mouth of the cave. Melvin's crew took up positions to get a better view. Vigilant scouts took up defensive positions outside the cave. They scanned the area using binoculars. Melvin and his crew flattened against the ground. Liz adjusted his pants and squatted down beside them, watching them yet saying nothing. The desert camo Liz wore worked surprisingly well, though anyone paying attention would see the massive rock crawling about.

"We save the trolls," Liz said.

"If we can, but not likely," Melvin said.

A series of thirty trucks rolled out of the cave and departed for the west. The gang moved in on the location, sneaking past the patrols. Each person showed up in a different area around the mouth of the cave. Melvin's team took positions at the top of the cave, watching through the holes above, while Melvin and Liz ventured inside. The cave functioned as a natural warehouse. A train track extended into the darkest recess of the cave. Two roads on either side of the rail track allow alternative travel to Vigilant's headquarters. Lights were set up through the caves, hooked up to a collection of generators lining the cavern walls.

"Train tracks? They have underground trains, big enough to haul trucks in 'em. That's nuts!" he exclaimed, immediately covering his mouth.

A skeleton crew of Vigilant patrolled the cave. Melvin moved carefully, knowing how well the night vision equipment he had stolen from them worked.

"Something tells me this is the tip of the shitberg," Melvin said. Liz looked at him.

"Party time?" he asked. Melvin let out a series of short breaths.

"Party time it is," Melvin said.

They quietly maneuvered around the cave and the Vigilant patrols. Melvin slinked his way behind some empty transport boxes where none ventured.

Hours passed without any sign of the train. One of the patrolmen caught a nap in an empty shipping container converted into a rec room. After a while, the patrols took seats and started a campfire near the mouth. The Vigilant men joked and snacked on canned beans and dried meat. Melvin lay quietly atop one of the containers.

A few hours crawled by. Something roared within the cave tunnel. Two white lights followed the sounds. The train emerged from the darkness at remarkable speed, slowing and stopping right in front of the snoozing men. Melvin and his crew moved on the train. A new round of patrolmen and trucks emerged from the large compartment at the back of the train. When Melvin gave the all-clear, everyone boarded the back of the train right behind the fresh troops. Skully went in first, finding no troops inside the vehicle storage area. The new troops argued with tired ones, which allowed Melvin's gang to hide among the storage. The doors closed automatically. The train jerked. The storage container shifted under their restraints.

With a loud clang and a jolt, the train sped off. Human sounds increased in volume and number from the other cars. The men quickly tired of the patrol and moved to other business.

An unknown amount of time passed before the train came to a halt. The storage doors opened. Melvin and the others waited a few moments to make sure men weren't waiting outside. They arrived at an underground station, putting the likes of Ellora to shame. Flood lights made stealth much more difficult. Three other trains set in the station with a dozen men gathered around each. Moments after leaving the train, large transport elevators doors slid open, filled with troop and supply trucks. The trucks drove into the backs of the other trains, giving Melvin's gang time to slip away.

Dozens of elevators and a handful of stairways, including some that moved, led up into the light. Captives held at gunpoint were escorted from the train opposite Melvin. The captives appeared to be men and women, many of which had metal enhancements visible through their tattered rags. All troops in the station pointed guns at the prisoners, the same weapons that pacified the trolls from earlier. With Vigilant occupied, Skully motioned the others toward an unguarded stairway furthest from the traffic. The team regrouped at the top.

"Here we go," Melvin said. "Be ready for a—"

Melvin told his gang of thieves he stepped out into the outside world. Suddenly the aspiring thieves' mouths collectively hit the floor when greeted with the sight of a floating city surrounded by waterfalls suspended over a massive basin.

"The legends are true," Melvin said.

Obelisks burned across the alien city. Melvin peered over the edge of the street in front of him. Buildings and streets like floating tiers descended to the waters below. Vehicles drove through all floors of the vertical metropolis, thankfully not enough to cover the whole city. Light flashed around a tower at the city's center. Screams soon followed.

A few thousand Vigilant soldiers moved through the city. Soldiers wore robes and the best government issue reinforced armor, repainted to match the crimsons and whites of Vigilant. Blue trails streamed from soldiers' rifles in an empty parking lot converted into a firing range. Liz practically glowed with joy.

"Cool," he beamed.

"The motherload," Melvin said, chomping at the bit for the

menagerie of treasures ripe for the plucking. Melvin sent Skully and Ed to scout the outer rings, telling them to meet at a location in the east that Melvin would mark.

Melvin and his companions chose not to dawdle anymore. Quietly they moved to the eastern part of the city, following the areas with inactive streetlamps. The duo stopped far too many times to gaze at the gravity-defying structures. There was a feeling in Melvin's gut, the same one he had experienced beneath the White Woods.

"Place creeps me out," Melvin said. "Let's be careful."

The pair walked through the darkened streets of the eastern districts. Melvin avoided the sides of the platforms to keep his vertigo in check.

"Wonder how many people took the express route," Melvin said. Liz gave Melvin a slight push. Melvin fell forward. After a few seconds, Melvin realized he was not falling to his death.

"Ass," Melvin replied, shaky. Liz chuckled at his expense.

Melvin unfroze and silently moved through the city toward the multi-story buildings on the east platforms with the least Vigilant activity. Soft blue light rose over the dense jungles walls around them.

"Let's set up a base and go from there," Melvin replied.

The two approached eventually stumbled across a building with an open door, narrowly missing the creeping daylight. A series of doors and stairways climbed up inside the buildings. Each door had no lock, only a small rectangular screen where a knob was typically found.

"Reminds me of one of those grocery scanner thingys," Melvin said, holding an imaginary scanner. Liz didn't know what a scanner was, nor ever experienced a grocery. "Food store," Melvin clarified.

Liz punched a hole in the first door and tore it off the sliding attachments. A couch, table, and three small rooms lay inside. The apartment had no decorations of any kind, a depressingly bland living space for such an ornate city. Melvin entered the kitchen and threw open the door of the thin refrigerator occupying half of the kitchen.

"No food . . . guess it was too much to ask from some wonder meat or space beans," Melvin said, not relishing another meal of dried meat and water that tasted about as old.

Liz removed his backpack and doled out the proper amount of meat and water. Melvin discovered a long time ago the perk of a troll able to carry nearly a thousand pounds. He walked into the bedroom, yet another bland, empty space.

"Got two beds . . . small beds," Melvin said, disappointed. "Probably won't support ya, bud."

"Okay," Liz said.

"Guess we'll hang out 'til sundown." Melvin and Liz took a seat on the unused couch. The couch groaned under the weight but held firm. Quietly the two ate their seasoned snallygaster meat. A few hundred meals ago, he loved the stuff, especially when he'd killed it himself. From the couch, the two had a view of the shuddered window. Melvin felt Liz's eyes on him.

"Where's your son?" Liz said. Melvin sighed, he grew tired of the question. Melvin kept tight-lipped about his personal life, even from his pal.

"Don't you want a better story, like the one about the singin' toaster?" Melvin asked with a hint of bitterness. Liz growled.

"All right, Mercy," Melvin said. Liz perked up.

Melvin looked down at the floor. He paused, looking for the strength to relive his past.

"My son is dead because of me," he said, drudging up the second set of events that led him to Joseph Kerr and the rebellion. He remembered skulking around Heartland after brain damage, and a few bad calls, got him ousted from command. His brain grew muddled at times. Without the support of his prestigious

Whitehall family, he relocated to a town a few dozen miles from his future home in Ellora.

Melvin's wife followed him every step of the way, even after the injury. They had a secret off-and-on romance during his career. Like him, she was damaged. Elsa was a daughter of a raider-turned-petty-criminal supposed to be reformed. She struggled to escape her old tendencies. After Melvin's fall, the pair changed identities and settled down in a small house close enough to necessity yet far enough to stretch his legs.

"Before I knew it, she popped out a wonderful little shit," Melvin continued.

Melvin spent lazy days with his son, teaching him hunting, fishing, and the small things that made life worth living. The double-edged sword of medication left his mind clearer, though it quickly drained his wallet. He felt the flashes of anger to this day. He relived only the bad moments of his life.

"Not sure where it went wrong. She came to loathe me. In truth, she started hitting me first. I tolerated it, knowing how much worse I could hurt her. We brought out the worst in each other. Meds only worked so long. I never wanted to hit back, even after everything she said and did to me. I found myself not being able to control myself sometimes." His mind flashed back to those times; he felt his fist connect with her jaw as clearly as hers would on his.

"Decided to bug out for a bit. I spent one night drunk and ended up in some hay bales behind a barn. I came back the next morning . . . " Melvin paused.

"My son was gone. He snuck out and went looking for me. My wife despised me, but Willy loved me through and through," Melvin said, still holding back the sorrow wanting to leak out of his eyes.

"I found him two days later. Fell down a hole in the woods.

Used all the money I had left to bury him," Melvin said. Melvin blocked the memory of holding his body from his mind.

"She went back to crime, killed during some deal gone wrong, I heard. When she left, I picked a direction and walked until I fell into Mammoth Cave. I found a city in there. I decided to stay," Melvin said.

Melvin looked back out the window, the sense of vertigo buried under years of mistakes. He let out one huge exhale. A bit of sorrow leaked from Liz's eyes as well.

"When you found me out there, part of me wished you hadn't," Melvin finally said. "But some good came out of it. It's good to have you here Wil . . . Liz" Liz placed a large gorilla arm across Melvin's shoulder for comfort.

"Friends," Liz said with a toothy grin.

"The best," Melvin said. Liz yawned, washing Melvin in his swampy breath. Sleep tight."

Liz sprawled out on the couch while Melvin handled the first watch and prepared to contact Skully.

ZORA

DRAKE'S TRUCK CRUSHED the thick growth of the jungle floor under his treads.

"Smooth ride, they said," he whined, bumping his head on the roof. Zora tried not to laugh at Drake, despite flailing around herself.

"Told you to recheck the map," she said.

The pair drove east to the Yucatan peninsula, a tourist attraction for the adventurous that was littered with ruins from the time preceding the Old World. They traveled without Thos, who emphatically told them not to worry about him and go enjoy themselves. Drake navigated the jungles back to the roads cutting through the areas of jungles used for travel.

"Thought you wanted excitement? There's a whole lot out here," Drake said with a smirk.

"I wasn't *dying* to see the sights," Zora replied.

Zora needed a break from civilization with only Drake. That wasn't her only reason for setting up this trip, but she'd timed it for a bit of fun. Discovering no signs of any more secret labs, she opted for more satisfying exploration.

She soaked in the majesty of the lush jungle. Trees of all sizes spiraled up the sky into a thick canopy raining light through any hole available. Streams wound down hills, going under bridges and dropping into enticing pools. Car-sized leaves left her in awe. Zora uttered wows of childlike amazement at rainbow-colored birds, monstrous snakes, giant turtles, striped snallygasters, and black cats lazily judging them from the trees. Crumbling stones peeked out from behind distant trees.

"No matter where we go, there's always beauty," Zora said.

Drake eyed her and smiled, a sign she had come to understand as him fumbling to say nice things yet not be overly sappy. A few bumps forced his eyes back on the road. Statues of the unknown, shimmering material peppered the area, bizarre against the ancient structures of the Maya.

Drake and Zora stopped periodically throughout the jungle trek, making sure to take in every marking, ruin, and natural formation of note. Drake captured each moment with his camera. The two made a pit stop at the azure waters of an unnamed pool at the bottom of a waterfall pouring down from a stone face.

They snacked on chicken tortas courtesy of Drake's "food guy," and cherry soda courtesy of Thos. Zora dipped behind a bush, to Drake's confusion. She emerged in a two-piece swimsuit and dove in the tranquil waters.

"You wanted me to have some excitement, right?" Zora asked. Drake sighed, a sign he was about to be pushed outside his comfort zone.

"I didn't bring swimwear," he said.

Something about one of the nation's most formidable warriors fretting over swimwear made her laugh. She slowly removed her swimwear and tossed it onto the grass. She waved him in. Drake looked around and hastily popped off his clothes. Zora laughed as the only other vehicle in the region passed by in time to get a visual of the bare-assed Drake.

"Think I saw a flash," Drake grumbled.

Drake's rigid demeanor loosened. He sprinted toward the

waters, cannonballing in. Drake was as shocked at his actions as Zora.

"You're really taking my advice," Zora said, spitting out a mouthful of water.

"Gotta live sometime," Drake said.

Drake and Zora leisurely swam in the pool. Zora loved the spontaneity. It also helped seeing Drake not get lost in his own head, although she saw the shakes and sleepless nights of the man's past clawing away at him.

"I needed this," Drake said. "I've been seeing Anselm, Aric... all the people I've killed."

"Counseling?" Zora asked.

"Been slacking," he replied, showing his disappointment.

"No more slacking," she said, incentivizing the action with a kiss.

"Won't happen again, ma'am," he replied, with a rare second smile.

A few kisses and an hour of floating later, they pressed on. The joy quickly vanished as masked statues came into view throughout the jungle.

"These can't be Mayan. I can't tell which is worse, the smiling ones or the frowning ones," Drake said.

"I can't get away from him," Zora said.

A few more rest stops later, the two arrived at the ruins of Chactun. Pieces of the ancient Mayan city Chactun stretched out across over fifty acres in the jungle areas furthest away from modern civilization. Drake parked the truck in the designated area. Zora and Drake proceeded on foot. They marveled at the remnants of step pyramids, plazas, living areas, and what appeared to be basketball courts. The growing thoughts of the masked horror vanished at the sights of structures that had now survived the end of the world twice over. People walked across the ruins of the pyramid in front of them. One of the women atop the pyramid saw the two approach.

"Welcome, glad to finally meet northern Freemen," she said. Hundreds of people moved through the ruins of the ancient city.

"I gotta say, you guys pick wild places to live," Drake said.

The Freemen of eastern Mexico lived in the area a few dozen miles west of the ruins of Chactun, serving as the protectors of the most complete set of Mayan ruins still in existence. Like many pockets of Freemen, they lived simply to avoid becoming so large the government would violently object. Drake stopped and scanned the trees, keeping his fingers on his gun. Zora laughed.

"No monsters this time," Zora assured, glancing at her host to make sure it was true. Drake waited a few moments just to be sure. He cracked a nervous smile before allowing himself to relax.

Various tents and wooden buildings covered the areas around the ancient structures, though no one lived inside or altered the original architecture. Drake and Zora walked through the city, taking the wonder of the ancient ruins. Freemen across New Prosperity, regardless of culture or clothing, shared a desire of escaping overcrowded cities and overbearing laws.

Drake and Zora walked over to areas between some of the most enormous pyramids. Curious citizens approached them, offering them snacks and bombarding them with questions about the northern Freemen. They overate and drank the Freemen's exotic delights. Zora spent some time taking in the local color. They walked up the steps of the largest pyramid where everyone liked to gather. As with all Freemen communities, respected members offered advice but held no official power. The two took the time to look out over the jungle domain. Zora breathed in deep yet another alien world hidden from the rest of New Prosperity. A voice from behind caused them to jump out of their skin.

"Never ceases to amaze" the voice said.

Both turned around and nearly fell off the pyramid at the

hulking, shirtless man. The man was muscular, with a head disproportionately small to the rest of him. Zora was starting to wonder
how many trolls existed in the world. The man's friendly smile
diminished his intimidating stature.

"Welcome to Freemen jungles," he said. "I'm Ix."

Ix gave Drake a welcoming pat on the back, almost knocking
him on his ass. Drake reoriented himself. This troll was far more
articulate and well-adjusted than Liz. Ix waved his two guests to
the others conversing atop the pyramid. After small talk and sight-
seeing stops, Zora switched to a more serious topic.

"Have you had any run-ins with Vigilant?" she asked, her
question directed squarely at Ix.

"No, though I've heard they're active in the west," Ix said.

Drake explained the situation to the Freemen. Ix walked over
to the western edge of the pyramid.

"Quite disturbing," Ix said.

"I think it's connected to that," Zora said, pointing to a
masked statue in the distance.

"And silver obelisks," Drake added. Zora described the objects
in question.

"My uncle has destroyed a few of these. Said Gideon worship-
ers revered them," she said.

"Very disturbing," Ix said.

"I've heard reports of such things out in the deep jungles," Ix
said. "We've had a few scholarly types out over the years. According to the last one, this thing is almost as old as New Prosperity
itself." Drake and Zora perked up.

"Who was the last one?" Drake asked.

"I forgot her name, but she was completely out of her gourd,"
Ix said. "Kept muttering about falling from grace. Explored the
jungle for years. And looked it. I remember she had orange eyes.
Couple years ago."

Zora had an inkling that things at hand were far beyond what anyone could have expected. Zora theorized the meanings of the statues, Zora's encounters, cults, worsening conflicts, and Vigilant's presence in Mexico. All the theorizing left her with no answers, only frightening possibilities. Zora had more to say, though she was afraid of Drake's reaction. Ix sensed it too; he knew the other reason why she was here. Both Ix and Zora looked at Drake. His brow shot up.

"What's this?" he asked. Zora had made numerous trips to various Freemen communities over the past few years, not just for pleasure.

"The reason I've been meeting…" she said. Drake didn't need to hear the rest.

"No," he replied.

"We both know the government won't tolerate us much longer," Zora said. "We'll soon be labeled enemies. They'll bring war on us and we'll be ready." Drake frowned.

"I respect what you're doing here," Zora continued. "But the government is the enemy and you know it. They'll come after us once this is over."

Drake cursed.

"I hate to admit it, but you're right. I . . . guess I can't ignore it anymore."

"Will you stand with us?" Zora asked.

Ix cleared his throat.

"There'll be time for that tomorrow. Enjoy the day while you can," Ix said.

Drake and Zora dropped the subject for now, choosing to spend some more time relishing the exotic paradise. Zora made sure to analyze as many structures as time allowed, and Drake struggled to keep up with Zora's supercharged enthusiasm.

Exhausted, they climbed the pyramid currently unoccupied. They sat atop the pyramid. Side by side, they watched the sun go down.

GREGOR

GREGOR AWOKE IN a giant feather bed with silk blankets, naked and exhausted. The Mexican sun beamed through the window. His eyes widened when he realized what he'd done. He rolled over and flung his hand out, connecting with the supple flesh of a raven-haired Mexican woman. He vented his frustrations by letting out a slew of curses. Meridiana rolled over onto him, resting her breasts upon his arm. It only worsened the sensation that he still lusted after her. The woman looked down at the rising covers and giggled. Gregor threw his hands over the spot.

"Did we?" he asked. She nodded.

"Did I?" She nodded.

"Shit. You enthralled me!" Gregor said.

"Not exactly," she said. "I illicit strong emotions in humans, I succumb to them myself. Had we not lost control, you would've killed me." *I would have*, he thought.

Gregor's sat up and rested his head in his hands.

"I broke my oath," Gregor said. Gregor stared at the floor while he gathered his thoughts. Meridiana hugged Gregor, her skin feverishly warm.

"You needed to see her again," she said.

"That wasn't her," Gregor said.

Meridiana's human form melted away. In its place was a feminine albino with no face and horn-like appendages extending from the top of the head and wrapping down around the ears. Her appearance morphed into that of a horned mannequin. Gregor realized he didn't like mannequins. He let out another loud curse and barrel-rolled off the bed. The demon flashed back to the form of the buxom Mexican woman that she, and most clients, preferred. She frowned, suggesting the form reveal was an accident.

"Shh. You'll wake the others!" she scolded. "You've been out almost two days, you should be recovered. I'll bring you some food. Eat then leave."

"Two days? Others?"

"Your companions are safe and untouched. They have been given rooms. And yes, they know my nature and that I'm no killer . . . otherwise we wouldn't be having this conversation. They await your orders," she said.

Meridiana crawled out of bed, threw on a silk nightgown, and seductively walked out of the room. Gregor watched her. She laughed as if she had seen him. Gregor bit his lip to stop another cavalcade of profanity. Meridiana returned a few minutes later, rolling a cart with a platter of roasted corn, braised beef, buttered bread, and sickly sweet cherries.

Gregor ate like there was no tomorrow, trying to forget he'd spent the night in the throes of passion with a demoness. He found the strength to hobble over to the bathroom for a hot shower. After his shower, he returned to the bedroom, finding Merdiana at the window.

"Wouldn't kill you to be a little more grateful," Meridiana said. Gregor rolled his eyes. *It was a spell,* Gregor told himself.

"I'll be grateful when you answer my questions," Gregor said. "Where are the runaways, why are you protecting them, who from, and what in the holy hell is going on around here?"

Meridiana approached Gregor and extended her hand. He did

not accept it. Together they walked through the halls of the castle, past a locked door that roused his suspicions. Meridiana took Gregor into the western tower that served as a laboratory. Inside, a man sat at a table with a set of tools. When he noticed Gregor, he gave a wave and returned to his business.

"I'll leave you two boys alone," Meridiana said, closing the door.

"It was only a matter of time," the man said.

"Vigilant suffers not a single demon to live," Gregor said. *Was a spell, definitely a spell,* Gregor thought.

"You weren't sent here for that," she said. "You were sent you here for someone else."

"And you are?" Gregor asked. The man cleared his throat.

"Paulo Ramirez . . . of Vigilant," he replied. Gregor swore he saw his life flash before his eyes.

"I think my brain finally gave out," Gregor said, placing his hand on his forehead at this horrible fever dream.

"You know if they find out what we've done, they'll kill us both!" Gregor exclaimed, possibly tipping off everyone in greater Mexico.

"They already wanted me dead," Paulo said. "A few of us started questioning our CO's methods, not sure he has our best interests in mind. I heard about Meri protecting Vigilant's enemies. I figured this would buy me a little time. The other defectors were all killed, so I guess it helped. I'm curious how they found out she was a demon . . . or that we were here." Paulo increasing sweat decried his anxiety. *Why is he not mentioning the witch? He protecting her?*

Paulo made even wilder claims, including using troll labor and conspiring with the Void. Gregor threw up his hands, expending what little precious energy remained in him.

"That's absurd. Trading guns for slaves?" Gregor asked, hoping hearing the words a second time would help him process them. Paulo leaned back, leery of his guest.

"He needs them to expedite Killswitch," Paulo said.

"If what you say about Matthias is true, I'll investigate," Gregor replied, not hiding his annoyance. Gregor walked over to the table. "But I'm still hunting a witch." He noticed Paulo's brow furrow at the mention of witches.

"No witches here," Paulo said. Gregor sensed the lie.

"We'll get back to that. Tell me about Killswitch," Gregor said.

Paulo, self-described as one of Matthias's top researchers and inquisitors, explained in detail the nanomachines found in all forms of life. He handed Gregor his notebook. Gregor thumbed through the notes about these genetically engineered organic, artificial, and cybernetic cells. With the right frequency, demon cells could be destroyed long-distance with better efficiency than their special swords. Matthias's impalement spikes overloaded the city's barriers and got him closer to the signal drawing him to the inner sanctum where the mask hid the source of the world's woes.

"He talked about some kind of false god controlling the Compact . . . was hoping that's a bad joke," Gregor said.

"I've never seen it myself, but all the masked statues we've found across that nation suggest it's real," Paulo said. "He calls it Eon, the arch-demon. He believes he can destroy it at a cellular level." It all made sense.

"So he's turning the city into a giant EMPX. What about the Compact?" Gregor said. Paulo nodded.

"The Compact will continue, albeit not in the hands of demons."

"Doesn't sound bad to me," Gregor said.

"Human hands can be just as bad, though," Paulo said. "And that's not counting the ways this could go wrong. I used to believe in him. I was there, when we found the city. He led Vigilant through the Uninhabited. He made it through the storms untouched. Whatever that signal was, it helped him avoid every bolt. That mask has given him power, but I think it's taken his mind. He's growing paranoid. He went out on a mission with Sentinel Alvarez. Only one of them came back. The closer he gets to the heart of the city, the worse it gets."

Gregor walked away from the table and ran his fingers through his beard. Though Gregor understood Paulo's feelings, he felt the ex-crusader was hiding something important. Paulo stiffened, further validating Gregor's concerns.

"Seems a bit crazy for him to want you dead for protesting, but Anselm once pushed me out a window for similar reasons," Gregor said.

"Then you understand," Paulo said, fingers easing off his sidearm. "Desperate leaders and world-shaping technology don't mix."

"In my experience, using Old World machines seldom turns out well," Gregor said. "This could backfire to horrific effect. On the other hand, a chance to eliminate all demons . . . this may be the first time I'm in favor of taking the risk. Maybe this is dementia." Paulo laughed.

"Whatever is locked up inside the city could be for good reason," Paulo said. Gregor cocked his eyebrow and folded his arms. It wasn't Gregor's place to question his CO. He wasn't one to tolerate it either, but there were numerous ways this operation could go wrong. He needed answers from the source and to prepare for the worst.

"I appreciate the information," Gregor warned. "Don't interfere with this mission or you'll be coming' back with me."

"What about Meri?" Paulo asked, showing his infatuation with her. Gregor toyed with the possibility of sparing a demon.

"Worry about yourself," Gregor said. Paulo sneered.

Gregor walked out of the room and into the main hall, where his subordinates sat in plush chairs drinking coffee. Raul held two mugs, handing one to Gregor when he drew close.

"Hard at work," Gregor said.

Gregor took a swig of coffee, a delightful mixture of cinnamon and crème compared to the usual bland roast that tasted like beans straight from grave dirt. Gregor allowed an "mmm" to slip out. The young crusader smiled at him.

Gregor took a moment to savor his coffee and chilaquiles. He greedily ate fast and wild, practicing what Cedric called "prison rules." Gregor shared what he learned from Paulo, including the disturbing notion of the murder of Sentinel Alvarez. Raul shared information on Meridiana's other clients, none of importance and all fleeing the castle.

"Good work, soldier," Gregor said. Neither showed any physical characteristics associated with joy.

"If what Paulo says is true, why would Matthias send us after someone willing to spill the beans on him? Especially if he told me about my father," Raul asked.

"Probably think he's dead. Meridiana is protecting someone else, think he decided to join in. There's a locked door not down the hall from her chambers," Gregor said.

"The witch," Raul said.

"Has to be. Not sure why this one is so special," Gregor said, finishing off his morning beverage.

"Apostates are an interesting thing," Raul said. "I never understood why the Compact forbid it, but this Eon seems to welcome a certain few into his flock. Is it based on skill or something?"

"Let's ask her," Gregor said.

"What's the play?"

"Search around the castle, make sure there are no other surprises," Gregor said. "And find our weapons. I'll speak with the demon again, kill her if I have to. I can distract her while you find a key for that door."

Raul cocked an eyebrow.

"Distract?" Raul said, with clear implications. Gregor raised his hand.

"Find our damn weapons," Gregor replied.

Gregor made his way to the courtyard and the blurry dots belonging to Mexico City. Meridiana wandered through the garden.

"Come to *pump* me for info again?" she asked. Gregor gritted his teeth, fighting himself on his decision. He denied his goal wasn't purely altruistic.

"No. I need . . . I wanted to see her one more time," he said. The demon turned to face him, morphing into the visage of Daniela precisely as he remembered her. The naked woman approached him with the same loving smile he'd treasured and lamented. It had been almost three decades since he had abandoned that life for duty.

"I feel the love you had," Meridiana said.

She pressed herself against him. Gregor told the story of first encountering Daniela in the city outside of Niagara Falls after a mission. The mission mattered little, an Old World machine in the earth leaking poison into some local farmland. He passed back through town and met a local merchant girl. He spent a whole day chatting with her, and from that day on, he made numerous trips to visit her until her place became his part-time home.

"I never married her, but I wanted to," Gregor said. "I thought I could juggle home life and run Vigilant. My brother told me I'd have to make a choice eventually. Someone once told me we had to sacrifice such things for the greater good. She wanted children . . . and so did I. I knew it'd get in the way of my duties. I broke it off. Little did I know my brother chose to do the same thing he told me to forsake; happened a few years later, so he was probably just as surprised, to be fair. He quit the order and started the Freemen village outside of the capital. I returned to the falls when I found out, but she had left. Eventually my brother ended up with two little girls and a wife that died way too young. After denying myself the chance for a family, I couldn't bear to see them. I severed contact with them for years."

Gregor looked into Meridiana's face, letting the layers of guilt welling in his chest to wash away.

"I never saw you . . . her again." Gregor held onto the imitation of his wife for a few moments longer, wishing he could believe in the lie. "Thank you," he said.

"Maybe not all you labeled as demons are as you believe," Meridiana said. Gregor shook his head.

"Perhaps not," he replied. "The whole world is mad." The demon smiled and took the form of an unassuming middle-aged woman.

"Now go and don't trouble us again," she said.

She walked back inside and threw on a simple cotton shirt, jeans, and worn-out shoes. Meridiana disappeared down the hall.

Gregor met up with Raul and his troops, carrying undamaged gunblades and all of Vigilant's tools. Raul handed Gregor his gunblade and utility belt.

"Key?" Gregor asked. Raul shook his head. "Then we break it down."

Gregor led his team to the locked door. Harsh sunlight created beams through the open windows that guided him to his destination. In front of the iron door stood Meridiana in her native form, with Paulo at her side.

"Still you persist?" Meridiana asked, words tinged with genuine disappointment.

"We came here for the witch. Get out of my way and I'll let you both live," Gregor warned.

"Don't let him have her," Paulo said, pulling out a rifle. Gregor and the Alvarez siblings raised their weapons and pointed them at Paulo and Meridiana.

"This witch you harbor has killed dozens. That can't stand," Gregor said.

A series of faint pricks danced inside Gregor's skull. Meridiana's skin blurred and shifted into a new form. Hot blood surged through Gregor's body when the demon shifted into the form of his niece.

"Don't you dare!" Gregor said, his tone lowering to an animal growl.

"I can't control it!" Meridiana screamed.

Paulo's arms trembled. His face contorted. He fought against himself. Raul tackled Paulo as he battled with his muscles. A revelation hit Gregor.

"They're enthralled!" he exclaimed. Meridiana's form continued to shift.

"Lora, no!" Meridiana cried.

Paulo's finger pressed down on his rifle trigger. Raul kicked the rifle away from the thrashing Paulo. He hit Paulo's face repeatedly until consciousness left him. Meridiana's transformed into a vaingloria, her fingers extended into flesh-rending claws. Gregor turned the dial on his gunblade to the max. The sword-gun hummed to life. Meridiana rushed toward Gregor, slashing wildly at anything in her path. Meridiana's swipes were clumsy. Gregor continuously jumped back, waiting for an opening.

"Leave, please!" Meridiana said.

For the first time in his life, Gregor pitied a demon. The witch gained full control over the demon. Meridiana increasingly precise attacks came hairs away from dicing Gregor to bits. Gregor dipped below Meridiana's swipes. With a single stroke, he cut straight through Meridiana's thin waist. Meridiana's top half shifted back to her human form. She looked back up at Gregor. Meridiana died with her eyes locked on her killer. Gregor took a moment to collect himself. Raul got to his feet and grabbed the cutting torch.

"Get the door," Gregor commanded, walking away from the dead demon.

Sparks flew from the cutting torch as it made easy work of the iron door's lock. The lock hit the floor. Gregor returned to the scene. He gave the door a hard kick, but it didn't budge. Vigilant pushed with all their might. The door rattled and grew warm.

A loud crash reverberated from inside the room. The door gave way. At the back of the room was a simple bed. Lying on the floor was a woman, machine from head to toe. The intricate, complex nature of various metals woven through the body suggested this was a witch unlike any he'd encountered before. Gregor scooped up the woman, thankfully much lighter than she appeared. With their business concluded, Vigilant left the castle with the unconscious bodies of Paulo and the witch.

CASS

Cass sat alone in her empty house, staring at her cellphone. The news of Yadira's miscarriage hit Cass much harder than expected. Cass attempted call after call to reach Thos. Out of the twelve times she called, only twice did the signal survive long enough to get through.

Cass stayed busy as often as possible with her only friend in the locked-down wing of the Prosperity Medical Center. Time spent in soup kitchens and with the Habitat for Prosperity community projects soaked up most of her off-the-clock time.

Cass prepared herself for a different kind of meeting. She colored her hair and popped in her contacts, her daily morning routine whether she left the house or not. She touched her side, feeling the sting of the bruises on her sides. The bruises had begun to happen much more frequently over the last few weeks, as did the bleeding. Already having access to the best medicine and elite care money could buy, she began to worry her defects were spiraling out of control. For the majority of Cass's life, she had suffered from numerous ailments that included hemophilia, a common issue for defects. It was easy to despair, but Thos always pulled her out of the darkness, and she strived to return the favor.

There wasn't time to concern herself with ailments for the

moment. Cass cleaned herself up, threw on some clothes, and prepared for her meeting. She walked out onto her private marina. A few small boats sailed across the clear waters under cloudless skies. Kane waited on the pier and nervously tapped his foot while using binoculars on all things. The knight wore shorts and a dark polo shirt. Something about hardened warriors in shorts made Cass chuckle. Cass devoured a protein bar and a glass of orange juice.

"Guards give you trouble?" Cass asked. Kane turned his binoculing on Cass.

"No, probably think we're having an affair," Kane said, placing his binoculars into the pouch of his harness.

"See anything?" she asked.

"People enjoying life. Nice day to go fishing," Kane replied. Cass invited Kane into her home and the two sat down at the kitchen table.

"Am I being forced into something else?" Cass asked.

So far, Cass gained no valuable intel during her spy missions at Prosperity Hall. Kane sighed. Cass stared daggers at him.

"Mr. Abaddon wants to speak with you; he sent me to give you a heads up. A car will pick you up; they will cover your head and take you to him. I want you to know I was against this."

"Even with my influence, I'm still being pushed around. His protection better be worth it," Cass said. Kane turned away, suggesting he understood better than she realized.

"I'm going to visit Yadira, so he can wait a bit," Cass said.

"Fine, but reveal nothing," Kane warned. "And keep the recorder on."

Cass drove herself to PMC with a gaggle of bodyguards not far behind. Throngs of well-wishers and obnoxious journalists clogged the streets around the hospital. In the crowd, Cass was unable to decipher friend from foe. Journalists bum-rushed Cass when they saw her. Cass hated journalists; the title meant nothing more than professional defamer. Bodyguards shoved the journalists away.

Cass walked up to the front doors. The crowd, and overzealous guards, made it difficult to get in the hospital hassle-free. Yadira's guards gave invasive pat downs to everyone entering, including Cass.

"Sorry, ma'am," the guard said, uncomfortable at groping a member of the country's number one family.

At a time like this, she imagined what witty remark Thos would say. Cass said nothing. Inside she walked past the wall of guards by the receptionist's desk. The receptionist consulted with the head guard.

"You can go up," she said.

Cass weaved through the excessive protection filling the lobby to the elevators. Cass rode the elevator to the tenth floor. Government agents walked through the halls, giving Cass a second pat-down and no apology. The agents motioned Cass to the largest room at the back. A sullen Enton came from the opposite direction, giving her a solemn nod.

Cass knocked on the door. She opened the door after she was met with no response. Yadira stared out the window. Cass took a seat and placed her hand on Yadira's.

"I was going to name him Horus, after my father," Yadira said in a tone drained of feeling and will. Cass sat with Yadira in silence for a while. "If not for Enton, I don't know if I could go on."

"There isn't anything I can say that'll help, but I'm here for you," Cass assured.

"I appreciate that, but you should go to Mexico and spend time with your husband. He may need you more than I do," Yadira said.

"I'm needed here," Cass replied. "Just like he's needed there." Yadira faced Cass, her eyes red and dry.

"You need to leave while you can," Yadira said.

Cass watched the crowd below. Cass sensed Yadira wasn't talking about the gathering horde.

"What's wrong?" Cass asked. Yadira wanted to say more, but Cass wouldn't press the issue.

"I'd like to be alone now," Yadira said.

Cass left the hospital to find a black car with two guards waiting. She took her spot in the back of the car with another man in a black suit. The man placed a black hood over Cass's head. Cass sat in a world of black on her way to an unknown location. Twists and turns made it impossible to discern where they were headed. The blindfold made her face itchy. She understood gang protocol and complied without hesitation. The pitter-patter of raindrops on the car gave Cass some comfort.

A man helped Cass out of the car. She heard the swift bloom of an umbrella shielding her from the rain. The man at her side did not remove her hood. He guided her through a building with the distinct sound of automatic doors. Machines hummed, beeped, and spat wet heat at her.

"Stop," the man said.

The hood rose from her face only to leave her in more darkness. She heard footsteps growing fainter. She stood alone in pure darkness. She could almost taste the metal all around her. A low rumble traveled through the room. A deep growl boomed in the dark. The growl became a deep voice.

"Forgive the theatrics. Caution is a necessity for one such as me," the voice said. The voice rattled her bones.

"Mr. Abaddon," she said.

"Once again, the Averills find themselves mired in the shaping of the world." Cass hid her fear, her imagination running wild at the man in the dark.

"We definitely have a knack for it," she said.

"Which is why you're here," he said. "Making an enemy of Vigilant is no small feat. You poked your nose into the wrong business, but it has been to our benefit."

"Glad I could help, why summon me?" she asked. She sensed movement.

"We still need you, and you still need us," he replied.

"No," she said. "Joe pulled that shit on us, and we won't repeat that mistake," Cass protested. She sensed more movement.

"This time it is not just your life on the line; everyone is at stake," he said.

"Why is Vigilant such a threat, and what more do you need from me? Is the regent involved?"

"I can't say, however, it's no secret he plans to remove the advisors," Mr. Abaddon said. "What I do know is that Vigilant has gone astray. Your surveillance is fruitless and no longer sufficient. They're playing with things that threaten this city. A threat against the city is a threat against me. They have taken much from me, and I need your help to take it back," Mr. Abaddon said.

Cass made out the silhouette of something above her like an impossibly long outstretched arm.

"Hold out your hand," Mr. Abaddon said.

The man beside Cass dropped a thumb-sized stick into Cass's hand. Cass looked at the object, confused.

"This little thing has the power to turn the tide in the conflict, and make no mistake, it is coming. This device is crude, but sufficient," Mr. Abaddon said.

Cass held the object up to her face.

"What am I supposed to do with it?" Cass asked.

"All you have to do is give it to the right person. And all they have to do is plug it into the city's central grid," Mr. Abaddon said. "With that, I can drive them out."

"Not sure I like the idea of you having system control," Cass said.

Mr. Abaddon let out a monster laugh that reverberated through the building.

"I've had access to the system for many years, my dear. I only use it in situations like this. You may disapprove, but I keep this place running; it would crumble without me. I held the locks on the systems they will abuse. I need back in. It's a temporary measure."

Cass didn't exactly like idea of giving the nation's crime king access to a city-wide defense system.

"Sounds like you're putting me in grave danger," Cass replied.

"You already are, more than most if they succeed. It requires little work from you, my dear. All you have to do is go to Prosperity Hall and hand it to one of my men. They will be coming after me so I must entrust it to you before my location is revealed. As of right now, my agents have been exposed. Only you can slip through undetected. Give it to Knight-Commander Theodore Vaughn. Kane will tell you when its time. He will be in the building lobby most days. Hand it to him and go about your business. That's all I require."

"And if they figure this all out, what happens to me?" Cass asked, fearing this move.

"Exactly what you think," Mr. Abaddon replied. "There's a man that'll come to your aid soon enough. An outsider like yourself." Cass placed the small device in her right pocket.

"I'll get it done," Cass said.

"Good. That's all," Mr. Abaddon said.

The black mass in front of Cass disappeared from her perception. The hood was slipped back over Cass's head. The guards lead her back to the car. The hood came off, and Cass found herself in front of her house.

MATTHEW

MATTHEW WATCHED THE crowd gathered around the hospital supporting Yadira after the loss of her child. The guards were more lenient toward crowds on the second day. Matthew wanted to chalk it up to a random tragedy, but there was too much going for coincidences. He scouted the city of Kingsbury, learning about the various faction spies always around the movers and shakers.

Knights on horses trotted along, bearing the national flag. The parade reminded the people of the power and glory of New Prosperity, strong even when tragedy struck. Throughout his years as Kami Rayntree, Matthew brought his daughters to parades in the small towns at the Heartland border. They were once mesmerized by the glistening armor and white horses, enamored by stories of his glory days as a monster-slaying hero. He thought of those days more and more as of late. Matthew was never a fan of city life, but he wished he had spent more time watching useless spectacles with his girls.

"It's amazing what I miss, B," Matthew said to himself.

He took a seat outside a steakhouse, casually people-watching while having a small meal. Cassandra Averill left the hospital, heading toward her car. Matthew kept his eyes on Mrs. Averill when he could, knowing she may need his aid before long. He identified the men around her as agents of Mr. Abaddon. Matthew felt the presence of a man taking a seat at his table. He continued to eat, not bothering to show respect for his guest.

"You said you'd leave her out of this," Matthew said, turning to face Proxy. "And you're rather brazen walking around when you're so desperate."

"Plans have been updated," Proxy said. "Vigilant is not aware of my presence or yours. I can deal with them if need arises."

"You can handle it yourself but better to use others," Matthew said.

"Of course," Proxy said. "You should worry about yourself. Until we replenish our forces, this is all on your shoulders. Tell me what you've found. Don't hold back; we'll find out whether you play along or not."

Matthew begrudgingly revealed Vigilant activity beneath the city. He knew that Mr. Abaddon was likely aware of the under-city since he first rose to power. Proxy listened, again showing no emotion.

"Most concerning," Proxy said. Matthew smirked.

"So you don't know everything." Proxy's mouth curled into his version of a smile.

"We know some things," Proxy said. "Your wife, for example. A storybook romance, predictable and cliche. Not exactly a wise choice for one such as you. If that info were to get out, Vigilant would have something to say about it, your brother, too. Maybe we should divulge this information to them and get you working faster."

The blood drained from Matthew's face. His vision went red for a moment.

"The other thing we know is tampering with the machines will be disastrous on a scale not seen since the Collapse."

"I'll get it done," Matthew said.

"Do whatever you must. The clock won't tick much longer. Good day," Proxy said, leaving with a bow.

"Oh, and one other thing," Matthew said. "You contacted me. You know I'm very good at what I do. When I have a target, they don't get away unless I let them."

Proxy stopped for a minute at the comment but didn't turn around. Proxy vanished around the corner, gaining not a single glance from anyone else in the area. Proxy unnerved Matthew, like someone who'd be on the end of his blade.

Matthew finished his meal and made another trip to the undercity. He slipped past Vigilant easy enough since they lacked the numbers to cover every nook and cranny of the underworld. Strings of lights gave Matthew clear indications of the main paths Vigilant used. Incoming trucks rolling through quickly made up for their lack of foot traffic in the darker areas. Apostates burned around the central structure. Matthew made out a smaller figure in a silver mask, what he surmised to be the CO. Light surged through wires feeding into the metal tower. Matthew slipped from building to building when Vigilant drew too close. The masked figure vanished from sight during Matthew's repositioning. For hours, he inched closer, studied troop movements, located weapon caches, and saw mounting frustration as Vigilant tried to open the central structure. Their machines stuttered and sputtered.

Lights flickered. Chatter filled the chamber. Vigilant immediately took defensive positions. One by one, the lights turned off, creating a domino effect all the way to the heart of the undercity. The fires around the central structure died. Vigilant in the area mobilized around the tower, aiming large flat guns at the long stairway.

"He's coming again!" a man said.

A single set of rhythmic footsteps reverberated through the silent chamber. Matthew scoured the streets for the body to match the sound. A sound of static preceded the shape taking form on the main road. The shape became a man in white, wearing a mask with a nightmarish grin. The earth shuddered beneath the man's feet. Matthew felt his heart stop, and a sense of terrible familiarity came over him.

"Get it running!" another voice cried.

Vigilant troops at the central structure attacked while others behind them rushed to the stuttering generators. All across the metal ruins, Vigilant troops split into attack forces and repairmen in a desperate scramble to re-power the city. Streaks of blue cut through the chamber, going straight through the man in white. The figure disappeared and reappeared halfway across the chamber to everyone's horrified dismay. The man in white raised his hand and re-directed the volley of bullets back at his attackers. The line of soldiers atop the stairs in front of the central structure hit the ground.

"Get it running!" the voice cried.

The figure flickered again, now the man stood at the stairs leading to the central structure. Machines began to hum throughout the city. The tower roared to life; green light spilled out from small openings traveling up the structure. A second volley of bullets from the new line of troops hit their mark, knocking the masked entity back. The entity fell to his knees, bloodless but wounded.

The machines stuttered again and the entity rose to his feet.

"Almost got it!" a soldier said.

The witch-burners started to bend.

"Almost got it!"

The central structure groaned. The engines roared back to life, stronger than ever. The entity stopped. His head turned. Matthew felt the black, empty eyes staring straight at him.

"What the—" Matthew said.

Matthew's head throbbed. Millions of invisible fingers stabbed his head. Matthew fought against the unprecedented power of enthrallment. He blinked. In an instant, he was back in the restored version of the chamber. Green energy ripped open the ground in the distance. Thousands of people gathered in the square were screaming and clawing at their heads. The land shifted again to Vigilant tower.

Matthew blinked again and once again stood in the ruins. The man in white now wore a frown. Bullets tore through the man in white. The buildings around Matthew started to fracture and buckle. The entity vanished and this time, he did not return. Building began to crumble around Matthew. Matthew sprinted from the collapsing ruins toward a decline leading to the empty waterways. With all attention on the road and chaos, Matthew hit the waterway and dipped inside the nearest tunnel. He felt the energy leaving him, and he wasn't sure why. He hurried down black tunnel, with no signs of Vigilant activity. He felt his consciousness fading. Matthew crawled into a small alcove and soundly went to sleep. There was far too much ground to cover for Vigilant to find him this far from the action, but being a light sleeper would ensure he'd be ready just in case.

THOS

THOS ROCKED BACK and forth in the old chair, creaking loud enough to annoy yet not enough to stop. He hated this memory the more he relived it, and he relived it quite a bit. His father, Cynward, rocked in a chair much quieter. Cynward saw happy retirement fast approaching, with no idea of what else was coming.

Thos and his brother, Etan, felt their dad's increasing frailty and the time to take the reins finally here. His father began to show the same signs mom did right before the end. Thos and Cynward made the rounds to the various mom-and-pop stores and community areas stretching across their farming kingdom. Business boomed for the Averill family. Other smaller farms to the west expressed interest in joining up after record-breaking harvests.

Cynward yawned loudly, taking a well-earned rest. Etan headed off to the fields. Thos stayed on the deck on the western side of the house with his father. Three chairs and a table made the deck a frequent dining room before the untimely death of Thos's mother. With his grandfather's death just a few years away, the Averill house was becoming a lonely place.

Etan tilled the fields. A consistent workaholic, Etan lived and breathed for this place. Thos lost his passion for the family business. Thos exchanged a few words with his dad.

"Been doing all right?" Cynward asked. Regardless of how he really felt, he always had the same response.

"Yep," Thos replied.

"Sure you don't want to go? You never go north," he said.

"Nah, ain't nothin' there for me," Thos said. Cynward frowned.

"Well, got some time left should ya reconsider," Cynward said. Thos's father rested a while longer, sipping on black coffee. The two sat in comfortable silence, watching the country world go by. Cynward reluctantly pulled himself up.

"Better get to it," he said. Thos hugged Cynward tightly, catching his father off guard.

"I know I don't say it much, but I love you," Thos said.

"I love you, too," Cynward said. Cynward walked over to the stables.

Thos waited until, by estimate, his father would be miles away. Picking up his rifle, he made his way east to the woods. Thos veered off the path cutting through to Greenfield to the lesser-traveled routes.

He came to this part of the woods often. Thos waited. He knew it wouldn't be long based on hunter reports. He wanted to do something that mattered, to feel like a part of it all again. Predators seldom hung around the paths during the day, but the occasional snallygaster skulked about. There was one too close, he knew. A presence behind Thos brought his worst fear to life.

"Thos? The hell are you doin' out here?!" Etan said.

"I have to do this," Thos said.

"Are you crazy? No, you don't," Etan said.

"I won't be long," Thos said. Rustling in the growth behind Thos caught their attention. He heard the gunshot, the shot that failed him.

"You don't have to prove anything."

Thos sat in a waking nightmare that replayed daily since his first night in Mexico. Constant reminders of his brother brought the memories kicking and screaming to the modern-day. Reports of more shrills made his dreams a deadly reality. Thos shrugged off the darkness by Duke's mini lake.

He lightened up more throughout the day, allowing himself the undeniable pleasures of the Mexican high life. Workers brought Thos shrimp and wine. A lone truck arrived at the main gate. The truck rolled into the garage housing the Duke's military vehicles. Thos went to greet Drake and Zora. Thos, as always, put on a happy face.

"Have fun?" Thos asked. Thos devoured his last shrimp and flicked the tail into the nearby trashcan.

"We did. Shoulda came with," Zora said. Thos understood the trip was designed for the pair.

"Too much work to do," Thos said.

Drake, Zora, and Thos walked into the guest house and out of sight from overzealous guards. The pair followed Thos to his personal floor of the guest house.

"Any word from Mel?" Drake asked. Thos shook his head.

"Not a peep," Thos replied.

Drake and Zora recounted their time with the Yucatan Freemen and the disturbing statues of masked figures. A tingling in Thos's brain drew him to a hazy image of Kingsbury Square.

"I've the strangest feeling I've seen a masked figure before," Thos said.

"I do too, in Mexico City," Drake said. Both looked at Zora.

"How do you remember yours so well?" They both asked. Zora shrugged.

"I wish I didn't. Maybe it has to do with father being in Vigilant?" Zora theorized.

"When you meet up, you can grill him on it," Thos said. "Mel'll run into him, just gotta wait."

"No point in dwelling on it, now," Drake said.

The trio concluded the serious discussion for a while and went about friendly chats and taking advantage of Duke's extensive hospitality. They hit all the villa areas, including the pool, once the other guests left. Each also tried their hand at the various types of military firearms at Duke's personal gun range. Thos sampled rifles, pistols, and the highly coveted flamethrower. He hit the bullseye ninety percent of the time.

"Training paid off too well," Drake said. Thos realized his abilities were quickly becoming on par with soldiers like Drake.

"Get captured a few more times and I'll be right there with you," Thos quipped. Drake's face soured.

"The way you keep throwing yourself into my operations you'll get there," Drake replied. Thos grinned.

The trio exhausted activities at the villa and made an evening trip to Mexico City for a night of lights, costumes, food, and binge drinking. Thos donned darker jeans and a different brand of shirt, his version of street clothes. The three rode across the desert under the sinking sun that painted the sky in tangerine beauty.

"Good to be out with you guys again," Thos said. "Been over a year since we've all been together without some battle goin' on."

"It has," Drake said. "We should take it all in tonight; things will probably get dicey from here on."

Guards followed Thos and his friends to the city until Thos sent them away. The guards left Thos, Drake, and Zora a few miles from the city. Drake guided Thos and Zora through the neon world. Fireworks peppered the sky non-stop. Dancers lined the streets in the areas not flooded with people making human roadblocks through a chunk of the city. There wasn't a single iota of tension or violence this night, but everyone knew to be ready.

The trio admired the vibrant colors of the dancers twirling with reckless abandon. The roadblock crowd parted for a grand parade. Images of various Mexican heroes from before and during their time assimilated by New Prosperity were plastered across multiple buildings. Fire-eaters dazzled with flames as vibrant as their clothes. Music streamed from speakers on a band on the stage a couple of blocks away.

The three took places in the crowd until the parade ended. A food truck rolled up near Thos, offering succulent meats. The food cart owner noticed Thos. Thos raised his finger to his mouth then reached for his wallet. Thos handed the cart chef a hundred Prosperity dollars for his silence and a couple of steak skewers.

Drake and Zora held hands. The image of the couple's joy made Thos painfully aware that Cass wasn't here. The trio moved on. Drake pointed out the best spots in the city, and they navigated the crowds to the statues, monuments, and the few remaining Old World structures.

Per Zora's request, they visited Chapultepec Castle, an Old Worlder's home converted into a museum. Thos lost himself in the checkered flooring with hypnotic power. The three made stops at the Ancient, Old, and New World exhibits. Mayan tools, Old World robot limbs, and car parts repurposed into crude armor provided three distinct trips through four thousand years of human history. Thos grew parched and wanted some strong drink.

He took the helm and directed Drake and Zora to a three-story bar called the Dirty Jackal, complete with a mascot of a shifty jackal wearing a comically large sombrero. Thos walked up to the bartender and leaned in.

"Roof open?" Thos asked.

"Yes, sir, Th-Thomas," the bartender replied.

Thos ordered bottles of tequila and Terrorizer, a potent concoction of alcohol, cream, and night terror blood. The bartender looked at Thos with disbelief at purchasing an entire bottle of the most expensive drink.

"Drinks're on me tonight," Thos said. The bartender's disbelief grew exponentially. Thos handed the bartender a few thousand in

Prosperity bills while no one watched. Thos weaved through the crowd toward the stairs.

"Thomas? That's your alias?" Zora asked.

"Cobra was taken," Thos said. "We're fine. Nobody has seen me up close." Drake shook his head.

The trio went up to the rooftop area. Thos sped over the lone free table near the railing. Drake and Zora plopped down on the metal chairs beside Thos. The trio chatted about all the usual things and plans for more excursions into the untamed places of the state.

The bottles and glasses arrived, carried by a waiter dressed up as Dirty Jack. Thos pointed at the man's hat and pulled out several bills to encourage a trade. The waiter happily traded the large hat for a week's pay.

"If your boss gives you trouble, send him my way," Thos said. Thos placed the monstrous sombrero on his head and twisted the small skull-shaped cap off the bottle of Terrorizer. He sniffed the drink.

"Woo, you can smell the power in that bad boy," he said.

He poured the three each a shot of Terrorizer. The red, syrupy liquid gave each of them pause.

"Down the hatch," Thos said.

They sucked down the alcohol. All attention turned to them as they hooted and hollered at the liquid's spicy punch to the throat. Thos reminisced about the fun times, especially his secret gift of a fart in a jar to his former rivals at Dullen Farms. The happy times decreased in response to the insatiable monster called Averill Estate Farms, though the work made it worth it.

Drake and Zora slowed their drinking before Thos. The endless pink and green explosions eliminated the need for any electric light. Thos maintained a steady pack of shots until his vision blurred, though his mind's eye view of Etan's death was crystal clear.

"Time to call it quits," Thos said.

He pushed himself up from the table, stumbled around, and laughed it off. He held out his finger and powered through the disorientating haze.

"I'm tired, too," Zora said.

Drake nodded. Thos walked into the bathroom and into a stall. He peeked out under the door to make sure he was alone. He pulled the cell phone from his pocket and alerted his driver to meet him out back. Thos met back with Drake and Zora and proceeded to it at once.

He sat quietly in the car for most of the ride, fighting the feelings on the verge of a cataclysmic eruption.

"I know something's bothering you," Zora said. Thos requested the driver roll up the soundproof shudder between himself and the driver.

"Been thinking about my brother," Thos said. Again he heard the gunshot that failed.

"Pain like that never leaves you, not even when you have vengeance," Zora said. Thos grimaced, no longer able to contain it.

"Dammit . . . it was my fault," he said.

Thos rubbed the back of his head and forced the words out. "I was not a happy person. Happiness was always something I couldn't get unless I was out in nature. I had no reason to be unhappy; maybe that's my defect. The silly, easygoing Thos is a character I play half the time." He rested his head in his hands for a moment before continuing.

"I felt useless. I wanted to prove myself. Thought it would make things better. There were times I considered using a gun on myself. That's why he followed me." Inside his head, he heard Etan's pleas. Thos was transported again to that fateful day. A rustling behind Thos instinctively turned his head toward the direction of the sounds.

"My gun jammed. I shoulda checked it," Thos said. Etan got his own gun ready. Thos struggled. "He killed the thing, but he died before I could get him back home. I shoulda died that day, not him."

Thos sighed as the pain devouring his very being came pouring out.

"My dad wasn't the same after Etan died. I...never told him the truth." Thos turned his gaze to the desert whizzing by. Drake's eyes widened at the revelation.

"The shrills . . . " Drake said.

"Were after me," Thos said. "Drawn to my guilt. Didn't make the connection until after you found one in the woods."

"Thos . . . I had no idea," Zora said.

"Now ya do."

Thos watched the night-drenched world outside and hoped that was his cathartic first step in putting his demons to rest.

ANSELM

Anselm wandered the endless green and blackness of the world beneath the surface, telling himself it would all be worth it. He thought back to the citizens of Durenburg, helpless without him, now seeing them as something that had held him back. Pain, anger, and hunger were the only family he required.

Anselm moved between the winding tunnels and the forest mesh of the world above. He found joys where he could. He ran through the forests where few humans dared tread. Etherflies danced in the green labyrinth, creating a sea of earthbound stars. He listened to the nocturnal symphony that gave him a sliver of peace. Afterward, he raided a small camp. Signs of snuffed campfires and gear lay strewn about the camp, clearly Vigilant. *Never thought bandits would work in my favor,* he thought.

Patchwork tents with sleeping bags covered an area on the edge of the woods. A handful of men slept in tents. Anselm quickly dispatched the men and scavenged for a new weapon. Their flesh and blood called to him. His thoughts turned to Rosalie Crowe. He ignored the gruesome call. Anselm found a stained executioner's blade on the ground. He effortlessly swung the two-handed weapon with his right arm. He discarded his sword for its bigger cousin. Anselm debated waiting to dispatch the campers, but something told him they weren't coming back.

He made camp in a clearing by a small pond a dozen miles to the west. He sat by the pond, imagining his wife and three young children laughing by the fire. Fake Aric laughed and played with his younger brothers. Edgar ran around with a vigor not known in his real life. Anselm pictured the timeless staple of roasting marshmallows, a family activity forever closed to him. The children lay in the grass under the starlight and etherflies sailing through the forest. He held Abigail by the fire when the children slept. He let the conversation play out in his head.

"I wished we could've done this," he said, unable to grasp the imaginary hand.

The flames danced in front of Anselm and the faux Abigail.

"We had our moments. More than most," she said. Her face glowed as bright and beautiful as the day they had met.

"I suppose we did," Anselm said. His mind struggled to recall the many years of happiness he'd nearly forgotten.

"Hard to see those days anymore," he said.

Anselm's mind battled with itself to picture his family as they were. He heard a real voice on the wind, a tone warm and very much unlike Eon's. Abigail's hand crumbled to ash. His faux camping trip became a nightmare when Aric lay dead, soaking in the piss of others. The rest of his family withered and blackened. Anselm performed his nightly duty. He thrust his arm into the flame and let his arm roast. He grimaced. It was an odd feeling to smell oneself cooking. It blackened only for seconds before returning to its standard pale color only to blacken again. Anselm let his arm roast and heal a dozen times. He ripped into the flesh to make up for his increasing resistance to the flames. Anselm no longer felt the urge to cry out at the agony. Anselm satisfied his dark addiction. He could never have his wife and sons, but he always had pain, anger, and hunger.

With his nightly torture concluded, Anselm doused the fire and gave himself a few hours to rest. He moved on, headed northwest to Vigilant headquarters. Eon went silent since the visions of Alexander. Anselm wondered what else the entity withheld from him. For now, he saw Eon as the means to help him exact his revenge.

Anselm passed the rusted skeleton of a logging bot with its saw-hand stuck in an ancient oak. He couldn't shake the sensation of onlookers studying him; he applauded their ability to avoid detection. Anselm veered into the network of tunnels to escape unwanted spectators. Darkened tunnels led into a web of cracked organic bones and the skeletal frames of long-dead machines. He moved through the black world for hours. A whisper flowed through the tunnels at steady intervals.

"I'm in no mood for games," Anselm said.

Anselm followed that gust of spectral voice into the hole. His eyes adjusted fast to the oppressive darkness, seeing a glimmer of light. He drew his beastly weapon and prepared to face another demon haunting the dark places of his former domain.

In a moment, he stepped into a dazzling new world. The underground chamber dropped off around him in a grassy clearing with plants unlike any Anselm had seen before. Neon flowers glowed with divine brilliance. Transparent bugs fed on the plants, taking on the colors of the flowers they touched. Small childlike creatures with branch-like bodies pranced across the underground fields while yellow-eyed birds flew in and out of the holes in the ceiling. The lifeforms paid the intruder no mind.

The underworld forest crawled up the sides of the chamber walls. An underground stream snaked through the bottom of the chamber into a large pool at the back. A tree sat near the other end of the underground grotto. Chunky roots greedily sucked up the waters. Dozens of branches ascended to the light, like a great monster stretching after a long slumber. Luminous white leaves covered the great tree. Anselm marveled at the subterranean haven.

He followed the lone natural walkway that went straight to the heart of the tree. Upon closer inspection, the tree looked much more fleshy than he anticipated. He noticed an all-too-familiar shape intertwined with the mass; a human head and torso.

"Welcome, Anselm," she said. Anselm braced for combat. "I'm no threat to you. My name is . . . I don't remember anymore, but I'm fond of Mandragora," she said. Anselm lowered his weapon. He gauged the witch's intentions.

"What's this place?" he asked.

"My grave and my home," she said. "It's where I came to rest once upon a time. I fled Vigilant decades ago, they wounded me. I fled here and died. My enhancements mingled with this tree; genetic mods were more unstable than I believed. We're one now."

"Fascinating," Anselm admitted.

"It took many years for me to adjust to this life, but being connected to nature is not the hell I once thought. I built my own world here."

Anselm jumped from the walkaway onto the grassy bottom. The strange lifeforms all approached Anselm. Hearts pulsated inside the branches. The creatures had no faces, only pits for eyes. Anselm bent over to touch one of the beings; it stepped out of range.

"Are you one of Eon's followers?" he asked.

"I freed myself from Its poisonous influence," Mandragora said.

"I wasn't aware that was an option," Anselm said.

"One you should consider while you still can," Mandragora advised. "The man I loved lost that chance years ago." Anselm knew who she meant.

"Gideon," he said. She nodded. "So that's why you called out to me. I assume if I don't heed your warning, I'll end up like you or him," Anselm said.

"No, I believe it'll be much worse," Mandragora replied.

"Enlighten me," he said.

"The details of your fate are not fully clear to me," she said. "But I'll share with you what brought me here."

Mandragora recalled the fragments of her previous life. Like many of the other purported apostates, she had been an ambitious scholar at Lewell Sanctum. She became enamored with Gideon, attending many of his private studies for those fit to further the world and skirt the limits of the Compact. He wanted to love her back, but transcendence became his mistress.

"Gideon theorized something in our bodies determined our fates," she began. "He called them Godseeds, an evolution of Old World nanomachines that had become organic. Knowledge, memory, and power stored in these cells took genetic blood memory to new heights. He believed they were connected to the Compact and could be hacked into. With the right know-how, our bodies could be altered and programmed to break free of these laws."

"Blood memory," Anselm said, holding on to those words.

Mandragora told Anselm of Gideon's disappearance and the events that brought her here. She went after Gideon when he had fled the capital, sacrificing her career to follow him. She took odd jobs in Eddington after he vanished.

"He came to me one night," she said. "Wearing a silver mask. Called it a piece of God. Told me I could be a master of the Algorithm and not its slave. I lived on that lie for so long." She hid from the public eye and Vigilant's wrath. The years passed. Gideon's visits dropped steadily.

Eventually, she gave up, moving from city to city, living on the streets and in hovels.

"One night It came to me, wearing white robes and a golden mask," she said. "It connected to my mind, showed me things I still can't decipher." The sadness filled her eyes.

"Gideon was there, too. I asked him to remove his mask," she began. "He wasn't there anymore, only an empty shell. I rejected the offer and left. My mods kept It from wiping my mind. Vigilant came for me soon after."

Light surged through her body and out into the roots and branches. The waters illuminated with the witch-tree's power. Her white eyes scanned Anselm.

"Abandon this cause while you can," she said. "You will lose yourself. Don't be shackled to Its design," she warned. Anselm considered her words.

"Will you stop me if I go on?" he asked.

"It's not my place. Should I interfere more than I have, Eon will destroy these lives I've created as punishment," Mandragora said. "Letting Vigilant succeed may not be so bad. You can simply walk away." Anselm nodded.

"I'll think on what you say," he replied.

"That's all I ask. You may stay here for the night," she said. Anselm felt the energy draining, he wouldn't refuse this to be his place for a recharge

"Thank you."

Anselm unpacked his sleeping bag and placed it among the radiant flowers. Soon, he drifted off to sleep, holding on to the words blood memory.

GREGOR

GREGOR AND RAUL sat in the bullet train with gunblades pointed at the witch named Lora. Hogtied on the floor, Paulo shouted curses.

"Stop bitchin', or I'll knock you out again," Gregor threatened. Gregor pulled out the marvelous tech called duct tape from his travel bag and silenced Paulo. Gregor stared out the window as the bullet train cut through an unknown body of water. Gregor saw the fish with vaguely human features gleefully zipping around. *We're all abominations,* Gregor thought.

Raul studied the unconscious witch. Lines segmented the different parts of her face as if they were connecting points. Like the other witches, her slender body was reinforced to withstand everything save Vigilant weaponry.

"Wonder who she was?" Raul said.

"She may not know. Some with half as many mods destroy their minds in the process," Gregor said.

"The energy he'll get from her must be off the charts," Raul said. "This must be the last ingredient for Killswitch." Energy surged through Lora's body. Raul gave her a shot of his gunblade to be safe.

"Never seen one with the power to enthrall demons," Raul said. Gregor ran his fingers through his beard, the sign of theories shooting through his mind.

"A dangerous precedent," Gregor said grimly.

Gregor had no qualms about putting this woman to death, but Matthias's methods were distasteful. Paulo mumbled his objections through the tape.

"Perhaps you could answer a few questions and help us both out? Give me some more good intel, and I might be convinced to drop you off somewhere," Gregor said. Paulo clammed up. Gregor pulled the tape from Paulo's mouth.

"Tell me more about the Godseeds," Gregor said.

"Marvelous little devils," Paulo said. "They're in everything we've studied to some degree." Gregor sat up. The subject of machines and hybrid cells in the blood intrigued and terrified him.

"They work like supercharged versions of normal cells," Paulo continued. "Communicating in all bodies like a super network. Human durability, memory, life span. I think these machines have the power to cure diseases or even kill the host. And if they can do that, then ones in water and soil could control the very Earth. The hubris of our ancestors to think they could have molded the world as they saw fit.

"I believe they were both willingly and unwillingly injected into the populace. They contain the memories of thousands of years. They can be manipulated, connect to machines, and be controlled remotely, as we've come to learn."

The pieces sloshing inside Gregor's head started to fit. The blurry memories, controlled leaps and bounds in human understanding, and a mysterious being at the center of it all.

"A network of machines that connect us all to Eon," Gregor said. "A network you can't quit."

"Perhaps those that violate the Compact have their nanos overloaded or shut down, which would explain the mysterious deaths. This is why Matthias intends to kill the controller," Raul said.

"We're being controlled through these little bastards," Gregor said. "They pop in the desired information and wipe out the encounter."

"And who knows what else they can do. You want Matthias to have this power?" Paulo said. "You think his intentions are true? That killing Eon won't leave a void for him to fill?"

Gregor looked at the witch.

"I'll find out soon enough," Gregor said. Paulo scoffed in disgust then grew despondent.

"The cameras don't work well here, yet. We can disrupt them and let him off," Raul said. Gregor brushed it off.

"You know the law," he said. "Conspiring with our enemies makes you one, apostate or no. Enemies must be dealt with." Raul didn't argue. Paulo looked at the floor.

"I know I'm not getting out of this," Paulo said. "All I ask is that when you learn the truth, you kill Matthias before it's too late."

Paulo didn't speak the rest of the trip. The train arrived. Vigilant soldiers waited outside the train at the stairs leading up to the city. The station guard alerted the grand crusader the second Gregor emerged from the train.

Matthias came down the stairs with arms extended in joy at the witch being carried past him.

"Excellent work. And you brought a traitor," Matthias said, joy flying off each word. I expected nothing less from the legendary witch-hunter."

Matthias's orange eyes studied Raul Alvarez.

"Did he give you any useful intel?"

"Nothing we didn't already know," Raul said.

Matthias gave a single nod to the man beside Paulo. The man raised his gun and planted one round into Paulo's head before he could utter last words. Soldiers quickly carried the body off.

"We've waited long enough," Matthias said, bubbling with excitement. Dozens of apostates and non-modded humans exited the train at gunpoint. Gregor followed Matthias out into the city. A soldier carrying a large case approached Matthias. He held the case out and unlocked it. Matthias placed his hands inside, removed the silver mask, and attached it on his face. Vigilant speakers lining the streets screeched.

"It's time. Take positions," Matthias said calmly. His voice boomed through the speakers. Matthias ordered his elite troop to the undercity. He pried the mask off his face, leaving cuts and drops of blood running down his head. Matthias, his lieutenants, and Gregor walked over to a see-through elevator.

The elevator descended into the chasm and through the waters. Under the lake, a machine at the center cut through to the bottom of a large room. Large panels, not unlike Vigilant weaponry, were attached at various points of the machine. The tower section of the machine funneled into a smooth base like an Old World reactor. Thousands of transparent slugs fed off the faint energy traces inside the machine.

"So this powers the whole city. Big as Blackthorne Castle," Gregor said.

"There's a way to access the grid down there. I bet there's another in the heart," Matthias said.

A massive heap of parts lay in the corner of the room, Gregor made out limbs among them.

"You do that?"

"Yes," Matthias said. "Got the head back in the lab. Some kind of guardian."

The elevator hit the ground floor. Matthias sped up, determined not to wait a moment longer. Gregor followed suit. The lieutenants massed behind their leader. Gregor pushed his way to the head of the group.

A massive door was on the western side of the room. Vigilant soldiers forced the door open. Trucks rode in. Each truck carried half a dozen prisoners in thick restraints. A platoon of Vigilant soldiers marched behind the trucks with gunblades to encourage prisoner compliance. The soldiers lead the prisoners to dozens of poles around the base of the reactor. Vigilant prisoners tried to bolt only to be coaxed back into submission. Grunts of pain drained the last vestiges of will from the prisoners. Members of Vigilant fastened the prisoners to the poles.

A second platoon brought forth Lora, very much awake. Unlike all the other heavily modded humans Gregor battled, Lora's eyes were a flaming orange instead of ethereal green. With head down, the witch shuffled forward with the spark of life long gone. A thicker witch-burning pole waited for Lora at the head of the machine. Vigilant soldiers attached her to the pole. Thick restraints shot from the sounds and wrapped around Lora.

"I've waited so long," Matthias said. "The world has waited too long for this." His words reverberated through his mask and across the city.

"For nearly two millennia, we've fought to preserve the world. We had no idea the true extent of the Compact. With this city operational, we can destroy the false god and those that pervert our destiny!"

Cheers erupted around Matthias. With hands shaking, he placed the mask back on his face. He grunted in pain as it wrapped around his head. Gregor understood Paulo's concerns watching Matthias.

"I can feel Its fear," Matthias said.

The prisoners cried out for mercy. The metal poles came to life. Lights flickered from within the reactor. A voice cut through the celebration. All eyes were upon Lora while hers were on Matthias.

"This isn't the way," she said.

"It's the only way," Matthias replied. Matthias raised his hand toward her.

"Wait!" Gregor said. "At least let her say her peace."

"No," Matthias said. The lights flickered faster inside the

machine. Bursts of flames shot from the metal poles. The humming continued to grow louder.

"I regret everything," Lora said, speaking over the groaning machines. "I know you mean well. We've been living a lie. All I wanted was to be more than a slave. I thought I changed my fate. Had I stayed . . . maybe it wouldn't have come to this." Matthias paused and lowered his hand.

"Can't you see what that mask is doing to you? You're connected to It, same as us," Lora said. The air rippled around the machine. The internal lights became a rhythmic pulse. The organic flesh of prisoners blistered and burned.

"You bring death," Lora said.

"Silence," Matthias said.

Matthias thrust his right arm forward and opened his palm. Sparks flew from the machines and showered Vigilant. Everyone jumped back, dodging the rain of fire. A mechanical growl shook the earth, followed by screeches and screams.

"Please stop this," Lora said. "I know I've done so much wrong this life. Maybe I'm beyond forgiveness, but you aren't. I'm sorry, dad. I hope one day you can forgive yourself."

"Shut up!" Matthias roared.

The witches and warlocks wailed, save for Lora. Matthias thrust his second hand forward and opened his palm. The ground beneath them splintered. Steam shot from the exposed pipes. Flames enveloped Lora. She closed her eyes. Matthias looked away. Machines roared to life in the city above. The transparent slugs fell from the machine, fried by a power too great for their bellies. Matthias tore the mask from his face and hit the ground. Blood ran down from the cuts around Matthias's head. Gregor rushed to Matthias's side.

"The mask, get it," Matthias said.

"It's time to destroy it," Gregor said. Gregor helped Matthias to his feet. Matthias pushed Gregor back.

"I still need it!" Matthias exclaimed, with a half-wild look in his eyes. Flames shot out uncontrollably from the metal pole. Gregor scooped up the mask and helped Matthias to the service elevator.

Vigilant retreated from the flame-throwing witch-burners. Matthias fell to the ground again. Gregor tossed the mask on the platform and picked up Matthias. He hopped onto the platform and hit the top floor button. The elevator rose steadily up. The electric poles exploded at the base of the reactor.

The elevator hit the top floor in front of the central structure at the heart of a city no longer silent. Electric life surged across the city. It glowed with a neon splendor greater than any in the known world. Vigilant soldiers investigated the top of the city, checking lights and utilities. Machines planted seeds in the soil of the gardens in all areas of the city. Vigilant went off in all directions to test the functionality of the city. Green light shone through the slits inside the central building. More buildings separated from platforms and floated in the air. Beams came from the platforms to connect them to the floating structures.

"Is the console intact?" a man said over the radio. "Go make sure. Looks like the barrier is still up. Delayed at every step."

Matthias lay unconscious on the elevator with his hand on the silver mask. Gregor picked up the mask. One of Matthias's lieutenants approached Gregor and demanded he hand it over. Gregor relinquished it. Vigilant soldiers rushed over and tended to the wounded Matthias.

"We'll contact you when we're ready," the lieutenant picked up the mask and followed the troops carrying Matthias to his quarters.

MELVIN

MELVIN SLEPT WELL given he was in a machine city full of enemies. The previous night proved uneventful, accomplishing nothing except getting into a building closer to the center. Liz grabbed the underside of the bed and flipped it over. A disoriented Melvin snapped awake with his bed a protective bed shell over him. He took a minute to process the situation and rubbed his eyes.

"Wakey," Liz said. Melvin heard guests come through the door.

"Come on in," Melvin said. Skully and Ed grunted in response.

Melvin rose to his feet, clumsily falling around for a few seconds. He relieved himself in the bathroom, happy to have a flushing toilet. He conversed while he peed.

"Sounds like Vigilant is moving in for good," he said.

"Void won't be happy with that. This partnership can't last too long," Skully said.

"Then let's get 'em when they're both here," Ed said.

"We need to get a layout of the armories, escape routes . . . " Skully advised.

"And set some nice little traps," Ed added, looking through his pack of death. Liz nudged Melvin, knocking him forward a tad.

"And contact Zora's uncle," Melvin said. "Have you found him?"

"Came back from a mission hours ago. Seen him near the center; elevators go through the water, I think. All covered though. From the chatter, they're about to launch their operation. Think he can be trusted?"

"I do," Melvin said. "I bet a fair amount of these guys are too."

"Burn 'em all, safer that way," Ed said.

"A tad harsh," Melvin said. "Some of them could be lovable like me."

"One Melvin is enough," Skully said, only half-joking.

"Yeah, yeah. Let's hit it," Melvin said.

The group hurried out of the apartment complex. Outside rose more buildings that floated in the air. Strange energy bridges connected to the once inaccessible, floating structures. Vigilant troops cautiously moved across the energy bridges. Bridges flickered, leading to panicked curses from those upon them at the time. Trucks emerged from ramps heading into the various tunnels going the waterfalls. Greenlight oozed from the central building at the city's heart.

The team split up again. Melvin and Liz took the job of contacting Gregor. Liz picked Melvin and dangled him over the suspended bridges that gave him the view of multiple floors, all explored by Vigilant.

"This whole damn city runs on autopilot," Melvin said. "Wonder if this place has a giant brain somewhere. Should find the off switch." Noises above had the three scrambling for cover.

"Why are they being so thorough?" Melvin asked. "We may not be the only assholes sneaking around."

The group passed restaurants, hospitals, office buildings, factories, and literally every building active but empty. Melvin found the architecture off-putting. Many of the buildings were domed or spiral-shaped and some rose at odd angles that made him uncomfortable.

Melvin evaded patrols of the tier halfway down the vertical city. Liz pulled out some retractable hook ropes from his backpack. The pair crept behind the tallest buildings in the area. Together they rappelled down the buildings tier by tier. Descending through the vertical city with the chance of being caught provided an indescribable rush.

Melvin and Liz reached the platform on the lake. The lake platforms served as a park, with benches, metal buildings for food, and a large empty spot likely for a garden. The three picked a staircase and went through the lake into a large room with a machine that stretched to the floor. The machine surged with power and hypnotic light. Vigilant troops circled it, aiming weapons toward the trolls fitting large objects to the structure.

"Kinda looks like their guns. We're in for a world of hurt if they use that," Melvin said.

Other Vigilant members gathered around the melted remains of a silvery human attached to a pole. A low growl from Liz threatened to ruin the operation. Liz felt a kinship with trolls and exiles. Melvin doubted they could be saved; he kept that feeling internal.

The pair hurried to the bottom of the stairs while the troops were preoccupied. Reaching the bottom, the group slipped into one of the smaller machines near the walls. A cavalcade of trucks rode through the underground chamber and vanished into a tunnel not far from them. A few more caravans of trucks came from other tunnels, all heading to the same location. Liz kept his eyes on the other trolls.

After a few moments, the duo followed the trucks through the tunnel. The trucks parked at the tunnel exit a warehouse area, going off into an underground road leading away from the city. Nearly a thousand Vigilant soldiers stood guns ready in the warehouse, one of which held a metal case. A red armored man wearing a silver mask was at the head of the army. The man paced then stumbled, others ran over to help him to his feet.

"Cheeseman," Liz said.

They waited for an hour. Black trucks and motorcycles bearing the image of Death eventually came from the other end of the tunnel. A woman in a red dress with a face tattooed up like a skull stepped out of the lead truck. The woman and her guards approached the Vigilant army. Melvin and Liz watched and listened.

"You aren't supposed to be here yet," Matthias said. Tension rose between Matthias and one called Valeria. Her tone grew accusatory.

"You're not delivering on your promises," she said with booming authority. Her skull-faced enforcers nodded in agreement.

"Patience," Matthias said. "Here's what we have ready."

The side of the warehouse groaned, and then it lowered, revealing it to be a freight elevator. Upon the elevator were six large white vehicles with treads. A huge cannon protruded from each vehicle.

"Mercy, they got tanks," Melvin said.

"See? Here is what you've asked for. More'll be ready in three days," Matthias said.

Valeria's enforcers walked over to the tanks and analyzed them. "I'm sure you'd like a demonstration," Matthias said.

A soldier approached the tank, it's inside opened, and he went in. The tanks roared to life. Another soldier brought a prisoner forward, a troll with no fight left in him. The soldier forced the prisoner up against the wall. Matthias and Valeria stepped back into the safety of the troops. The man in the tank powered up the gun and aimed it at the prisoner. A blue charge shot through the gun. The blue charge flew forth, sending troll pieces in all directions.

"Perhaps I responded too quickly," Valeria said.

"I can forgive that," Matthias said.

Matthias raised his hand. Valeria clutched her chest and fell to her knees. The Void aimed their weapons at Matthias and his people responded in kind. The tank groaned as its gun changed direction toward the Void.

"What . . . is . . ." Valeria said, words coming out between pained breaths.

"But some things I can't forgive," Matthias said. "This is a reminder who holds power here. Do you think me blind to your scheming? I've eyes everywhere. Sending agents to steal from us is not wise and your last mistake."

Matthias closed his fist as if he was crushing an invisible heart. Valeria screamed and thrashed for only a moment, then ceased doing both.

"I think she's dead. So much for the new death queen," Melvin said.

"What we're doing here is for the best of everyone," Matthias said. "Go fight your futile war. We're here changing the destiny of the world. I'll say this only once. Get in our way again and I'll gladly provide you the death you so desire."

After the Void left, Matthias pried the mask off his face and stumbled back. The man with the case rushed up, placed the mask into the case, and hurried off with a team of his own. Others helped Matthias to his feet and escorted him out of the tunnel.

"They're gonna attack Mexico City. They'll roll right over it," Melvin said. "We need to contact Greg and get out."

"Okay," Liz replied.

The duo moved through the tunnels back through to the room with the big machine. Melvin and Liz stuck to the darkened corners to avoid the numerous vehicles going through the tunnels. One truck parked away from the tunnel. The driver and passenger got out to discuss the progress of the retro-fitted machine with a white-haired man approaching them.

"Gramps?" Liz asked.

"Probably. Let's crank up those binos."

Melvin pulled the headphone cords from the sides of the bin-oculars from the headphones and placed them in his ears. The older man's demeanor reeked of bitterness. The man cursed repeatedly. The man voiced his disbelief at the sight of troll slaves reinforcing the large machine with Vigilant tech.

"Sounds like he don't approve," Melvin said. "Says some of the others don't either. Gotta be him. We need to get him away from them. Zora told me there was a surefire way to get his attention," Melvin said.

The other men walked off to speak with a group of soldiers. The older man went over to inspect the machine far from the others. Melvin and Liz slinked around to get within earshot. The two got behind an unguarded truck.

"Greg," Melvin whispered. The man looked around, confused. "Gregory Lynn." The man looked around, confused and angry. Melvin peeked his head out from the side of the truck.

"The hell?" Gregor said. Melvin waved Gregor over. "Hurry."

Gregor turned around to see if anyone was watching. He walked over to the vehicle, jumping back at the sight of Melvin and a troll.

"Oh, you," Gregor said, annoyed before the surprise hit, "You? Better have a good reason for me not to shoot you because you already made me twitchy." Gregor reached for his gunblade.

"Zora sent me!" Melvin cried. Gregor lowered his weapon.

"She here?" he asked. Gregor craned his head around the duo.

"At Duke's villa with Drake and Thos," Melvin said. Gregor's confused anger only worsened.

"On top of all . . . you guys need to stop meddling in shit," Gregor snapped.

"Growl at me later. There a place we can talk?" Melvin asked. Gregor ran his fingers through his beard.

"I'll get a truck," Gregor said. "Actually, I'll take this one. The trio hopped in the back and flattened themselves on the truck bed. Gregor drove them to his quarters. When the coast was clear, Gregor motioned them in.

"Start talking," Gregor said.

Melvin filled Gregor in on Zora, Drake, the gun for troll exchange, and Vigilant rolling out tanks to assault Mexico City. Gregor paced around the room. Liz made the occasional one-word response to make up for his wandering mind. Gregor had his own equally disturbing intel to give. Melvin spoke aloud to help process the information overload.

"Let me get this straight . . . Matthias is turning this place into a weapon to kill some demon that's been controlling humanity through the Compact?" Melvin asked.

"That's the gist," Gregor replied.

"Okay. Thought I was going crazy for a second," Melvin said.

"That's the good part," Gregor said. "He needs to get into the central building to activate it . . . that's if what's in there's what he thinks and not something horrible. I agree with his plans . . . Mercy help me. But using slaves and helping gangs I can't abide. There's too much to ignore. I've a terrible feeling about this."

"You need to deal with him," Melvin said.

"If it comes to that," Gregor said. "His critics are growing. If he goes nuts, they'll be resistance. There's still much he has to answer for. Matthias will get through the final door before long. I'll handle whatever happens next. If things get bad we'll need you guys to send backup, get 'em ready." Gregor hit the wall, knocking a spiral pot off its stand. "Things always have to be so damn complicated." Liz picked up the pot and shoved it into his pack.

"All right then, we gotta get out of here and alert the regent," Melvin said. Melvin pulled a few black sticks from his pocket, detonators for remote explosives. Gregor knew the drill.

"Got these too if we need 'em," Melvin said.

"Might," Gregor said. "All right you better go. Train Four, get on that. I'll have it set for you. I'll reach out when I can."

Melvin and Liz prepared to depart. Liz made a quick scan of the house for a few things to steal. Gregor stopped them.

"Oh, and in case I don't get the chance, tell Zora I love her."

Melvin and Liz walked away. Gregor hollered at them right before they hit the door.

"Wait! There's something else you can do."

YADIRA

Yadira's attention split between fear and pain. She felt hollow inside. She touched her stomach, now devoid of life. She spent two days in the hospital then went straight back to work. In the safety of her office, she cried when time permitted. Sorrow gnawed at her core. Yadira made herself stay busy. Enton's best efforts provided little comfort, leaving both him and Yadira to drift apart in their grief. Yadira had to move, had to work. She hurried to the audience chamber. One figure sat on the central chair belonging to Mr. Derbin: James Dumas.

"The advisors see you and you're dead," she said. James waved it off.

"They aren't here. Anytime there's a whisper of trouble, they bunker up," he said, growing too comfortable in the seat of power. He extended his arm to the chair beside him. "There's a place for you, too."

Yadira rejected the offer. Armed guards lined up in front of the Advisor's chairs.

"Why am I here?" Yadira asked.

"There was a skirmish near the dam. A few corpses were recovered," James said, a hint of accusation in his voice. "I've also heard reports of more abductions and activity in the sewers."

"I'm aware," Yadira said.

She hid her mistrust of James. James looked at her with not so hidden mistrust.

"Martial law may be necessary. Locking down the city will show us who serves and who doesn't," James suggested. Yadira shook her head. *Is he making his move?*

"You're already too used to that seat if that's your answer for everything," Yadira said. "The people would reject that and revolt again."

James nodded in consideration.

"I'll handle it," Yadira said.

James shifted nervously. Yadira understood James's trepidation after his subterfuge destroyed the last king. James was now effectively a king on the receiving end of the schemes. He straightened up, taking on the posture of someone preparing to pass judgment.

"What?" Yadira asked, fearing what came next.

"Someone is conspiring with them, someone powerful," James said. Yadira knew this wasn't exactly a profound statement. Many influential people conspired against each other all the time. The web of deceitful manipulators didn't exactly narrow it down. The two stared each other down. Yadira wouldn't be intimidated by James's unsaid accusations. Yadira provided him with a list of suspects.

"The *guilty* party will be found," Yadira said.

She stood her ground, she wouldn't be accused or intimidated. James paused for a minute. She considered this may the moment he started rounding up anyone he deemed guilty.

"Indeed. I'll alert the agents. You send more men to search the underground. We'll have them before the day is out," James said with disturbing confidence. Yadira nodded.

James stepped off Mr. Derbin's chair and went to the regent's chair a level below. James and Yadira returned to regular duties and relaxed demeanor upon the arrival of the scholars, businessmen, administrators, and secretaries bombarding them with lesser problems. Yadira's scattering attention affected her ability to govern, worsening with each meeting.

"If you're unwell, then leave," James said.

"Yes. My apologies," she said.

"It's all right. You've shown exceptional strength to govern after all that's happened," James said.

Yadira was taken aback by words resembling admiration. An escort led Yadira to her car. A man hurried to open the door.

"It's time," she said before stepping inside. The man acknowledged this and hurried off.

Though scatterbrained and barely holding it together, Yadira became acutely aware of her surroundings. Her escort drove her home while others cleared the streets for her.

"It's okay to take time off. If I may be so bold, you're no good to the country fighting yourself," her escort said.

"There's too much to do," she said. *I have to reach Enton,* he thought.

Her escort learned long ago the futility of dissuading her. Yadira felt a presence, always out of sight yet always right around the corner. The fear swelled inside. Arriving at her house, Yadira rushed up the stairs and to the wall safe. She stopped in her tracks. Enton set on the bed, head low in disappointment.

"Heard a rumor you were leaving. Planning on telling me?" Enton said.

"I was coming to get you," she said truthfully. She rummaged through her belongings. Enton stood up. When they looked at each other, they tried not to think of the son they lost. Enton placed his arms around Yadira and kissed her forehead. She wanted his love, yet nothing could pull her from doing what had to be done.

"We have to leave now. They're coming after me, now you, too," she said.

Enton clamped his arms on her shoulders. A loud bang came from the ground floor.

"They're here!" she cried. Yadira dashed to the wall safe opposite the desk. Yadira trembled, repeatedly bumbling at the passcode. Enton went for the gun on Yadira's desk.

"What's going on?" Enton said, turning the safety off the handgun.

"James—" she said.

She heard crashes below. Glass shattered behind them. An agent burst through the window via a rope. Enton fired at the invader, only to be shot by another man coming through the door.

"I'll kill you all for this!" Yadira snarled, rushing over to clutch the hand of Enton in his last seconds of life. Yadira wept, losing her sole reason to go on. A commander stepped into the room. He gave the gunmen in the room a stern glare.

"He was innocent!" she said.

"Your fault for getting him involved."

More soldiers barged in the room, checking every nook a cranny. The commander strolled over to the wall safe.

"Crack it. If it's not done it in sixty, we'll resort to other methods," he said.

Yadira inched close to the gun, only to have it kicked away. The safe beeped. The soldier opened the door to find firearms, Toth and Gloire passports, and the damning evidence the commander sought. The soldier pulled out a silver mask. He handed the mask to his CO. They both looked at each other in bewilderment.

"Got a thing for theatre?" he said to Yadira.

The commander ran his finger through the inside of the mask, receiving a shock for his trouble.

"You have no idea what that is," Yadira said.

The commander flipped the mask over. She didn't bother to stop him; it bought her a bit more time. The man raised the mask to his face. His eyes widened. His mouth went agape as he saw the same dark things she had seen. The commander pulled the mask back.

"What the?" the commander said.

A steady thunder drew the soldiers to the windows and the door. Vigilant soldiers surrounded her house. Vigilant marched into the house, killing the government agents without hesitation. Yadira took advantage of the commander's distraction and scrambled for the gun. Yadira shot him dead. She sat by Enton's lifeless body. Yadira looked up at the Vigilant soldiers in the room. The first, High Crusader Wren, extended his arm and helped her to her feet.

"I'm sorry about Enton. James caught on faster than expected," he said. Yadira washed her sadness away for the mission.

"Are we ready?" she asked.

"We can hold off the regent for at least a few days," Wren said.

"That may not be enough time," Yadira said. She held back the tears even when the full weight of Enton's death hit her.

"If you need a moment...." Wren said. Yadira regained her composure.

"They were why I fought," she said.

"You can't give up now. We have to get back underground and prepare."

Wren picked up the mask and handed it to Yadira. Vigilant followed Yadira through the escape hatch in her basement. One of the many perks that came with being the regent or vice regent came in the form of the repurposed board member estates complete with escape tunnels that fed into the sewers. Yadira and Vigilant followed the sewers through the freshly drilled tunnels into the secret world. It took Vigilant the better part of a year to drill through to the sealed underworld.

Yadira and Vigilant descended into the chamber of the unfinished city to the circular platform around the central tower. Soldiers on the platform removed charred remains from the metal poles attached to the tower. Yadira took her place at the tower door and awaited the signal. The time arrived, but the radios didn't respond. She knew the alternative. A jolt from the mask traveled up Yadira's arm into her brain. She understood the meaning. She held the mask up to her face. The mask warmed.

Through the mask, she felt the presence of masked figures in two different locations. Her brain tingled. She could see them. One man wore the white clothes and red markings of a lord crusader, while the other man wore the crimson armor and gold trim of the grand crusader.

"What news do you have for me?" Matthias said.

Matthias commanded respect and power that reverberated through the mask. Yadira hated the vile object, but relished the idea of using it against its master. She sensed the inhuman presence desperately trying to reclaim its parts. Yadira briefed Matthias on the progress made unsealing the last chamber and the unfortunate developments putting her branch on the offensive.

"Dig in as best you can," Matthias said. "Today we're unsealing the final door. I'm unsure how long it will take to activate the system, but be ready."

Jaren Hart gave his reports of trouble with the locals. Matthias's anger carried through the mask.

"I told you not to mess with the locals. Your petty revenge will destroy everything we've worked for!" Matthias growled.

"Petty? My father, my mother, my baby sister!" Jaren snapped.

"The people of Durenburg aren't responsible. We're trying to save them, save everyone," Matthias said.

"I'm not," Jaren said. Matthias's anger burned through the mask. He raised his hand out. Jaren clutched at his chest.

"Fulfill your oath. I won't ask again." Matthias said.

"F-forgive me, sir," Jaren said, panting heavily.

Jaren collected himself and continued his report, providing information far more disturbing. Jaren detailed accounts of a stranger in the frontier and a trail of eaten corpses left in his wake. The stranger in question currently evaded them.

"So it's true," Matthias said. "The Adversary has risen. Eon must be tired of the witches. We can't wait anymore." Yadira knew what he meant; she feared it would come to this.

"He must be eliminated or incapacitated at once," Matthias commanded. "Yadira, double your efforts underground. Keep the government busy a little longer. Drive James out of the city and kill any who know. These are your top priorities. Don't forget why we're here. We're at the end now. Ever Vigilant."

"Ever Vigilant," Yadira said.

DRAKE

Drake felt the old demons stirring, pulling him into a past yet to let go. He reflected on one of the missions where his troubles took root. Drake navigated trees to the side of the enemy location. Drake was handpicked by Aric Blackthorne to carry out a rescue mission. To reach the highest level of knight meant a person must handle a variety of situations to prove their ability to operate solo. A small group of disenfranchised souls was holed up inside the mayor's house outside Godwin Crossing. Godwin's Crossing was named after an ancient Blackthorne that had once camped here on the way to quell an enemy force from the neighboring country of Gloire, the onetime enemy and now ally.

The wooden cottage lay atop a hill with woods on three sides. A single dirt road transformed into a concrete path up to the mayor's domain. Intel suggested four targets held the mayor and his wife hostage. Drake understood the flaring tempers upon the election of a man who happened to be the son of the last mayor everyone seemed to hate. As Aric predicted, pockets of angry citizens formed small bandit groups when attempts to create a more significant rebellion in the east fell flat.

With dozens of windows, a second-floor balcony in front, and a third-floor balcony at the back, the cottage served as a rifleman's paradise. At seventeen, Drake had plenty of experience dispatching small groups of enemies, infiltration missions, and settling petty disputes, though seldom hostage situations. Drake had to be put through the wringer to be the best of the best. Aric's ranking knight-ambassador in the area went so far as to forbid anyone from helping Drake.

Drake made two attempts to negotiate with the captors, but they didn't utter a single word. He talked his way, and others, out of violent ends a dozen times across his career and treated each failed negotiation as his failure; this wasn't one of those times, though. Every failure meant Drake needed to work harder.

He wore his traditional black gambeson. Camouflage armor and top-of-the-line gear weren't always available in the field. The best soldiers needed to work with such limitations. Drake disapproved of handicaps that could risk the hostages. He crawled through the forest floor to avoid detection. He spied three enemies moving from window to window, a man for each foot. Drake studied the patrol patterns, not professional but relatively consistent. No armor protected the enemies.

He slowly crawled forward in the brief gaps when the men switched windows, making steady progress, telling himself one hasty step spelled doom for the hostages. Drake noticed the agitated movements inside the building, evidence they feared their inevitable fate. Shooting was a last resort. A stray fawn darted across the road, catching a bullet from the second-floor window. The sniper cursed in frustration.

Drake made it to the cottage wall and flattened himself against it. He zipped past the window when the bottom man continued his clockwise pattern. He approached the door, quickly picking the lock and slowly pushing it open when the man passed by. Drake closed the door behind him and crouched beside the stairs. He unsheathed the survival knife at his hip. The bottom floor man walked by one last time, receiving a knife across the throat. With catlike swiftness, he dispatched the second with a quick knife jab in the back of the neck.

Drake listened for the footsteps of the last gunman and eliminated the threat with record time. Drake checked his corners for surprises. He navigated halls, checking each room for signs of the final man and the hostages. He walked into a large room with a long table holding an icebox with two wine bottles. A couple and their young son lay on their stomachs on the other side of the table with mouths taped and limbs bound. A third body was too late to be saved.

A short figure with a high-pitched voice aimed a shotgun at the head of the mayor. The boy holding the gun appeared no more than twelve and basted in his nervous sweat. Drake aimed his gun at the boy. The boy's eyes widened in fear.

"You don't have to do this," Drake said.

"What did you do to my brothers?" he cried. Drake's heart sank.

"You're a fuckin' murderer!" the boy screamed.

"Please let these people go, this is not the way to handle it," Drake said, realizing this would only end with forceful disarmament.

"Stay back!" the boy said, cocking the shotgun.

"Let them go. We'll talk this out, I promise," Drake said.

"He got our dad killed," the boy said, not lowering his weapon.

Drake sympathized with the boy; however, he learned that a person can be accused and not be guilty even when they're quite abrasive. The job of a Blackthorne soldier was taxing on Drake's soul. Drake kept his nausea at bay, aiming a gun at a boy.

"We'll figure it out. You have my word," Drake said. Drake saw the fear in his eyes.

"Liars! You're all liars!" the boy cried.

"Please stop," Drake said. He saw what was coming. The boy's finger tightened around the trigger. Drake acted on instinct. His shot connected with the boy's chest, dropping him dead. He told himself he could've aimed at the legs or disarmed him, but that would've only ended with him or the others dead. Drake placed his arms on the game table. His chest constricted with serpentine force. Drake's arms trembled. The nightmare had ended.

Drake aimed the gun at the series of targets at Duke's private gun range. He fought through the images. The blackest moments of his life rushed back, hitting with a newfound fury. He dwelled on all the kills during his bloody career. Petty criminals, bandits, corrupt soldiers, and low-level politicians. Drake had over 200 kills to name and witnessed dozens of friends die. Justified or not, each one gnawed at him. The dead pulled him into an abyss that threatened to drown him. He lowered his gun and panted heavily. Zora and Thos practiced their rifle skills beside Drake. Zora and Thos stopped firing when they noticed Drake.

"You all right?" Zora asked.

The gunfire in his head didn't stop. Knights slashed and fired at him. Anselm lunged at him, forcing him out into the courtyard. Drake fell back, fighting against his own to the amusement of others. Blackthorne Castle exploded. For a second time, Drake murdered his king. Drake's heart pounded. Voices cut through the bloody haze.

"It's not real," Zora said.

"It's not real," Drake repeated. Drake's breath slowed. "I'll be back."

Drake walked to his room in the guest house. Drake maintained deep, steady breaths and went straight for the medicine cabinet. Drake poured himself a cup of water and gulped it with a double shot of pharmaceutical relief.

He spent his off-hours with Zora and picked up a few of her habits. He performed his version of meditation. The blood-soaked memories dulled, leaving Drake alone in the peaceful dark. The images of Anselm lingered for a time, as they always did.

Zora came in, wordless, and sat beside Drake. Drake appreciated her support. The two sat in comfortable silence while Drake slew his internal demons. Drake took Zora's hand.

Her sweet smile glowed in the darkness, giving him the extra boost to fight through the pain.

"I tell myself I do this for the good of the nation," Drake said. "I was proud to fight and ready to die if that's what it took. It was always so easy to go along with it. I believed in what I fought for. I . . . don't have that anymore. All I have are nightmares and ghosts." Drake clenched Zora's hand tight.

"You're protecting the people," she assured. Drake knew she wasn't wholly convinced of that either.

"These people wouldn't need protecting if not for groups like the Void or the advisors or Aric." Drake looked at the officer's badge he kept on the nightstand. He never wore it anymore. *I keep this system going,* he thought.

"I've never been fond of institutions of power," Zora began. "Even Vigilant no longer seems to be what it was meant to be. Most Freemen believe that ultimately government must be reduced to the basest functions of protecting people. Some want none at all. People say it's unrealistic. We say going on like this and expecting it to get better is. I can't tell you what to do, but what I can say is do what you feel is right."

More and more people flocked to Freemen areas or looked to start new ones. The wounds from the last war weren't healed, and recent conflicts threatened to rip them open once more. Drake felt lost. Drake held no doubts he was needed here to stop the madness, but he faced an uncertain future.

"I'm glad you're here with me," Drake said. "You, Thos, and me are our own little support group. Guess Melvin belongs in there too," he said.

"We all fight our pasts."

"No better people to suffer with," Drake replied.

Zora slowly introduced small talk as Drake overcame his darkened mind. The duo made plans for other trips around Mexico when time permitted. Drake and Zora rested on the couch for an hour before meeting back up Thos. Thos swapped his jeans and shirt for tacky smiling jalapeno decorated swim trunks and lounged in the hot tub by the pool. Drake and Zora approached him.

"Feel better?" Thos said.

"I do," Drake said. "You?" Thos drank a glass of wine in response to the rhetorical question.

He dried off and followed Drake and Zora to a table in the garden for a light lunch of pork sandwiches. The three laughed and joked their way out of both past and present negativity. Yelling outside interrupted the pleasant day.

"Sounds like we're gettin' a turd for dessert," Thos said.

The three walked out to the sight of two dozen armed guards and Duke staring down Melvin, Skully, Ed, and the giant Liz carrying an equally giant sack full of goodies. All eyes, and guns, aimed at Liz.

"Don't shoot!" Drake cried in the nick of time.

"Why the hell not? This man has been AWOL and, correct me if I'm wrong, has been stealing from us!" Duke said. Melvin belted out a laugh in disbelief.

"You guys are bigger thieves than I could ever hope to be. And you fucknuts tried to kill me after fighting the gang *you* powered up and couldn't shut down because they got a better dealer," Melvin growled. Duke scoffed.

"Melvin found out where the Void's getting their hardware from," Drake said. Duke covered his face with his hands.

"You hired them . . . aiding traitors makes you one," Duke said, directing his hateful glare to Drake.

Drake hid his smile, relishing the small jabs at the state's armchair general. Duke's actions were causing some to question his leadership. Liz bore his teeth when Duke's men entered his personal space.

"Let's skip the standoff. We got big trouble," Melvin said.

"Fine. Your pals go with my men. Collateral, let's say," Duke said.

"Liz stays with me. You can try to stop him if you want," Melvin said.

Duke motioned Melvin, Drake, Thos, and Zora to his spacious office. Melvin's human cohorts were escorted to the barracks by Duke's troops. Melvin told them the mythical metropolis out in the wastes was very real, and two factions in Vigilant were probably about to fight for it. Melvin laid out the imminent attack on Mexico City using Vigilant weapons. Zora perked up at the mention of her uncle and his doubts about the grand crusader's intentions. Melvin assured Zora that Gregor would contact her after he gathered more intel.

Duke mulled the looming threat of Mexico City reduced to a smoking heap. He realized how engaging or fleeing the enemy would enflame the situation.

"Got us over a barrel," Duke said.

"Same play you used on Anselm," Drake said. Duke sneered. Drake bit his tongue before inflaming the situation any further.

"I'll radio the army and Mexican officials. Those fools want a war, they're gonna get one," Duke said, letting out a hint of Red Devil viciousness.

Drake knew how things were about to play out. He hated the idea of letting people die in the city to encourage the populace to accept Duke's rule.

"That isn't the worst part," Melvin said. "They're being used by Matthias, a distraction from a massive operation. They've activated the Silent City, converting it into a super weapon. Gregor isn't sure of the boss's motives, so he sent me here to warn you and prepare to fight the deadheads. He'll arrive soon as he can."

Melvin dished out the even more alarming news of Vigilant activating the very real Silent City to destroy a demon-controlled Compact.

"If things go bad, how do we stop it?" Drake asked.

"Not sure, but we bought some time on that front. We damaged part of their weapons factory and took out one of the tunnels." Melvin said. Melvin untied the bag attached to his belt. "And that's not all. Wait 'til you get a load of this."

MATTHEW

BRIELLE WAS RIGHT in front of him, screaming and clawing at her own head.

"Just make it stop!" she screamed. "I can still see it. I can see it all! Make it stop! There's only one way to sever the connection."

Even one as mighty as Matthew Pavane was powerless to help his wife in this internal war.

"Don't make me," he said.

Matthew stood, sword in hand, prepared for the worst. He jolted awake at the killing blow. It took a second to realize it was a dream, and a few seconds later to remind himself Brielle did not meet her end that way. The resurfacing memories didn't completely alleviate his fear.

Matthew grunted as he fought off the grogginess and the sounds of Vigilant forces getting far too close for comfort. Matthew snapped alert and crept out the sewer tunnels and back through the maze of buildings in the undercity. Troop activity increased since the appearance of the masked man that had invaded Matthew's head. He considered himself fortunate he wasn't found, maybe too much so. Matthew wondered if his foes were too busy scouring the buildings or if the masked creature had something to do with it. Images of mass death hastened his steps.

Matthew dipped and ducked through numerous buildings to a better vantage point of the central structure. Matthew climbed through a collapsed warehouse and took the position in a hole in the roof. He lay on the top and used his binoculars. A large opening at the central tower base pulsated with green light. A petite female figure holding a silver mask divvied orders outside the building. Matthew zoomed in and identified her as Vice Regent Yadira Khouri.

"No wonder they've gotten away with this," Matthew muttered.

Soldiers around Yadira hastily strapped new prisoners to the incinerator poles, serving as generators for the lone machine at the city's heart. The tower groaned with power and was finally open.

Matthew looked inside the tower, barely able to make out circular objects. His off-kilter position didn't provide a view straight through the structure. Something on the edge of his perception gnawed at him like a buzzing gnat. Matthew followed the sensation. Something far above the floor caught his attention, something that moved. He squinted, though it didn't help.

Yadira hurried into a truck pulling up at the base of the stairs and quickly absconded to the world above. Matthew needed answers, and time was running out. He cursed and preceded to a vantage point near heavy Vigilant activity in a warehouse a mile from his location. Pops and creaks from the dark corners of the chamber had Vigilant shooting at shadows, forcing Matthew to move quickly at the paranoid scanning of every inch of the place.

He watched soldiers move into another building and emerge with weapons that appeared to be both gun and sword. Soldiers in helmets gave Matthew an idea. He detoured to the storehouse to speed up his recon and waited for gaps in the patrols. Matthew searched for nearby scrap to expedite the process. He climbed back onto the ground and reached into a patch of exposed earth for a tried and true rock. He chucked the rock with all his might into a hollowed-out tunnel feeding into a buried section of the city. The apocalyptic pang sent every soldier in the region to the potential threat source.

Matthew slipped in behind them and pilfered the crates. Next, he donned some Vigilant light armor and helmet for added protection in case someone saw him from afar. Matthew snatched a gunblade.

"So they finally got it working," Matthew said.

Matthew scanned the weapon for some on-the-fly training. He kept the weapon in gun mode as the other soldiers did. Footsteps getting louder forced him to strap it on and leave. Dipping out of sight, he discarded his old sword and hit the main road. It felt good to not be shuffling through life anymore. It felt less good to be working against his once prestigious order.

Vigilant paid no mind to anyone dressed in their colors. So Matthew blended in fast, thankful he hadn't let himself go during his retirement. He glanced up at the central structure along his way to the warehouse, maintained pace, and kept his eyes forward. He took the long way to the warehouse to avoid the final wave of troops. Matthew slipped in through the back. Electric lanterns hung from the ceilings.

"Like our first date, B," Matthew said. "Got a little better after that."

More memories came rushing back. The memory from before continued, this time of the woman he loved altogether different than he remembered. She approached him, weapon in hand. Matthew shook off the unearthened past bubbling up, there was no time for such things.

Matthew got back to business. Tables covered with lab instruments and iceboxes filled the room. The warehouse served as a mobile lab for the operation. The lab was bare-bones but neat with stacks of books and boxes.

Matthew pulled open the iceboxes. The first two contained

red and black blood. The following three boxes contained various human organs and unidentifiable masses. This haphazard cold storage wouldn't last long. Matthew couldn't linger. Vehicles passing too close and the occasional flickering light kept his head on a swivel.

He approached the books on the table and skimmed through research on demonology, cybernetics, gunblades, and a plethora of info there was no time to analyze. He picked up a fat red journal, having that old-fashioned gut feeling he'd hit paydirt. The first page listed numerous Vigilant operations, the first being Killswitch. Matthew powered through the info as truck activity increased outside. Diagrams of cells labeled "Godseeds" filled the pages, notated with genetic makeup and potential cybernetic components. Cryptic notes and questions covered the following pages. The next page contained a list of names. He read past the targets and saw one different from the others as a person of interest: Cassandra Averill. He quickly studied diagrams of silver masks, the witch-burning devices, and the man in white tied to it all. He wondered about the connection and the visions of mass death. It all clicked. His eyes widened in horror at the revelation. Matthew couldn't stop this alone. He had to act fast.

He stuffed the red journal into his satchel as best he could and rushed out the back of the warehouse. The central structure growled with life. Matthew doubled back to the armor for an explosive solution to his immediate problem. He found precious little, save for a few bags of grenades. He dodged patrols and climbed the side stairs of the central structure. Matthew strapped the weapon to his back. He homed in on a lone guard at the elevated edge section serving as the tower's base. He hesitated for a moment. It had to be done. Matthew snuck up behind the man and wrapped his arms around his neck and head, stopping short of killing him. The other soldiers huddled around the door of the tower.

Matthew removed the gunblade from his back. He dropped the gathering of soldiers. Though he was ex-Vigilant, he held back the growing vomit at the notion of killing them. Matthew removed the bag of grenades from his belt. For all Vigilant's plans, the mission always ended in a wild Hail Mary.

Matthew pulled grenade after grenade out and chucked them at the witch-burning generators powering Vigilant's machines. One by one, the poles blew to pieces. Matthew's grenade stash ran out two-thirds of the way through his attack. The hum of the tower stuttered and died. A dozen soldiers burst from the tower door, hollering and dashing to the destroyed machines. The soldiers hollered out, bringing their companions to bear on him. Matthew hopped off the elevated platform and hit the ground running. The hail of bullets nipped at his heels and whizzed by his shoulders. He weaved through the remnants of the old city that provided him ample cover. He picked out the nearest truck, forcing himself not to hesitate. Hundreds of Vigilant troops amassed and zeroed in on the lone intruder. Matthew ran. The ground shuddered; he hoped this wasn't a mistake.

The army stopped dead in its tracks. The echoing thuds on the main road directed all gunfire to a far greater threat. Matthew plowed his way through the reduced forces in his way. Metal screeched and bent. Cutting across the main road, Matthew unloaded shots into a soldier running toward a truck. Matthew rushed to the corpse and ripped the keys from his still-warm hand. He fired up the engine and headed through the tunnel leading to the fields near the amphitheater. Matthew had no pursuers, but he had a hunch his maneuver had bought him precious little time. He couldn't fight the whole of the Vigilant army. Matthew followed the tunnel to the source: Vice Regent Khouri.

GREGOR

GREGOR LOOKED OUT the window, fearing what the day would bring. He alerted trusted soldiers and prepared for the worst-case scenario. There were plenty of men on his side, as many out of respect as there were doubting Matthias. Outside his temporary home, Gregor saw the thousands in the crowd of frozen robots awaiting Matthias's arrival. He protested not dismantling them all, but Matthias decided that was a waste outside of taking some for study or scrap when needed. There was a knock at the door. The time arrived, the man told him. Gregor walked through the city buzzing with electric life. He entered the lab. Matthias sat alone, staring at the case holding the silver mask.

"You wanted to see me?" Gregor said. Matthias continued to stare at the floor.

"Do you ever doubt your commitment to the order?" he asked. Gregor thought about the life he had given up for the job.

"I do," Gregor admitted.

"I never thought I'd have a child," Matthias said woefully. "After my service in the army, I became a fisherman. It was a fine life, nothing special. Married a fine woman who tired of our life. Sought out knowledge and power, an escape from mundane existence. Was convinced a sacrifice would get her a life outside of fate's shackles. I did what needed doin' and saved my daughter.

"Eventually, she learned the truth and got too close to the same knowledge that corrupted her mother. Maybe my actions even pushed her to it. That set me on the path. Hard to believe that same little girl could become a murderer. A now he's taken her from me as well. He's about to learn what that feels like." His last word burned with hate.

"At least she regret it in the end," Gregor said.

"Was I wrong to kill her?" he asked. Gregor sighed.

"I'm not sure. She violated the Compact . . . but there's nothing wrong with desiring to be free. What I do know is that you need to destroy that thing," Gregor said.

Gregor knew he wouldn't. Matthias didn't take his eyes off the case.

"In the beginning, I tried," Matthias said. "It's surprisingly resilient. I decided to use the weapon of the enemy against him. I believe I've done good with it. My visions are stronger and I take knowledge from the host. We never would've gotten this far without it. We'd still be scurrying around, reprogrammed at the whims of a monster."

"Believing you do good doesn't mean you do," Gregor said. Matthew showed no signs of anger at Gregor's overstepping.

"You're the only person here that's honest with me," Matthias said. "You never ask permission to speak freely. I wouldn't tolerate that from anyone else, but I respect you. You're a hero, you know that? If not for you, I wouldn't be here. Most of us wouldn't."

"You're too kind," Gregor said. Matthias stood up and picked up the case.

"I understand your concerns, but today the doubts will vanish, I promise you," Matthias said. "It's time."

Matthias and Gregor walked to the impossibly tall front doors of the cylindrical building at the city's heart. Each soldier put on a breathing mask. A soldier handed Gregor and Matthias breathing masks. Trolls, two on each side, pulled on the doors.

The doors groaned from unimaginable strain. They slowly opened. Green light poured out, bathing the forest of dead machines in otherworldly splendor. A few men with square devices analyzed the ancient world spilling out. No acrid wind came out to greet them. Everyone removed their masks.

Matthias ordered a team to accompany him and Gregor, including a man holding the case. The remaining troops, including Raul, were ordered to wait outside. Gregor and Matthias walked into a ring-shaped room circling the area. A giant screen hung above a second door leading into a larger chamber. Discolored images of organic, synthetic, and cybernetic humans adorned the walls.

"Imagine the world had they not failed," Matthias said. "Had they channeled their efforts into something good. But they desired control over every aspect of human life, and they partially succeeded. They wanted a New World Order. Thought they needed it. Unfortunately, It didn't feel the same way about them," Matthias said.

The last door slid apart. Matthias stepped in, followed by Gregor. Gregor stopped in his tracks, and the blood left his face. Thousands of eyes watched him. Large bubble-shaped pods filled with liquid crawled up the walls. Inside in each bubble was a living organism with a dozen wires and tubes inserted into vital parts of the body and connecting them to the walls. The lifeforms wore no clothes, likely destroyed over the ages. They were withered to the point of being skeletal, atrophied beyond repair. Kept alive by this structure, the beings floated in their pods. Their sorrow-filled eyes begged Gregor to end an existence they could no longer bear and were powerless to stop.

"Are these Old Worlders? This place has been keeping them alive for two thousand years!" Gregor exclaimed.

Gregor's long-festered hatred of the people he believed ruined the world softened in the face of this fate worse than death.

"I never expected . . . " Matthias said, dampening his mood.

"Planned to ride out the end of the world in these support pods . . . didn't work how they intended," Gregor said. "They fled to avoid the world becoming a wasteland, ironic this is one of the only places that did."

Gregor walked over to the row of pods on the ground floor. Gregor placed his hand on a pod. The person inside watched him, trying to move his useless arm to reach out. Matthias flew into a rage.

"This can't be the signal. Was it from them? Was it all just a cry for help!?" Matthias fumed, drawing his EMPX and repeatedly striking the ground. Gregor analyzed the pods and those trapped within the living tombs.

"Pull the plug. They've suffered enough for their crimes," Gregor said.

"I've no sympathy for them," Matthias said. Gregor scowled.

"You intend to use them as part of your machine?" Gregor asked. Matthias turned his head to see Gregor then the thousands of pods filling the room.

"If necessary," he replied. "Don't forget the countless lives they ruined while they hid here waiting to do it all over again." The images of Matthias's daughter dripping to the floor haunted Gregor. He bit his tongue while Matthias's temper raged white-hot.

A machine with keyboards and screens lay in the center of the room. Thick wires spiraled up the device, running along the walls into the pods and other unseen locations outside the room. The other Vigilant members worked through the facility, following the wires after a few moments of gawking at the Old Worlders.

"I'd almost given up," he said, heading straight for the machine. Matthias tapped on the keyboard. "For years, I struggled. Lost in the dark. I lost my daughter and wife. I joined Vigilant and gained purpose. I followed in the footsteps of the great heroes of our order, men like you and your brother. Now we can set Vigilant on the true path."

The screens came to life. Words and numbers flew across the screen. Like a man possessed, he typed away. The machine awakened. Matthias flew through applications and coding Gregor didn't understand. Gregor approached the machine. Matthias grunted in frustration and rammed his fist into the side of the console.

"Gonna take longer than I thought," he said, more to himself than Gregor. "But this will work."

The man holding the case moved beside Matthias.

"I think now is the time you told me exactly what happens next," Gregor said, unintentionally demanding. "We kill Eon"

Matthias stopped typing and turned to face Gregor.

"Not just It. All of Its agents. Others are still paving the way for his next stage of the world. There's one greater than all the rest. A man has been chosen; no, not a man anymore. He was deemed worthy beyond the apostates. He's every bit the threat as Eon, maybe worse. He's not an adversary, he's *the* Adversary."

"How do—" Gregor began. Matthias raised his hand.

"I can see him. This mask is a piece of Eon; the mask connects It to the chosen and each other. We have two more, one in Kingsbury and the other not far from your old home."

"Who is this Adversary?"

"I'm not sure. I see a trail of corpses everywhere he goes, picked apart like roast chicken. I feel pain, unceasing pain. I think it's his pain. I see the pain he brings to others. This man is becoming a demon or something worse. He's Eon's crowning achievement. There's a small connection to him, but it is weakening. Our chance to destroy him is fading fast."

"Fine, we kill him too," Gregor said.

"It isn't as simple as that," Matthias said. "Eon is connected to many things, including every part of us. It has the power to control our lives, our deaths, how many children we have, what we know, and when we know it. It is the new Collective. Everything in this world is part of this thing's Algorithm. So long as those are inside us, then It lives."

"What're you saying?" Gregor asked, clenching his fist in irritation.

"I'm saying we have to destroy every single trace of Eon on this planet, including what's inside us," Matthias said. The revelation hit Gregor full force. The weapon had the power to disable or kill anything with a strong enough frequency.

"You're going to wipe out all nanomachines? But destroying them may kill everyone! Have you found a way around that?" Gregor exclaimed.

"Not completely," Matthias said. "We've managed to eliminate the target cells in myself, Yadira, and some of the others, but many have died. There'll be casualties. Many casualties. You object?" Matthias asked, his voice almost disgusted with Gregor's questioning.

"I want them out too, but . . . this is too risky, too self-destructive. There has got to be another way," Gregor said. Matthias sneered.

"We can't wait any longer," Matthias said. "If we succeed, we'll helm the evolution of the world. I'll make the Compact what it should be. And if we all die . . . perhaps it's better than the alternative."

"We can free ourselves another way. I know we can," Gregor said.

"There's no time. The Adversary has risen and his power is growing," Matthias said.

"Don't do this. You're making a huge mistake," Gregor pleaded. Matthias sighed with disappointment.

"I expected more resolve from you. To make it this close and bow out is unacceptable," Matthias said, taking a step toward Gregor.

"You nutty little shit," Gregor said, raising his weapon. "I'm not gonna let you do this."

"You aren't willing to do what's necessary," Matthias said.

"Yes, I am," Gregor said.

Gregor shot the man holding the case and activated the sword mode of his gunblade. Matthias stopped, not reaching for the case. His fingers twitched. His head jerked. Gregor felt Matthias's anger rising like a hurricane of fire.

"You think hiding it will stop me?" Matthias asked with sinister calm. "I can sense it."

"You've used that thing too long. It's eating you up," Gregor said, bracing for a confrontation.

"It'll fail," Matthias said. "When this is done, the only thing that'll be left in here is me. The Compact will be in its rightful hands. Vigilant will guide the world."

Matthias hollered for reinforcements. Gunfire erupted outside. Raul and a team of Vigilant burst into the chamber. Matthias's people came running back to aid him. Gregor lunged at Matthias. Matthias kicked Gregor, sending him backward. Matthias drew his gunblade. Raul pointed his gun at Matthias, stopping him in his tracks.

"You've only slowed me down," Matthias said. "I'll succeed." Vigilant backup stormed into the building, quickly overwhelming Matthias forces. Matthias nodded to a man behind Gregor. The man sped away. Matthias fell back into his calm and collected state.

"I'll get it back. You can't destroy it, so it's only a matter of time. Your niece is shacked up with Duke. Such a shame to get her involved. The Void'll probably get her before I do," Matthias said with sorrow. A metallic roar shot through the city outside. Gregor switched to wave mode. He fired his gunblade, knocking Matthias to the floor. Gregor cranked the knob up to max and fired again. Matthias rose to his feet.

"Do you see? My power is growing," Matthias said. Gregor pointed at the machine in the center of the room.

"Blow it," he commanded.

Raul bombarded the device with blasts from his gunblade. Gregor pulled out the long range detonator from his satchel and turned it on. Gregor hit the button. Explosions boomed outside.

"The factory!" Matthias said.

Vigilant surrounded Matthias. Troops poured in from the other doors. Gregor and Raul fought their way through the enemy line. Vigilant soldiers with rifles, railguns, and EMPXs fired upon each other. The two barreled through, firing at any with guns aimed in their direction.

"I'm not sure who's on our side!" Raul said.

"Shoot who shoots you," Gregor said.

Together they weaved through the forest of robot corpses and to the trains. Gregor heard Matthias shouting in the chaos.

Vigilant soldiers sprinted off to intercept Gregor at the station. Soldiers hopped into trucks parked at the gate and hurried to the station, cutting off Gregor's escape. Gregor chose the next closest train.

"This one!" he said. "The coast right?"

"Yeah," Raul said.

Some Vigilant soldiers came to Gregor's aid. Gregor sprinted hard. A shield of pure energy formed a shell of energy around the city, separating it from the outside world. A truck hot on his heels closed in.

Gregor and the survivors of his Vigilant allies fled to the train station leading to the east coast. Enemy forces gathered in the station to block their escape. Enemies broke off from the other locations to close off the second exit. Gregor and his team rushed through the station, taking cover and firing when they could. Enemies behind them forced them forward. Gregor's team dodged what they could, making it to the train with a few casualties. Men behind Gregor took positions to defend him. Raul hurried inside the bullet train. Matthias's men blasted them with every type of weapon they had. Gregor and his men backed into the train while firing at the incoming enemies. Gregor, Raul, and his soldiers piled inside the train. Raul fired up the train. The sides of the train caved from the railgun shots.

The train charged up and began to move. Soon, it picked up speed. A rail blast clipped the front of the train, barely missing Raul's head.

Gregor and the survivors collected themselves in the temporary comforts of the bullet train zipping through the earth toward a city soon to be under siege. Sweaty, bloody, and angry, Gregor plopped onto a bench and lay back against the wall. Raul left the head car and sat adjacent to him.

"Any luck contacting Duke?" he asked. Raul shook his head.

"Keep trying," Gregor said. The train cut through earth, caverns, sewer systems, and water. Hot bile sloshed inside him.

"I'm fighting my own people," he said.

Gregor sat powerless in the train car as his men attempted to contact the world above. Gregor had no idea how much time they bought stealing the mask, and if it would come at the cost of Zora's life.

ZORA

"Touch it," Thos said, from a good ten feet away.

The silver mask lay on the table in Duke's office. Thos, Drake, Liz, Zora, and Duke stood around the mask. All of them hesitated to step forward.

"This thing?" Thos asked. He nodded in the direction of the mask. "This thing."

"Gregor told me this is what Matthias used to control the city and will use to kill the thing that controls the Compact," Melvin said, trying to believe the words himself.

Melvin put a lot on info on them. Out in the Uninhabited, her uncle was battling for control of Vigilant; from the sound of it he would need help. Whatever was about to happen, her uncle didn't want this vile thing anywhere near it. Drake approached the mask and stuck out his finger.

"Some kind of demon artifact. The way Gregor talked, it may even be alive," Melvin said. Drake's arm fell to his side, and he returned to the group circle of trepidation. Melvin's speech of demon masks controlling minds was a hard pill to swallow.

"So . . . can we destroy it?" Thos asked. No one made the slightest movement.

"We tried," Melvin said.

"It hurt," Liz said, turning to show the purple splotch on his back.

"We considered dumping it in a chasm, but Gregor was sure they'd find it soon enough," Melvin said. "He wanted us to hold it if we couldn't smash it."

"So we're stuck with it," Thos said. "And Big Cheese will be coming after it."

"Yep. Ol' Greg didn't trust Matthias with this power," Melvin said.

Zora picked up the mask to examine it.

"What're you doing?" Drake asked. Though not a member of Vigilant, Zora learned much from her father and uncle.

"If we can't destroy it, let's study it. We may learn something. We're going to need everything we can get if we have to fight Vigilant, especially with Old World tech at their disposal," Zora said.

Drake lowered his head and cocked an eyebrow, suggesting he knew there were more reasons.

"This thing will haunt me no more," Zora said. *I have to know,* she thought.

"Nobody touch the devil mask!" Thos cried.

Zora analyzed the mask front and back. She felt the heat from one thousand invisible pincers. She placed the mask on her face. Her heart leaped into her throat. Through the mask's eyes, she caught images from elsewhere. Eyes that weren't hers looked through binoculars at a pale man with a large sword in the wilderness. The binoculars zoomed in. The man wore different clothes, but it was unmistakably the stranger that showed up on her doorstep after the fall of the Blackthornes.

"I'm looking through the eyes of someone else. I think he has one of these masks on," she said. "He's watching that stranger I met right after the castle fell."

Other references to what sounded like a prisoner piqued her interest. The man in the other mask stopped and scanned the area, mentioning voices in his head. Other voices and images flashed through Zora's head. Again, she felt the tingling sensation probing her brain. Zora explained the sights and sounds.

The mask shifted to another person with a female voice in a deep underground chamber with unknown machinery like what Melvin described as the Silent City, though in far worse shape. People on metal poles screamed and burned. Zora listened as the mask wearers conversed with each other about the final phase of Operation Killswitch. The tingling in Zora's head turned to stabbing. Her vision shifted again, this time to a golden mask in the darkness. She heard a new voice in her head. *You again,* it said.

"Shit's about to hit a huge fan," Melvin said.

The other two wearing the masks cried out. Vigilant soldiers around the woman approached a metal structure. A hiss inside the machine signaled a geyser of energy growing from within. The golden face disappeared. Zora heard references to Prosperity Hall.

"We need to contact them now!" Drake said. Duke pulled his phone from his pocket and made the call while everyone else focused on the bizarre mask in Zora's hands.

There were cries around Zora before she realized what was going on. Silver tentacles burst from the sides of the mask, wrapping around Zora's head. Drake rushed to Zora's side. Drake tried with all his might, but the mask didn't budge. Liz ripped the mask from Zora's head. As the mask came off, the thrashing tentacles latched back onto Zora's head. The mask once again came to rest on her face. She heard the voice again. *We're made for each other,* it said.

A surge of energy sent Liz crashing into a table holding a two-hundred-year-old lamp gifted to Duke from the Toth ambassador. Drake screamed for a medic. Everyone, slack-jawed, turned to Zora.

"You all right?" Drake asked. Zora shook her head, still in complete shock herself. She couldn't hide her fear.

"I don't know," she said. "What do I do?"

"Remain calm. We're here with you," Drake said. A low rumbling came over the horizon. By the steady, constant pace, it wasn't thunder.

"We gotta go," Melvin said. "Either he found us or its deadheads."

"You have a place? Can you marshal a counterattack?" Drake asked. All attention shifted to Duke.

"Of course," Duke said, "to both."

Zora, Drake, and the others hastily gathered essential belongings and loaded them into the back seat of a truck for an unfortunate team on luggage duty. Melvin and Liz ran to gather the rest of his gang. Drake took stock of the weapons, trying not to be distracted by Zora's condition. The voice continued to taunt her. *Only certain people can connect to us; do you know what kind?*

"It's speaking to me," she said. *He knows where you are. Better hurry.*

"It says Matthias knows where we are."

Zora did her best to keep calm. While Drake procured an armored truck, Thos, Zora, Melvin, and his gang grabbed weapons. The group lost track of Duke and his men, growing uneasy. The thunderous rolling was upon them. Duke's convoy didn't wait. Drake rolled up with a truck. The sound took the form of motorcycles and a white tank.

"We gotta go now!" Drake said.

"Uncle," Zora said.

"He won't make it in time. Will find him later," Melvin said.

Zora and her friends loaded up and sped off. Melvin took the wheel. Explosions boomed in the west. Behind them, smoke rose from the direction of Mexico City. Four motorcycles broke off from the tank and came after them. Liz picked up his stolen railgun. He lined up the first target, taking his sweet time. Liz fired, obliterating the bike at the head of the pack. For every blue trailed bullet he fired, three came back at him. Melvin veered off the road to avoid the blue death.

Liz fired a second, well-placed shot. The blast collided with the bike, sending the skeleton-paint driver into the air. Liz hollered out at his perfect shots. The other two bikers broke off the pursuit.

"They have the villa. We probably aren't worth the trouble," Drake said.

"They don't care, but Matthias does," Melvin said.

The group rolled on through the night to the southeast. Each hour removed from civilization resulted in steadier breaths, though each person noted the rock formations potentially conceal-ing enemies.

"Where we going?" Thos asked.

"I got a place," Melvin said proudly. Drake's brow furrowed at Melvin's tone. "It's something else, believe you me. I didn't steal it . . . it was abandoned."

"It keeps us off the grid. I'm on board," Thos said.

The truck veered off due east to the Mexican coast. Hours upon hours rolled by until the group hit a sea of rocks forming jagged towers. Melvin navigated the rocky maze.

"No one come out here to the ass-end of Hell's Teeth," Melvin said.

"Of course not, look at it," Thos said.

Hell's Teeth was a desert of endless rock on the coast, sepa-rating the cities of the northeast coast from the jungles of the Yucatan. The truck arrived at a wall of rock with an opening just large enough for a single vehicle to squeeze through. Liz flattened himself against the truck bed. Melvin drove through the entrance in the ancient wall.

The rock wall stretched around the flat area with a massive structure in the center larger than Duke's villa. The long beast of a machine had a series of cannons on it, slight rust damage in spots, and patches of various plates around its sleek, black frame.

Two large wings protruded from the bottom of the structure. A staircase of scrap metal served as the side ramp inside the jury-rigged marvel.

"What in the? You found a battleship . . . plane . . . thing," Thos said, not believing the sight.

"We've been cleanin' the old gal up and putting 'er back together. Welcome to the Air Mel!" Melvin said, beaming with pride. "There are ruins of other ships all around out here, but this is the one most intact."

Melvin thrust out his arms in the direction of the ship's side, with his name poorly written on the side as well as a winged version of himself. A dozen men and women stood armed and ready for his arrival, while another two dozen worked on fortifications.

"How in the hell did you find this place?" Thos said

"Heard about it from a treasure hunter, former scholar," Melvin said. "We went looking for tech. He tried to screw us, we ended up with the whole thing, and he ended up dead."

"It work?" Drake asked. Melvin grinned.

"Hell yeah, sorta. We got some of the guns working," Melvin said.

Dozens of crates were stacked high on trucks, and skull-painted armored motorbikes were parked in a makeshift garage beside the ship. Drake's particularly lustful glare at the bikes made Zora slightly jealous. *I have a devil on my face and I'm jealous,* Zora thought.

"If you fellas are lucky, we might be able to grab a few of these for you. Know a guy that fakes licenses too," Melvin said. Melvin patted Drake on the back.

Melvin led the guests into the ship, providing a grand tour of his home and reminders there was room for more employees.

"Get some rest," Melvin said. We'll find Greg. The rest of my crew have the guns ready in case shit gets wild," Melvin said.

Melvin directed them to the next cabin deck. Drake and Zora

took the room near the stairs while Thos headed to the back. Drake closed the screeching door behind him when he entered the bland quarters. Zora caught wind of Drake's staring. Her heartbeat quickened.

"What?" she asked. Zora seldom liked the stares from Drake, though they weren't nearly as bad as the invisible other probing her mind. *How sweet,* the mask said.

"You remember that story you told me about your uncle?" he asked. Zora sat confused for a minute until she recalled Gregor's tale of ferrying a witch's head across the country and the mask she now protected.

"Seems like you're destined for the family business," Drake said. Zora smiled.

"Maybe. Back when I was little, I pretended I was fighting alongside my father and uncle," she said. "My dad used to bad-mouth uncle all the time, but he missed the order sometimes. He loved the adventure. I did, too. He taught me how to fight and about technology, but he never wanted me to be a part of it."

"Yet you're in the thick of it all the same," Drake said.

"Maybe this is the life I was meant for," Zora said, contemplating her purpose in life; the voice in her head pondered this as well. *You will serve our purpose. You all will.*

"Has your opinion on Vigilant changed?" Drake asked.

Zora thought back to vanquishing imaginary demons and swinging around wooden swords with her father while her sister ran around with the other children. Every bump and bruise didn't deter her from the life of an adventurer.

"Strict tech regulation goes against Freemen belief, but I loved the adventure and stories of heroes killing villains. I wanted to live the life in his stories, probably why he stopped telling me them."

Zora's happy childhood battled tooth and nail to quell the images of Matthias's regime on the march. She thought of the days she had listened to her father's stories, her feet dangling from the hanging courtyard and a belly full of peanut butter and jelly sand-wiches. She considered them one of the few good things from the Old World. Meanwhile she saw an orange-eyed man command-ing a legion, and she heard screams and flames behind him. The younger her would've champed at the bit to be here fighting, but she couldn't find that now. She understood Drake as the fantasy faded and the reality set in; there was no adventure, only death on its way. The voice in her head laughed.

ANSELM

ANSELM PARTOOK IN one last trip to the neon gardens of Mandragora's lush underworld before the seeping daylight stamped out the wondrous colors. Denying his hunger required more sleep, and the heavenly domain enticed him to linger.

The gardens extended a great deal through the cavernous domain, enveloping green tunnels spilling into glowing pools for well over a mile. Anselm arrived at another pool in a large area. Stripping off his clothes, he took the opportunity to bathe in soothing crystal-clear waters.

He washed his dirt-crusted, sweat sticky body to the sounds of weird birds and Mandragora's golem children prancing through her domain. Part of Anselm's brain yearned for a round of self-inflicted torment, but also fonder things. When Anselm tried to picture his family, he only saw them in their last moments. He floated in the waters, looking out into the harsh summer light in the mesh walls above.

A faint stabbing inside his mind caused him to rise from the waters and don his clothes. A static mist rolled off the waters, forming into the shape of a man. Black pits in the head widened into eyes and a mouth. Eon said nothing. The needle-pricks in Anselm's head caused his vision to blur. He felt Eon attempting to connect to his mind. The connection failed. Eon fell to pieces that dissolved into mist. His new advisor grew weaker by the day. Anselm questioned his role in the new order and the bitterness at being reduced to a henchman for this entity. He told himself Eon was a necessary evil for now. Eon concealed too much from Anselm; he wanted the whole story. Two words would lead him to the whole story: blood memory.

There was hunger, anger, desire, and pain stirring inside Anselm. He could feel very human blood, or a substance close enough, flowing through Mandragora's fleshy roots. The hunger, the desire, and the hatred of the world above were powerful motivators. Mandragora sensed Anselm. Mandragora's children gathered behind him, preparing for what was coming.

"There's no need for this," she said, a desperate plea for his sake and hers. "You don't have to be what they want." Anselm doubted Eon's grand plan.

"I'm no fool. I know I'm being used," Anselm said. "I accepted this so long as our goals align. This is for what I want." Anselm learned much during his northern exile and not from Eon. "Which is why I need more information. I'm sorry."

"You're not," she replied.

The earth groaned beneath him. Mandragora's massive fleshroots ripped out of the ground. One of the earthen tentacles smacked the unprepared Anselm, sending him through the air. It took seconds for Anselm to recover, this time leaving Mandragora unprepared. Anselm hit the ground running, dodging and hacking the incoming root arms. Sappy, amber-colored blood ran from Mandragora's wounds. He chopped at her trunk, drinking in the strength and knowledge spilling out. Her children leaped onto Anselm. The diminutive golems tore and sliced his flesh. Anselm dropped his sword to tear the creatures off his back and threw them hard into the walls. The creatures exploded in pieces only to reform around their cores. They rushed him again. Anselm grabbed hold of one and pulled the heart out. He gripped the heart tight with his right hand. Anselm swatted at the other golems dog-piling him. He applied his full pressure. The heart burst and its earthen shell fell apart. The golems shrieked and let go of Anselm.

Anselm returned his attention to Mandragora. Her wounds healed, though not nearly as fast as his. Her blood gave him boundless energy. Her root arms came at him. Anselm jumped on and ran up the tentacle root arm. Using it as a launching pad, he latched onto the human part of the fleshtree. Anselm ripped through her neck with teeth, drinking the powerful blood. He felt her flesh closing. He clawed at the neck to keep it open. Memories that weren't his flooded his mind, information Mandragora and Eon had withheld from him. He saw great machines in the earth, one beneath his former home. He understood these machines and their destructive potential, something he could use as well. The more he drank, the slower she healed. Her roots withered.

Anselm thought of Rosalie and stopped; part of him didn't want to be the monster. Her wounds began to heal. He let go of her and hit the ground. Anselm left through the tunnel, wondering why he still spared those in his way; part of him wanted to be the monster. He didn't want to stop; he reminded himself he could always come back later. Anselm soldiered on through the unfinished passageways that, according to Eon, were designed for safe and secret travel for the continent's elite as they braced for the uprisings. Anselm emerged into the outside world at the faint sounds of gunfire.

Anselm quietly followed the sounds. He scurried up a tree when he got within range. Vigilant men with bloodstained robes executed a group of bandits clutching to their tech, including another executioner's blade. A handful of soldiers reclaimed the stolen tech while Vigilant gathered the bandits for a meeting with a firing squad. A set of Vigilant soldiers in the group caught Anselm's eye. They wore bulky red armor and pointed bizarre gunsblades at a collection of people bound and gagged. A few prisoners were a patchwork metal and flesh that decried their apostate nature.

One of the red-armored soldiers pulled the trigger on his weapon at the protests of a male prisoner with the top of his head transparent like an egg cooker. No bullets came from the gun-blade, only rippling waves. The prisoner grimaced and went silent.

Vigilant took the prisoners north. Anselm followed from a safe distance, sticking to the trees when able. Vigilant marched throughout the day and night, halting for quick breaks and shooting prisoners refusing to budge. Anselm quietly pursued them. As they progressed northward, more troops and prisoners joined the procession. The commander of the group communicated via short wave radio with other soldiers in range.

Engines growled in the east and west. Camouflaged trucks carrying white panels rolled to crumbling ruins surrounding a metal obelisk far larger than the Hell Gates once described to him. Anselm hung back without the protection of the trees. Anselm surmised he approached what remained of the state's Vigilant headquarters.

Anselm waited for night to sweep its dark hand across the North Frontier, letting his dark urges fester in the meantime. His desire for ever-increasing pain was beginning to extend to not just himself but others. Anselm crouched low and moved across the swaying grass. Patches of clouds gave him extra protection from the moonlight illuminating his deathly pale skin. Anselm carefully worked his way to Vigilant tower. A lone truck and a half dozen men scanned the grasslands with night vision goggles. Anselm was flattered he garnered such attention.

He arrived at a few dozen yards from Vigilant tower. Not much remained of the previous structure. One small building and the base of a tower were the last pieces of the old fort that once held watch over neighboring Highland. Highland was the northernmost country in North America, consisting of parts of Old

World Canada, Alaska, Greenland, and home to powerful clans with a penchant for waging war on everyone. Without defenses up north, invading clans and now Vigilant could conquer the state with relatively minimal effort.

Tents covered sleeping areas, weapon crates, trucks, carcass-cleaning stations. A pile of white metal with thick treads and heavy wheels made Anselm raise an eyebrow, this was his first encounter with a railtank. Men and women were attached to poles around the central structure. Other prisoners were tossed into a massive pit at the edge of the compound.

Anselm circled the compound and took stock of the enemy. He noticed each member of Vigilant carried a sidearm and a gun-blade. The Vigilant faces stirred a vague familiarity in Anselm. A pang of fleeting guilt knocked on Anselm's gut at killing former members of his army that refused to support his betrayers.

A cylinder rose from the tower base. A black and white cannon perched atop a turret station provided a last line of defense for the base. Anselm recognized the retrofitted cylinder matched the designs of the Vigilant gunblades, creating a super weapon designed to burn out all traces of Eon from the world, with those connected as collateral damage.

Anselm spied Jaren, wearing a light armor of shining crimson, at the front of the machine. He tapped on a keyboard attached to the structure and the poles via wires. The man analyzed information appearing on the screen after each keystroke. He turned away from the keyboard when another man approached him with a black case. Jaren unlocked the case and placed the mask on his face. Jaren looked to his left and spoke to an invisible figure. He discussed the situation in Kingsbury.

"Any word from the Matthias?" Jaren asked.

Jaren paused and replied to a response only he heard. Anselm listened to Jaren's half of the conversation. "Dammit, something must've gone wrong. Perhaps we should continue without him."

Jaren's demeanor grew tense, energy crackled around him. "I don't care if it kills them; why do you think I'm here? I'll take out as many as I can."

His demeanor relaxed while he continued sizing up the invisible person.

"It won't work without him. He's got the juice. We do this right," his underling replied.

"Very well," Jaren said. "But the plan was in two days, I'm activating it, whether I hear from him or not. You know what'll happen if the government, Mr. Abaddon, or the Adversary catches you. We can still take them out without him."

Anselm hadn't heard the name of Mr. Abaddon in well over a decade, believing he had been killed in a military operation masterminded by Mr. Derbin. Anselm knew that Mr. Abaddon would eventually butt heads with the new regime without the checks and balances. Anselm savored the idea of his foes weakening each other, but he wanted them all alive for his terrible retribution.

Jaren's gazed at the metal cylinder jutting out of Vigilant tower. One last man was brought before him, wearing the dirty shreds of a white suit. Anselm caught the blank stare and dead eyes of the man once called Gideon Grey. A series of deep indentions in the sides and back of Gideon's head told Anselm whose mask Jaren wore. Vigilant soldiers attached the compliant, lifeless Gideon onto the pole in front of him. Jaren waved the mask in front of Gideon.

"Not so tough without your toy," Jaren taunted while striking Gideon repeatedly.

Jaren addressed Vigilant, commemorating the final phase of Killswitch. Anselm counted over two hundred members of Vigilant at the compound. He estimated a few thousand preparing to engage the military.

Jaren cursed and went back to typing on the keyboard. The air around the bound prisoners crackled. The bodies went alight in the roaring fires greedily embracing them, all save for Gideon. The segments of the metal tower spun and screamed. White light shined with a blinding light from where the pieces connected.

"Initiate test fire," Jaren said.

A pillar of white light shot into the sky, sending a white wave in all directions. Anselm felt a sharp pain in his chest that traveled through his body and set his blood afire. His energy left him. Anselm collapsed, becoming as helpless as a newborn. Most of Vigilant fell to the ground, including Jaren. To Anselm's dismay, Gideon winced and convulsed in agony. A disoriented Jaren stumbled about. He pulled the mask from his face and threw it to the ground.

"Keep working," Jaren approached Gideon and wrapped hands around his throat. He squeezed, though Gideon responded only with a dead gaze.

"I promise you'll burn," Jaren said. *I'll do so much worse to you,* Anselm thought.

Anselm began to regret not taking everything Mandragora had, wondering why he spared any in his path anymore. It grew harder for Anselm to feel compassion for the other beings of the world.

He walked away from Gideon to the big tent guarded by two thick armored soldiers. Anselm laid out a plan to eliminate his foes and use their weapons against them. He spent a good chunk of the night studying patrol movements, noticing movement patterns that might allow him some advantage in dispatching Vigilant before they'd know what hit them. Anselm's body grew sluggish from fatigue and hunger. He was too weak to face his foes. Anselm prepared to kill Vigilant and destroy their machine tomorrow night.

He broke off his recon at the coming of dawn and doubled back to scour the woods for a hidden place to rest. The pangs of hunger nearly took control. He considered giving in and laying into the succulent flesh of his enemies. His thoughts turned to the injuries he'd sustain in the future. A sickly part of him was excited to experience and dish out new forms of pain.

CASS

Cass took a seat on a bench in Advent Park: a collection of rides, stalls, junk food, and fountains that offered a more wholesome experience for those with families or weary of the bar and prostitute scene. Cass battled heart-bursting fear as she prepared for her mission for Mr. Abaddon.

Cass sat by the water fountain spurting a rainbow of colors to the heavens. A man approached her in casual clothes with a shaved head; it took a moment for her to recognize Kane Turce. Kane took a seat beside her.

"Me and Thos always planned to come out here, but we never do," she said. "In the early years, we'd always go to the Greenfield Fair. Never thought I missed stuffed animals and fried cheese. Even on our 'vacations,' we rarely make time to enjoy things anymore."

"I've always loved this place. My parents brought me here all the time when I was little," Kane said. "I couldn't get enough of those doughnut sticks. I often fantasized about having a son and bringing him here." Kane frowned. "Forgive me for asking, but why don't you have kids? Seems like the perfect time."

Cass now imagined herself and Thos watching a pair of little ones hollering and laughing at the Whack-a-Witch, a cartoony take on a rather dark reality one could face.

"I can't have one," Cass said. "Part of my defect. Thos blamed himself for the longest. Took a long time for me to accept it and longer to tell him. We wanted them so bad. We even had names, Andrew and Mary. We sank a fortune trying to fix it, fix me, but nothing worked. Guess we could adopt, but we let life pass us by so far."

"I let life go by, too," Kane said. "Toured the country. Got to spend time in Gloire for a bit too. Planned on marrying when I left the service. When I came back, I had a hard time. Didn't marry, relied on meds to help- the wrong kind. Fell back into the life, working for Mr. Abaddon. Lot of thrown away soldiers find their way to him. He snatches us lost souls, fitting for the king of the underworld. Drake nearly joined. Couldn't cope after Anselm died. Always recited his oath to help. Mr. Abaddon wanted him, but I told Drake to decline because when you join, you're his 'til your dying day."

"And he may be our only ally," Cass said, sickened by the idea.

"Working with crime bosses to fight Vigilant. What a mess," Kane said. Cass nodded, keeping her head lowered when troops came by. Cass and Kane watched the fountain as the soldiers made the rounds.

"Lot more activity than usual. Things are getting spicy," Kane noted. Cass kept her cool. Cass and Kane casually strode through the park to the commercial district when the soldiers passed. Kane and Cass passed men loading various trucks, including those with Thos's grinning mug plastered on the side.

"I see your husband's face so much it haunts my dreams," Kane said.

"He overacted for that shoot. Can't believe they went with it," Cass replied.

Cass walked with Kane for a bit until he fell back into the crowds of people. Cass steadied her breathing.

"In and out, that's all you have to do. No one will have a clue until it's too late," Kane assured.

Cass glanced over at Kane only to find him swallowed by

the group. Cass stuck her hand in her pocket to ensure the all-important prize remained. Cass pushed herself forward toward Prosperity Hall.

Stepping into the building, everyone carried on business as usual. Cass saw no trace of her contact, instead finding Yadira at the base of the left stairs. Yadira looked flustered, like she had run all the way here. Cass waved and Yadira waved back.

"Nice to see a friendly face today," Yadira said.

"Likewise. Thought you were confined to your office?" Cass asked.

"I try to step out once a week," Yadira joked.

"Heard there was some chaos in your neighborhood. Everything okay?"

"It's nothing." Yadira's demeanor changed on a dime. "What brings you here today?" The tone was no longer friendly, like Cass shouldn't be here.

"I have a meeting with the housing commissioner," she said, a real meeting plan for the same day next week.

"Wasn't that next week?" Yadira asked. Cass around and shook her head, feigning confusion.

"Was it? Too many meetings," Cass said.

Cass scanned the area, finding vaguely familiar faces among the soldiers. There was a different air about Yadira. Cass recalled these soldiers as those that attacked her house. All at once, the revelation hit her. Yadira didn't fail to notice. Yadira pulled the device from Cass's pocket, threw it on the floor, and crushed it.

"I told you to leave it alone. Not only did you persist, you conspired against us," Yadira said, confirming Cass's fear.

"You sent those people after me," Cass said.

"They were under strict orders not to harm you. They only wanted the switch," Yadira said.

"You killed people," Cass said. "You killed Adrienne." Yadira placed her hand over her stomach.

"She was agent of the enemy, even if she abandoned the cause her crimes had been unpaid until now," Yadira said. Cass let out a single laugh of shock.

"How did you get involved in this?"

"I defied the Algorithm," Yadira began. "I survived Toth. I survived demons. I survived Aric. My family was never supposed to endure, but that's how it happened. I thought it was all bad luck until I met Matthias. Years ago, he reached out to me and revealed the truth. Matthias freed me. We fought to change destiny. As his second, I came here to legitimize Vigilant's power and activate the city below. Then I met Enton. I had new reasons to fight. Thanks to the grand crusader, that monster couldn't kill me but... It took my son instead. I couldn't stop it." Yadira sucked back the tears, letting determination burn them away.

"I don't understand," Cass said.

"The Compact is a sick joke," Yadira began. "Our destiny is in the hands of the most egregious violation of that order. Our bodies. Our minds. Our lives are under Its control. It can help or hurt us whenever It wants." Cass's head spun.

"That's madness," she replied, trying not to be drowned by the grim reality of the world. Faint images of a masked horror and paralysis flickered in her mind.

"You've seen It. We've all seen It." Yadira said. "The being that appears as one and many. With our new tech, we can block Its powers. Killing the bastard's followers is just a bonus. There are ancient unfinished cities where the best and brightest gathered to escape and fight back. We found two and salvaged what was left of another, I hope that's enough."

"The Collapse," Cass said.

"They didn't realize what they created. They tried to kill It. Eon endured, but our world did not. It took a part of us with It. This time we kill It and break our shackles for good."

Cass debated telling Yadira about Mr. Abaddon's plans, but

she knew better. Again the guilt returned. Yet another person that had risen to power after Anselm had become a threat to those that aided them in gaining their station.

"All those people . . . what's to say you won't end the world again?" Cass asked.

"We've been making strides," Yadira said. "We're destroying Eon in those we can, but our time is up. I've seen the next stage of the Compact. The Adversary is coming and will unleash horrors the likes of which this world has never seen. He's becoming a perversion even the false god didn't intend. We're killing Its agents, but more will come. It will use whoever It has to stop us. The Compact took my son from me, and James took the man I love. It may be the reason why you can't have children. Gave you a defect because having kids doesn't fit into the equation. I was too late to save my son.

"It's taken countless lives and won't stop. I'll end this cycle. I'll burn down this world if I have to. I'll kill this thing for good. It will pay for my son. Many of us will die, maybe all of us. If we die, we'll die free rather than at the whims of some devil."

Cass saw a new Yadira emerging. She saw the friend vanish and in her place was vengeance and determination.

"I suppose you'll kill me now," Cass said.

"If I must," Yadira said.

"Were you ever my friend?" Cass asked, hurt.

"At first, no," Yadira admitted. "I monitored you because Adrienne got too close, thought you were an agent too. We suspected she was a witch, but weren't sure. But during that time . . . you've been my only friend in this terrible place. Even so, I won't let you interfere anymore. You will be held prisoner until the mission is done."

Yadira's guards moved on Cass. Doors flew open behind Cass, and a storm of G-men burst in, led by Kane.

"Make one move and I'll drop you," Kane said.

"We've already taken the city. Vigilant is everywhere. If you stop us here, other groups work in tandem here and across the country. We will end the cycle no matter what it takes." Vigilant soldiers and government forces converged on Prosperity Hall, with Cass caught smack in the middle. Mr. Abaddon's forces were quickly outnumbered.

"We're willing to die. Are you?" Yadira asked.

"We have your little hideout surrounded," Kane said. Yadira extended her hand toward Cass.

Cass stepped back, showing too much hesitation for the emotionally compromised Yadira. Yadira darted behind the cover of her troops. Cass hit the floor just as the bullets began to fly. Kane's forces moved up and pulled Cass from the exploding brick, flesh, and glass. Cass caught a glimpse of the disappointed Yadira fleeing in the direction of the elevator leading to the Vault. Most of Yadira's troops fell back to the meeting hall leading to the elevator. Kane escorted Cass from the building. Crowds fled Prosperity Hall, getting in the way of Kane's army.

"She smashed the device," Cass said, still in shock at the world screaming around her.

"We gotta get to Mr. Abaddon. Only safe place," Kane said. Cass struggled to keep up with the near sprinting Kane on his way to a black car. Kane ripped the keys from his pocket and hit a button on the side. A dozen men were running straight for Kane and Cass. "Can you drive?"

Cass nodded. Kane threw the keys at her.

"Then get to it. Red building on 22nd. Find Proxy, got purple eyes. I'll keep 'em busy. Can't let them find it."

Before Cass could protest, Kane fired on the incoming foes. Kane took cover inside a restaurant. All enemies broke off to engage Kane. Cass sped off toward the red building, leaving her companion to die.

GREGOR

THE TRAIN ARRIVED at Mexico's east coast, the spot where Melvin and his massive troll friend managed to sneak aboard. Unlike last time, Vigilant was ready for them, and they knew it. Gregor subsisted on little sleep. He never got the numbers of Matthias's forces, but there were at least ten thousand and growing. Gregor managed to get a bit over two thousand of those men on their side. Eight thousand soldiers was a small number compared to the military forces, but Vigilant tech and violence across the land more than evened the odds. Gregor had endured many injuries over his long career, but they all paled in comparison to the pain of fighting an order he devoted his life to. Time spent recovering from injuries was time Mathias spent taking Vigilant down the wrong the path. Gregor wouldn't let this happen again. His army engaged the enemy forces in the cave station. Gregor's head hurt. He wanted to throw up.

Raul stayed by Gregor's side, also struggling with the notion of them having become their order's number one enemies. Raul performed a weapons check.

"When dad didn't come back," Raul began. "I told myself it happens. Men die in the field all the time, even the best. He was bullheaded and questioned Matthias more than he should. I'm not

325

sure if he killed our dad, but that was when we should've known something was wrong. When he burned anyone deemed an apostate. When he used slaves. We thought it would be worth it."

Gregor looked into Raul's eyes; it hurt to know he would've been the age of his son or daughter had he not sacrificed that life for duty.

"I tell myself that, too," Gregor admitted. "I was right there with Matthias for a time. To think that the Compact is all the design of some self-ordained god is enough to drive anyone over the edge."

"Do you still believe in the cause?" Raul asked.

Gregor breathed in deep and looked out the window into the cave station.

"I do," Gregor said. "We protect the world from those that use technology to do harm. That part hasn't changed." Gregor pulled himself off of the seat. Raul finished his business inside.

In the cave, Gregor's men looted the dead and prepared the commandeered AATVs and trucks for departure. Raul stepped off the train, fighting with his portable radio equipment.

"No luck?" Gregor asked, not needing a reply. "It's amazing how we got laser tanks and robowitches, but we can't ever get our fuckin' radios to work." Gregor suppressed the urge to smash the radio.

"Gotta get near a city or straight to the villa. Not sure how safe those are at the moment," Gregor said.

"If your friend came through, your niece is on the run I'm sure. We aren't close enough anyway. We need a base while we figure this out."

Raul pulled a folded-up map out of his pocket. He unfolded it and pinpointed their location. A few dozen miles north was Alvarado, the site of Gregor's first mission in the state.

"No way the deadheads got this far. Maybe we can get a signal up there. Your thief friend's probably trying to hail us."

"Not exactly a friend. And he's been stealing from us," Gregor said.

"Weren't you a pirate back in the day? Plundered Meridiana pretty good from what I hear," Raul said. Gregor's stone-faced expression did the work it needed. "Nasty gossip I heard, complete lies, sir," Raul replied.

Gregor and his team headed for Alvarado. The occasional voice came through the radio as the Vigilant caravan moved east, though never more than a few garbled words. Drawing close to the city, the radio chatter increased. Raul kept up with communications and managed to contact Duke's men holding up in a city a bit further up the coast. Unfortunately, Zora and her friends were not with them. They had heard nothing about them.

Gregor sent his troops to town to gather supplies while he pressed locals for more info. The locals were extremely forthcoming after Gregor's dispatching of the vaingloria for them, though it was easy to divulge information when you don't have much. The one piece of information on everyone's lips was the bloody conflict ravaging northern Mexico and about to bleed into southern Heartland.

Gregor's men were more successful when it came to supplies, getting a decent amount of food and medicine. Gregor's head throbbed when he thought about the insane world swirling all around him. Things had turned out differently than he ever imagined. He pined for the days of hunting mutant beast-men and jury-rigged golems. He spent a few minutes at the waterfront to collect himself. Despite chaos to the west, the people of Alvarado carried on with business as usual, albeit with a few more barricades and guns at the ready. He admired people who refused to cower. If Gregor and his people failed, many of these people could die. Gregor would not let that happen.

Gregor pushed himself up and went over to Raul Alvarez. Raul paced while chewing on a stick of jerky, the extra chewy kind Gregor always left for everyone else.

"Well?" Gregor asked.

"We got through," Raul said. "He's going to meet us at an encampment west of here."

"Let's head out now," Gregor said. Raul contacted the Vigilant teams and quickly rolled them out to the new destination. The Vigilant caravan arrived at a large encampment of deadheads.

"I thought he cleared this place!" Gregor said. The confused deadheads hesitated to shoot. Gregor's men didn't. Vigilant dropped a few thugs and received only minor wounds. No deadheads took the place of their fallen brethren.

"That can't be it," Raul said.

Vigilant closed in on the encampment. Gunfire roared from the opposite end. Vigilant parked cars. Some took up defensive positions while others followed Gregor inside. Gregor appreciated the well-oiled machine of Vigilant. Everyone knew their place. Gregor was the spearhead. He slipped through the barricades. Raul gasped at the sight of a dozen headless bodies at Death's altar.

"Focus," Gregor said.

A cluster of explosions rocked the edge of the camp, sending pieces of barricades in all directions. The gunfire ceased. The infiltration team moved through the soundless camp, passing a handful of bodies shot or chopped to bits. Gregor heard the faint hum of a railgun. The attacker would die, but not before taking him out. A roaring thunder came from Gregor's side. Gregor watched bewildered as a smashed-up truck rolled like a bowling ball over the equally bewildered deadhead. Gregor turned around to see Liz and Melvin. Liz had a massive ax made of car parts strapped to his back.

"Hi," Liz said with a wave.

"Hey," Gregor said.

"Don't shoot!" Gregor said to his men.

Raul had no words, clearly unprepared despite Gregor's explanation. Melvin strode through the devastation.

"They don't like death so much when it's bowling over them," Melvin said, surveying his Liz's handiwork.

Melvin's compatriot, Ed, approached from the other side. "Sorry we're late. Few more deadheads than we thought. I didn't want to radio you guys again because I'm pretty sure they know all our frequencies."

"Quite the hellraisers for a small gang," Gregor said, speaking directly to Liz.

"Employee of the month every month," Melvin replied. Liz's awkward grin made him smile, too.

A few of the Vigilant troops grimaced and voiced displeasure at Melvin's gang taking stolen Vigilant hardware, but that wasn't a priority.

"Don't give me that look. We put it to better use than your friends spit roastin' people," Melvin said. "And there's plenty to go around. Probably gonna need every bit of it." Vigilant took the opportunity to snatch up excess hardware. Melvin explained the situation with his people and Zora, including the indestructible demonic mask latched onto her face. The words hit Gregor with the same force of a golem's fist. Melvin assured Gregor she held up well and insisted he tried all he could to destroy the silver mask. Gregor threw his hands up in the air.

"It gets crazier and more dangerous by the minute," Gregor said, accepting this mad new world.

"That's right. Yer just another turd in the shitshow," Melvin said. Gregor frowned, annoyed at the truth in the disturbing statement. Ed placed a few landmines in the encampment for the next round of deadheads.

"Overkill," Gregor said.

"Absolutely," Melvin said.

"Footsteps to Hell," Edward said.

"Sure," Melvin agreed.

With the place stripped clean, Melvin hopped in a truck and

led the Vigilant caravan to his hideout. Raul shifted uncomfortably when they passed into the jagged rocky lands. The jagged rocks curled upward, creating skeletal rib tunnels through the wasteland. Gregor marveled at the formations, wondering if man or machine created this place. The trucks went single file through the claustrophobic tunnels, inches from scraping up the vehicles.

"A web of tunnels like these out here. Even I get lost sometimes," Melvin said. Everyone looked at him. "I mean not now, though." Melvin pulled out a piece of paper with a series of wavy lines on it, representing the path to his base.

"You have to be mad to live out here," Raul said.

Melvin belted out a maniacal laugh. *This can't be Victor Whitehall,* Gregor thought. Behind them, Liz lay in the truck bed, staring up at the rocks.

"Save the rest of your gawkin'," Melvin said. The trucks weaved through tunnels until arriving at massive natural walls. Gregor once again found himself dumbfounded.

THOS

THOS TRIED NOT to crush his cell phone. He also had Melvin's acquired radios and was one step away from good old-fashioned shouting. Drake had stayed with Zora, easing her fear of the demonic mask stuck to her face. With the possibility of Cass under the same threat as his friends, Thos grew antsy. He spent his time at the practice range outside of Melvin's base. Six automated guns, waiting for Thos to hit the activation button, protected them from outside invasion. A horned snallygaster crawled over the rock wall. Thos heard the sound of falling pebbles. He hit the button. The guns located the target and swiftly sent chunks of lizard all over the place with surgical precision. It provided Thos a brief outlet for his powerlessness. He commended Melvin for acquiring such an impressive collection of toys.

Thos wandered around the perimeter, battling with thoughts of his business's future, his wife's safety, and the looming battle with Matthias. The thoughts assaulted him. Should he have stayed at home? Was it right to fight? Was Cass alive? Did she think he was dead? Would they survive the coming attack? Were his thoughts getting in the way? His heart beat as rapid-fire as the autoguns. He focused on breathing and walking for now. *I'm worrying about worrying,* he thought.

Thos made lap after lap around the ship until his legs hurt. He took a seat at the table under a pink umbrella, not unlike the actress's back at Duke's villa. The autoguns moved back and forth, set to alarm mode and not attack. On the top of the aircraft, Skully kept vigil with a high-powered railrifle in case Vigilant appeared earlier than expected. Drake came down the ramp.

"She okay?" Thos asked.

"So far. No more pain or visions," he said.

Thos buried his questions on that matter, seeing Drake suppressing his anxiety.

"Shooting helps. These guys have tons of bullets," Thos said.

Drake agreed and approached the table with the hardware Melvin entrusted to them. Drake analyzed the EMPX. Part rifle, part wave gun, and part sword, the gunblade was the souped-up version of an Old World Swiss army knife. A knob on the side handled the wave intensity, a button under the barrel switched to AR mode, and a button on the right side extended the blade. It was a tad clunky yet impressive all the same.

"You check this out?" Drake asked. "Pretty cool." Thos pointed to a beheaded target in the corner and another in pieces.

Drake spent some time using the blade function of the EMPX. He fumbled at first to get used to the weight. Thos watched, not in the mood to laugh at the awkward jerky motions. Drake sliced the air until he became comfortable.

"It's a mess, ain't it?" Thos said. Drake lowered his weapon.

"Is it ever not?" He replied. Thos laughed.

"Guess it wouldn't be home otherwise," Thos said.

"True," Drake agreed.

"And not even all this," Thos said, clearly talking about everything since the Aric showed up in Heartland. "We were supposed to be free. Things were gonna be better without the kings, queens, and boards. But we didn't get rid of those things, did we? All we did was pick a few more and change the names." Drake frowned, then resumed his sword practice with a bit more angry fervor behind the attacks. The more Thos thought about it all, the angrier he became as well.

"Joe meant well," Drake said. "A free society is a great thing to strive for. I used to not think so. I thought the world needed authority to keep balance. It can be heredity, won in battle, or elected, but it seems that the result is the same. All we do is ensure the power to rule over someone else continues, and the Compact is just another master."

Thos faced Drake, taken aback. Drake's tone was laced with doubt and defeat.

"I didn't expect that from you," Thos said.

"Neither did I," Drake replied.

"Sounds like we're all becoming Freemen," Thos said.

"I'm not sure what the future will be; hard to think it'll be anything good," Drake said. It hurt Thos to see the stalwart knight doubt his mission.

"You breathin' right?" Thos asked. Drake nodded. "You can still fight. My dad used to say that when the chips were down. It was a reminder that I could always make things better as long as I lived. You're still breathin', so keep fightin'."

"Look at you being inspirational," Drake said. Thos laughed heartily, waking Skully.

"A one-time deal," he replied.

Drake raised the EMPX and gave a hard vertical slice, cutting straight through the target dummy with the image of Duke's face taped to it. Thos hollered at Skully for a second EMPX. Drake and Thos dueled, adjusting quickly to the awkward gunblades. Thos gave as good as he received, showing the value in his training. Thos knocked Drake back.

"I'm starting to regret training you," Drake said.

"It's good to have competition."

Both men noticed Zora sitting on the ramp, watching them

like a typical day in a typical place with a typical demonic wrapped around her head.

"Need cheering up?" Thos asked. "We were talking doom and gloom."

"I'm good," she replied.

Drake put his weapon on the table and went to Zora's side. Thos switched over to the "demon killer" function of his EMPX and proceeded to explode another target. Distant rumbling outside the rocky walls caught everyone's attention. Skully snapped to full alert and raised his rifle. A truck emerged from the tunnel, followed by another and another. Some trucks were branded with Vigilant colors, some Void, and others still with the image of an crudely drawn Melvin. Liz sat up in the first truck bed and waved.

The doors popped open; out stepped an unknown member of Vigilant, Ed, Melvin, and an older man in white robes that brought a hint of sourness to the area.

"Honey, I'm home!" Melvin said. "Got company!"

The corresponding groan from the older man confirmed him to be Gregor Pavane. Zora rushed to him and threw her arms around him. The bewildered old man quickly softened into a loving uncle trying to keep the anger from that mask at bay.

"It's good to see you," Gregor said, catching her by surprise.

"You aren't going to yell at me for this?" she asked.

"Oh I will, but let's have a nice moment first," he replied. Gregor analyzed the massive aircraft, his Vigilant troops pouring in, Melvin's gang, and Zora's friends.

"So this is our ragtag group, eh? Could be worse," Gregor said.

"Guess I'm not the only motivational speaker," Thos said.

Thos met with Zora's uncle a few times before his reinstatement in Vigilant. He came to know beneath Gregor's hard exterior was a slightly softer interior, and beneath that was a kind man. Gregor and Thos shook hands.

"Decided to throw yourself back in the fire, I see," Gregor said.

"What can I say? I like it hot," Thos replied. Gregor sized up Drake before extending his hand.

"Drake," Gregor said.

"Sir," Drake replied. Gregor cleared his throat.

"Let's not waste time," Gregor said, immediately taking charge.

"Hold on a sec; this is my operation," Melvin said. Gregor cocked his eyebrow. Liz growled. Gregor growled back, startling Liz.

"We'll do it together," Melvin said. Gregor shook his head and followed Melvin through the aircraft to the bridge.

ZORA

MELVIN'S GANG SPENT a reasonable amount of time renovating the Old World ship. Zora admired the massive vehicle the size of the water-bound aircraft carriers, dreaming of taking to the skies or the worlds beyond. Newly acquired seats filled the bridge. An oversized, deep, spinning chair lay in front of the main control area. Melvin plopped down in his captain's chair. Everyone else, except Raul, chose to stand.

"Wait 'til we get this bad boy running. We'll be the terror of the skies," Melvin said.

Everyone waited for Gregor to comment. Gregor focused on pressing matters. Zora felt the faint probing in her head. The probing became a pulling.

Melvin contacted Duke, who contacted Regent Dumas. The three factions exchanged information and realized the gravity of the situation. Together they concocted a plan to launch a war on three fronts.

"Let's recap," Melvin said. Melvin gave a brief rundown.

"This mask was his way of doing it, at least as fast as he was," Gregor said. Zora stepped forward.

"Wait," she said. "Matthias said that only apostates can use the mask like this." The revelation hit everyone else. Gregor sighed.

"That means you're a defect, apostate, or the descendant of one," Gregor replied. Everyone looked at Zora.

"To be fair, we're all defects to some degree," Raul added.

Zora had a sinking feeling it wasn't the former. Zora took a seat, visibly shaken by the news.

"My mother, she never . . . how?" Zora asked. "Did father know? Did sis? Is that why she followed that woman?"

"We'll chat with your dad about it," Gregor replied.

Zora remembered her mother well enough. Kind, sweet, and able to make her father forget the order. Zora felt a pinch in her temples. She voiced her pain.

"Zora!" Drake said, rushing to her side.

Zora looked through foreign eyes. She could almost feel the person behind the eyes, a man whose mind was slowly being enveloped by something inhuman. She sensed his mind one tap away from shattering completely. The mask's finger-like appendages bore deeper inside his head.

"I'm in another's body, not wearing a mask," she said. "I can't explain it, but neither is this person." Zora described the scene as it happened.

The man addressed two women and another man. One young woman had long flowing hair, and an aura of kindness and warmth Zora knew well.

"Mom?" she asked.

Her mother pleaded with the man to abandon the cause. Zora became dizzy inside the man's head. He was another soul lost in the pursuit of power that went nowhere. The man argued with Zora's mom. She gave one last desperate plea. The man refused, summoning a wheeled golem to quiet her for good. Zora's mother renounced the group and fled.

"Maybe this thing wiped her memories," Drake said.

Zora heard a voice in her head. *You're just like them,* the voice said.

An unknown force pushed Zora back in her seat. Zora clawed at the mask. It grew hot.

"Get out of my head!" she screamed. *You're gonna need this power.*

Zora reached out through the mask, mustering all of her will. She pried the mask off her face, but the tentacles squeezed tighter. Zora visualized the tentacles weakening, giving her the power to fight back. Gregor scrambled for the closest EMPX.

"To think our fate would be in the hands of people like you," the mask said, this time speaking to everyone.

Gregor adjusted the knob on his weapon and fired at the mask. The voice in her head screamed. A vision flashed through her head, a white tank and an army rolling across the desert.

"He's on his way," the mask said as it fell to the floor. The mask now bore a frown.

"Sure we can't throw it in a chasm or something?" Thos asked. Gregor shook his head.

"He's connected to it now and we've found no way to break it. He'll find it," Gregor said. Zora described the vision of Matthias's army driving under the black clouds of the Uninhabited, with the apocalyptic storms that halted just for him.

"A weather control defense system," Gregor said. "Not to mention a bona fide force-field around the whole city. And we gotta shut them both off."

"My guess is we have about a little under a day 'fore they get here," Raul said. "We can try to radio for backup or at least get some of the military to engage them outside the Rocklands."

"He won't send his full army; most will be preparing the city so Killswitch happens even if he dies. He'll send a force greater than ours plus a tank or two. We got two thousand men; I expect him to send no more than three. He thinks that'll be enough to take us out," Gregor said.

"If he's coming to us, then we have the advantage," Melvin

said. "My pal Ed here can booby trap the hell out the paths in here. Right Ed?"

"Seas of blood and flame," Ed replied.

"Got railguns too, plus Liz," Melvin said.

"I'm the best," Liz replied.

"Don't get cocky, but yes," Melvin said. "With the guns on this bad body we can wipe him out right here and then figure out how to smash that evil thing." Melvin opened a can of Averill's Own soda and dumped it in a goblet at the captain's station.

"And the deadheads?" Drake asked.

"Or Kingsbury?" Thos said.

"We can't worry about that right now," Gregor said. "Let the government do its job for once. They'll protect Kingsbury, at the very least, to maintain their seat of power. The full force will come down on Vigilant there. As for the deadheads, we'll deal with them later. Matthias is willing to kill half the damn world to end the Compact. We don't know what the exact death toll will be, but even Matthias expected it to be high. We cut this off at the source. Everything else is secondary."

Gregor looked at Raul.

"The machine here amplifies the others," Raul said. "Destroying this one will weaken the others."

"But Kingsbury," Thos said.

"Kingsbury'll be fine," Gregor said. "You won't make it back in time anyway. We have to stop Matthias. I need you all here for this."

The group stood on the bridge in silence, contemplating the overwhelming odds against them. Zora couldn't help thinking about her mother and her newly discovered heritage as a Witch-kin. Gregor and Zora held back.

"All right, let's get ready to party," Melvin said.

"I'll get my troops ready," Gregor said. Drake hesitated at first but chose to aid in preparations.

"All this time," Zora said. Gregor shook his head in disbelief.

"No need to be sad. Your mother's past is not yours, nor did it define her life," Gregor said.

The words proved a little difficult for Gregor to speak. He walked over to the view window. Melvin gave orders below while Liz performed the necessary lifting for heavy weapons and barricades.

"A few weeks ago, if you'd told me my niece, daughter of Vigilant's finest, was a witch, my heart would probably give out. I mean your dad and I are technically super soldiers by Old Word definition, so I can't be that broken up about it. World isn't so simple anymore."

Zora hugged her uncle. At the moment, the past was irrelevant: it was time to prepare for war.

MATTHEW

MATTHEW WEAVED THROUGH the tunnels, plowing over two surprised troopers setting up barricades for their final stand. A gathered force sent him on a detour directly into tire spikes. Matthew's swearing echoed through the tunnels. Matthew ditched the truck and hit the road on foot. Distant explosions and gunfire from below suggested Vigilant was still busy with Matthew's last play. Without a vehicle, Matthew lost hours trekking through the underworld. He reached a fork in the underground road and hit the path on the right that went up and east.

The tunnel emptied into the old passageways under the amphitheater and not far from what was once the Blackthorne mausoleum. Matthew drove to the outskirts of Kingsbury and parked his car a few blocks from the red building on 22nd. He discarded the Vigilant armor in case the government were fine targeting those in red and white.

Voices echoed over the speakers declaring an attack on the regent and vice regent had been thwarted, though James was injured in the fighting. They were declared a band of Blackthorne loyalists and summarily defeated. The world moved on. The story would stick long enough with James driven from the city. *This'll be over before anyone knows it started,* Matthew thought.

He weaved through the back alleys when soldiers drew too close. Matthew braced for inevitable fighting in the streets. A lone car sped past in the same direction as Matthew, followed by another. Then another. Matthew picked up speed.

The cars stopped in front of a red brick building in the middle of 22nd Street, beside one other empty vehicle. Camouflaged soldiers ran into the building before Matthew could catch up. He cautiously moved in on the building. The building had no markings. Matthew pulled the gunblade from his back and crept inside. He checked the corners, but he heard no sounds and saw no movement. Instinctively Matthew went toward a lock-picked door that led down, where things always seemed to end up.

Matthew pushed on to flights of stairs going well past where a basement would be. He placed both hands back on his gun. Several flights of stairs later, he arrived at the bottom floor of yet another formerly locked door. Matthew stepped through. The walls were made of large stones and covered with electric torches. In the center of the room were the fresh corpses of camouflaged Vigilant troops at the feet of a man in a black suit with purple eyes. An astonished Cassandra Averill stood beside Proxy. Matthew lowered his weapon.

"Ah, Mr. Pavane. Mrs. Averill just arrived as well," Proxy said. "I feared the worst, especially since your mission is incomplete."

"I'm working on it. Bought us time," Matthew said.

"Indeed. James has a few black ops teams picking up your slack. The enemy is delayed, but not for long."

"Nice place. I figured Mr. Abaddon was one for dungeons," Matthew said.

"It's what's left of the original Kingsbury wall," Proxy said. "We installed a bunker right below it. But we're not here about that. Tell me what you've found."

Matthew laid out the facts.

"I must say even I didn't know all that. Most concerning," Proxy said with a touch of human emotion.

"I assume you already know about the nanomachines? Will it kill everyone?"

"We do," Proxy said. "And to your other point, I can't say. These wave weapons are dangerous and can do fatal damage to the intended host. They brought an end to the Old World network. Matthias is a fool to think he can control it."

"You know of the arch-demon too?" Matthew asked.

"Indeed. We'll discuss this in full in a moment. Follow me, please," Proxy said.

Poxy turned and walked to an old pulley elevator. He motioned for Cass and Matthew to follow him. Matthew and Cass reluctantly followed.

"Nice to see you again, Mrs. Averill," Matthew said.

"Another one of them days," she said.

The elevator took off the second they entered. When the elevator hit bottom, they followed Proxy into a void-black room. Proxy took position at the other end of the room. Matthew felt a fourth presence in the room. The presence moved up ahead, drawing closer with a low growl. Matthew's imagination ran wild, trying to visualize the dreaded gangster mere feet from him.

"They're here, sir," Proxy said. "Please continue with your findings, Mr. Pavane."

Matthew explained the situation to the shadow-cloaked Mr. Abaddon. The growl intensified.

"Their infiltration was more effective than I realized." Mr. Abaddon spoke with disturbing calm.

"They aren't yet ready to finalize their plans. Our interference has forced their hand, but they still hold the advantage. They will fortify the tunnels until they've acquired enough power to fully activate the machine. As long as no one knows they've compromised the government, they need only to focus on hunting those that do. They intend to launch before we can mount a counteroffensive, but the regent's ops, and your stunt, bought us precious time. I'll reach out to the coward regent; he owes me greatly."

"All right, I'm tired of being strung along," Cass said. "You're going to give us another mission and hide in the dark. I'm sick of it. If I'm going to die soon, you could at least give me a face-to-face."

Cass couldn't see the alarm on Matthew's face but it was there.

"Take it down a notch, Mrs. Averill," Matthew said.

"Boldness and bravado are not always virtues, my dear. You're an expendable asset when I've none to spare. When that's no longer true, you can be fully spent," Mr. Abaddon said. "As can an ex-Vigilant soldier who married a witch."

"Wel—" Cass said.

"Now wait just a—" Matthew said.

"The dreams you have, the images that conflict with your memory, are quite real," Mr. Abaddon said. "Not an overwrite, but a removal of certain key pieces. It seems Vigilant's tampering has worked to your benefit."

Matthew clenched his fist as he learned about his own history for the first time.

"How do you know about my life when I don't?" Matthew asked. He heard a cacophony of metal in the darkness.

"There are many things to which the great Pavanes are wholly ignorant. You're very limited in that way. Unlike you humans, I don't share this flaw."

Two large purple orbs burned in the darkness. Matthew's heart skipped a few beats. A faint hum permeated the area. Blinding yellow light roared in. Matthew used his hand to shield himself from it. He heard a loud curse from Cass. Matthew lowered his hand. The light illuminated a long metal face with purple eyes, a square jaw, and a triangular protrusion clearly meant to be a nose. The face had a skeletal quality, though it had no teeth. The slick, navy skin shined in the light. The head was thrice the size of

Matthew's. Proxy stood unmoving beside his boss. Mr. Abaddon's head was attached to the wall by wires and a large metal neck. The head lurched forward.

"Mercy . . . you're—" Matthew said.

"A survivor of the Old World," Mr. Abaddon said.

Mr. Abaddon explained that he was a GARDEAN AI tasked with defending and running the city in the elite's absence. He recounted the last moments of the Old World, his "death," being reactivated by an aspiring wizard, the subsequent killing of his would-be owner, and his assistance building a foundation on which the city, and by extension, the nation, could thrive. Mr. Abaddon explained his role as the administrator of the city's various systems, keeping things running when the government got in the way. Cass looked around in confusion for his missing body.

"You now understand what Vigilant took from me. I am somewhat compromised," Mr. Abaddon said.

"And you wanted me to plug you into the city's systems? Giving you control of everything," Cass said.

"And you failed, which I expected." Mr. Abaddon said. Cass went red.

"You just wanted to flush out Yadira!" Cass said.

"Either outcome was acceptable," Mr. Abaddon said. "The enemy has been revealed, she can't hide that for long. I must admit I'm surprised it really was Yadira, empowering Vigilant was bold and made her seem too obvious. It was clearly her objective and not just a demand from her constituents."

"You toyed with my life!" Cass said. She crossed her arms, trying to shake off her fear of the machine with her anger.

"Not a decision I came to lightly," Mr. Abaddon said. "I could've put this city under complete control centuries ago if I wanted. The pros for not doing so have always outweighed the cons. I'll relinquish control when this is over. Unlike the rulers above, I understand how to sustain this place."

Cass wore her doubt on her sleeve. The long metal neck connecting Mr. Abaddon to the wall extended, putting him inches from Cass's face. Cass stepped back. Mr. Abaddon's thunderous laugh bounced off the room and cut straight through to the bone.

"You have little choice in the matter," Mr. Abaddon said.

"Because I'll die? I'm well aware they'll kill me," Cass replied.

"You may not make it that long. Did you think the worsening defect was completely unrelated?'" he asked.

Cass pushed herself up, not considering the disturbing possibility.

"The nanomachines in your body may be responsible for your defect or what keeps it at bay, human genetics post-Collapse is very tricky. Simply tampering with them can have devastating consequences, like creating trolls, for instance. If Vigilant succeeds, you could be cured, you could die, or things could stay unchanged; who knows how the machines affect you specifically. There'll be consequences for severing the connection, especially in such a hasty manner. The more they tamper with the Algorithm, the more people will die, including your beloved Thos. Can you sit by knowing that? I calculate up to a 42% mortality rate if Killswitch is completed."

"You know I can't," Cass said with a defeated sigh.

Abaddon's long neck swung, placing his face directly in front of Matthew. Matthew didn't step back.

"And you," Mr. Abaddon said. "Bedded a witch and your order's number one enemy . . . well number two after your brother." Matthew's stern expression vanished. "Yes. I've received word he's on the run as well. Vigilant would've come after you sooner or later. You can't help him there, but you can here . . . with my help."

Matthew's skin grew hot. For a brief moment, he missed his buffet of psychedelics.

"Back in the fire," Matthew said.

"In time," Mr. Abaddon said. "The pieces are falling into

place. You two will be contacted when we're ready. Proxy will show you to your rooms for the time being. Don't leave the premises. Goodnight Mr. Pavane, Mrs. Averill. Sleep well."

The head retracted into the wall.

ANSELM

ANSELM FELT RENEWED after the best sleep he could get on old jerky. He required substantially more rest in his weakened state; he grew too accustomed to the two to three hours that served as good as the nightly eight before. He grew to regret putting restraints on himself, he knew his old life was gone. With his enhanced abilities, Anselm covered large swaths of ground fast. He spied on Vigilant, learning of government forces marshaling to challenge them. His hunger only grew.

Vigilant forces broke off from headquarters to engage the military setting up bases at the edge of their territory. A few infiltrators penetrated Vigilant's perimeter, though they met quick ends. Anselm left the bodies this far up alone to maintain the element of surprise. It was a curious thing to see people once loyal to him on two different sides. Anselm's enemies were killing each other; he wanted to engage them personally, but he preferred neither side to know he was alive and well.

Anselm sat in the treetops breathing in the damp morning of the wilderness. He'd lost more hours than he'd planned with his extended sleep. Vigilant activity increased throughout the afternoon, seeing dozens more troops and a few tanks. Chatter from his time gave him the impression the Freemen communities in the north were also gaining members; they'd be the next government target when Vigilant was gone.

From what he heard, chaos brewed all across New Prosperity. Lines were being drawn. He always knew if his family fell, the elite couldn't help themselves from overreaching. His rivals bred chaos to gain power, and they always wanted more power. They could never stop and were destined to destroy the world men like Alexander worked so hard to build. *I'll build a new kingdom from their ashes greater than even him, Anselm* thought.

Anselm watched them like a hungry predator. The government held the advantage of numbers; however, Vigilant's high-tech weaponry could keep their foes at bay until Killswitch was ready or Jaren was forced to launch prematurely. When Anselm dispatched them, the rest of his enemies would fall in short order. He prepared himself for tonight. Eon made no appearances and Anselm no longer cared. His mission remained the same.

Skirmishes between Vigilant and government infiltrators came to an end. Vigilant's armored trucks drove out to the edge of their territory to hold off the regent's forces for now. Anselm maneuvered his way back to the transformed Vigilant tower. Anselm sized up his foes.

When night arrived, Anselm waited for the clouds to bring another onslaught of summer rains. Vigilant forces were divided into three groups: the front line near the logging camps, the tower, and the forests in between. The bulk of Vigilant departed for the front lines. There were fifty men around the tower, with no sign of Jaren. Anselm devised a plan to clear a path to the tower. Once it fell, he could slaughter them without worry.

A dozen Vigilant soldiers gathered around a large pit to the west. More troops left their posts to join the crowd. Anselm could destroy the machine and lure them all to the woods; he was eager to refine his hunting skills. He hopped from his treetop perch and crouched low. He knocked the first patrolmen to the ground and quickly reduced his head to a pulp with a single blow. Anselm rushed forward and snapped the neck of the second patrol, who hit the ground before anyone noticed. The third and fourth fell just as quickly and easily.

Anselm eliminated the fifth, sixth, and seventh guard with fast decapitations, leaving nothing between him and the restrained Gideon Grey. Anselm approached the control panel of the jury-rigged doomsday machine. He moved the sword to his left arm and raised his right fist.

"Poor excuse for a hunter," Jaren said from behind.

Anselm cursed his arrogance. Jaren wore a silver mask and carried a massive rifle like the heavy versions of Old World railguns that Gideon created for him. The irony of it all was sickening.

"One never expects much from the rats in his walls," Anselm replied. He felt the pain and the anger; the hunger would come later.

"Rats can carry plague enough to kill a kingdom," Jaren said. "That arrogance is why you lost and why you keep losing, my king."

Anselm dropped his guard.

"I thought I was crazy at first," Jaren said. "Matthias still doubts it, but I don't. The way you talk. The way you look, so much like Aric. I've seen crazy things up here, but resurrection is new. Of all the people that got to come back it was you. So many people died for you, and you wasted your second chance."

Jaren's troops surrounded Anselm.

"I failed your father, it's true," Anselm said. "But my second chance isn't over. I'm here for revenge, same as you. Against them and this worthless order. This machine of yours is in the way of my plans and I can't have that." Anselm paid little mind to the Vigilant grunts.

"They died for you! They died because of you!" Jaren cried. "You let your enemies surround you same as now. If you had been a strong king, none of this would've happened! My family would still be alive." The words hit Anselm square in the gut. The truth was a different kind of pain.

"And I pay for that every night," Anselm said. *No. Now I'm starting to enjoy it.*

"It's not enough. Not for me," Jaren replied. "My father could've taken the deal. He was loyal to the end. I don't see why. You were always a weak king, and you came back just to die again."

The Vigilant bullets and waves pummeled Anselm. He put one foot in front of the other. Soldiers with EMPXs dialed their weapons up to max. Anselm sliced and diced any too close, though he felt his momentum fading.

"You aren't as invincible as you think," Jaren said.

Jaren raised his hand. Anselm braced for the attack. Vigilant tower hummed to life. "We aren't ready for the main event yet. That test last night wasn't for the witches, demons, or false gods but for mutants like you. All we needed was a little fine-tuning."

Anselm struggled to move. Jaren raised the heavy railrifle. Blue energy zipped through the large magnet-like protrusions from the gun and shot forth into Anselm. Anselm felt intense heat in his midsection. He looked down to find a gaping hole in his chest. The wound closed, only to be blown open again. The healing slowed. Jaren set aside the rifle and brandished his sword. The wound closed one last time.

"You can't—" Anselm's words were cut off by the sword piercing his heart. Anselm fell to his knees. The continuous waves from the gunblades negated his healing. Anselm's arms became like noodles, too feeble to pull the blade out of him. The soldiers lowered their weapons. Anselm didn't heal.

"I didn't kill your family," Anselm said.

"Maybe not, but close enough. I'll deal with the rest soon. I'll make do with you for now."

Anselm thought back on the day he died, kneeling in front of

Drake Hale, a man he considered a son. Jaren pulled the sword from Anselm. A man approached Jaren and handed him an object. The object was a metal circlet large enough to fit around a man's head. Long jagged bits of metal protruded up, down, and inside. Anselm knew the meaning behind the object. Jaren took it.

"Every king needs a crown," Jaren said.

Jaren pushed the crown down onto Anselm's head. The bits and pieces of sharp metal ripped and cut their way into his head. The metal went deep into Anselm's head, effectively locking it into place. The blood streamed from the wounds. Jaren's men carried Anselm over to the large pit and tossed him in. Anselm collided with wet, muddy earth. People screamed around him. Anselm lay in the muddy hole, his body desperately trying to heal. Flesh began to weave through the crown pieces and became embedded in his head. Bones grew in the gaping hole in his chest. Anselm's vision blurred, but he could make out the shapes of others in the hole with him.

It took Anselm several hours to regain a semblance of strength. He thrust his right arm into the dirt wall and pulled himself to his feet. Once on his feet, he thrust his other arm into the wall so he wouldn't topple over. Anselm expended all of his energy to stand. The eyes of the prisoners were upon him, staring in horror at the pale man with a crown hooked and nailed into his head. Anselm growled; his animal roar devolved into a sickly cough.

The other prisoners pressed themselves against the walls across from him. Anselm recovered enough strength to push himself from the wall and face them. He knew they were men, women, and children from Durenburg. Anselm saw the blame and hate in their eyes, deservedly so for the lives he took. Once upon a time, these looks would have hurt him. There was no imaginary family or masked strangers to comfort or provoke him; an altogether different voice spoke to him.

"Anselm. King of New Prosperity. Durenburg devil. Murderer."

The voice was a hateful growl Anselm now envied. Anselm opened his mouth to speak only to receive a hard fist in the jaw from Ezra Crowe. The young Cameron hid behind two women while his father pummeled Anselm's face. Anselm hit back, though his attacks were no better than the average man's. Ezra relented.

"I told you to live your life," Anselm said. "You and Cam are here because you wouldn't let it go. Betrayed your people and still wound up in the dirt with me." Anselm gasped for air between words.

"We're here because of *you*," Ezra snapped back. It hurt too much for Anselm to laugh; Ezra wasn't entirely incorrect.

"This fate is your doing and mine," Anselm said.

"We're shackled to the fates of kings. I heard about the things you've done. I saw it. Turned yourself into a fuckin' monster! And you still failed!" Ezra said.

"Then I should've done it sooner!" Anselm growled, mustering enough strength to frighten Ezra Crowe. *A strong king must be a monster*, he thought.

The dark urges stirred within Anselm, yet he denied them. He didn't want be that monster, but he was losing that battle. The energy left Anselm and he hit the floor. Anselm lay motionless and defeated. Ezra spat on him. In the dark hole with the rain starting to pick up, Anselm awaited his next punishment.

GREGOR

GREGOR WOKE EARLY. He climbed his way through the ship's bowels and up past the spacious captain's quarters where Melvin resided. Patches of the ship, namely what Melvin used, were as clean as the day the vehicle set off for the last voyage. Gregor knew some about Old World ships. This was a Caelus, a flying aircraft carrier. The Caelus matched its water-bound brother in size and could launch dozens of fighters. The Caelus was the first in the line of Pantheon vehicles that included spacecraft designed for aerial, interplanetary, and intergalactic travel. Intergalactic mega-ships like Zeus never came to fruition.

Gregor passed a shift of soldiers catching a few winks on his way to the mess hall. A handful of pristine coffee makers provided Gregor with the liquid smack to the face he required to get up and running. The late shift tinkered on powering up the Caelus's weapon systems. Raul lay face down on a table in the center of the room. Gregor admired his gung-ho efforts to get the ship operational. Raul also spent some time attempting to weaken the mask with wave attacks, hoping that with enough of them, some progress could be made. Gregor adapted quickly to the notion of powering up an warship, considering it less taboo in the face of Killswitch. The teams worked in shifts, getting only a few hours of rest in between. Gregor walked past and poured himself some hot coffee, trying not to disrupt Raul's much-needed sleep.

He rummaged through the pantries containing Melvin's dry goods. Gregor ate excessively chewy jerky, at this point he'd eat a bullet over jerky. He finished his breakfast and headed up to the deck where the smaller fighter ships would launch. The soft orange and purple of dawn crept over the rocks. A few night-terrors howled in the distance, the signal that their day was at an end. Gregor wandered the deck to find two individuals sitting on the edge of the ship. Gregor avoided edges with long drops after his trip to Kingsbury. One was a bulkier yet normal-sized man with dark hair, and the other was substantially larger and greener. Drake and Liz watched the sky together.

"Welcome to the club," Drake said.

Gregor approached but maintained some distance from the edge of the ship. Drake whispered something in Liz's ear; Gregor caught the words "no pushing."

"Ready for tomorrow?" Gregor asked.

"No," Liz replied.

"I appreciate your honesty."

"Ready as ever," Drake said. "This reminds me of the attack on Fort Alexander, except this time we're the ones with no way out."

"Last stand of the Witch-Hunter. I like the sound of that, not enough for it to be true," Gregor said, thinking on his glory days. He feared those days were long past, but he had to fight on as long as could. It wasn't just glory, it was duty.

Gregor enjoyed the sunrise. Gregor faced overwhelming odds quite regularly and today was a day like any other to him.

"Hell of a thing fighting your people," Drake said. The words were meant for Gregor, but he sensed Drake spoke about himself as well. "Does it make you rethink your life?"

"No," Gregor said. "It makes me question my methods and some rules, but the goal to bring down those that use technology to control and destroy remains. I'll kill Matthias and get us back on the path." Drake stared off in the distance. Liz listened intently, happy to be part of the conversation.

"Wish I had that clarity," Drake said.

"You will," Gregor assured. "Takes a long time to reach those moments. I was a little younger than you when I had my first one. I terrorized the coast, did the things a pirate does."

"Did you have a hat?" Liz asked. Gregor shook his head. He shifted the conversation back on track.

"Some people have their moments in quiet," Gregor said. "Others face down in the mud or being sucked into the sea, but they come, and then you'll find out where you need to be."

The three talked until Gregor sensed movement from behind. Gregor looked back to see Zora and Thos approaching, dressed for war.

"What you guys talking about?" Zora asked.

"Purpose," Drake replied.

"Girls," Liz said. Zora raised an eyebrow.

"Don't listen to him; he's an instigator," Drake said. Liz grinned.

The screech of speakers got everyone cursing. Everyone shot angry glares in the direction of the bridge and its new captain.

"Sorry," Melvin said.

Everyone heard him whistling while he fidgeted with the sound system. "All right, here we go. All hands to battle stations ye dogs. Get yer coffee and all that 'cuz it's gonna be a long day. Hopefully not our last one." Melvin cursed, not intending the last bit for public consumption.

Gregor, Thos, Drake, Zora, and Melvin's gang headed to the bridge for one last meeting. Melvin sat in the captain's chair, sipping from his goblet full of straight black coffee with the odor of motor oil.

"You look comfy," Thos said. Melvin took a big swig.

"I am," Melvin replied. "I presided over Heartland for quite a while, if you recall. Only when I left did things go to shit. Don't forget I led the attack on Kingsbury when Joe died." Gregor heard stories of Victor Whitehall's capabilities, a man once considered a leader on par with the famed Witch-Hunter himself. Gregor fought plenty of battles in his day but never a full-blown war. Gregor hated being out of his element. Melvin went over everything one last time.

"We ready?" Melvin asked.

"We are," Gregor said. Melvin let out a huge breath.

"Here we go," Melvin said.

Everyone took positions. Vigilant formed battle lines at the aircraft's base, with snipers on the ship's sides and decks. Thos, Zora, Skully, and the rest of Melvin's gang took positions with the deck snipers. Raul worked with the smattering of technicians to power up the rest of the ship's guns, so far getting almost half ready. Liz took center stage at the head of the army, wielding a heavy railgun and a homemade ax strapped to his back. Melvin took his place beside Liz, carrying a lightweight railgun. Ed went to the ground armed with a grenade launcher and a few different bomb triggers on his belt. Ed cackled like a madman at the side of the army. Gregor switched his EMPX to standard rifle functionality; Gregor took the helm of his troops. Drake embraced Zora, giving her a last kiss before joining the ground team.

In silence, they all listened and waited. A gentle wind rolled across the jagged wasteland. Rocks fell from the wall of the crater hiding the battleship. Time slowed. An hour felt like an eternity.

A faint boom echoed across the desolate land. Everyone stirred. Gregor's heart beat a little faster. A second boom echoed, followed by another. After the explosions came the sounds of rocks falling. The bangs and crashes happened faster and grew louder. The sound of wheels and metal joined the symphony. Gregor's heart danced faster.

"Get ready!" Gregor hollered.

Liz replied with a bestial grunt. Thos repeated the message far above. The roaring of machines was upon them. A truck drove into the crater, followed by another. Edward shot first, pelting grenades at the incoming vehicles. High-powered grenades rolled under trucks, resulting in a shower of metal and rock. The enemy trucks stopped. Loud shrieks of energy heralded the arrival of the railtanks. Blue energy blasted holes in the rock walls, turning them to mesh. Snipers shot through the holes at the Vigilant troops scrambling to get out of the way. Matthias's forces retaliated with volleys from their railguns, forcing Gregor's men to break ranks. Enemy tanks focused efforts on the rock walls.

"They're in position!" Skully said.

Ed giddily hit the button on his back remote. The rock floor cracked and burst under the enemy. Trucks and soldiers went flying, but the tanks remained whole. The tanks continued to assault the foundation of the rock walls. The earth trembled as the front area of the wall fell. The fighting began in earnest.

Matthias's troops rushed through the newly created door. Gregor's team engaged them. Matthias's tanks aimed at the ship. Even the superior firepower of railcannons did nothing to the vehicular monster. A nonstop barrage of cannon fire proved fruitless. Gregor hailed Raul through the radio to fire.

"Something's wrong; the guns aren't working!" Raul cried.

Vigilant forces clashed with Vigilant forces, only told apart from Matthias's red troops and Gregor's white. Liz sprinted into the thick of the enemy, blasting them to pieces with his gun or splitting skulls with his ax. Liz acted like a tank himself, massacring a dozen foes in a matter of seconds. Gregor killed foes long-distance, scanning the battlefield for Matthias. The first wave of enemies went down, with only minimal losses on Gregor's side.

In the middle of the enemy force was one red tank, standing out from the two white ones on either side. During the lull between the battle, Gregor estimated a thousand more troops waiting in the wings to attack. The airship's guns weren't yet operational. A loud screech came from the red tank.

"You're outnumbered," Matthias said. "Don't throw your life away like this. There's still a chance to survive and build a wonderful new world. His crisis of faith is not worth your life."

"Crisis of faith!?" Gregor yelled back. Gregor stepped forward. "Our faith is strong as ever. We stand for what we always have, protecting the world from humans and demons alike." Gregor heard Raul's voice through the radio.

"Guns almost ready. Keep him talking," Raul said.

"We're putting an end to the demon, to his world. I've connected to him. Working with those gangster scum. Using slaves. I didn't want to make these choices, I had to. We have to risk it all or be part of it forever. The loop ends now." Gregor thought back to the witch attack right after he escaped from Kingsbury. The witch had said something similar.

"I can't accept that," Gregor replied. "I understand your desperation; I do. I saw it with Anselm. Your fear is real, but the cost is too high." Gregor heard Raul through the radio, targeting the three tanks. Raul gave the signal.

"I wish it didn't have to be this way," Matthias said, with genuine sorrow in his voice. Gregor pitied the man; he understood and respected unwavering conviction.

"Me either," Gregor replied. "Fire."

The guns came alive. The guns at the sides bombarded the two white tanks. The tanks popped like old melons. The airplane-sized main gun of the ship hummed to life. Blue light glowed from inside the spinning parts. The parts moved faster and rotated into place like a puzzle coming together. A white-hot beam spewed forth, disintegrating all his troops caught in its path. The beam took out hundreds of the enemy troops. The relentless beam hit an invisible force in front of the red tank.

"He's got a shield too!" Gregor cried.

The excess beam not absorbed by the shield went around like a river of hot death, wiping out the nearby troops and trucks. The cannon beam devastated both land and troops, but not Matthias. The cannon parts spun faster and groaned louder. Both sides watched the beam pummel the shield protecting Matthias's tank.

The beam pushed the tank back. All of Matthias's men concentrated fire at the base of the airship's beam weapon. Pieces of metal fell from the airship. The beam continued pushing the tank back. The invisible shield around the tanks became a transparent white.

"The shield! I think you're breaking it!" Gregor hollered through the radio.

The shield flickered. Matthias's tank returned fire. The airship's supporting guns ground to a halt. Raul called out the need to reload.

Gregor's men re-engaged the enemy. Liz ran headfirst into the approaching second wave. Gregor provided cover fire for the railgunners aiming at the charging troll. Explosions rocked the airship's main gun. The gun came loose, sending the death beam off to the side, killing dozens of men on both sides. The beam bore through the ground ahead with a fury more incredible than any drill. The spinning pieces of the gun came loose. The gun exploded in blinding white light. A few more of Gregor's men were smashed and impaled by the debris.

"Zora!" Gregor and Drake both cried.

"We're all right up here," Thos replied through the radio.

Melvin ordered the men under his charge to eliminate the enemy soldiers while Gregor took control of the reserves.

"Heavies, bring down that shield!" Gregor cried.

Liz and the others concentrated fire on Matthias's shield. The tank was forced to attack the ground troops. Soldiers ran to Matthias's aid. Liz effortlessly cut through enemy forces, spraying them in all directions. Drake joined him on the front lines. Along with Melvin, the three became a whirlwind of death. Gregor took on the enemies heading toward the ship's ramp.

The tank shield disappeared and didn't come back. The railguns pelted the tank, finally putting a few dents in it. The tank got off another shot and blew apart three of the attackers. The tank aimed back at the airship support guns and destroyed one. The other gun laid waste to a group of enemies before reloading again. Ed walked out from beside Gregor. He threw off his jacket, revealing numerous explosives foreign to Gregor. Gregor nodded.

"Last ride is the best ride!" Ed cried. He sprinted toward the occupied tank and dove under. Ed erupted in brilliant flame. The suicidal bomb knocked the tank over, rendering the mighty weapon useless.

The hatch at the top of the tank fell upon and out stepped the grand crusader in glistening, ruby-red armor. Matthias wielded an EMPX, he hit a switch and it transformed into a sword. Matthias engaged his enemy. Matthias severed the arms of the nearest gunner and the legs of the second. More attackers pulled Gregor's attention away. Using burst first, Gregor eliminated his targets. Matthias dispatched the other men at the ramp and entered the ship. With everyone else occupied, it was up to Gregor to pursue.

"He's inside!" Gregor shouted into the radio.

Gregor chased after Matthias, quickly falling behind the younger, and faster, grand crusader. He followed the trail of death through the ship. Gregor yelled through the radio as he ran.

"Everyone regroup on deck!" Gregor said. Gregor heard the sounds of fighting behind him.

"Too many. They're scaling the walls!" Drake said.

Drake engaged the forces entering the ship. Gregor rushed to the deck. Resistance snipers, including Thos, shot the Vigilant soldiers using grapple guns to climb onboard the deck. A collection of troops gathered around Zora and the silver mask in her hand. At the head of them was Raul Alvarez.

"I'm so disappointed in you," Matthias said, addressing Raul.
"Likewise," Raul said.

"You lack conviction, just like your father," Matthias said.
"When he turned on me, it broke my heart. Shame I have to kill
you too." Gregor realized Matthias provoked Raul to attack.

"You son of a bitch!" Raul screamed.

Raul charged. He swung his blade. Matthias easily deflected
the blow with his gunblade. Matthias disarmed Raul. Raul hit the
ground. Gregor rushed forward, locking swords with Matthias. At
the edge of the deck, Vigilant forces pushed Thos and the snipers
back to the center. Matthias pointed his gunblade at Zora.

"The mask if you please," Matthias said.

The fighting in the ship grew louder. Drake was pushed on the
deck near Gregor. Vigilant surrounded them. He heard the bulk
of the resistance fighters led by Melvin and Liz holding their own
below. Gregor needed to distract Mathis for a moment.

"You've lost your way," Gregor said. "This is madness, can't
you see that? You're killing innocent people . . . your own daughter!" Despite her being a witch, even a former one, Gregor couldn't
stomach filicide.

"She wasn't innocent," Matthias said. He pointed his sword
at Gregor. "Ms. Pavane, I'll ask you one more time. Return the
mask to me."

Zora made no movements. Matthias shook his head and
lunged at Gregor. Gregor deflected the first blow. Matthias struck
again and again. Gregor deflected, though losing steam and the
nonstop assault. Matthias troops and Gregor's were at a standstill,
none with the numbers on deck to ensure victory. Gregor fell to
his knees. Gregor looked at Zora.

"To think I ever believed in you," Matthias said. Gregor
ignored him, preparing one last vain attack on the mask.

"Now!" Gregor said.

Drake launched himself at Matthias. The two furiously

clashed. Thos and the snipers fired on the distracted troops. Zora threw the mask down. Every resistance member with an EMPX cranked up the power to max and fired on the mask. The mask shuddered and cried out. Matthias pushed Drake back and immediately countered Gregor's attack. Drake attacked again, receiving a slash through his arm and chest. Drake stepped back, wounded but not mortally.

"You can't destroy it," Matthias said. Gregor smirked.

"But maybe we can cripple it," Gregor said.

Matthias sprinted toward Zora, forcing her to defend the gunmen. She knew she'd lose in a straight clash. Zora moved with swift speed, using her one advantage against a stronger foe. He slashed at Zora. Zora hit him with a series of attacks, putting him on the defense. She relented and opted for safer, surgical strikes.

Matthias slowed, leaving him open to attack. She attacked. Matthias deflected and disarmed her. He struck her. The second she hit the ground, he switched his weapon to rifle mode and fired upon the resistance before anyone could say a word.

Matthias picked up the mask, practically glowing from the elation. He held the silver horror to his face. Finger-like appendages emerged from the sides and wrapped around his head. He raised his hand. Everyone hit the ground. Zora reached out in desperation. Gregor had a revelation.

"Witchkin can use it," Gregor said.

Matthias's hand shook. He clutched at the mask. It began to crack. Zora went unconscious. Matthias thrust out his hand again, this time to no avail. Matthias cursed.

"A minor setback," he said.

He walked over to the edge of the deck and the nearest grappling hook. Gregor's army re-mobilized, though retreating enemy forces kept them from delivering or receiving the final blow.

"We'll stop you," Gregor said.

"You know where to find me," Matthias said, grabbing the rope.

Matthias reached the ground. Vigilant took positions around him and escorted him to one of the remaining trucks. Vigilant continued firing at the resistance as they fled. Drake rushed over to the unconscious Zora. Though Gregor's forces had won the battle, the enemy had what they required. The attack on the mask gave Gregor and the others a bit more time. So far, all Gregor did was buy more time. He couldn't play defense any longer. It was time to go on the offensive.

CASS

VIGILANT SEIZED CONTROL of the city fast, once again proving
a government could be toppled in a matter of hours. The world
above was utterly oblivious to the Vigilant's plans. Cass was now a
high-value target of Vigilant occupiers and shared a bunker with
one of their legendary former members. She laid low in a safe
house hidden beneath a shipping yard. She wouldn't hide forever.
She prepared to aid Matthew in taking down Yadira. The Averills
should help, too, obligation or guilt be damned. Her surroundings were quite comfortable, a cozy underground house with all
the amenities and even a pool, but not her medicine. The sporadic
headaches and bruises worsened. She had no other contacts, leaving her to reveal her orange eyes.

The door to her area of the underground mansion flew open;
in came Matthew Pavane. Matthew stopped and frowned at the
curses of the startled Cassandra Averill.

"Sorry. Habit," Matthew said.

"A pretty bad one, yeah," Cass said, letting the brief moment
of pure hate fade.

"My wife hated it too. Either I creep in really quiet or full
force apocalypse. No middle ground," he said.

"Yeah, you don't seem like a happy balance kinda guy." Matthew took a seat opposite Cass.

"Definitely not," Matthew said. "I spent much of my life with an all-or-nothing mentality. You and your husband seem the same." Cass nodded.

"It's not purely noble," Cass said. Matthew leaned forward, a sign she had his full attention. "After I found out I can't have children, I had a rough go of it. For a very long time, I sat on the sidelines. I always wanted to help people but couldn't muster the strength. There was so much I could've done. For years Thos picked up the slack. He had his own demons, so he knew. He got me through it. We always did what we could to bring out the best in each other. Staying busy helped. Maybe we stay too busy."

She saw Matthew looking at the table, reflecting on his life.

"I love my time with the Freemen. I fought and trained them to defend our city or community or whatever people want to call it. We always made time for our daughters, but it never felt like enough. I can't complain. It was a great life. When they grew up, that slipped. I never got the chance to make up that time. Used drugs to cope when my youngest died, then everything slipped. Freemen value hard work and not laziness. I needed a reason to fight again. Never thought Vigilant would be that reason."

The door swung open, garnering another loud curse from Cass. Through the door came Kane Turce. She received no word on the whereabouts of Kane; she held no doubts he'd left this world. Cass underestimated the resiliency of soldiers.

"Sorry. You understand," Kane said.

"Sure do," Cass barked. "But glad you're alive."

"Me too," he replied.

Kane gave a brief and vague description of his street battle and status as a terrorist attempting to murder the vice regent. Kane carried a large backpack. Cass braced for orders from his, and currently her, boss.

"We being summoned?" she asked.

"Not yet. He wanted me to keep you in the loop. Some of it will put your mind at ease," he replied. Kane told her everything he could. He began with Kingsbury, now under complete lockdown with the regent mysteriously absent. Vigilant only harmed civilians that attacked them. There was very little combat in the city proper, with the fighting centered on Prosperity Hall and the recently uncovered tech city connected via the Blackthorne Vault.

The government fought Vigilant on two fronts and prepared for a third. Each Vigilant base had a super weapon designed to amplify each other and burn this supposed arch-demon that held power over bodies and minds of the known world. On top of that, Thos, Drake, and Zora worked with Gregor's renegade Vigilant to launch an attack on the grand crusader responsible for all the chaos. Her head spun at all information. Everyone's life was topsy-turvy. She wondered how Matthew was processing the madness. Matthew seemed unphased, though concerned for obvious reasons.

"Anything else?" she asked.

Kane removed his backpack and took a seat at the table in Cass's decently comfortable bunker. Cass saw the instant relief without the load. She learned about numerous safehouses across the city, some used for hiding and some they may retreat to. Cass poured herself some wine to calm her nerves. Kane opened the backpack and pulled out a large metal head. Kane held the head for a minute before the eyes became a glowing purple.

"Mrs. Averill," it said.

"Mr. Abaddon," she replied, partially shocked.

"I fear our time grows short," he began. "Your husband and his friends were attacked and driven out of Duke's villa. They're alive; however, Killswitch is nearly ready. The enemy's weapons are damaged; however, based on my calculations, he will be ready in less than 48 hours.

"We're the only ones available for this mission," Kane added. Cass couldn't help experiencing a little fear at Vigilant's effectiveness at unseating a two-thousand-year-old gangster.

"Which means you need us for? What about Proxy?" she asked.

"He has a special task, a backup plan you could say," Mr. Abaddon said. Matthew laughed.

"My brother went through this same thing," Matthew said. "Carting a head around."

"You won't be carting me around for long," Mr. Abaddon said.

A series of metal legs grew out of Mr. Abaddon's head base. The head skittered onto the table, to the disgust of everyone. "The bag is simply a cover while I conserve energy and prepare my defenses—hide in plain sight. We need to get my body back," Mr. Abaddon said. Cass had a feeling this machine also took some pleasure at making his underling carry him around.

"Surely Vigilant smashed it by now," Matthew asked.

"It's very durable. I've been improving it for centuries now for such an occasion. Help me get me to it. With them occupied by the army, we can slip in unnoticed." She realized exactly where this would take her.

"They have it underground," she stated.

"Correct. Behind enemy lines," Mr. Abaddon said. The new recruits are working with the army." Cass had a feeling the term recruit did necessarily mean willing. Cass quickly drank the rest of the wine in her glass.

"We may die either way, but better to go out fighting," Kane said.

"Couldn't this be a trap?" Cass asked.

"No, they're busy preparing for the attack. They only need to hold them off just long enough. The defenses inside will be rudimentary. Help me get to my body and I'll deal with Vigilant," Mr. Abaddon said with icy confidence.

"Never thought I'd be a reserve soldier," Cass said.

"Indeed," Kane said, showing his disapproval from behind Mr. Abaddon.

Mr. Abaddon let the comment go. After all the stories of death and disappearances for hundreds of years, it was amusing to see such a scary figure reduced to a head. Mr. Abaddon skittered over to Matthew Pavane.

"And what of you of Mr. Pavane, is this acceptable?"

"The enemy of my enemy," he said.

"Good. We'll be in touch," Mr. Abaddon said, climbing back into the bag.

Kane bid farewell and carried his boss out of the room. Matthew shot Cass a look, the kind suggesting that the enemy of his enemy was likely also his enemy.

ZORA

People screamed and burned around her. A wounded man with orange eyes sat inside a metal car speeding through the earth. She felt the thousands of jabs in her mind beginning to lessen. It all felt so real. It was no dream. She felt what remained of the dark presence inside the silver mask, telling her to get on with it already. Zora sat up in the bed to see Drake sitting in the lone chair. Drake hopped up from the chair and was on her in a second.

"Always rushing in to save me," she said, appreciative

"How you feeling?" he asked. Zora's jaw hurt. "Matthias got you pretty good."

Zora analyzed the bruises on her body.

"He got us all pretty good," she said.

Drake handed Zora a bottle of water from Melvin's extensive storage. Gregor entered the room not long after. Zora smiled at the notion of the stern old man waiting outside her doorway.

"I'm fine. You don't need to worry about me," she said assuredly.

"I think we do," Gregor said. "Helluva thing you did."

"I'd rather not do it again," Zora said. *But I'll have to, I'm sure,* she thought.

"What exactly did you do?" Drake said.

"I'm not sure. I could feel myself still connected to the mask or the network or whatever you call. I wanted to destroy it. I was desperate and reached out." *Like a witch.*

"Somehow, you made it real. That lends credence to apostates being able to manipulate those things. Not sure how emotion ties into that. Still, so little we know. We definitely need to have a talk with your father about this."

"I never realized," Zora said. "She wasn't even a fighter. My mother seemed normal. If dad knew that, why would he let Naia leave with that witch?" At that moment, Zora wanted to see her mother, and not simply for answers.

"Who the hell knows at this point," Gregor said. "Anyway we'll get to that later. We're getting ready to go after Matthias," Gregor said. "I'd tell you to stay out of our counterattack, but since I know that won't work, you can meet us on the bridge in five."

Drake and Zora followed Gregor to the bridge where Melvin, Thos, Liz, Skully, and Raul scratched beards and pointed at maps.

"They gotta have the tunnels covered," Melvin said. "Big risk. Might as well put some targets with points on us."

"Well, we can't go through the storms," Thos said.

"We can. I've seen the defense controls in the city," Raul said. "There are two consoles, one at the power source and one in the main chamber. Matthias will be at the latter but we have a shot at the other. If we can find a way in, I can deactivate it. Matthias walked through with just that mask. It's a system, any system can be shut down. Without the storms to protect them, they're done. Will Duke come through?"

"Yes, but he ain't happy," Melvin said. "Diverting so many troops. They may lose Mexico City."

Everyone stopped when Gregor, Drake, and Zora joined the discussion. Zora got the obligatory "I'm fine" out of the way. A faint tingling sensation distracted her. Though her connection faded, it wasn't gone completely. She saw her mother in a circle with two others. She saw a man staring at a person strapped to a large machine. She fought to see her mother.

"You connecting?" Gregor asked.

"Sorry," she said.

"Let's keep the reach-outs to a minimum," Drake said.

"I think I can fight him," Zora said. "I have to try."

Zora closed her eyes and reached out. She thought of Matthias. Her head grew hot. She couldn't explain the sensation but it came with eyes. The sensation became floaty, like suddenly submerged in water. There were dozens of connections in the invisible web of a network. Figures were blurry and out of focus. She concentrated on the lest blurry figure, also the only one with orange eyes. She looked through his eyes. She felt him and he felt her. Matthias appeared erratic; his exposure to the mask was taking its toll. She felt sorry for the man.

"I can see what it's doing to Matthias. He hasn't fixed it yet. I feel his panic."

Zora heard Matthias's voice in her head.

"I can play this game too," Matthias said.

Her chest tightened.

"I'm in control now, not Eon and most certainly not you," Matthias said.

Zora engaged in the mental battle with Matthias. She began to sweat. Matthias began to sweat. Zora fell to her knees. Though she didn't win the battle, she realized the exhaustion went both ways. The last thing she heard as she disconnected was Matthias screaming in anger at the realization.

Drake helped Zora to her feet.

"I can't stop him, but I can drain his power. That buys us more time," she said.

The group discussed the precious few options they had; none were very appealing. Melvin relayed the info from his radio contacts with Duke. Everything now rested on their shoulders and their call.

Raul detailed the master control system at the bottom of the Silent City and pointed out the approximate location of the city on the map. The plan consisted of sending half their forces through the tunnels and the remainder of the army after the shield fell. The first team would undoubtedly suffer heavy casualties.

"We've tried the ship. Totally byffed," Raul said. "Matthias destroyed what you managed to get running. Can't even crash the thing," Raul said. "Plus, none of us are pilots. Would've made this easy."

"Can't have that," Gregor replied.

A plan formed. The group formulated a plan to use tunnels to invade, getting control of trains if possible. Melvin contacted Duke's men, telling the locations to hit. Duke's forces numbered in the tens of thousands, far more than Vigilant possessed. It took much persuading to convince Duke to reallocate fifteen thousand troops from contested regions to this assault. Two infiltration teams were created. The first would disable the shields while the second would play defense. Raul and Gregor detailed the nearest train tunnels.

"There's nowhere we go that won't be defended," Gregor said. "And we gotta hit them all at the same time."

"Won't they blow the tunnels?" Thos said.

"Possible, but I don't think so," Raul said. "Melvin collapsed part of a tunnel so the ones we hit are the only way in or out. Their factory is damaged and they aren't fully stocked yet. They'll starve and many aren't *that* willing to die for the cause. I'd wager they'll use barricades and bombs." Melvin nodded in agreement.

"Either way, we gotta use 'em," Melvin said.

A pin-drop could be heard in the room and a dozen miles outside. Zora felt the enormity of it all. Somewhere in Kingsbury, her father also planned his last-ditch effort to stop Killswitch. Across the nation, a simultaneous attack on the grand crusader's Vigilant came to fruition. The faint tingling remained in Zora's head. She lacked the power to destroy the mask, but she'd do her best to hold Matthias at bay for a bit longer.

ANSELM

AIR WHISTLED, ROPES cracked, and red spewed forth. Whip strikes cut Anselm's flesh to pieces; though he loved the punishment, he despised the man that brought his plans to a grinding halt. Flesh healed slowly. Jaren waited each time, eager to re-open the wounds. Waiting on his orders, Jaren unwound with a bit of sadism. Anselm watched his blood feed the grass. Swords pierced his hands, feet, and chest, pinning him to a tree. Anselm's belly roared with hunger and heart burned with hate. Anselm fought against his nature, but seeing Vigilant gathered before him made that a losing battle. He tried holding onto his humanity, but it was flowing out of him as quickly as the blood. Being human wasn't worth it anymore.

Crucifixions, stabbings, de-limbings, shallow cuts, deep cuts, and nails, Anselm found it disturbing how such horrors were now like addictions to him. Jaren took out his frustrations on one of those he blamed for his father's death, with the former king providing him the best outlet. Anselm understood the sentiment; he couldn't deny doing the same to any in-range during his bad days. Anselm fulfilled his torture quota for the month courtesy of Jaren. Sapped of energy, he was more powerless than ever.

Jaren walked over to Vigilant tower, now converted into a

super EMPX called a Killswitch. Jaren tapped on the terminal that powered the goliath machine. He targeted Anselm with test fires, allowing Anselm to recover enough to have a rejuvenated body to deconstruct. The unresponsive Gideon no longer provided Jaren any amusement. Jaren's men were not keen on his side project getting in the way of the grand crusader's goal. Anselm listened and learned.

"Sir, is this really necessary?" one asked.

Jaren finger's twitched near the hilt of his weapon. Others noticed and came to the scene.

"I'm the boss here, don't forget that," Jaren said. "I kept those shits down there alive, that not enough for you?"

"They're prisoners, not your playthings."

Fellows rallied to his side, most of them being his former troops once part of the Blackthorne army. Others came to the aid of the dissenter. *Disloyalty in my favor for once,* Anselm thought.

"You forget your place," the man replied. "We're agents of Vigilant; our orders are clear if you get in the way of that. This is for the greater good." Anselm sensed the opportunity.

"Why do you fight for these fools?" Anselm asked, directing the question at the ex-soldiers at Jaren's side. "You see what I'm capable of. We have the same goals. The same hatreds. Abandon this quest and help me re-establish my kingdom."

A Vigilant crusader stabbed Anselm in the side. Anselm replied with a grin.

"Don't speak, demon," the crusader said. Anselm looked at Jaren.

"I didn't kill your family. I wanted to save them. Your father stood by me through thick and thin. If not for him and the loyalty he inspired, I probably would have died long ago. He would be fighting on my side, not theirs. He recognized strength and new the long game. I was a weak king before, but not this time," Anselm said. Jaren's fingers left his weapon. Jaren shook his head.

"Stop," Jaren said.

"No," Anselm began. "This pain you inflict on me is something I've done to myself every night since. I've wasted away for two years letting those piss-ants destroy everything we built. You really willing to kill countless innocents for your revenge?"

"I am. And I'll have it. They'll be dead," Jaren said.

"That's not good enough for me," Anselm said. "You can be a part of something greater than this suicide pact, or I'll show you what true suffering is. Accept my offer while my moral code remains."

The malice swelled in Anselm. His heart blackened a little more. He limited the casualties in his path; he fought that part of himself getting hungrier. He spared the people, but deep down he hated them. Jaren pointed up at the beaten and bloodied Anselm.

"This is your enemy," Jaren said, trying to rein in his dissenters. "He's a demon now, and none will be swayed by your words." Anselm sensed the kernels of fear and doubts inside Jaren.

"I'll get free," Anselm said. "And I'll share this pain with you."

Anselm's wounds healed. His energy returned. His muscles tightened. Jaren's eyes widened. He sprinted to the Killswitch terminal and quickly activated it. Witches burned around the machine. Anselm's energy faded and left him powerless once more. The two sides of Vigilant united.

"Nice try," Jaren said.

Jaren rammed his sword into Anselm's stomach and twisted it around. Anselm grimaced, then smiled.

"All it takes is one mistake and I'll be free. You're wasting resources. How can you be sure your machine can truly kill me?"

Anselm watered the kernels of doubt. Even Anselm wasn't sure either if Killswitch could truly destroy him. Blood filled Anselm's mouth, he let it run freely down his chin. Jaren pulled the sword out of Anselm. Jaren proceeded to the hot iron phase of Anselm's punishment. Anselm's senses took in the aroma of his flesh roasting.

"Let's put that to the test," Jaren said. "If you can't die, then I'll give you all the pain you want."

Jaren's men pulled the swords from Anselm and tossed the broken man back into the pit. Anselm's brittle bones snapped upon impact. The other prisoners made no attempts to help or hurt him. Anselm lay in the mud, waiting to heal. The hunger kept Anselm from passing out long. He fought it every second. Anselm wasn't sure if Jaren's prisoners were an ingenious form of torture, and if it was, Jaren had no idea how spectacularly it might backfire.

Anselm lay in the mud for hours. The rain came again to turn the pit into an aspiring well. Anselm's bones reformed and broke continuously until reaching the proper configuration. Anselm repeatedly fell during his body's slow rebuilding process. Anselm fumbled like the frail man he once was.

"Perhaps I'll die a second time," Anselm said, laughing in despair.

The words of hundreds filled his head. Words from civilians, the board, and his family drowned out the world around him. He heard the words as clear as Ezra's insults.

"You're a good man," Abigail said.

"I tried to be," Anselm said to the imaginary voice. "I wanted to be, once."

He needed to see her one more time. In his mind, he saw her as she was before everything went wrong. He kept her image clear, refusing to let it blister and burn. He kept it alive long enough to say his final goodbye. She disappeared, staying as beautiful and loving as the day they first met.

"Salvation has a price," Eon said.

Even in his temporary grave, he heard them coming to mock him, heard them talk of desecrating the remains of his family. He heard them laugh about throwing them in the garbage after promising a respectful end for the other Blackthornes. He realized they desired a bit more humiliation first.

"You were always weak," David Westerfield said, emptying his bladder on Anselm's sarcophagus.

"When you deal with an enemy, you act without mercy," Aric said. "They won't fight fair. You shouldn't either." Anselm no longer saw the young, quiet boy he remembered. Conspiring forces and overbearing responsibility sent him on the same dark path Anselm walked. Percival and Edgar were beside him; like Abigail, he imagined them as they lived. He said his final goodbye to them.

He heard Blackthorne Castle collapse. He saw it. He found the one form of pain he could not yet bear. The anger, sorrow, pain, and hunger reached a horrific crescendo. He refused to wither and die in a pit with those that despised and would betray him. The internal locks he placed on his inner demon began to crack. He told himself his urges were wrong. He fought this monstrous side for years. Government forces would arrive soon. There was still time. Jaren would lose; the number of deaths, including his own, was the only real question. There was still a way out for Anselm. He knew what it was.

MELVIN

MELVIN SAT PERCHED atop the overlook a few miles from the Hot Land's entrance to the Silent City. Government forces gathered below for the quickest mobilization in the nation's history. Duke sent troops to each of the four closest entrances to the Silent City. Another vehicle-bound force headed to the Uninhabited, waiting outside the storm wall. The remainder of Duke's army engaged the deadheads across the southern cities with the worst of the fighting in Mexico City.

Melvin surveyed the government army that betrayed him, now awaiting his command. He remembered the days like this. Standing above a mighty army. For many years of his life, it was perfectly normal. He planned for that life to return when the Blackthornes fell. That plan was intended to be a bit more long term than it ended up. Melvin spent his days in the new order as nothing more than a foot soldier. The once adored Victor Whitehall spent his time as a thief getting revenge when the opportunity presented itself. He reminded himself that he wasn't still in the middle of a slow, hallucinating death in the desert.

On one side of Melvin, Drake and Zora checked their weapons; on the other, Gregor ran his fingers through his beard while Thos stared off into the horizon. Liz made his best attempts at conversation with the astonished troops below.

"Amazin' where we end up, isn't it?" Melvin said. "Thought I'd be the head of the whole damn military. Thought I'd be a dad in nowhere. Thought I'd bring freedom to the nation."

"You're tellin' me," Gregor said. "I intended to plunder and pillage 'til I was dead. Ended up a monster hunter. Thought it'd be me and my brother, side by side 'til the end. And now I'm waging a civil war on my own order to stop it from killing half the world." Thos followed the trend.

"Thought I'd sell my farm and hit the coast with my wife and two sons," Thos said. "I hope Cass is okay."

Everyone looked at Zora, holstering her gun. The stares intensified.

"I thought I wouldn't be a witch," she said, not wanting to play along. "I thought I'd be traveling the world with my sister."

"World's a shitshow, ain't it?" Melvin said.

"Not all bad," Zora said, looking at Drake.

"Wouldn't want to be attacking a robot city with anyone else," Thos said.

"Me either," Drake said. Vigilant troops brought each of them an EMPX gunblade and a radio.

The group watched Gregor's troops and government forces mobilize. Trucks and motorcycles lined up for the long drive. The trucks for Melvin and his friends rolled up, driven by Skully. The preparations were completed. The soldiers turned skyward to Melvin, Gregor, Drake, Zora, and Thos.

"Men," Gregor began. "I'll keep it short and sweet. You know what's at stake. You'll be fighting, killing your brothers. I wish it didn't have to be this way, but they pose an unprecedented threat to the world. Our oath demands we fight back against any villain, even one of us. Even if we have the same cause. Stay focused. We don't stop 'til the mission is done. From this day, until our last. Ever Vigilant."

"Ever Vigilant," his troops replied.

Melvin cleared his throat to address Duke's officers and soldiers under his command. Somewhere in Mexico, Duke cursed loudly at empowering Victor Whitehall. Melvin breathed in, puffed up his chest, and channeled his old self.

"Funny world, ain't it? I know a lot of you aren't thrilled to be here under me, though that usually changes when you get to know me." Melvin laughed at the innuendo and then waved his hand. "The world is falling apart. Our friends and brothers are fighting everywhere. Many of 'em probably won't survive the next few days. Hell, we may not. Some of us hate each other and are about to fight our friends. Some of you had to leave friends behind for this. What we ask of you is more than you should have to give, but sometimes we gotta give it all for what's right. We're needed here. This is for the good of the many, for the good of all."

Melvin felt the old energy surging within him. He felt the spark in the crowd.

"It's easy to wonder if what we do is worth it. It is. I forgot that once. The fate of everythin' we know and everyone we love depends on what we do right here, right now. Regardless of how ya feel about me, don't forget what we're fighting for. That whacked-out asshole is willing to kill millions for his perfect world; I ain't gonna let that happen! You? Hell no!" Melvin moved back and forth, getting animated.

"I don't know about you, but I'm sick and tired of the others decidin' what our lives should be. Be it masked creeps, witches, or government clowns. It's time we get back to what we do, and what we do is stop bad guys. So let's go do that!"

Melvin raised his arms heavenward. The soldiers erupted in cheers. Liz thrust his right arm into the air and roared. Gregor leaned in.

"Not bad," Gregor said. Melvin smiled.

"Totally winged it, but damn it felt good," he said.

Melvin buried his sorrow, knowing that there would be heavy

casualties. Melvin gave the signal. Melvin, Gregor, Raul, and Liz got in the lead truck; Drake, Thos, and Zora got in the one behind them. The two kept in constant contact via radio. Melvin and Gregor's army drove toward the mesa, the most remote of the four locations. The armies gathered around the entrances to the Silent City. The door remained closed.

"Doing everything they can to delay us. Bet they're behind that door," Melvin said.

Heavy trucks moved to the sides of the door. Troops attached hooked cables to the insides of the door. Heavy gunners positioned themselves in front of the door. The door buckled and groaned. Wheels screeched. The doors began to slide apart. A stream of blue bullets spewed forth from the opening. Melvin's army retaliated. Melvin rationed the grenades, particularly the remote variety, for the thicker fighting in the city. Liz lobbed a single grenade through the hole, curses and an explosion soon followed.

Gregor's Vigilant attacked from the sides, firing as the doors were pulled open. Matthias's forces retaliated with their stores of grenades, less frugal than Melvin. Skully dodged the explosive rain.

Gregor's railgunners blasted the soldiers inside the mesa to bits. Melvin sent a team forward. Inside the mesa, they drove the enemy back. A group of a hundred soldiers guarded the entrance, knowing they would die just to delay Melvin a bit longer. Potshots dropped a half dozen more of Melvin's team. Liz rushed through the enemy line with the support of gunfire. The startled men fell back. Liz split and de-capped the unprepared enemy, pushing the rest into Gregor's firing line. Melvin lost another half dozen men in the first excursion. The army moved forward into the train station. Raul exited the truck and ran to the station controls.

"Busted," he said.

"Was worth a shot," Melvin said.

Melvin hollered through the radio for news from the other fronts. The Alvarado army arrived inside the passageways a good half-hour later. Like Melvin's team, the train controls were disabled. The third group in northeast Tamaulipus, however, had a fully functioning train station.

"Gamble paid off," Melvin said, praising Raul for his idea to take the station furthest away.

"Whole thing is a gamble," Gregor said.

The fourth and main team came through the northern tunnel that extended through to Heartland. Team four was double the size of the other teams, with almost as many troops as Matthias's entire army. The northern tunnel was the one closest to the main army headquarters for the region. The team attacked from an unguarded entrance hidden in the rocks, much like the mesa tunnel Melvin hit. Team four arrived in an empty station with no train.

The army formed a convoy of vehicles. They moved slowly at first. Riflemen used scopes and night-vision to scan the dark corridor ahead for surprises. Teams one, two, and four rolled through the tunnel. Team three divided its forces, sending vehicles through while ground troops summoned the train.

Team four proceeded through faster than the others, with a scant resistance for the size of their army. The team leader detailed barricades that forced vehicles into lines. Anxiety crawled up Melvin's spine.

"Not so tough," the leader said.

"Don't get cocky fellas," Melvin said.

"You worry too much." Vigilant troops were decimated by Duke's men, even with their superior firepower. Team four gained speed. Melvin heard the beeping through the radio. The chatter increased.

"What's going on?" Melvin said. Melvin couldn't make out the words from the cries and curses. The bangs and booms followed.

"Guys?" Melvin said. After a few minutes the radio screeched to life

"Bombs. They got bombs," the man said.

"How bad?" Melvin said

"We lost some, but we're trapped. They sealed it up."

"You better plow yer way through cuz we can't get to you," Melvin said. "Everybody hear that? Keep yer eyes peeled." Melvin fought the urge to punch a hole through the dashboard. "A third of our infiltrators crippled right outta the gate."

Raul immediately took on the duties of explosive ordinance analysis. Raul provided updates through his radio, identifying strange devices he surmised were IEDs in the tunnels. Gregor suggested EMP waves to disable the explosives. Melvin relayed the intel to the other teams. An EMPX line of Vigilant became the bomb squad to test Raul's theory. A brave Vigilant soul threw himself onto the IED, sighing in relief. Gregor scanned the roofs for explosives with the power to collapse the tunnels.

"Think they'll blow more?" Melvin said.

"If they get desperate," Gregor advised. "But this slowdown might be enough."

Team two clashed with enemy checkpoints. Team three met with no resistance with their scouts reporting the train fast approaching. Thos poured over Raul's hand-drawn map, providing estimates on their progress. Melvin's convoy picked up speed. After a long slog, the train arrived at station three. The train-bound troops gave the word and headed off to the enemy base. Raul advised them to operate the train manually and watch out for any surprises likely waiting for them. Team two lost a dozen vehicles in the checkpoint battles. Melvin's team gained momentum, speeding and disabling traps faster and faster.

Team three arrived at the destination, wisely using manual mode to avoid an explosive volley from enemies in the station. The team played defense in the station, slowly pushing through to the city. Team two lost a fifth of their forces along the way, while team three lost two hundred in their uphill battle. The surviving team four made steady progress unclogging the tunnel.

Melvin's team suffered no casualties en route to the enemy base, unleashing a storm of bullets the minute they hit the final stretch and saw the enemy rushing to meet them. Bullets and grenades flew past Skully, wiping out the five trucks behind him. Liz jumped out of the vehicle before it stopped. Hitting the ground running, Liz swung his ax with all his fury. Liz decimated ten enemies in his path in a matter of seconds. He switched to the railgun strapped to his back. With an army at his back, team one cleared the station. Melvin and Liz lead the charge up the stairs into the city. Gregor, Drake, Thos, and Zora hurried up after them. Thousands of Vigilant troops and a dozen tanks gathered at the main roads leading to the thick, circular tower at the city's heart. Zora closed her eyes.

"Matthias has fixed the mask but can't get it working yet," Zora said. "I feel his anger. He's trying something new. I'll do what I can to stop him." Melvin looked at Raul.

"They know you can break the shield?" he said. Raul shook his head. Melvin looked at Gregor and the others.

"You guys get down there then," Melvin said. "We'll keep 'em busy."

"No need for heroics. Come with us," Drake said.

"They need me up there. We'll draw their fire. Go pop that bubble," Melvin said.

"Mel—" Zora said.

"No time to argue, miss, get your asses down there," Melvin said.

"I'll join ya," Thos said, stepping up beside Melvin. "We got this."

Liz took a position on the other side of Melvin. Gregor nodded.

"Stay alive," Gregor said.

Gregor, Raul, Drake, and Zora got back in the truck. Together with Vigilant and a few hundred government troops, they broke off through the tunnel descending into the city's defense grid. Melvin, Liz, Thos, and the army at their back climbed up the stairs and roads to face the enemy entrenching themselves in front of the city's core.

GREGOR

GREGOR TOOK CHARGE of the convoy heading through the depths beneath the automated city. Drake and Zora held guns ready if any foes caught wind of the plan. Raul provided directions through the maze of passageways. A skeleton crew patrolled the underground; Gregor expected something would compensate.

"This is one of two consoles that control the defense systems," Raul said. "The second one is in the main chamber. We can push most everyone through before Matthias can get the shield back up."

"I hope you can get this done fast. I doubt we'll be alone for long," Gregor said.

"No pressure," Drake said. Raul didn't laugh.

"Good thing you learned all this stuff," Gregor said.

"Now I get to pay that asshole back, picked the wrong guy to betray," Raul said.

Raul guided Gregor and his team through the underground web to a tunnel filled with white light. Gregor veered hard left when he emerged into the main chamber far beneath where Matthias's prepared Killswitch. A single white tank guarded the control system at the machine's base. Gregor's team divided around the chamber to avoid the blue beams. The last truck in the convoy wasn't so lucky. The two sides of the convoy circled the tank. The circle of firing put nary a dent in the resilient machine. The treads went horizontal, allowing it to follow the desired target. A second blast from the tank sent pieces of a truck flying into the circling convoy, colliding with another truck. Drake avoided the tank blasts. The tank cannon broke off from pursuing Drake's bike and focused on obliterating any trucks it could.

"Running out of trucks. Any grenades?" Gregor called out, dodging the tank blasts increasingly fixated on him. Raul conveyed the message. Three grenades bounced and rolled into the tank treads, locking the vehicle in place.

"I got an idea," Gregor said.

He directed the trucks to the machine itself. The tank fired before the gunner realized the plan. The tank blast hit the side of the central machine. The machine shuddered.

"These things are too automated," Gregor said.

Raul activated the wave feature of his EMPX and cranked up the power output to maximum. Raul hit the tank with an energy wave. The gun jerked around. Raul unleashed continuous waves at the tank. The front of the tank popped open, revealing a man in a seat typing on a screen. The man grumbled curses and he put the tank in manual mode. A series of bullets from Zora's rifle ended the man before he could engage manual controls.

"Cutting edge doesn't always cut," Gregor said.

Gregor and his convoy stopped the vehicles and formed a perimeter around the central console. Gregor, Drake, and Zora took aim at the tunnels. Gregor took the radio. Melvin's responses came faintly through the raging death above them. Gregor made out a few words, including "battalion." Raul's furious fingers hit digital buttons on the screened console. A waterfall of sweat flowed from him. Zora winced.

"Matthias is doing something, hooking himself up to a machine. There's screaming," Zora said. "I think he's got some kind of backup plan. He's . . . hooking himself up to those witch-burning machines."

Zora screamed out and fell back.

"I'm trying to hold him off," Zora said. Zora sweat and strained.

Gregor ran over to the tank and ripped the body from the seat. Gregor's knowledge of tanks was decent but not up-to-date on the space-age kind he plopped into. Gregor scanned the seat and the hatch up above him. He performed some trial-by-fire learning. The sounds of a wheeled army echoed in the tunnels. Five trucks and two hundred soldiers emerged from the darkness. Gregor's men and Matthias's troop filled the chamber with blue bullets and red flesh. Gregor hastily unlocked the hatch.

"They know what we're doing!" Drake said.

Gregor grabbed the lever at the side of his seat. The seat rose upward. More troops rushed into the chamber. Gregor's troops began to fall at the onslaught, losing one for every man they took out. Gregor studied the rail weaponry during his time at the city and Melvin's fortress. The massive cannon appeared more or less the same as its smaller cousins. Gregor's fingers wrapped around the handles with triggers on both sides of the back of the monster gun. A large square screen with a reticule in the middle served as the manual scope.

"Hold 'em off a little longer!" Raul said.

Enemy troops rumbled through another tunnel on their way to the chamber. Gregor pushed down the triggers. A barely audible hum came from the gun. The one-for-one death ratio continued. The buzz grew louder and traveled through the weapon. Blue energy surged into the gun and gathered at the end of the barrel. The gun jerked and flew blue destruction into a series of trucks too close together. The blue became an orange domino effect as the trucks exploded, wiping out the gunners on the back and the stream of troops coming in behind them.

Gregor pulled the triggers. The slow-to-fire cannon wiped out a second mass of vehicles and troops. The other vehicles broke off. Drake covered Raul on foot, killing enemy forces slipping through the lines. Zora dipped behind cover, having an unseen battle with Matthias.

"Shield is down!" Raul cried with joy. "Just a bit more and I'll have the storm wall."

Gregor's men started to outpace their foes in killing. He heard the unmistakable rolling of tank treads and a subsequent blue beam punching a hole through his team's defenses. Gregor swung the cannon and pressed the triggers. The hum of both tank guns reached a fever pitch. Gregor's few-second head start connected with the enemy gun. The gun erupted in a shower of blue fire that quickly traveled to the rest of the vehicle. Gregor was quickly running out of men.

"I . . . I think I got it!" Raul said.

Gregor scrambled for his radio.

"Melvin? Can you hear me? Confirm the shields are down."

Gregor heard no response and sent another blast at the enemies coming through the opening in their truck wall. Ten minutes passed. Gregor's blasts prevented the enemy from gaining any more ground. A screech through the radio provided hope.

"Can you hear me?" Melvin said. "Shields are down! Cavalry's comin' through! Get yer asses up here!"

"Hi," said a second voice through the radio.

"Liz says hi."

"On our way," Gregor said.

Gregor yelled at his surviving companions as the enemy did the same. The enemy made a hasty retreat through a side tunnel leading back up to the city. Zora winced again.

"Matthias isn't ready, but whatever he's doing is creating a ton of energy," Zora said.

"Time we put an end to him," Gregor said.

Drake, Zora, Raul, and a few dozen survivors boarded the trucks and went up through the tunnels to meet the army. Gregor took one last shot at the power console, ensuring no one could turn it back on, and then he jumped into the back of the last truck.

MATTHEW

WITHOUT THERAPEUTICS TO calm his mind or a mission, Matthew feared for his daughter. He did his best to prepare her for a harsh and dangerous world, but a father couldn't help but worry. He'd lost his wife and one daughter already; even his resolve would fail should he lose the other. He couldn't rest. Matthew sat up in the bed and propped himself against the wall. Proxy's words bounced around in his head. Matthew's daughters never knew their heritage, and neither did he.

He struggled through the haze, growing tired of reaching the same dead end. He breathed deep, seeking help from Freemen meditation. He smiled at some memories and blushed at others. He focused his thoughts on the ones out of place. Matthew stood beside his wife in a half-submerged cavern staring up at an elevated platform. Matthew vaguely remembered this moment. There were nine blurry masses, vaguely human in shape. He couldn't make out the words, but felt the anger swirling around him. The being in the center held something in it's hand, a spherical object. The witch held the sphere up. A bang outside the room broke Matthew from his concentration, though the anger remained. His sword arm itched for a fight.

Kane stepped inside the room without a knock. The head of

Mr. Abaddon with its spidery legs climbed up onto Kane's back and flattened out into a sort of metal backpack with the legs as the straps.

"Bag too much, was it? Good thing you have strong employees," Matthew said.

Kane grumbled but said nothing. Matthew tangled with a few robots in his days and realized Kane carried the burden of an at least 50-pound head.

"Don't worry about him. The regent's forces and almost ready. We move now," Mr. Abaddon said.

Matthew and Kane went to the elevator where Cass waited. Cass wore light, black body armor. Matthew hated endangering civilians, but she was the only other person available for this last-ditch stealth op. The elevator took the four up into a large room filled with containers of various arms. Matthew donned a set of the stolen military gear but decided to stick with his gunblade. Kane opened a small container and handed Cass a suppressed pistol before grabbing a modified AR. The trio returned to the elevator and emerged into a faux shipping container leading to the outside world.

The dark cloudy night provided ample cover. Sticking to the corners and back alleyways, they avoided dozens of Vigilant trucks with mounted machine guns patrolling the city.

"Looks like they caught wind of the operation," Matthew said.

A platoon of Vigilant troops set up an MOB in the city square leading up to Prosperity Hall. The troops carried the EMPXs and railguns. A substantially large force surrounded the building itself, managing to cobble together watchtowers and two searchlights.

"We wait here," Kane whispered. "The army'll be launching an attack shortly, should draw everyone here and give us access to the tunnels. The infiltrators are already in the sewers, so we will, fingers crossed, have a clear path." He pointed over to a spot between two building west of the fountain.

Within minutes came the monstrous thunder of the army.

APCs, and mounted trucks drove through the main street, with a host of a few thousand men. The army outnumbered Vigilant five to one; however, the more advanced technology would at the very least buy them enough time to complete their mission. Some infiltrators crawled across the rooftops to size up the Vigilant snipers near Prosperity Hall.

The city square erupted in bloody violence. Bullets and blue trails of death dropped and obliterated troops on both sides. Heavy railgun fire collided with army trucks. Army machine guns pelted barricades. Grenadiers launched their payloads behind the barriers, forcing Vigilant out and into the path of the mounted guns. After a few minutes, Vigilant troops ran to replenish their mounted gun being sniped from above. Kane saw the opening.

"Go!" Kane said.

Cass, Kane, and Matthew ran full speed past the distracted troops. Kane pried open the sewer drain. A Vigilant soldier caught a glimpse of Cass. Matthew shot the man twice in the chest and hurried into the sewers.

He took the lead. Gunfire from behind right on schedule gave them no resistance. With no enemies in sight, the trio sprinted until they reached a hole in the side that fed into the undercity. They followed the tunnels. Green light surged through the underground. Cass rubbed her eyes, shrugging off unknown pain.

"Hang in there. You'll get through this," Matthew said, channeling his fatherly side.

They emerged from the tunnel in front of a toppled building. The three inched to the gaping hole formerly housing stories of glass. They stopped for a minute to get their bearings. In the distance, a structure lorded over all the others, emanating an ethereal green light. A heavy Vigilant presence guarded the structure.

"My body should be in their paltry lab," Mr. Abaddon said.

Matthew mapped out a path through the empty alleyways to a long rectangular building. A handful of troops ran from the building carrying railguns and EMPXs. Matthew moved in, with Cass and Kane providing him support.

"Don't shoot if you can help it," Matthew said.

They moved in after Vigilant troops rushed to defend against the army. Inside the long building, they found dozens of empty containers and one man in the back observing multiple large metallic objects attached to the walls. Though large and separated, the pieces resembled a torso and limbs. Matthew rushed the scientist. Matthew pulled the knife from his belt and rammed it into the man's throat. Another man came around the corner, receiving a bullet from Cass. Cass kept herself together, but her skin went a shade of green after killing a man.

"I'm still not used to it," she said.

Kane approached Mr. Abaddon's dismembered body. The arms retracted from Kane's back. Mr. Abaddon's head hit the ground and skittered over to his body.

"This will take time," he said.

Mr. Abaddon's head climbed up onto the torso. Tiny wires slithered out of his head and connected with the neck. Multiple footsteps outside came at the worst possible time. Cass and Matthew readied their guns. Kane followed instructions, tapping on keys. Cass breathed in deep and steadied her aim.

"How many people you killed?" Matthew asked.

"Including today, three," she said.

More green light surged through the room, reigniting throbbing throughout her body. Kane grimaced at the same time. Enemies rushed in.

Kane knocked over the table. Cass quickly dipped behind the cover, immediately doubtful Vigilant bulletproofed their tables. Kane drew all gunfire to him. A couple Vigilant soldiers ran into the room, receiving bullets as their greeting. Wires snaked out of the torso sockets and connected to his limbs. Metal, bone-like cylinders attached each part to the torso.

A scraping bellow from Mr. Abaddon put all eyes on him. He tore his arms free of their restraints. Vigilant directed all gunfire to him. Kane stood in shock as Mr. Abaddon broke free of the leg restraints. Fully complete, Mr. Abaddon stood ten feet tall with a wide body like a vertical tank. Intricate plating around the body connected in a form resembling a skinned body, with sections not unlike human musculature and plate connectors serving as the bone and ligaments to hold it all together. The frame protected the system of wires fed into whatever served as Mr. Abaddon's artificial organs. Matthew appreciated the design—reminded him of the most advanced body armor from the Old World. Matthew had a feeling Vigilant intended to replicate this design for their future endeavors, or couldn't yet destroy it. Mr. Abaddon was an unparalleled robot, far beyond what Matthew battled over the years, a complex body that seemed to rival his human counterparts. At that instant, Matthew feared that whatever Mr. Abaddon's capabilities were, they would be used on him if the opportunity arose.

Frantic Vigilant soldiers adjusted the knobs on their guns. Mr. Abaddon raised his right hand. The palm opened up, revealing six gun barrels. The barrels spun and hot metal death sprayed forth, shredding nine of the twelve assailants. Two of three survivors managed to power up the wave functionality of their guns. Invisible waves sent Mr. Abaddon into the wall and onto the floor. Kane fired back at the attackers, killing one. Matthew fired two shots and dropped the last two soldiers. Mr. Abaddon's hands dug in the ground. The metal bones coming out of his hands extended and pushed the rest of his body up. When he got back on his feet, the metal bones retracted, connecting the hands back to his arms.

"Follow me to the main terminal," he said. Kane dropped his rifle and swapped it for a railgun. Cass followed suit and picked up an EMPX, amazed at the lightweight three-in-one death dealer. Cass played around with the weapon for a minute with Matthew's help.

"Move," Mr. Abaddon commanded.

Mr. Abbadon set off out of the building. The metal giant strode across the ancient streets. The ground shook with each step. Loose debris fell from the collapsed buildings nearby. The noise directed all Vigilant attention within earshot to the mechanical monster. Matthew struggled to maintain pace with the machine's long gait. Kane and Cass quickly caught up. With enemies blocking the exits, Cass and Kane pushed forward. Mr. Abaddon maintained a brisk pace for a machine of his size. The more he walked, the more human the movements became. The three passed through the alleys and out into the underworld's equivalent of the city square. Green light continuously spewed from the tower. People tied to poles burned in a ring around the structure. The trio climbed the stairs. The Vigilant army gasped at the behemoth robot moving toward the central structure. A door at the tower's base slid closed; Matthew caught a glimpse of Yadira inside.

Cass and Kane used Mr. Abaddon as a walking shield while Matthew did his best to keep up. The plates on Mr. Abaddon's back slid apart. A third arm with an end similar to the railguns extended up and over his head. Mr. Abaddon raised both his arms, unloading more death from his hands. The enormous robot annihilated everyone in his path.

A cluster of Vigilant troops switched their guns to wave mode. Cass and Kane shot back at them. Matthew held forces from the right at bay. Mr. Abaddon's mouth dropped. A yellow flash preceded a beam. Vigilant screamed and melted from the intensity of the blast. One sneaky crusader from the side sliced up some of the robot's arm plating. Mr. Abaddon gave the man a hard smack. The robot raised his foot and brought hundreds of pounds of metal onto the man's chest.

Matthew glanced back and his human companions, all starting to regret empowering the mechanical monstrosity. In a matter of minutes, Mr. Abaddon decimated all the Vigilant troops protecting the tower. Vigilant soldiers across the city converged to rescue Yadira. Mr. Abaddon turned to engage the oncoming wave of foes. The machine bellowed his bone-rattling laugh before unleashing his full fury. Beams, blasts, and bullets eviscerated wave after wave of Vigilant. Hundreds fell at the hands of the war machine turned crime boss. The rest of Vigilant scattered at the maelstrom of death.

"Cowardly vermin," Mr. Abaddon said.

The third arm retracted into his back.

"This is *my* city," he said.

Mr. Abaddon's guttural call echoed across the underground city. Mr. Abaddon resumed his walk to the glowing tower. He ripped the door open like paper. A second later, he was flying backward. Everyone jumped out of the way; Mr. Abaddon tumbled down the stairs. Out of the tower stepped Yadira in Vigilant robes and a silver mask.

"You won't stop us," Yadira said.

Yadira raised hand and thrust it up. Kane's gun snapped back and hit him square in the face. Cass raised her gun and received the same treatment. On the ground, Kane convulsed. Matthew seized the chance to hit her with an EMPX wave. Yadira's hand shook. Her breathing grew heavy.

Yadira backed into the tower. Kane and Cass rose to their feet and joined Matthew's pursuit of Yadira. The tower hummed louder. The earth above groaned and fell, revealing a metal ceiling sliding apart. Light seeped throughout the floor and rushed to the central structure. The light shot into the sky. Kane clutched at his chest and fell to the ground. Cass focused on putting one foot in front of the other.

Matthew entered the tower and froze at a chilling sight. Thousands of liquid-filled pods adorned the walls. Shriveled remains of mummified remains were entombed in the pods. attached via tubes in their mouths and backs. The empty black pits of their eyes stared at the machine that failed to save them. A few dozen of the floating, shriveling beings clung to life, their fully functioning eyes watching the showdown below. Yadira latched onto the terminal and pulled herself up.

"Stop this!" Cass said, spitting up blood.

"Is this the world you want?" Matthew asked.

"How dare you judge me. How many have you killed for the Compact? Do you want to be part of a system where you or your children die based on some monster's equation? The sick game ends here. The survivors will rebuild the world. We will live and die on our own terms Vigilant will lead the way."

Matthew moved in for the kill. Yadira thrust her hand forward, halting Matthew's killing blow. Matthew's neck constricted. Paralysis took hold.

"You're a slave to it too. I feel the evil rising. This is our only chance!"

A shot rang out from Cass's gun. A red spot grew on Yadira's stomach. Matthew gained control of his body. He lunged forward and tore the mask from Yadira's face. A wave of enemies stormed the tower. Matthew dipped behind cover. Cass got off a few shots and Matthew did the rest. Cass got to her feet. Matthew turned back to Yadira, finding nothing.

"Dammit!" Kane said.

"We'll get her later. We gotta blow this thing!" Matthew said.

Kane scavenged for heavy ordinance scattered about the area. Matthew held the mask tight to be safe. The quakes grew closer. A hulking shadow came into view.

"I'll take it from here," Mr. Abaddon said.

Mr. Abaddon lumbered forth unopposed. Cass, Kane, and a begrudged Matthew stepped out of his way. Mr. Abaddon arrived at the terminal. Cass clutched at her chest. Kane shrugged off the pain but maintained his composure. He picked up a railgun. Dozens of small wires slithered from Mr. Abaddon's head and into the terminal. The beam went white. The mask burned Matthew's hand; tentacles shot out and flailed. Cracks began to form. The tentacles grabbed hold of Matthew's arm and squeezed tight. He fought through the pain as the octopoid nightmare wrapped tighter around. More cracks formed, severing the tentacles from the rest of the body. The arms fell apart when they hit the ground. Matthew heard a voice in his head, warning him of the world he was ushering in. The mask shrieked before shattering like glass.

The beam thinned until it was nothing. The machine was deactivated but still whole. Mr. Abaddon had complete control over the underworld. Guns rose around the tower and throughout the city. Matthew questioned Mr. Abaddon's intent, and from the look on Kane's face, he agreed. Kane nodded. Matthew nodded back. Cass slowly walked over to the nearest EMPX. Matthew motioned with his hands how to prepare the weapon. Kane raised his gun. Mr. Abaddon's back plates slid apart; out came his third arm.

"How predictable," Mr. Abaddon said.

Military forces hadn't reached the underground chamber. Many Vigilant soldiers were trapped between the army and Mr. Abaddon. In a matter of minutes, Mr. Abaddon wiped away all traces of Vigilant in the underground city. The guns around the tower pointed at Cass, Kane, and Matthew.

Kane fired at Mr. Abaddon, pushing him back into the terminal. Mr. Abaddon became unbalanced. Cass fired a wave into the robot. Kane got a second shot off before diving. Cass dove as well. Matthew fired a wave. The waves stunned Mr. Abaddon. His purple eyes flickered. Matthew risked it all to engage the robot up close, slashing through the plates and the exposed wires serving as his veins. Matthew hacked away at the arms until the limbs hit the ground. The autoguns targeted Matthew and fired. Matthew dropped to the ground, leaving Mr. Abaddon in the path of destruction. On the ground, Cass and Kane pelted the robot with waves. The combined assault sent Mr. Abaddon through the central structure. The bullets tore through the robot's thick armor as well as the central structure. The purple of Mr. Abaddon's purple eyes went black. Mr. Abaddon flew back, going straight through the tower and into central machinery. The tower groaned and tilted like a cut tree about to fall.

"Run!" Matthew said, hightailing out of the area,

The trio ran as fast as their broken bodies allowed. The base of the machine bent. The insides crashed down onto Mr. Abaddon. The last image Matthew saw of the dread gangster was him caving under the weight. The falling machine smashed into the wall of the structure's outer wall.

The falling machine exploded, spraying shrapnel across the structure. The three escaped, barely avoiding the shower of metal. When the dust settled. Matthew checked for his companions. Kane was nowhere to be found. Cass lay unconscious on the ground, blood running from her mouth.

ANSELM

ANSELM LAY IN the sludge after yet another round of torture. His body struggled to heal from the constant on and off attacks of Jaren's test fires. His body was weakening, whether the machine was active or not. He no longer imagined his dead family for comfort, but the faces of his enemies were as ever-present as his hunger and pain.

Anselm's ears pricked at the radio chatter of the government army marshaling at the edge of Vigilant territory. Part of Anselm fought to hold himself back. Leaders constantly faced difficult decisions. It was a familiar line his father told him and he had repeated to his children. He never realized that gravity until the final days of his reign. He accomplished nothing here, withering away in the watery pit for a people he had come to despise. The more he thought about it, the less difficult the decision became. Indecisiveness and humanity put Anselm in this embarrassing position. New Prosperity needed a strong king.

The Durenburg prisoners recoiled when they looked at him, not out of fear but disgust. Ezra walked over to Anselm and gave him a series of hard fists to face. With each hit, Anselm saw the numerous faces that brought him so low. Anselm's face hit the mud.

"Fight back, ya piece of shit!" Ezra said.

The prisoners never attempted an escape and, like Jaren, seemed content to take out their frustrations on Anselm instead. Anselm hated them for not trying, as he hated himself for not taking the actions necessary. *Why am I holding myself back for these dumb cows?*

"Weak and pathetic, the lot of you!" Anselm choked out the words, adding dark red to the muddy water. His stomach roared, startling his attacker. Ezra kicked him repeatedly, yelling at one of the women to distract Cameron.

"Yer words are hollow," Ezra said. "Coward! Ya hid up here all this time. Ya outta make their sacrifice mean something. That should make you strong!" Anselm looked at him, taken aback by the words.

"Their sacrifice . . . makes me strong," Anselm said.

Anselm never would've used the mutagen on himself had Aric not died; he would be in the ground with the rest of his family. The Blackthornes would fade from memory, wiped from history. Pain and loss had driven him on for so long. Loss gave way to hate. It gave him the strength to reestablish the Blackthorne order. Anselm had potential greater than any Blackthorne that came before, and it was only possible because of the actions that led him here. Morality was a crutch he didn't need.

"I've been looking at this wrong," Anselm said, hit with the revelation. "Their sacrifice was necessary. That was the price for my salvation. That drove me to be greater than any man. Love was weakness. Compassion was weakness. Humanity was weakness. Pain made me strong. Strong enough to be a true king."

Anselm lets the tears fall. Ezra turned Anselm over and threw himself on the old king. Ezra pummeled Anselm without mercy.

"Their sacrifice was necessary," Anselm said. "I should be thanking them."

For a second time, Anselm had a moment of clarity. The

sobbing of a broken man became a twisted laugh. Ezra stopped his assault, confused.

Anselm tired of caring about these pitiful creatures. Ezra threw another punch, but Anselm caught it. Anselm's right hand clamped around Ezra's fist. He channeled what remained of his strength into his right hand. There was great power and knowledge in blood, and there was one above him who possessed more than any other; Anselm coveted that power, but he couldn't get it on an empty stomach. Ezra howled as his hand flattened. Anselm pushed Ezra off of him. Ezra's stared in shock at the fingers dangling from the mush he once called a hand.

Anselm rose to his feet. He had a new calling. A greater calling. A calling that wouldn't be without the death of his family. There was so much more he could accomplish in a life without end. There was darkness festering in the deepest parts of him; he surrendered to it.

"It's time I embrace who I really am," he said. "The pain has made me strong . . . and I love it. I think I love it more than them."

Anselm looked at the prisoner on the other side of him. He threw himself upon the prisoner, burying his teeth in the tender flesh of the throat. The sweet nectar rejuvenated him. This time he was in complete control. The stiffness of his muscles began to fade. The others gawked in horror as Anselm consumed parts of the neck and head. Anselm's muscles expanded. The bones of his victim broke so easily they lacked the satisfying cracks he desired. Limbs came off easy, like pulling apart a roast chicken. Anselm savored it.

He moved from person to person, saving Ezra for last. He had forgotten all reservations about hurting this man. Throats opened easy, keeping the screams to a minimum. Each bite, each drink, fueled him; once a feeling of loathing now lustful joy. He didn't have to deny the pleasure he took in it any longer. Anselm heard Vigilant troops on route to investigate the screams; it added an extra thrill to the slaughter. Anselm's victims became unrecognized blobs of meat. The sadness faded with each cut and slice, he stopped for a moment to wonder how it was so easy to turn that part of him off; after another moment he realized he no longer cared. Anselm felt the joy of their pain as well as his. Muscles tightened and bulged. Attacks became effortless. Ezra remained. Ezra fell to his knees and wept at what pieces of his grandson he could discern in the gory meat buffet.

"You're everything they said you were!" Ezra screamed. Vigilant was getting closer.

"Oh, I'm far more than that. I have much to accomplish, free of notions of family and other weaknesses. So much to do and so much I need to do it. This is hungry work, after all."

Joy and pain became one to Anselm, opening himself to a whole new world of possibility. Anselm's ears tingled at the sounds of soldiers rushing toward him. He thrust his right hand into Ezra's thick body and spilled him onto the pile of leftovers. Anselm knelt down and quickly devoured the dying heart of Ezra Crowe. He soared out of the pit. Vigilant forces gasped in horror. Anselm allowed them to attack.

Soldiers in slashing distance rammed their blades into him. Anselm responded with a grunt bordering on delight. Anselm knocked them back with a swing of his arm. Gunmen unloaded everything they had on him. Anselm stretched out his arms, welcoming each shot.

"To think I feared this," he said.

Anselm was upon a swordsman in a flash. He grabbed hold of his head. Anselm applied pressure soldier, gradually at first, there had to be pain and most certainly screaming to make this any sort of fun at all. His fingers went deep. Anselm pulled the head apart, letting the red wash over him.

Dozens of gunmen ran to a safe distance to fire at the villain, killing two of their own swordsmen in the way. Anselm walked forward, pulling the blades from his body. Anselm threw a sword at a gunman, who failed to dodge in time. Anselm cut a bloody swath through the Vigilant with the last sword, cleaving through their bodies like butter.

Out of the corner of his eye, Anselm noticed a wounded Jaren holding the silver mask. The mask had softened him up, Anselm felt a bit disappointed. Jaren's face became awash with horror at the visage of the blood-soaked king with an embedded metal crown digging into his head. Anselm had warned the arrogant Jaren about this future. He was glad he hadn't listened.

"Ah, Mr. Hart, I believe we have an appointment," Anselm said.

Jaren placed this mask on his face, willing to risk it sucking all the life he had left. He sprinted toward the behemoth EMPX. The machine growled with power. Anselm pulled out the final sword and took off, making detours to remove a few arms and legs from the outmatched Vigilant. Long-range fighters with EMPX rifles blasted him. His blood boiled inside, hurting but not stopping him. Anselm moved swiftly, eviscerating the battalion guarding Jaren's super weapon. Anselm severed the head of a soldier, catching and throwing it at Jaren. The head collided with Jaren, knocking him to the ground.

"Stop him!" Jaren said, struggling to get to his feet.

The desperate gunmen moved to intercept Anselm. Anselm swapped the sword for a rifle. The army made the push across the plains, attacking him all at once. Hot bullets ripped through his flesh. Anselm ignored the bullets. He focused on the EMPX gunners first.

Enemies fell fast, but not fast enough. The machine growled behind him. Green energy surged through the machine and into the sky. Anselm grunted in pain as his cells burst and reformed. With the troops behind him dead, he turned back the teams on either side of the tower and Jaren Hart. Anselm fired at Jaren, who callously used his men as shields. The soldiers fell in droves. Anselm saw the fear in their eyes; he loved it. He was at one with his true self now, he thought. Anselm didn't bother to negotiate. He fired until he ran out of bullets and ran up to attack his foes up close. His foes scattered, leaving a startled Jaren with no one but a shell named Gideon Grey.

"Survival trumps loyalty. I learned this lesson well," Anselm said.

Jaren sneered at Anselm through the mask. Anselm's heart beat erratically. White-hot fire tore him apart inside. His insides were rebuilding slower. Jaren picked up his sword. He ran Anselm through, but this did little. Anselm smiled and ripped the mask from Jaren's face. Anselm bit into his neck a took a little drink. He pulled back.

"Such a waste," Anselm said. "Or...maybe not."

Anselm hit Jaren with a force to incapacitate, but not kill. Anselm walked to the console unopposed. Anselm analyzed the rudimentary computer hooked up at the base of the machine. Anselm read at length volumes on old technologies after his first meeting with Eon. He punched in a code on the keyboard. Commands appeared on the screen. He moved through them with ease, knowing nanoblood memory contributed to his abilities, and he entered the commands to disable the machine. The green light dissipated.

For the time being, Vigilant was neutralized. What remained of the enemy battled government forces miles from his location. No one would disturb Anselm now. Anselm approached Gideon Grey strapped to the front of the machine. Gideon's dead eyes regarded him coldly. Gideon had no expression, not relief or sorrow or fear.

"Looks like your ascension wasn't want you wanted. Your gift helped me achieve what you failed to do." Anselm said. Gideon's black eyes didn't move. Gideon was unresponsive.

"You have the answers I seek. I'll take them, bite by bite," Anselm said.

Gideon was unresponsive. There was power in blood, flesh, and nanomachines. Anselm bit into Gideon's neck. Gideon didn't fight back. Anselm felt something very similar to blood sustaining him. Gideon's possessed great knowledge, more than what could be gleaned in blood. Anselm took the divine blood into his body; he reveled in the power. Anselm let go of Gideon's neck. Gideon looked up, showing no expression. Anselm's teeth bore into Gideon's skull. Gideon had much to give and Anselm wouldn't waste a drop.

THOS

THOS RAN OVER a bridge of pure energy, with no time to concern himself with the absurdity and impossibility of such things. Beside him, Melvin led the charge to the center of the city. Vigilant had three lines of defense for the cylindrical tower. Liz demolished the enemy, as lethal with the ax as the heavy railgun. Enemy tanks minimized progress. Melvin yelled out orders through the radio. The two other teams from the train stations joined Melvin's to create one unified front. Melvin's army used the buildings on each floating platform for cover. Blue energy from the tanks dented the space-age buildings, slowly but surely wearing them down. The tanks more than made up for Vigilant's lack of numbers. Most Vigilant fell back to defend the central structure, but Melvin alerted Gregor of the battalion heading their way.

Thos added a dozen kills to his name. Thos handled this battle much better than the ones before. Top-tier military training paid off in spades. For the first time in decades, the specter of his brother's death was gone. He could finally give the here-and-now his full attention. Thos refused to die, nor would he let the people he cared about die. In Kingsbury, Cass fought for her life too; he would see her again even if he had to take out the whole of Vigilant himself. A Vigilant stealth unit crept around the windowless building next to him. Thos added another kill to his name while his support unit did the rest. Snipers on the floating towers picked off the soldiers behind him.

"Eleven o'clock high," Thos said, directing the others to the threat. Snipers rained from the floating towers. The sky became a solid pink that extended to the city entrances. The pink wall flashed.

"Hold on a bit longer!" Melvin said.

A blood-soaked Liz dodged tank blasts. Liz leaped onto the tank hatch and ripped it open like a madman. Liz effortlessly tossed the driver out and off the energy bridge. The tank on the next tier caught wind of Liz and took aim at his head.

"Heads up Liz!" Thos cried.

Liz jumped off the tank, barely avoiding the vehicle exploding in all directions. Liz gave Thos a thumbs up. The pink wall grew brighter and flashed faster before disappearing completely. Melvin contacted the desert forces.

"Storms're still up. Little bit more!" Melvin said.

Vigilant fell back to the next section of the city, where half a dozen tanks halted them. Melvin took position on the other side of the long street. The rest of Vigilant's forces all gathered into one single army.

The battle came to a standstill. Electricity and fire shot from an object connected to wires at the door of the central structure. Vigilant tanks kept Melvin at bay. Thos and Liz took places by Melvin.

"What's the word from below?" Thos said.

"Not a peep," Melvin said. "Must be busted again."

Melvin, Thos, Liz, and the army prepared for the final assault. The rest of the government troops joined Melvin and surrounded the city's outer ring. Melvin pulled the radio up to his face for one more address.

"They're outnumbered three to one, but don't get careless. They'll throw every gadget they have at us!" Melvin's cry echoed through the city. The Silent City transformed into a hurricane of death. Thos heard a few words through the radio.

"Me . . . shield," the voice said.

Bullets and beams came from all directions, blasting soldiers to bits. Buildings collapsed from the unending railgun fire. Enemy tanks rolled forward, decimating the first line of enemy vehicles. Melvin hailed Gregor again.

"Can you hear me?" Melvin said. "Shields are down! Cavalry's coming through! Get yer asses up here!"

Melvin's army concentrated fire on the tank. A tank burst into blue flame. Each lost tank was a nail in the coffin of Vigilant. But Vigilant held their ground, fighting to buy Matthias every second they could. A convoy of vehicles filled with familiar faces joined the fray.

"We saved ya some!" Thos said. Thos welcomed the sight of the unamused Gregor and always chipper Drake.

"Get me to Matthias. This ends when I kill him," Gregor said.

The companions united at the head of the army and made a final push to the central structure. Liz ran ahead and hopped onto the tank rolling to meet them.

"Save as many 'nades as you can," Melvin said.

Liz hopped onto the tank cannon charging. Thos once again gave Liz cover from the heavy guns even he was unlikely to survive. He turned the cannon downward at the driver's seat. Liz hit the ground running as the tank fired before it could be stopped. Melvin's army arrived at the final tier of the city. The second tank fell without the support of the other. Melvin's team decimated the enemy ahead, splitting the rest into two forces.

He directed troops to divide and assist the others teams held at bay by the tanks. Melvin left two battalions to cover their rear just in case. Each step forward for Thos was one step closer to his wife.

Melvin and his team arrived in the sea of dead robots between them and the door of the central structure. Melvin got a sitrep through the radio and smiled; the battle was all but won. Wires from witch-burning poles ran across the ground into a flat, upright device holding a man. Electricity shot from the man stepping off the device. The man was Matthias Rehnquist, wearing a repaired silver mask. Matthias approached them.

"Dude's gone full warlock," Thos said.

"So the slaves have come to fight their rescuer?" Matthias said. Gregor stepped ahead of the group to face Matthias.

"Don't give me that shit," Gregor said. "You would kill half the world and install yourself as dictator."

"Who better? I fight to save us all," Matthias growled; energy crackled off him. "If we don't do this, know we'll be lucky to die when the Adversary comes to power. This is our last chance!"

"I'll deal with him and Eon, right after I kill you," Gregor said, activating his EMPX's blade mode.

"It's over, Big Cheese. You failed," Melvin said.

Thos fumed at the idea this man endangered his wife and friends' lives. Thos switched his weapon to wave functionality and nodded at the others.

"I haven't failed," Matthias said. "Those that threaten the stability of the world should be fought without mercy, with whatever tools we possess."

Metallic groans dominoed throughout the robotic crowd around them. Thos hit Matthias with a full-blast wave before he could attack. Matthias recovered quickly. Thos saw the white of Matthias's toothy grin. The robots twitched and jerked. The one beside Thos lurched forward and swung its arm at him. One by one, the machines attacked in zombie-like fashion. Arms swiped at the group, forcing them to engage in melee combat. The robotic corpses shambled to attack. The dead faces bore blank expressions. Matthias sprinted into the central structure to finish the mission and leave his enemy to the new army.

The robots separated the group and became an active maze.

Thos dodged the awkward swipes, chopping his way through the labyrinth of machine dead. The robots fell easy, but thousands were shuffling in for the kill. He fought his way to regroup with Drake, Zora, and Melvin. The mindless machines swiped at any and every organic in sight. Robots piled onto Gregor's troops, separating them from Thos and the others.

Thos made it to Drake and Zora. They went back-to-back, moving and hacking through the onslaught of machines. Pieces flew over the crowd to the sounds of Liz's triumphant growling.

"Head for the door!" Melvin said.

Massive ax swipes cut through the machines in front of them. Liz took point, dismantling scores of robots. Melvin hollered out to get a bead on their location. The foursome pushed on, trying to close the gap between themselves, Gregor, and Matthias. Melvin burst through a crowd to the left side of the group. Together the five battled through the robots. As one unit, they stepped over the pieces of fallen machines and powered through. Thos could see nothing but disconnected faces of twitchy machines mindlessly reaching out for him.

Robots lunged and swiped, clawing at Thos's flesh. Thos felt the heat and red dripping out of his sword arm.

"Keep fightin!" Thos said. A blast of green filled the skies. Zora grunted in pain.

"Uncle, you have to get in there!" Zora cried.

"I can't leave you!" Gregor said. The group made slow progress through the mechanical hordes.

"There's no time. You gotta hurry!" she said.

Gregor looked back at her and cursed. The last thing Thos saw before the machines completely surrounded them was Gregor running into the heart of the Silent City.

GREGOR

GREGOR SPRINTED AFTER Matthias, trusting his niece and the others to handle the army of robot dead. Gregor couldn't stop; too many would die if Matthias succeeded. He felt a crushing pressure on his chest. In three separate areas of the nation, people fought back against Vigilant. Reports of victory in Kingsbury eliminated a large chunk of the threat, but the Silent City was the source. It was Gregor's duty to stop this.

Matthias tapped furiously on the terminal keyboard in the center of the structure. The ceiling opened. Green energy spilled out of the machine's innards up into the sky. Gregor focused on the moment, taking calculated shots. Matthias seemed unaffected by the beam, suggesting that he would survive Operation Killswitch unscathed. The beam itself also proved a minor nuisance to Gregor. *Am I Witchkin?*

"Still ticking, eh?" Matthias said.

"Old dog's not going down yet," Gregor said, raising his sword.

Matthias shot at Gregor. Gregor deflected the bullets with his blade. He ran forward, deflecting every shot to the surprise of Matthias. The imprisoned Old Worlders helplessly watched the final conflict. Matthias flipped the switch on his weapon. He got his sword up in time to catch Gregor's incoming strike. Their blades collided over and over. Gregor stayed on the offensive, leading Matthias away from the terminal. The green beam pierced the clouds above. Invisible fingers prickled Gregor's insides.

Matthias pushed back with faster strikes. The sword fight became a tug of war. Every time Gregor drove Matthias from the terminal, he fought right back to it. Gregor's momentum wouldn't last forever as Matthias's stamina gave him the long-term advantage. Gregor sighed with relief as Zora, Drake, Thos, Melvin, and Liz came into view. The machine army lagged behind them. Raul pushed through the mechanical zombies while the surviving men engaged them. It took a moment to overcome the horror of the pods full of shriveled humans watching them. When the shock left, everyone fixated on the grand crusader.

"Shut it down!" Gregor said.

Raul sprinted to the terminal. Matthias kneed Gregor in the stomach, sending him to the floor. He then sprinted toward Raul. Liz bellowed a rib-breaking growl and ran to intercept Matthias. Liz gave Matthias a single, hard punch. Matthias's armor caved in and he flew back, colliding into an Old World pod before hitting the ground. Raul reached the terminal, and promptly, the green light disappeared. Gregor, back on his feet, readied his weapon.

"You're done," Gregor said. Matthias lay on the floor in defeat.

"Well, that's that. Time for a cookout," Thos said.

"Not yet, we're gonna blow this thing," Gregor said.

"And kill this dickhead," Melvin added, nodding in the direction at Matthias struggling to get to his feet. Matthias screamed in anger, then collected himself.

"Knowing everything, you'll let the people of the world continue to suffer and die? This is the only play we have left!"

"So we can all die anyway to leave the world in your hands?" Gregor asked, sizing up Matthias for the kill shot.

"Look at what has been achieved under my leadership. We took Kingsbury before anyone knew we were even there. Neutralized

Mr. Abaddon. Exposed the truth about the Compact. I know the price is high, but the world will be better when all is said and done. Vigilant will be where it belongs, charting the future and not simply killing for it. I can do that. You can do that. Vigilant *will* do that."

"The cost is way too high and the outcome uncertain," Gregor said. "Even if your plan works, which I highly doubt, I won't sacrifice these people. I'll find a better way."

"I won't let you damn this world," Matthias said.

Matthias's orange eyes glowed behind the mask.

"You won't stop me," Matthias said.

His eyes burned brighter. Matthias removed his damaged armor to the confusion of all. The building groaned. The robot parts scattered about began to shake. Everyone hit the ground, save for the spry Liz.

"I don't need the north or Kingsbury!" Matthias said. "As you said, I'm connected to this false god. I'll use his power! I'll take it all!"

Gregor and his companions ducked and dodged the incoming metal heap. The pieces of robots broke down and attached to Matthias. Blood ran from his body as the pieces snaked and weaved through him. Matthias grew as the cybernetics transformed his body into a flesh and metal monstrosity. Wires wormed into Matthias's skin. Skin tore. Machine filled in the gaps, extending his limbs. Plates became gauntlets and boots. The heads of the robots covered his torso.

"He's . . . he's using himself to power the machine!" Zora said. Liz ran headlong into the new Matthias, now twice his size. Matthias gave Liz a hard swipe, sending him through the room and into the wall.

"Liz!" Melvin said, dropping everything to check on his dear friend.

Gregor and his fellows stood up when the dust settled. Gregor frowned and shook his head at the monstrous form.

"How far you've fallen," Gregor said.

"Fallen!? I've transcended. Now I am the Compact! I'll take Vigilant to its rightful place at the head of this world." Matthias bellowed, his voice distorted from his enhancements. "I have the power to right the world."

The terminal activated and the central weapon hummed with life once more. Green light blasted into the heavens. A few more plates flew into Matthias's hand. Gregor saw the insane smile on the grand crusader's face as the plates melted into a new weapon. Matthias was on Gregor in a matter of seconds. Their swords clashed. Gregor's muscles strained to repel the grand crusader's newfound strength.

Zora and Drake joined the battle. Matthias slashed at the three, clashing with each blade. The trio deflected his attacks, though they were pushed back by the strength of his blows. Thos and Melvin also joined in, turning the tide in their favor. Matthias growled in frustration. Incoming machinery forced everyone to disengage. The parts wrapped around Matthias's weapon. Matthias shaped the new collection of parts into a massive claymore that made Melvin's old blade look like a toothpick.

Everyone scrambled out of Matthias's reach and took a defensive stance. The wounded Liz got to his feet, though now sporting a discolored side. Matthias's orange eyes were focused on Gregor. Gregor raised his sword while everyone else opened fire on the remaining fleshy parts of Matthias's body. Matthias raised his sword and lunged forward. Gregor rolled to the side, avoiding the ground-splitting attack. Matthias rushed forward again, taking a swipe at the gunmen. Everyone dodged the blade. Matthias pressed his offensive, keeping everyone moving. Matthias divided the group, creating two teams.

Matthias swung at Thos, Zora, and Melvin. Massive swipes from the blade kept all three diving and dodging. Thos popped off an EMPX wave. Matthias grunted in pain. He swung his sword relentlessly, his strikes vertical and cracking the floor. Thos, Zora, and Melvin narrowly avoided strikes capable of cleaving them in half. Liz bum-rushed Matthias. Matthias hit the wall hard. Drake and Raul pelted Matthias with waves. Liz pried the blade from Matthias's hand. Liz, gripping the weapon with both hands, hacked away at Matthias's cybernetics. The flesh and metal of Matthias's sword arm fell to the floor. Blood sprayed from the wounds of Matthias's remaining human parts. He knocked the blade from Liz's hand with his remaining arm.

Liz pulled off the breastplate protecting Matthias's vitals. The plates shuddered and fought to reseal. Drake switched back to sword function and ran to Liz's aid while everyone else focused wave attacks to incapacitate Matthias. Drake stabbed Matthias repeatedly in the chest.

Gregor noticed blood dripping from Raul's nose and Drake gritting his teeth. Melvin fought to catch his breath. Zora and Thos were unaffected.

"Destroy the machine!" Gregor cried.

Raul nodded. Gregor positioned himself between Matthias and Raul. More pieces of various machines shot forth to envelop Matthias and the weapon in the center of the room. Melvin and Thos were hit by the flying parts and fell to the ground. The machine rose ever higher, spilling out through the opening in the ceiling. Vigilant troops pushed through the depleting robots becoming part of Matthias's body. Robot limbs merged and reformed to replace his missing limb. Matthias's arm's fist collided with Liz's chest, once again sending him across the room. Refuse enveloped Matthias. More robot limbs formed on his body, transforming him into a centipede-like horror. The mass grew larger and wilder, losing any semblance of humanity. Matthias skittered toward Raul.

"Ew," Liz said, looking but still laying on the ground.

"Guys, a little help here!" Raul said when his peripherals caught Matthias closing in. Raul ditched the terminal. Matthias took the position as the terminal's guardian. Zora, Drake, Thos, Melvin, and

Gregor fought his extra arms. Gregor's head hurt. Pain in his chest left him gasping for air. Drake's nose bled.

Matthias moved swiftly, keeping his enemies away. Heavy strikes from the EMPX blades cut into his new legs. A leg swipe cut Thos across his chest. Thos jumped back and covered the wound.

"You all right?" Drake asked. Thos padded the slash.

"Not deep," Thos replied, wincing. Another swipe clipped Zora's shoulder.

"Don't stop!" she told everyone.

"I expected more from a Witchkin," Matthias growled.

Matthias knocked his attackers away and skittered over to Thos, isolating him from his fellows.

"This is this price you pay for interfering," Matthias said.

Matthias's numerous hands clawed Thos. In his madness, Matthias lost awareness of the others rushing to aid their friend. The oncoming attackers pulled Matthias from Thos.

"Help him!" Gregor commanded.

Some Vigilant troops pulled Thos out of harm's way, while others drove Matthias into Melvin's path. Melvin severed the tip of the leg he battled. Gregor severed another. The opening allowed the two men to hack through to Matthias's core. Matthias's attack grew wilder as he lost limbs. Liz stirred yet again and bellowed a monstrous roar. He collided head on with Matthias, gripping the metal frame of his torso. Matthias's remaining arms clawed Liz repeatedly. Blood ran from Liz's wounds. Liz lifted Matthias into the air and slammed him over and over into his death machine. Dents in the machine grew deeper. Matthias's limbs thrashed in all directions, Liz proceeded to tear them off. More wreckage flew into Matthias, melding him with the super weapon. Massive arms with thick, sharp fingers formed out of the structure.

"He's becoming the whole damn city!" Gregor cried.

Everyone stepped back and fired waves. Matthias cried in pain yet grew ever larger. The constant influx of scraps kept everyone dodging more than shooting. Dozens of arms of various sizes formed out of the structure. Orange light filled the machine and spilled into the beam. Tank parts flew into the chamber, including a railcannon. Drake and hit the floor. Zora fell to her knees. Gregor alone stood against Matthias.

"You'll die witnessing the new age," Matthias said.

Matthias stopped, confusing Gregor. Gregor looked to see Zora with an outstretched arm. Matthias convulsed and growled. Gregor's tank arm aimed and fired in random directions.

"Get out of my head, witch!" Matthias said.

Thos, scarred and bloody, got to his feet and picked up an EMPX, hitting Matthias full blast. Zora and Thos gave them the precious seconds they needed. Thos's gun flew from his hand and into the bio-mechanical monster growing in front of them. Melvin clutched at his chest, dropping a bag of remote grenades he tried to throw.

"Hail Mary," Melvin muttered.

Gregor ran over to the grenade bag, hoping these things were as resilient as he was told. Gregor saw an incoming plate heading to reinforce Matthias. He threw the bag upward into the flying plate. Melvin pulled a small gray remote from his pocket and flipped the switch. Matthias looked down at his metal body filled with parts of robots, tanks, city, and explosives. Melvin glanced at the activation button and smiled.

"Assimilate this, asshole!" Melvin said.

The wounded scrambled to the exit. Matthias aimed with his tank arm. All his others reached out at Melvin. Melvin hit the button. The orange light inside Matthias expanded, becoming a flame that traveled up through the machine. The tower ruptured. Explosions traveled up through the structure. Gregor scooped up the nearest metal plate and held it up like a shield. The tower buckled and fell in on itself. The floor around the central machine gave out, sending the remnants crashing to waters far below.

Gregor's breath returned, and he hobbled to his feet. Drake, Zora, and Melvin got out from their cover spots. Raul lay unconscious in the corner of the room. Soldiers tended to Thos's shredded leg.

"You okay, buddy?" Gregor asked.

"Picture of health," Thos said.

Liz didn't move. What remained of Matthias writhed on the floor. Wires from his missing limb latched on to nearby scrap, slowly replenishing him.

"Just won't quit," Melvin said as he checked himself for major wounds.

After Melvin checked himself, he ran over to his fallen friend. Gregor, sword drawn, walked over to Matthias. Matthias got up on his new mechanical feet. Gregor severed his reforming arms. Zora and Drake picked up their guns and fired waves at Matthias. Gregor latched on to the mask and gave it a hard pull. The mask flew off.

Matthias's body almost wholly regenerated before the mask left him. He stared down Gregor Pavane. He reached out for the mask; it didn't move. Matthias screamed in rage, scanning the area for his blade. He picked it up. Everyone took positions to engage him once more.

"You're fools!" Matthias said. "I'm freeing us from our chains. If I fail, you'll suffer in cages you can't escape!"

A mist rose from the gaping hole in the floor. The fog rolled across the room with the purpose behind the unaware Matthias caught up in his speech. The fog took the shape of a man in a white suit and wearing a golden tragedy mask like the smiling one resting on the floor. At last, Gregor came face to face with Eon. Matthias realized the presence and turned to slice him. Matthias didn't strike. He grunted and shook against unseen powers.

"You would undo two thousand years of work," Eon said. "Work necessary because of misguided fools like you."

Eon gave a careless wave of his hand. The silver mask shattered, the entity himself uttering a scraping sound akin to pain.

"We're willing to sacrifice for the greater good," Eon said.

Matthias's sword arm snapped back, the wires in his flesh and organs ripped free. He cried out in pain. No one moved to aid him.

"You're the enemy of this world, not the savior," Matthias said.

Eon gave another careless wave. Matthias's left leg below the knee fell apart.

"We were never meant to be its savior," Eon replied. "And neither were you."

"They'll know the truth," Matthias said. "You set on your throne playing with our lives, but don't get comfortable; you won't be there long. The Adversary you created will destroy you too. The Final Turning is upon us."

Eon snapped his fingers. Matthias looked up at the sky and burst into flames. Eon walked past the burning corpse of Matthias and analyzed the pods in the room. Eon walked over to the nearest pod. He stretched out his hand. Eon ran his long, pointy fingers along the surface. The human trapped inside regarded him with the tired eyes of someone ready for their torment to end.

"Why didn't you trust us?" Eon asked. "We're fixing this world, realizing your dream. We didn't want this for you. We wanted you to see what this world will be, what this world will soon be. But you sealed yourselves away, and it went so wrong."

The shriveled humans lacked the power to do anything. Eon spoke as if he read Gregor's thoughts.

"They came to places like this to ride out the Collapse, the fall they would ironically create soon after. These places were meant to be their castles, but it became their tombs instead. Had they not acted so rash . . . what a world this would've been."

Eon looked at all the pods, every eye fixated on this entity.

"You can rest," Eon said.

Gregor saw the relief in the eyes of the prisoners. One by one, the pods went dark.

Zora fired on Eon. Her bullets went straight through him. Gregor teetered on the verge of collapse; he lacked the energy to face this new enemy. Eon vanished, only to appear in front of Gregor.

"You have done well. The correction may resume," Eon said.

Gregor stared into the empty black eyes of the very reason for his existence. He stared at the perversion of what he had fought for. He held no doubts this thing was every bit the enemy Matthias said. Gregor's muscles ached. He raised his weapon and pointed it at Eon, the blade an inch away from his golden mask.

"Matthias was crazy and his methods wrong," Gregor said. "But he was right about one thing, don't get too comfortable."

Eon's head snapped back, then forward again. His mask now sported a wicked smile.

"The Algorithm needs a challenge," Eon said.

Eon looked to the side suddenly and dissipated into a fog. The fighting outside ceased. Gregor's men celebrated their victory. Gregor took stock of the dead. Vigilant's forces were halved in their civil war. Melvin's shouts echoed throughout what remained of the building.

"He's alive! Get the medic!" Melvin said. A medic ran over to the grumbling behemoth. Two soldiers carried Raul away.

Thos grew woozy, getting immediate support from Vigilant survivors before he fell over.

"Shredded up pretty good, but he'll survive," a medic said. Melvin hollered.

"Hot damn, we made it," Melvin said with relief. "We make a pretty good team."

Gregor was happy to concede that fact.

ANSELM

ANSELM SAT IN front of Vigilant tower beside the nearly skeletal remnants of Gideon Grey and an unconscious Jaren Hart. Gideon was a filling meal. Anselm had never enjoyed a meal this much in either of his lives. His body threatened to explode for the unbridled power coursing through him. Eyes, brain, heart, lungs, and blood were of particular value. He felt his cells absorbing them, learning from the quasi-divine warlock half assimilated by Eon. Out in the wilderness, Vigilant troops were being driven back to the base by the government army. Anselm processed the tidal wave of information torn from Gideon's mind. Gideon had the answers Anselm sought, things that Eon didn't want him to know.

Anselm entered a dream state to delve through the vastness of Gideon's and Eon's knowledge. His eyes rolled frantically as he searched for what he desired. Anselm stood within Gideon's lab. He smelled the mold, dirt, and meat. Gideon examined an amorphous blob filled with nanomachines. He prodded the blob with a long device. The blob took shape, becoming circles, squares, and a long worm that slithered off the table. Anselm followed Gideon through various labs, studying the living and dead masses. Anselm took it all in, gaining decades of knowledge in minutes. Anselm struggled to discern the dates of the information dump. He sifted through the information like Gideon did files on his computers. Anselm studied weapons, vehicles, locations of interest, demon hotspots, and machines that made the wizard nervous. Gideon analyzed drawings of an orb. He kept his head on a swivel, peculiar for a man in a cave far from civilization.

"Why does he fear this?" Gideon said.

Anselm made note of this orb. Gideon held the papers up to the torch and destroyed them. Anselm scanned through Gideon's studies on artifacts of particular interest to Eon. He ran through the fragments of Gideon's ascended mind, getting a static-filled, incomprehensible mess half of the time. The longer it went, the less of Gideon remained. He sensed Gideon's regret as he was slowly assimilated into Eon, the same fate Mandragora had avoided.

There was more Anselm needed to know. Gideon was connected to Eon, part of him, at least. Anselm exploited that connection. He grew sick of Eon's games. It was time Anselm learned the true nature of his part in the Algorithm. He walked within the halls of his castle and saw the newly established board of directors kneeling before Alexander. Alexander struck an imposing figure until his last days. Anselm witnessed his great ancestor's final moments. Alexander lay in his bed staring at Eon, wearing a frowning mask. Alexander's memories of Eon returned for this moment. Eon grieved for Alexander as one would a son. Eon bid Alexander farewell and disappeared as his wife and son came into the room.

Eon kept tabs on the Blackthorne family, making more than one appearance to his ancestors. Eon appeared to Adamina Blackthorne. The queen screamed at Eon, threatening war on him. The frowning entity assured her threats weren't necessary and mentioned his Algorithm.

"My children won't be part of your design," she said. She clutched her head. Eon vanished. Adamina was alone and confused, unaware the meeting had transpired. Anselm went through the ages to another king.

Godwin ranted and raved about ghostly visitors in the night. The once fierce king, a feeble man the world believed insane. Anselm knew his fate. Godwin stood on the roof of Blackthorne Castle. He walked over to the edge and turned back to the frowning Eon.

"Won't be in my head anymore," Godwin said.

Godwin stepped back and went over the side of the tower before Eon could stop him. Anselm reached the information he sought. Anselm's grandfather, Aldous, argued with the Eon. Aldous was gaunt and shook uncontrollably, not long for this world.

"Your machinations end here. I know the truth. I won't allow it!" Aldous said.

Aldous's eyes were a brilliant orange, not the brown Anselm remembered.

"He was a defect? Is that how he knew?" Anselm said.

Anselm marked this idea for further analysis later. Aldous hollered at Eon, declaring the monster would not use his family any longer.

"We believe the time is here," Eon said. "You have produced one that may correct the Algorithm."

"Leave my family out of this!" Aldous said. "I'll reveal your secrets to the world; you can't bury the truth forever. We rule. Not you."

"Chaos rules the land, not us or you. An adversary is what we need if your world continues down this path. If not you, then your son or grandson," Eon said. Aldous reached for something in his robe.

"You'll not manipulate us no longer!" Aldous said.

"Stop," Eon said. "This isn't necessary." *Could he not control his mind?*

Aldous sweat profusely. Aldous clutched at his chest and fell to the ground. Eon watched, frowning but not helping. *Could he not save him because of the defect?*

"I curse you," Aldous said, fighting for every second left. Aldous died, spending his last moments face down on the floor. Eon vanished. Anselm found one last memory. Eon watched Blackthorne Castle fall. He walked through the rubble as a specter. In the wreckage, a dying Abigail lay buried with the corpse of Edgar in her arms. The final revelation hit him. His grand purpose in life, the one Eon encouraged.

"It's a joke. All one big joke."

There was no sorrow inside him. A laugh bubbled up inside, consuming him. Uncontrollable laughter took hold of him. Both Vigilant and the army would be here soon; he planned it that way. He felt Eon. He knew the entity heard his words. The man in white materialized beside the remains of Gideon Grey.

"What have you done!?" Eon asked. Eon touched the leftovers of the fabled scientist.

"All this to get to me here," Anselm said. "You needed them to die, didn't you? You had the power to stop it all. Was this our destiny? My destiny? To fall?" Anselm said.

"Contrary to what you might think, the Compact does not control every minute of every human life. It adapts as required. Your failure as a king made this necessary. Chaos is in full bloom. There's only one thing that unites the world in such times. It is not fool notions of heroes or saviors. Your world has never been defined by good. The world needs an adversary, a boogeyman you would call it," Eon said. "You're a new kind. One that will break the endless loop. An adversary like no other, one that shall remain until the correction is finished."

"Why?" Anselm said.

"Because we...love you. You're our children. Your family is a driving force in this world and will remain so. We saw your family's potential from the very first moment Alexander found us. You, like your ancestor, must bear this burden for the world."

"All the pain? The loss?"

"They're powerful motivators. Love is sacrifice. Sacrifices test the mettle of a man. The exceptional endure." Retreating Vigilant and the army were getting closer.

"And I did," Anselm said. "I want to hate you for that, but it is the greatest gift. You've given me great freedom, perhaps too much." Eon cocked his head at the fallen king's lack of melancholy. Fingers probed Anselm's body. Eon stepped back.

"Your-" he said. Anselm smiled

"Filled with the blood of many: humans immune to you, demons, witches, and gods," Anselm said. "Becoming greater than you anticipated, guess I owe Vigilant for that. Seems like your mind never recovered from the Collapse to have such oversights; the god of our world, stricken with dementia."

Anselm thought of cells rupturing inside the masked entity. Eon jerked. Eon's screech pierced the heavens. Anselm heard a pop and then nothing. His eardrums quickly rebuilt themselves. The guns levitated around Anselm and turned on him.

"We don't need your nanomachines," Eon said.

"I don't need you," Anselm said. "But, as you said, the people of this world need me. Who am I to deny them?"

Vigilant troops arrived in the forest not far from Anselm, with the regent's army hot on their heels. Anselm raised his hand. Anselm had no knowledge of Eon's full capabilities, but he knew his weakness. Anselm turned his hand in the tower's direction. The console at the base lit up. The tower began to hum.

"You're a lesser god. A demented god. A failed god. Nothing but a collective of fools," Anselm said, growing power behind each sentence. "I thought I was some kind of savior, but I see now what a foolish concept that is. You wanted me to be the dreaded Adversary. I'll be that. I'll be more than that. This world you've created, this stupid plan for these stupid people, I'll tear it all down and build something new. I'll be the god these people deserve." Anselm let the machine charge slowly. With Gideon's knowledge flowing through him, Vigilant's haphazard devices proved easy to manipulate. Eon fell to his knees. Anselm savored this moment.

Gunfire ripped through the forest. Trucks cut across the plains to pursue the last of Jaren's army. Government troops picked off fleeing crusaders, having no qualms shooting them in the back.

"What was it you told me? My hell is just begun? It's time I share it. I'll rule this Hell. Farewell ant-god," Anselm said.

White energy shot into the sky. Everyone in the region stopped fighting to stare at the burning sky. Anselm's body tore itself apart inside over and over. Over half of Vigilant and the army screamed and bled. Anselm put all of his newfound power into the machine. Vigilant tower cracked. Energy spilled forth in all directions. Blood streamed from every orifice of the faces of everyone in range. More men fell. The blood streamed from every opening in Anselm's face. Anselm reveled in the unprecedented levels of pain. The unaffected fled. Anselm would hunt them soon enough; he needed a further test of his abilities. Eon's masked lost its brilliant luster, turning as dull as the first vision with Alexander. Eon fell into a mist. Anselm collapsed the machine in on itself with Gideon's power. Anselm reached out for the weapons nearby to no avail, his power still had some limitations. Jaren writhed on the ground.

"Jaren, my boy, did you forget our meeting?" Anselm said.

"Fuck you," Jaren said. Anselm gave him a tsk.

"Jaren," Anselm said. "You've been approaching this all wrong, like I have. I told you I can give you the revenge that you seek. Do you still doubt me? Look on my works."

Jaren rolled over to see men screaming, bleeding, and dying all around him.

"This power. You can have it too." Jaren looked back at Anselm. "Your father was my great general. I'm in need of a replacement, someone with passion." Jaren choked on his own blood. "You're dying. I need your answer rather soon, I'm afraid."

"What must I do?" Jaren said.

"All I ask is that you swear your allegiance to me," Anselm said. "Pledge yourself to me for all time, and this power will be yours."

"I pledge myself to you...for all time," he said. Anselm smiled, eager to begin his first new project.

"Then I welcome you to my new kingdom, Lord Jaren Hart. There's much for us to do. There's a long road you must travel, but first you must see the truth. This is my promise to you, I'll make you suffer and you will love me for it."

Jaren's cries were music to Anselm's ears.

ZORA

Zora sat on a bench in the floating gardens for a rest. She assisted the cleanup while her uncle toiled on numerous projects for a Vigilant that wasn't going anywhere. The green trees and running waters gave her the comforts of home in this bizarre, robotic world. She enjoyed the sounds of the waterfalls. She spent what time she could with Drake, though he was also occupied with eliminating the rest of the Void. They enjoyed some private time with plenty of empty houses available for use. This city had great potential, a veritable desert oasis. Zora wanted them to stay, but there was much for her and her friends to do. There was always too much to do.

A contingent of Vigilant carefully destroyed the pods filled with dead Old Worlders to ensure the city's integrity. Surviving trolls were released from the cages. Some immediately ran for the desert while others remained without anything in the outside world to go back to.

Thos paced nervously in floating gardens, trying his phone, radio, and any random crusader or soldier in range. She could only imagine the bandages covering his body. It was good to see him up and moving, after a full day in Vigilant's primitive hospital. He noticed Zora, calmed by her warming presence.

"She's all right," Zora said. *I hope it's true,* she thought.

"Probably," he said. "I'll be headin' out soon. Hope Cass likes battle-scars cuz I got a ton. Guess I'm lucky that's all I got. What about you?"

"I'm fine," she said. Zora sighed. "Still trying to figure out this connection I have." Zora closed her eyes. She calmed her mind. There were no masks but vague images and raw emotions. The visions were choppy, like a flip-book, with each picture creating action. She focused her thoughts on the past, on her mother. She felt anger. Saw a woman on the ground facing a sword. She then felt unconditional love. She wanted to see more. Her face wrinkled in a vain attempt to delve deeper into the past. An image came and went in second, but it was enough to make her stomach churn.

"I see a man. The one Matthias was scared of. He's . . . eating other men. Some are still alive. There are corpses all around him. Hundreds, maybe more," she said with revulsion.

Sharp, unbearable pain turned her insides into a pincushion. The pain was so great it knocked the breath from her. She couldn't scream. The sensation lasted seconds, far too long, in her opinion. A second feeling overwhelmed her. She went red. "That man that showed up after Kingsbury fell. I feel his joy. His pain. It's over-whelming." There was something in this man, and the way she could describe it was unrestrained evil.

"The Adversary," Thos said. "Guess we better rest while we can."

The two sat and talked to distract each other for the time being. Trucks growled at the tunnel entrance.

"Time for me to head out," Thos said.

Zora followed Thos to the trucks. Gregor moved to the head a group of Vigilant en route to meet Duke's army gathering at the train stations. Drake talked with Melvin and Liz. Most sol-diers quickly adapted to Melvin's leadership, and his respect grew. Melvin eased tensions between the two factions, part of one not fond any part of Vigilant survived. A sizeable portion of the army moved to Gregor's side, becoming part of the new Vigilant. A handful of soldiers pointed weapons at the defectors.

"Stand down," Melvin said. "Let 'em go."

"Vigilant is a criminal organization. The Duke—" a soldier said.

"Duke is the head of a criminal organization that funded terrorists long before Vigilant, so I don't give a fuck what he thinks," Melvin said. "These guys ended a threat, more than he's ever done."

"That's treason!"

"Oh, who cares," Melvin said. "Stand down! That's an order. I'm the CO of this operation, going against me is treason. The guilty one is dead. Vigilant will be pardoned; you got a problem take it up with Duke. Gregor will handle it from here."

"Vigilant is not outlawed yet," Gregor said. "The law remains. Some things have changed, but the core tenant is the same. I'll get my house in order, and it will stand. Don't think Matthias's actions change that, nor that I won't fight back."

"That's—" the man spoke again only to be cut off by Liz getting a little too close for his comfort.

"Everyone stop!" Melvin said. "The mission is done. We're heading out. We can war over this later. We still got deadheads to kill."

The majority of Melvin's troops fell in line. Zora had a feeling this powder keg would blow any moment. Melvin's army prepared to depart, with Thos leaving with personal medics to Kingsbury.

Gregor's and Thos's friends were all here to send him off. He went from person to person.

"Quite the ride," he said.

"You're practically one of us now," Gregor said. Thos scratched the back of his head.

"I'm sure we'll be doin' it again 'fore long," he said. Zora gave Thos a hug. Thos winced.

"See you in a few days," Thos said. "I should probably get to a real hospital."

Liz scooped Thos in a monstrous hug and spun him around.

"See you around, big guy," Thos said. "Stop on by the house sometime." Liz nodded and grinned. Drake approached and gave Thos a firm handshake.

"Always a pleasure," Thos said. "Don't get captured when I'm gone." Drake frowned, then nodded.

"I'll do my best," Drake said. Thos walked up to Melvin and extended his hand in friendship.

"Take 'er easy," Thos said.

"She won't be easy, but I'll try," Melvin said.

Thos gave everyone a last wave as he was escorted into the station leading north. A small army followed him through and awaited him at the other end, making him the safest person in the state.

Zora spent the next two evenings with Drake as he prepared to join Melvin at Duke's villa and stamp out the deadheads. The two lay in bed the last night. Blue light from floating streetlamps doubled their level of distraction. Drake was less talkative than usual.

"Wanna talk about it?" she said.

Zora threw her arm over Drake's chest to give him a better distraction than the little blue suns floating outside the window. It was good to help someone else with problems while hers were set to linger for who knows how long.

"Not sure how tomorrow's gonna play out," he said. "Not looking forward to it."

Zora kissed him.

"Still not looking forward to it, but that helps," he said.

"We'll keep working on it," she said.

After a night of pleasant company, the two fell asleep. Images of witches and adversaries infected her dreams. The images were much clearer in her sleep, in the case of the evil man too clear.

Zora jolted awake numerous times. Each time Zora woke, she checked her body for wounds. Searing pain in dreams followed her to the waking world. She got up to spit in the toilet numerous times to hold the vomit at bay. Drake couldn't help her now; she didn't want his attention divided while there was one war to finish and a second on the horizon.

The morning light rose up over the waterfalls, making them sparkle as any good oasis would. The light orbs floated off to a square building on a platform above them. Zora saw Drake off to the head of Melvin's army. Zora gave them both a hug then Liz gave her another suffocating embrace.

"Take care of him," she said to Melvin. Drake busted out his trademark amused frown.

"Yes, ma'am," Melvin said.

Zora bid them farewell, leaving her with Gregor and Vigilant. She went to the lab where Gregor and Raul carried out analyses. Zora recoiled at Raul dissecting an Old Worlder. Zora cringed at the silver fragments of something once latched to her face. Gregor assured her some fragments were already melted.

"Still see through that thing? Or the others?" he asked. Zora attempted to connect to it and sighed with relief at the failure.

"I think they've been destroyed. I don't feel Eon's presence anymore," she said.

Zora did, however, possess the ability to connect to other things. Zora explained what she saw to the best of her ability. Gregor walked over to the empty table and placed his hands on it for support.

"The hits don't stop," Gregor said.

Zora's images gave her snippets of the evil man moving with purpose to places unknown. "Won't be resting anytime soon," Gregor said.

Raul compared Zora's abilities, visions, and experiences to ones from the notes compiled by Matthias.

"It does match up, but you don't have cybernetics, so that's something. The mask must've triggered your ability to 'interface,' as the notes call it. Matthias apparently did the same. Shame we can't talk to your mother about this."

Raul theorized where nanomachines might fit into the equation and what might've happened to them while Killswitch was active.

"I think your mother and some of the other apostates learned to alter their nanos. Maybe this allows them to connect to each other and this Eon monster. End of the day, we're taking shots in the dark on this," Gregor said. "Your dad can shine some light. He better."

"Since you're stuck with this 'gift,' we can use it to track this Adversary," Raul said. *It might help the Freemen*, she thought.

Gregor stared at him for a moment, and grumbled in agreement.

"It could be useful; just be careful with it," Gregor said.

"I will," she said.

Raul indulged Zora's curiosity on demons and machines until Gregor called it quits for the day. He had worked a double shift, leaving Gregor the night to spend with his niece. Gregor took Zora to the largest park on the highest floating platform in the city. Zora fought disorientation as she traversed energy bridges and floating staircases. Gregor, scourge of the demon world, carried two small brown bags with ham sandwiches and Averill brand potato skins.

"You make these?" Zora asked.

"My hidden skill," he said.

The two ate and watched the sunset. Without the walls of kill storms, Zora saw miles and miles of wasteland. The reds and purples bringing the night brought out beauty in the desolation.

"Elena or Matthew," Gregor said to Zora's confusion. "Your

dad got your name from me. That's what I was gonna name my kids if I ever had one."

Zora and Gregor watched the emerging stars and distant sounds of life in the wasteland. Zora's carefree life dwindled since she fled her home. "Me and your dad never wanted our kids to be involved in all this shit. I'm sorry you got dragged into all this."

"I'm not," she said. "Everyone else is out there fighting for a better world, and I'm happy to do my part. Maybe I'm destined to be in Vigilant."

"I wouldn't say destined. Life can get pretty crazy; who knows?"

Her father was becoming less and less Kami Rayntree, and she was becoming less and less Zora. Vigilant and the Freemen needed people in the days to come. Zora held no illusions she was some great heroine, but she could help those she loved. Whether they were Vigilant, Freemen, or something else she would fight beside them, and that was what mattered. Zora and her father didn't need to hide who they were, cowering under false names. She would be Zora no longer, it was time to be Elena Pavane.

DRAKE

DUKE'S VILLA CAME up over the horizon. The villa suffered very little damage and became an outpost for the Void. Without Vigilant, the deadheads were about to live up to their name. The bulk of the army drove to Mexico City to engage the Void, while Melvin led a force to take back the villa. Government vehicles and troops surrounded it. Some of the Void refused to surrender, killing as many as possible before the inevitable. Drake accompanied Melvin's assault team. Duke's black car was escorted by four trucks with heavy machine guns, reducing the Void to shredded meat. The battle was decided before Drake and Melvin arrived. Melvin looked at Drake.

"Ready?" Melvin said. Drake nodded.

Duke's cavalcade filled the road through the villa, forcing Drake and Melvin to approach on foot. The corpse of a Void priestess wearing nothing but a robe was tied to a large metal pole, a grim welcome sign for the Duke's residence. Blood ran from deep cuts in the arms, suggesting a self-inflicted fate.

Duke's troops rounded up those who surrendered. The whole thing made Drake sick. A state in tatters, enemies plotting more destruction, and a government becoming more powerful made his head hurt. Duke practically salivated at the thought of taking

Vigilant tech for himself. Drake's vision blurred. Little information came out of Kingsbury save for the fact that Matthias failed, though rumors of mass casualties suggested the victory hadn't come fast enough.

Duke's forces pulverized Void thugs, matched them blow-for-cruel blow. Drake felt no sympathy for the gangsters but came to despise his superiors just as much, who time and again authored these problems. He saw two distinct factions within the military forming. Some of Duke's men carried out their orders no matter how heinous without question. Drake saw in others the same doubt and distaste that had been plaguing him for years now. They, like him, no longer believed in what they killed and died for.

Drake knew what he was going to do and the risks that came with it. Part of him felt his indecision had in the end contributed to what New Prosperity now was. A younger gangster at the villa screamed as he was dragged by his leg and dropped at Duke's feet. *Another child soldier, just like I was.*

Drake had seen too much of this predicable cycle for one lifetime. All he wanted now was for it to stop. Duke pulled a revolver from the belt at his hip, silver and engraved with bony arms stretching out the length of the barrel. The boy pursed his lips. Bloody phlegm spewed forth onto Duke's flawless suit. The boy whispered Death's prayer, barely starting as Duke buried hot lead into his skull. Duke laughed, the kind of laugh Drake heard from the men and women that treated this country and everyone in it like condoms to use and throw away.

Drake breathed in deep. He walked over to the gloating Duke, who noticed his approach.

"The man of the hour. Look at this man. He's a shining example of what you can be," Duke said.

"Can't take all the credit. Melvin did quite a bit. Gregor too," Drake added. Melvin didn't approach Duke; he stayed at the head of his army.

"Vigilant helped solve the problem Vigilant had created," Duke said. "As for Victor . . . I doubt the government will be throwing him a parade. He'll get a pardon and get to live. But worry about that tomorrow. We'll restore order and stability after some celebration."

"You sure about that? With everything going on? Plus a third of Mexico City is gone. Tens of thousands died in the city alone. Our troubles are far from over," Drake advised. Duke scoffed.

"They'll be dealt with in time. Our retaliation will be merciless. There'll be no more talks of Vigilant, secession, rebellion, or Freemen. Time these people remember who they serve." Duke revealed the advisors' list of targets. He wasn't sure if it was unintentional or an arrogant threat.

Drake wore his doubt so much he feared it became his default outfit. Duke gave him a pat on the back.

"Don't be so sour. I've something that'll cheer you up," Duke said. He led Drake over to the armorer's shop. This was the first time Drake saw the bulky man, an apparent defect with red-brown skin with a set of different colored eyes, and a mouth slightly too big. The armorer diligently sharpened a sword on his electric grindstone. Drake remembered the faulty grindstone from before; it required a certain amount of pressure on the pedal lest it become a wheel of death. The armorer showed no interest in anything except his craft.

"This is Wayland, he was a prisoner of Trinity for years, designed much of their melee weapons. Doesn't talk much. What he lacks in personality he makes up with impeccable skill."

Wayland's foot left the pedal. He handed Duke the blade for inspection, who analyzed it with everything except an actual fine-tooth comb. The blade was slim with a hilt in the shape of a dragon. Duke gave the nod of approval. Wayland stood up and, wordless, returned to his quarters.

"A fine officer's sword. Beautiful with the lethality of the ancient katanas. Made from pure heavenstone," Duke said. Drake gave a quick vertical slash, the air rippled around the blade.

Drake admired the weapon. He yearned for the days of fighting with swords. A certain romantic grace and skill came with melee engagements compared to impersonal distance killing. Internally he scolded himself for relishing any kind of battle.

"A fine addition to the collection," Drake said, sad the weapon was a prop destined for rust and ruin.

"Not for me, for you," Duke said, handing the blade to Drake for his own inspection.

Drake found joy in testing it out in future sparring. With no means to carry the weapon, Drake handed it to a trusted soldier for now. Duke, in his infinite generosity, bequeathed Drake one of the Void's motorcycles. Drake hated the Duke, but he would gladly take the bike.

Men tied to poles at the end of the shooting range screamed curses at Duke. Drake noticed some of them not fitting the skeletal theme of Void enforcers. Soldiers quickly filled the prisoners with holes.

"Not all of them look like thugs. Who were they and what did they do?" Drake asked, his frustrations mounting.

"Came here to spy on us, got imprisoned by the deadheads," Duke said. Didn't crack for them or us. Drake had a revelation.

"Wait . . . they're Freemen!" Drake said.

"So? Came snooping around., decided to interfere. That makes them terrorists. Terrorists should get what they deserve."

The anger warmed Drake's body, threatening to set him aflame. Drake threw his arm over Duke's shoulder, surprising him.

"I couldn't agree more," Drake said.

Drake slammed his foot on the pedal of the electric grindstone. He kicked the back of Duke's left leg. Duke fell to his knees. Drake grabbed the back of Duke's head and thrust it forward, stopping an inch from the spinning wheel. Drake kept Duke where he was while the soldiers watched and waited for the knight to make the next move. Drake heard Melvin's swears of amused disbelief.

"I'm tired of killing for people like you," Drake said. "I've always done what I thought held this country together. Necessary evil, they said. That logic is only necessary for evil to thrive. I'm done with it, and all of you." Duke's arrogance disappeared around the spinning wheel.

"Shoot him!" Duke commanded. The soldiers raised their guns. The ones at the dead prisoners aimed at Drake. Drake heard the sounds of the guns from the men beside him. Melvin's troops shot men preparing to kill Drake.

The soldiers behind him moved to his side and killed the soldiers rushing to defend. Melvin entered the fray. Soldiers quickly took sides, the numbers began to favor Drake. With Liz approaching, the battle was preemptively decided.

"Looks like I'm not the only one," Drake said. Duke panted. Drake sensed the fear taking over vicious merc turned dictatorial regent.

"So what . . . you turning Freemen? They're a dying breed; we're only expediting the process."

"You're doing quite the opposite," Drake said.

"We run this country. Without us, there'll be chaos!" Duke's tone quickly lost its authoritative sting.

"You create the chaos," Drake said, feeling the pedal foot getting a bit antsy.

"You're a murderer, no better than Aric. This is a violation of your oath!" Duke said, trying to mask his fear.

"The oath doesn't condemn killing, only of the innocent," Drake said. "Aric made mistakes. I won't."

"Kill me, and you'll prove that you and your friends are terrorists. They'll be the first to go," Duke said, quickly developing a layer of stinking sweat all over his body.

Drake realized that this was inevitable regardless of what he did, people so drunk on power couldn't be reasoned with. Even facing death, Duke was nauseatingly cocky.

"What you gonna do? Put me on trial?" Duke said. "We control the courts. These people, this country, and you belong to us. The alternative is worse. Accept it because you won't win. We're their gods and they gladly licks our boots over helping you."

Drake's foot eased off the pedal. He took a moment to reflect on his career and how it rarely benefited anyone except people like Duke.

"You're not gods. Gods don't die," Drake said.

Drake slammed his foot back down on the pedal. The grindstone spun wildly. Duke's eyes widened just enough to get a full view of the grindstone connecting with his face. His head caved and flew off onto everyone nearby. Drake told himself he took no pleasure in killing even the deserving, but that was being dishonest. Drake pressed Duke's head harder into the grindstone, whittling it down a good deal further. Drake had his fill of justice. Drake let go of Duke's body, letting it hit the ground.

Drake and Melvin's army focused on Duke's supporters.

"Your move," Drake said.

The soldiers looked at Duke's corpse. Drake pulled the officer badge off his belt. He stared at it for a long time, contemplating his life. He threw it to the ground.

"This is treason!" a soldier said.

"So be it. I won't be their dog anymore."

"This is treas—"

A bullet rang out and the soldier hit the ground.

"I hate that guy," Melvin said. "If you guys wanna be technical we only fulfilled Duke's wishes. He did want Vigilant and Void conspirators executed, just not when he was one."

Slowly Duke's men lowered their weapons and Drake's men followed suit. Melvin laughed.

"Who would've thought you'd end up like this, eh? Welcome

to the shit list," Melvin said, giving Drake a pat on the back for comfort. Drake chuckled, trying to hide the disgust at his moment of vengeful weakness.

"Doesn't feel so bad," he lied. "The guys outside won't be happy."

"If they want to mindlessly follow orders, they can follow mine," Melvin said.

"What about the goblins?" Drake asked.

"Not sure. I'll burn that bridge when I get there."

Melvin puffed up his chest and addressed the army.

"We're at a crossroads gentlemen," Melvin said. "They'll come for you one day. They're already turning your children against you. All it takes is one wrong word. One wrong thought. One stinky fart and you'll end up in prison forever. You're tired of killing for them; otherwise, you'd be shooting."

"What do you suggest?" one asked. Drake cocked an eyebrow.

"I'm curious as well," Drake said.

"First off, we need to wipe out the Void. I'll continue as acting CO over military ops. We're needed for that, but that doesn't mean we *have* to be on the government payroll. Not for much longer anyway. After the mission is over . . . maybe we'll take this army on the road if you get my meeting. Got a feelin' a bunch of people are gonna need one."

"A mercenary army," Drake said.

"Bingo," Melvin replied. "The good kind that defends people, not the Red Devil kind. You fight for people. And the advisors don't have to know 'til we're outta here. This is a long-term project. Once the mission is over, I'm refusing the occupation. Start thinking about what side you wanna be on."

"Ridin' high after your victory, aren't you?" Drake asked.

"Thought I did pretty good. We all did. A lot of you were there. Duke wasn't. The advisors weren't. Why do we need them? High time we broke away."

The soldiers looked at each other.

"You don't like it; we can shoot each other up right now," Melvin said. "Or at the very least, you can help me shitcan these deadheads first. We keep this secret until the time is right. Gather support. This ain't gonna change unless we do something; it's about time we do. Those government assholes only have power cuz we allow them to. I don't think there's a right person for the job anymore. I say we stop makin' that mistake. You know they've already got some plots on us. Make a choice: freedom or slavery, you can't have both."

"What about our families?"

"We'll relocate them. When the government asks you to fire on your own people, don't. Tide is turning against 'em, much faster than I thought. I, for one, won't be firing on my neighbors. If enough people refuse their orders, they're screwed."

Drake wanted to walk away and be done with it all, but there were always people that needed help.

"Waddya say, Drake? We could always use some knights on our side."

Drake shook his head, surprised he considered this. Drake's heart pounded; he tried in vain to hide his shaking. *Am I really doing this? Who else will I have to kill?*

"The Freemen are growing," Drake said. "The government's only getting worse. If Mexico secedes, others might follow. I can't believe I'm saying this, but that's for the best. Maybe we all should. We're killing the Void, then we're out. I'm out."

The soldiers consulted each other.

"Get our families out and we'll do it." Melvin looked at Drake and waited for an answer. Drake took a moment to process his options. Drake was under no illusion that everyone was on board with this, he would have to watch them carefully.

"I was going to kill Duke and leave, but this is better," Drake said. "Actually, pretty smart."

"The magic touch is coming back," Melvin said proudly.

"Don't push it," Drake said.

Drake pondered his future as night began to crawl across the desert. He thought on his oath, Zora, and the Freemen. The Freemen sounded better by the day, and it was about to be his only option.

"To defend against foes both foreign and domestic," Drake said.

"And that's what we'll continue to do," Melvin said. "And right now this coup will be our little secret. Enough people turn on them, we won't have to do anything. All hearsay right now. Deniable Plausibility."

"Something like that," Drake said.

Melvin ordered Duke's loyalists from the time being, intent on winning them over and avoiding pointless death. Drake hid his shaking, but the disorientation was much harder to contain. He shrugged off the nauseous guilt. As Melvin headed into Duke's, or rather now his, office, Drake, he realized his devotion to his oath hadn't changed, and this time, nothing would get in the way of that.

MATTHEW

MATTHEW SPENT HIS days going back and forth between the woods and the city. With his cover blown, the need for secrecy was no longer required. He donned plain clothes and walked as an ordinary civilian. Though the threat was defeated, government soldiers patrolled the city in unprecedented numbers on orders of the advisors with Regent Dumas still mysteriously absent.

Matthew faced no push back in Kingsbury, a courtesy for his part in ending Killswitch . . . at least for now. Few knew who he was or the threat they'd survived. Matthew knew it wouldn't last. Scholars and soldiers mapped out the newly opened ruins of the old city beneath his feet while the government debated Vigilant's fate.

The city above didn't carry on like usual. People took stock of the dead and the damage. Houses were checked for bodies left by Killswitch. Hundreds were still unaccounted for. He could hear the hushed whispers in the areas without military activity. The government's walking back of religion bans did little to ease tensions, especially with talks of banning all civilians from owning guns in discussion. Matthew saw the disdain people had for those in power and was happy at the notion of the potential swell in Freemen numbers. The advisors were aware of the sentiment, but not the Freemen's preparations for the attack. He remained acutely aware of his surroundings in case anyone proved so bold as to attack him in full view of everyone. With Yadira and some of her followers at large, the government had another lingering foe to capture. Matthew intended to find her first.

Construction crews were already hard at work rebuilding the war-torn areas around Propensity Hall. Numerous buildings were reduced to rubble leading up the hall. Trucks fully loaded with their remains drove by Matthew to the dumping grounds outside the city.

Matthew had two reasons for being in the city. Matthew made a trip to the hospital for his first reason, a hospital filled with those injured by the Vigilant super weapon. Matthew left his pistol with the local guard and climbed the stairs to Cass's room, ironically the special one Yadira once occupied. A hefty guard held vigil at the door to her room.

"No entry," he said. "Mrs. Averill has had enough people scurrying about. She hasn't woken up anyway."

Cass was unable to grant access, leaving Matthew unable to check on her. Matthew decided not to press the issue. Cass remained comatose since her collapse in the undercity. Her husband would arrive in a few days. Until Thos arrived, Matthew would do his best to keep an eye on her. People outside the hospital gathered in support for one of the heroes of Kingsbury.

He set aside that task for now, he'd slip in later. Matthew headed off to the park for a meeting with his new contact. He walked through the masses to the center of Prosperity Park. Matthew took a seat on a bench under the most prominent tree by the crystal clear pond. Matthew enjoyed the light breeze after the choking, soupy heat. Matthew ordered a sandwich from the passing food cart going by while he waited.

Matthew's contact was late, but he didn't mind on such a pleasant day. An argument to Matthew's left distracted him for a moment. Matthew looked back to find a man in front of him. The man wore a black suit and hat. He carried a cloth bag containing a large circular object. The man's eyes were a brilliant purple. The man took a seat beside Matthew.

"Good to see you, Mr. Pavane," Proxy said.

"Sure it is," Matthew said. "Was hoping for a Vigilant survivor."

"You won't find those here. I've made more than sure of that," Proxy said. Proxy's manner of speech was different, like someone else.

"I suppose you also got some intel for me?"

Proxy told him about of the government's interests in Freemen strongholds and James falling out of favor with the advisors. Mexico was in shambles. The Void was in its death throes and the calls for succession were growing. Vigilant was on the verge of being outlawed completely, making his brother an enemy of the state permanently. Yadira vanished without a trace, responsible for eight thousand deaths in Kingsbury from Killswitch's brief time active. She would meet her end by the hand of Matthew or Gregor. Worst of all, Proxy told Matthew of the north. The north had an estimated two hundred thousand residents. For all intents and purposes, the state's population was effectively halved. Another twelve thousand soldiers died in the battles with Vigilant and the Void. Thousands more died from Killswitch. All in all, the death toll was nearly 200,000. Lastly, Proxy detailed reports on an individual Vigilant hunted, one they feared as much as the entity they tried to kill.

"That it?" Matthew said.

"Not quite," Proxy said. "I have a gift for you. One I'm sure you'll appreciate."

Proxy handed Matthew the bag. Matthew opened the bag. The stench hit him first, he knew it well. Inside the bag was the wide-eyed, open-mouthed head of Kane Turce.

"Thought he was smart. That he could steal and not get caught. He forgot who's city this was."

Matthew braced for the worst.

"There's so much ignorance and arrogance in this world. That's what has led to so much damage"

Proxy looked at a young family of four lounging by the water. There was something different about Proxy, a menace that wasn't there previously. Men in suits directed the nearby locals to exit the park for "Advisor business."

"These people know nothing of the world around them," Proxy said. "In those offices. In the forests. Beneath their feet. They think they're safe. They think their actions are just. That their actions went unnoticed. That I didn't have a backup plan."

Proxy turned to look at Matthew Pavane, cracking a wicked, unnatural grin. The skin bothered him, and he realized why: it was fake. The body was the same, but the inhabitant was not.

"Mr. Abaddon?" Matthew said, confused.

"Most of him," Proxy said. "Been improving my speech to boot."

"A backup . . . fuckin' robots," Matthew said, kicking himself for underestimating his opponent.

"I fully anticipated my body would be destroyed, why I had this one ready. There are others, should you try anything. It's an odd feeling losing one's body, I'm sure Mr. Turce would agree. While I lack the records from its final hours, there are things I find most concerning."

Matthew only had a pistol; he was well aware the weapon couldn't destroy a body-hopping AI. Matthew was at least thankful Mr. Abaddon lost his walking tank of a body.

"What're you planning?"

"Don't fret," Mr. Abaddon said. "No harm will come to you or Mrs. Averill; hurting her may be unnecessary from the sound of things. Whether you were involved or not, I owe you a great deal for saving this city, so this is a one-time courtesy. You can expand your colonies, but don't come after me or meddle in my affairs again. This city is, was, and will always be mine. It was a pleasure doing business with you, Mr. Pavane."

One of Mr. Abaddon's henchmen picked up the bag with Kane's head. Mr. Abaddon gave a bow and walked to a black car waiting on the street beside the park. Matthew sat in the park for a time, learning how to gauge your opponent was easier said than done.

Matthew said his farewells and left for the comforts of home. Word spread of his deeds in Kingsbury. Some Freemen stopped to shake his hand. Freemen began construction for the planned expansion, including hidden defenses when the advisors finally decided to strike. Matthew spent his time enjoying the beauty of the world around him when not making preparations with the other Freemen or picking up the trail of Yadira.

Matthew sat with his feet off the edge of his hanging courtyard, a simple pleasure he once shared with his family. Memories of a past he didn't remember flooded in his head. Matthew chalked up his memory gaps from herb usage. They battled in an unknown collection of ruins. Brielle had no cybernetics, but she fought him with the ferocity of a Grey Sister. He couldn't make out when this was, though he felt he had already known her for quite a while. Matthew knocked her off her feet and pointed the sword at her throat. He pitied her, but he wasn't sure why he stayed her execution. Matthew powered through the fog. The two embraced, the pleasant memory soon turned wrong. Matthew carried her body to an enormous cavern.

"I can't stop!" she said. She begun to convulse. Matthew placed her down in the center of the cavern. Nine figures sat on a platform floating above them.

"Help her, dammit!" Matthew cried.

Matthew remembered pain. Crippling pain brought him to his knees. He felt the connection to Brielle was no longer emotional, but physical and quite deadly. The figures conversed. Had their help not been needed, Matthew would've shortened them a few heads. Matthew crawled over to Brielle, her pulse faint on the verge of nonexistent. Matthew felt Brielle's cries within his mind. The leftmost figure held a large yellow orb and passed it down to each of the other eight members. The orb glowed like a miniature sun. Each of the members looked into the orb.

"The Council has decided," said the figure in the center. "We'll sever the connection, but it affects you both. This action can't be undone as decreed by the Compact. It will take part of your mind with it. To what extent, even we can't see."

"Just do it!" Matthew said, chewing through the words as the pain stabbed at his brain.

"Very well," said the central figure.

The pain intensified. Matthew and Brielle convulsed and then looked at each other, confused at where they were. Matthew looked up to find no figures at all, unaware what transpired. He explored through the fog to glean what he could, but the info came slow. Matthew made a note to learn more of these nine figures, and if they still lived. Matthew also wondered if there were others out there with newly emerged memories after the Compact's disruption.

After a few days, Zora arrived on his doorstep, putting his investigations on hold. Zora hugged him tightly.

"How was the vacation?" he said, already knowing the answer.

"Eventful," she said. Matthew sat back down and Zora took her place beside him. The two caught up on their respective adventures, laughing at the sheer absurdity of it all. All the drugs in the world couldn't give Matthew such a trip. They exchanged information on Yadira, the death of the north, the looming war with the advisors, Mrs. Averill's condition, and the "Adversary."

"Wow," she said, shocked at everything.

"Yeah," Matthew said, equally shocked. "Won't be resting

anytime soon. Your dad's gonna need therapy for quite a while; think I might too."

Zora divulged more information her father didn't laugh about.

"Connected to it? And can connect to others without it," Matthew said, fearing the implications. "I assume you've learned about your mother's former life?" Zora nodded.

"A bit. What can you tell me?" she asked.

Matthew took a deep breath.

"Not much," he said. "She was a witch . . . or something similar. I think my memories were erased, hers too. We met with something called the Council of Pythia . . . they did that to us. I think your mother had this sort of 'connection' too."

Matthew thought on that lost mission, an early encounter with an apostate group before they adopted cybernetics. He thought about that fateful day and the ones that came after. The fog would clear. Whether these resurfacing memories result from Killswitch or not, he was glad to have them back. He wanted to know about the missing pieces of his life, why they were taken from him, and what that meant for Zora's new ability to "connect." Matthew and Zora had much to do and much to learn.

The two sat and relished the chirping birds and swaying branches. There was another maelstrom on the horizon. Matthew would prepare for the future, but today he would reminisce about the past and enjoy the present.

THOS

Thos spent every waking moment he could in the hospital. He spent, however, precious little time in any form of medical facility in his life before now; each time gave his wife only bad news. Thos's body hurt. When he wasn't in her room, he was busy with his appointments and medication. Thos's body was a grid of permanent scars, thanks to Matthias. He'd gladly take a thousand more scars to have Cass back.

Thos held vigil over his comatose wife for days. He struggled to focus on Averill Estate Farms, but he refused to take off when there was so much to do. The business expanded at record speed. Thos gladly picked up Cass's slack as she did during his absence.

He occupied his time in the room, reading the local paper. It was difficult sifting through the hit pieces on anyone that criticized the advisors to find bits of honest information. Word of Victor Whitehall's triumphant return as Melvin was of particular interest to the media given the fact that a former elite was right in front of them this whole time undermined their omnipotence. The regent's absence was of particular note, sparking a lack of faith and fear in the aspiring dictator.

In Mexico, Melvin had stepped in as acting state regent after Duke's apparent murder by the Void. The government was fuming at Victor Whitehall's comeback story and there were whispers of plans being made to remove him. Melvin and Drake were exterminating the Void, but calls for secession remained steady. Tensions between Vigilant and the government ran high, and the order didn't plan on going anywhere. Regardless of the situation, Averill Estate Farms would continue to do business in the south. Meanwhile, the death toll rose with each passing day from the war with Matthias, and reports of the north suggested most were dead. Hundreds, if not thousands like Cass, were in rooms spending what could be their last moments with the people they love.

Matthew stopped by after a few days and gave Thos the truth about her involvement in the Kingsbury incident. Matthew assured Thos she faced no danger from Mr. Abaddon. He now realized he had a large enough influence, and capable friends, to give the gangster more trouble than he'd expect. Yadira was a different story. And there was the business with the Adversary, a powerful enemy yet to reveal himself. Reports of eaten corpses, both human and demon, were popping up throughout the nation; Matthew attributed these to this monstrous new foe. Thos appreciated Matthew's protection, as he did for aiding Zora. He advised Thos should he require more business with him that it be done outside the city. Matthew went for the door.

"Guess we don't get to retire, do we?" Thos asked.

"We do better that way," Matthew said.

Zora visited the day she arrived. For the moment, Zora was his only friend in the city. Thos appreciated her support, but he was in no mood for conversation. Thos forced himself to speak. He wanted to be honest. If he got the words out, he might believe them.

"The doctors don't know what's wrong," Thos said. "Her defects are getting worse. Good news is we can afford to be here a while, maybe till they figure something out." Thos repressed the urge to add some holes into the walls.

"She'll get through," Zora said.

"What I keep telling myself," Thos replied. "Got any other important topics?"

Zora was blunt with Thos, telling him the Freemen cities were next on the advisors' hit list.

"Sounds like you got a lot goin' on these days. Elena . . . Frigilant, or a Vigawitch," Thos said. *Not my best joke*, he thought.

"We'll just stick with Elena. My 'connection' might help us too. And I'll be careful," she said, cutting off Thos's obligatory response.

Thos realized his friendship with the Freemen would become a huge issue for his business and put him on the hit list. Thos wouldn't abandon his friends, and that support might cause him a world of hurt in the days ahead.

"I know it puts you in a difficult position," she said.

"They'll make it illegal to do business with you, but I won't abandon you guys," Thos said. "You'll have my full support when the time comes. They come at me they'll regret it. I fed a rebellion before."

"It may not turn violent," she said. "We get the people on our side the advisors won't be able to fight back. You guys took the country in a handful of battles in less than a month. I hope that's how it works."

"Hope ain't a winning strategy," Thos said.

"No, it isn't," Elena said. "That's why we're making a real one."

Zora stayed with Thos for time, giving him some emotional reprieve.

Thos spent his nights in the chair at Cass's bedside. Noises roused him in the middle of the night. His heart soared.

"Hey stranger," Cass said.

"Hey," Thos said.

Thos was all quipped out. Cass's eyes widened when reality set in. Cass panicked for a moment, instinctively grabbing at the tubes going into her. The deathly visage took Thos back to the Old Worlders. She noticed the small army of flowers and balloons on the table, all from Thos.

"Heard you like flowers," Thos said.

Cass's confusion turned to joy. Thos helped Cass sit up. It killed him to see her frail and listless, much like his father in his last years. She had already lost close to fifteen pounds since he was gone, and she had been rather slim to begin with. Bones were more pronounced as muscle and meat started to disappear. She looked like she had aged twenty years, even with her dyed hair. Her youthful beauty was fading despite her attempts to stop it. Cass didn't show how much it bothered her, but Thos knew it ate her up inside to be reduced to this. The formerly energetic young woman struggled to move. "I'd ask how you're feeling, but you're in a hospital." Cass laughed. The laughter gave him a precious moment to see her once radiant glow.

"Heard you were busy," Thos said. "Matthew told me you helped him save the city. You're a bona fide hero."

"I did my part," she said.

"It helped."

Thos cut the reunion short to alert the doctors. The facility's head doctor gave Cass his personal attention. The doctor gave every statement that boiled down to "We don't know." The doctor offered increases in medication and an extended stay at the hospital. Cass seemed hesitant to stay. She was eager to get back to work. The doctor became adamant that she remain here for the foreseeable future. Cass reluctantly accepted.

The doctors and nurses continuously interrupted Thos's time with his wife. Cass went in and out of consciousness many times and always woke up confused. Thos stayed by her side to comfort her; he prided himself on being an expert in that field.

Thos ran out of things to say. He seldom ran out of things to say.

"I'm scared," she admitted, starting to cry. Thos took her hand.

"Me too, but we'll get through," Thos said. "After all we've gone through, this is a bump in the road."

Thos assured her to the point he started to believe it himself; things did turn out okay more often than he realized. There would be many more happy days for them; he'd do everything in his power to make it so.

"We'll take it one day at a time," Thos said.

"You and me," she said, gripping his hand as tight as she could. Thos didn't finish the rest. *Till the end.*

GREGOR

GREGOR PACED AROUND the Silent City so many times he thought he may end up chair-bound again. His body was as stiff as the formerly dead robots. His muscles ached. He fought through the pain; there was too much left to do. There was always too much to do. Vigilant dismantled the city's heart and cremated the last of the Old Worlders. The rest of the city continued to function. Gregor wasn't concerned with the danger removed. He was no longer in a rush to dismantle all ancient technology, after all it was crazy not to utilize the tools at one's disposal to help and defend. Gregor was going to need answers and weapons. His niece was a witchkin, Yadira was on the run, evil lurked in the shadows, and the government may wage war on him. Raul carried out his duties in the labs, pouring over Matthias's extensive notes. Raul waved at him but kept focus on the texts.

"Matthias was onto something," Raul said. "Had he not been so hasty, he could've developed a large scale non-lethal solution eventually. Would take years, though." Gregor walked over to Raul's workstation. "Do you remember the Compacts?"

Gregor recalled fragments from them all; hazy memories from his youth were visible through the fog. Throughout the years he stood lifeless in fields, on streets, even in prison.

"Matthias wasn't completely unsuccessful," Gregor said. Gregor scratched his beard.

"No," Raul said. "Which means that this thing can't just shut us down or wipe our minds anymore, at least more of us. I'll do some tests."

"Keep up the good work," Gregor said.

Gregor picked up a text written by Matthias himself on Eon and the Adversary. Gregor kept going back to the two phrases: Final Turning and the potential names of his new foe, which included Anselm and Aric.

"Could it be?" Gregor said in a whisper.

"What?" Raul said.

"We need more on this Adversary," Gregor said. "Not sure what he's capable of. If Matthias felt he's as dangerous as Eon, we've got a serious problem. I'll divert more resources for the search." Raul cleared his throat. "Speak your mind already."

"Aren't you gonna help your brother? The Freemen may need your help if the rumors are true." Gregor let out a heavy, annoyed breath. "If that happens…"

"I'll help if I can. But this comes first," Gregor said, stunned by the words. Raul crossed his arms, doubtful Gregor could really put this first. "Let's hope there's no need for that. They'll be coming after us too; Vigilant may be outlawed before long, which means that'll be a third faction uniting against them."

"Being an outlaw hasn't stopped you yet," Raul said. Gregor rather enjoyed it.

"If they hate me, I'm probably doing something right."

Gregor left the lab and headed to the city's heart. Vigilant troops amassed at the base of the stairs leading to the central court-yard, not yet fully cleared of robotic debris. The troops all waited on him, including the three rescued trolls wanting some purpose in life. Gregor climbed the steps to address his men.

"I stand before you during an unprecedented time in our

history. We slaughtered our brothers. Our order is in shambles and nearly brought about the same destruction we've fought since the beginning. I've believed in this order. I bled for this order. I still believe in that order. We've learned the Compact is a lie, a manipulation by the worst violation of our order. But that doesn't mean Vigilant is worthless or dead. And there's much more to do. Bring forth the prisoners."

Matthias loyalists in tattered clothes were brought to the bottom of the stairs for his judgment. Raul moved to the head of the army. Designated gunmen took aim at Matthias's surviving men. Raul acted as Vigilant speaker for the moment. Gregor listened to the pleas and the crimes. Matthias had stood here once, as judge, jury, and executioner. Gregor took this situation very seriously. Vigilant required a strong, decisive leader, but he wouldn't follow the mass murdering path of the late grand crusader.

The speaker rattled off real crimes ranging from murder and slaving; e-drugs would go off Vigilant's radar. Gregor held court. Gregor listened to their pleas and curses. He took his time to analyze the cases. Gregor listened to the evidence.

The majority of Matthias's troops were quick to abandon him, citing the tried and true excuse of following orders. These men didn't resist arrest, even with numbers capable of fighting back. Gregor sympathized with them. He'd been guilty of just following orders plenty of times in his youth. He listened to their cases. Gregor identified the thugs from the soldiers. Gregor wanted to execute them, yet he hesitated; harsh punishment would've put him in line with them once upon a time. There were plenty in the ranks that fit neither category of guilty or innocent.

Gregor needed soldiers for the road ahead, making the verdict difficult. A handful of soldiers were unrepentant, flat out refusing to join Gregor. He hated the waste. Gregor passed judgment. The executioners led the guilty to the firing line. In unison, Vigilant executed the prisoners, using bullets on regular humans and waves on the modified ones. The bodies fell over the side and into the incinerators. He never relished passing judgement on humans. Quite often they were simply fools playing with things they didn't understand. Sometimes harsh judgement had to be made. He wouldn't let himself be another Matthias. Vigilant needed to eliminate threats, but never again be so willing to expend others in that pursuit. When the executioners were finished, he continued with the rest.

He looked over at the others on trial. Gregor took a moment to consider his decision one more time. The prisoners faced a moment just like he did, awaiting the previous king's judgment all those years ago. King Astor spared his life, seeing the potential future greater than the actions of Gregor's past. He breathed in deep. There was a consequence for every choice. He let out a deep exhale. Gregor allowed them to remain in the order.

"Consider this your second chance, don't waste it," Gregor said.

The criminals in question were escorted to Matthias's special EMPX mobile prison cells.

Vigilant brought the five surviving apostates to the edge of the platform. Some wept. All the witch-burning devices were in pieces, though they gave him ideas for improving Vigilant weapons further; Gregor would prioritize function over sadism. Vigilant drew weapons, both EMP and rifle functionality of their gunblades.

The apostates closed their eyes and prepared for the end. The executioners raised their weapons one more time. Gregor passed his judgment. Waves pelted the two apostates on the end, followed by bullets to finish the job.

"The guilty have been punished," Gregor said.

The other apostates opened their eyes, too shocked to be relieved. Everyone awaited Gregor's words.

"For years, Vigilant has enforced the Great Law," Gregor began. "There are many things about what we do I'm proud of, but I think we've lost the forest for the trees. Our mission is to destroy those that use technology to bring harm to others. We aren't here to kill people over trivialities. Technology is not the problem in and of itself—it's the use. Vigilant will be what it once was, defenders of people and not henchmen of false gods or corrupt states. The judgment is decided. You will be released." The executioners tried not to do a double-take. "That's an order." The men lowered their guns. The prisoners only got one foot.

"One last thing before you go," Gregor said. The prisoners all looked at him in terror. "I won't stop your pursuit of knowledge or whatever idiotic fate you bring on yourself. But know this, if you bring harm to others, there'll be no place on Earth you can hide from me. This is your one and only warning. Vigilant is here to stay. Spread the word."

Gregor gave the nod. A handful of troops escorted the prisoners to the train leading to the coast. Gregor had more to say to his troops.

"The government probably won't recognize us anymore. That's fine because we won't recognize them either. Our calling is higher than them. We protect people from those who would enslave or destroy them. Vigilant no longer follows what the Compact is but what it's supposed to be. To the Eons, apostates, advisors, and adversaries of the world, if you threaten this world your days are numbered! Ever Vigilant!"

There was a few seconds of silence; Gregor feared his new speech fell on deaf ears.

"Hail, Grand Crusader!" Raul cried. The trolls hailed him next, triggering a domino effect. The calls echoed throughout the city.

"Get to it," Gregor ordered.

The troops departed for the dozens of tasks at hand. Raul took his place beside Grand Crusader Gregor Pavane.

"So you established a rogue state. Bold direction," Raul said. Gregor struggled to process what he'd done. As time wore him down, he began to fear his place in the order. He wondered if it was time to retire. He knew the day was coming, but not yet. He would guide the order until he could no more.

"I did. Which means we gotta get our shit in gear. Are you ready, Lord Crusader?" Gregor asked.

"Yes sir," Raul said.

Raul wasted no time and went back to the lab. Gregor looked out over the Silent City, the first of his many planned Vigilant strongholds. The thousands of Vigilant soldiers toiled across the city, preparing defenses, acquiring new members, studying demons, and locating targets. There was a traitor on the loose and something wicked lurking out in the wilderness. Gregor wasn't sure what to make of his new foe nor was ready to accept he was the former Blackthorne king. It didn't matter who or what his adversaries were—Gregor would destroy them all the same.

EPILOGUE

ANSELM CHOMPED AT the bit to see what all the fuss was about when it came to the Deadlands. A demon wriggled at his feet, not so tough without pesky limbs. The demon was slender with numerous small faces wrapped around its head. His upgraded knowledge found no references to the nature of this beast, but it was surprisingly delicious. Anselm licked the black blood from his fingers, able to feel the power within it. He ripped out the pulsating orb that served as the demon's only organ. Anselm's teeth pierced the hard shell. He ripped into the tender meat inside. It tasted better than the others he'd consumed, a lot like fried chicken he once enjoyed with family on lazy Sundays. Anselm savored each bite of the organ to the sounds of the demonic death rattle.

There were demons everywhere in these blighted lands, some of which were a challenge. Demons preyed on humans, which seemed to be their only purpose in life. With this many demons, there most certainly had to be humans. Humans had less power than demons, but were no less valuable to Anselm in the long run.

Anselm accomplished so much more now that he didn't require sleep and reached speeds that matched cars. He traveled straight through his former kingdom in a single week, stopping to indulge himself on small patrols and fulfill his sadistic quotas. Anselm proudly displayed each body in unflattering and disrespectful poses, planting the seeds of fear to germinate for his grand return.

The putrid yellow sky thundered overhead. The Deadlands was a place like no other on the continent. With Gideon's knowledge, Anselm possessed a great understanding of why this nightmare land existed and thrived as it could. Fake environmental disasters hid black site projects with the potential for unrivaled creation and destruction. He felt them out in the dark waters. Great machines with the power to weaponize the very weather rotted in the abyss. Altered nanomachines filled the land, sea, and sky. Corrupted by the failed attack to kill Eon during the Collapse, coupled with his attempt to connect to the underground machines, transformed the southeastern coast into a hellscape none had conquered. These were unimportant to him. There were even more incredible things Anselm desired.

Blasts of flame shot up from the black water coagulating in pools across the swamps. Roots twisted up through the goop at odd angles, creating lopsided trees that looked like spirits wailing at the cruel sky. Anselm heard the faintest sounds of human life far off in the distance, in the exact same direction he headed. He sensed much human life in the lands even Eon had forsaken. The notion piqued Anselm's curiosity and an opportunity he couldn't pass up. Anselm followed the sounds.

Night washed over the swamps. Beneath a neon purple sky, he stalked the land. Dozens of masses gathered in the darkness, staying out of sight if not for Anselm's enhanced vision. Demons dogged his steps, curious at the new tourist. A menagerie of twisted shapes waited for an opportunity to strike. A serpentine beast struck him. Fangs from a disturbingly human face buried themselves into his back. The long body wrapped around him. The grip tightened and began to crush him. He enjoyed the pain more than the demon. Anselm let the game play out long enough.

He thrust his hands into the thick green body. His hands went deeper and deeper into the slick flesh. Anselm pushed his hands apart. The demon shrieked. Anselm pushed harder, feeling the meat of the beast separating. He thrust his hands deeper, cutting straight through the grotesque creature. Anselm pried the bottom half of the demon off of him. The top half clung on for dear life with its hundreds of saw-blade teeth. Anselm gripped the head latched on his back and tore it loose, along with shreds of himself that were quickly replenished. Anselm held the demon in front of him. The beast thrashed wildly. Anselm gripped the beast tight. He greedily ripped into the side of the demon's head, intoxicated by the surge of energy from the blood and flesh.

He threw the half-eaten remains to the ground. Anselm scanned the demonic crowd, eager to sample the buffet of power. The demons stayed far from Anselm's reach. He lunged at the inhuman crowd. The demons scattered and vanished in the deep dark reaches of the swamp where he couldn't see. *They fear me,* he thought, and took great pleasure of this.

Anselm moved through the swamps unopposed toward the ruins of civilization. He waded through the black muck. Corpse-white snallygators soared through the waters, wisely avoiding the superior predator among them. Anselm walked by the toppled structures Gothic in nature. Gideon had incomplete records of life here, only caring for the technology hiding in the darkness.

"Was there a kingdom here beneath my nose? Is there still one? Is the muck preserving the Old World?"

Anselm climbed onto a ruined castle tower and got a lay of the land. His goal was east. Electric lights hung from the stilted huts, a sign of very human life. He neither saw nor heard any humans in the area, only the sloshing from ulcerous bloatfish caught in the jaws of the pale gators. He moved between the wetlands and the cracked earth of the wastelands. He found numerous villages in his travels. It was no secret that the Deadlands was the home of exiles. Humans, ranging from normal in appearance to those with monstrous deformities, fished and hunted what edible life they could find. The scientific interest grew in Anselm since his Gideon meal. He doubted this was a coincidence. There were witches here, or something similar in nature to them; he couldn't explain it, but he felt beings that gave off an energy similar to Mandragora. Anselm counted nine of these unique signatures that warranted future investigation. He put the locals on the back burner for the moment; it was more fun to anticipate what he'd do to them anyway.

Anselm pressed on to his destination and the true beginning of his new life. He passed through the rocky crags to the darkest recesses of the black swamp. He found his goal, exactly where Gideon suspected.

Broken pipes jutted out from the ground and water. A mass of metal rose the heavens, twisted and perverted from the ages of torture in the dark lands. The structure reminded him of a pipe organ turned demonic like him. It was a perfect. The machine went deep in the earth, as all the interesting places of the world often did. Pieces of the great machine were a testament to Old World ingenuity. It was an old research station under the guise of cleaning up a disaster that never happened. It was in tatters. It would take much work to rebuild it. Anselm held no illusions he'd find all the knowledge and power of the ages, but there were definitely secrets here to unearth. He honestly didn't care if it held secrets at all; it was a spot he couldn't pass up. Anselm would explore the dark corridors from top to bottom. Before the consumption, Anselm didn't care how things worked, only that they did. Gideon's hunger for knowledge passed to him, and he felt genuine excitement to plumb the depths. He required many things for the next stage of his plan, but it would all begin here.

The world saw junk in sludge and filth, but Anselm saw something more. Anselm saw the bones for a mighty castle, a grand cathedral, the kind necessary for a kingdom the likes of which the world had never seen. Such a feat required work. It required workers. It required subjects, those willing to learn the truth of the world as he did. Anselm felt Eon's presence, now little more than a whisper after being neutered by Killswitch.

"The world does indeed require a correction," Anselm said. "I'll give them the paradise you can't deliver. The road to paradise begins in Hell."

Eon's presence left with the sickly wind. Anselm made an initial run through the structure. He tossed aside the wreckage blocking the passageways. He navigated the refuse maze to a room with chairs that led into a spacious room with its contents long gone. Holes peppered the walls, letting purple beams of light creep inside. He ripped a seat from the small room and placed it in the center of the larger chamber. The space was adequate for now. He saw its very important growth potential. Anselm's ambitions were grand; they were necessary for a king such as him.

He took a seat in his prototype throne room. He waited there and he planned. For days he waited and planned and fed. The anticipation built. His first guests finally arrived. Two forms approached. The first was a mangled, wiry mess of a human, like something out of a dream that wasn't quite right. His reconfigured bones protruded too far out at the joints. His skin cracked and bled while it processed the new gift. Massive horns protruded from the eye sockets and wrapped back around the head in an appropriately devilish fashion. The creature dragged the second form, a man bound, gagged, and soaked in urine. The monster tossed the man at Anselm's feet.

"Good work, Lord Hart," Anselm said.

Anselm knelt down and removed the gag from the prisoner's mouth. The man looked up in horror at the pale-skinned Anselm with a crown cutting and weaving through his scalp.

"It's good to see you again, James." James didn't respond, clearly overcome with fear and shock.

"You know why you've been summoned. You and I have a

problem, well mostly you. I had a son, a dear friend of yours. I had a whole family, something even the best men don't always get. We know what happened. Trust me, I didn't forget. Such a crime can't go unpunished, not even if it was for the best."

"Ans—" James said.

"Hush. There'll be time for . . . discussion later, and believe me, there's much to *discuss*. And I have all the time in the world. I wanted to welcome you to my humble abode. A bit of a fixer-upper, but I'm up for the challenge."

Anselm's unbridled joy and pain no longer shackled him to his pesky humanity. James wept.

"The man who would be king, Murderer of my wife and two of my sons, leaking at both ends," Anselm laughed.

"Kill me and get it over with," James said, almost pleading. Anselm smiled. His skin began to stretch. Anselm was changing and he willed it so. Anselm took all of Eon's words to heart. *Power over life and death, flesh and blood.*

"Oh, poor baby James I'm afraid you don't get that luxury. I've got something better in mind. Something more fitting. Utterly beautiful." Before Anselm stood the reborn Jaren Hart, his first subject. Anselm needed workers. He needed subjects. James would be neither of those. Anselm needed pain. He looked down at the whimpering James Dumas and knew he needed one more thing: examples. Not everyone would adapt to the pain, to be honest he hoped most wouldn't, but they needed to suffer all the same. He went to work on James Dumas, an altogether different project than Jaren.

"The king is dead. Long live the king. The King Beyond Death!" Jaren said, his voice as distorted and mangled as his reconstructed body.

"And forever shall he reign," Anselm said.

James's screams were the trumpet blasts that heralded Anselm's new world.

Thank you so much for reading my book.

Did you enjoy it? Spread the word! Please share your thoughts and leave a review on Goodreads and Amazon. Your feedback is greatly appreciated. Follow me on social media or on my website, www.aaroncolewilliams.com.

ABOUT THE AUTHOR

Aaron Cole Williams is a science fiction, fantasy, adventure, and third-person bio writer. When not engaged in creating the things mentioned above like what you just read, he likes to spend his time enjoying the science fiction and fantasy medium in all its formats and being out in nature. He currently lives in western Kentucky with his wife and two dogs.

www.aaroncolewilliams.com
www.amazon.com/author/aaroncolewilliams
www.facebook.com/AuthorACW
www.instagram.com/aaroncolewilliams/